Dance for a Diamond

DANCE FOR A DIAMOND

CHRISTOPHER MURPHY

Walker and Company
New York

First published in the United States of America
in 1986 by the Walker Publishing Company, Inc.

Published simultaneously in Canada by John Wiley & Sons
Canada, Limited, Rexdale, Ontario.

Library of Congress Cataloging-in-Publication Data

Murphy, Christopher.
  Dance for a diamond.

  "... Walker adventure fiction ..."--Colophon.
  I. Title.
PR6063.U729D3 1986   823'.914   86-13259
ISBN 0-8027-0925-7

Printed in the United States of America

10 9 8 7 6 5 4 3 2 1

For Rupert

'Tis the good reader that makes the good book
Ralph Waldo Emerson

With thanks to Michael W. and the Order of the Boot, also to all the other kind or inadvertent conspirators, even if only they know who they are. One or two are in jail and several others deserve to be.

M-L.G.A.
R.L.
J.T.
J.D'h.
R.W.
D.B.
P.R.
D.K.
D.S.
P.B.
P.&G.F.
J-D.&A.R.
B.B.
G.M.
A.W.
F.M.
G.T.
V.P.
A.J.
R.C.
J-P.E.
J.&S.S.
M.H.
L.S.
F.v.P.
P.G.
J.B.
C.M.
J.A.
R.J.
J.L.
S.C.
J.R.
W.A.
J.E.

I hate quotations.
Ralph Waldo Emerson

Dance for a Diamond

One

What a lass that were
to go a-gipseying through the world with.
                    Charles Lamb

A large, intricate stone was poised to tumble into a pool of quiet domesticity. A slim young woman lay on the floor in front of the fireplace, chin on hands, reading a spread newspaper. She wore green cotton trousers, loose-fitting for ease of movement but their softness emphasising her body-tone, a tautly rounded rump, a natural arch in the back, a lithe definition. Her face was hidden from him by a mantle of tawny hair yet she sensed from his stillness that he wasn't reading.

"Want some more coffee?" she asked without looking round.

"I'll get it. Stay there."

He flung his paper aside and made for the kitchen. Lately she'd begun to notice his new restlessness; he hadn't enough to occupy him now that their renovating was virtually finished. It was the third house he'd converted, a useful and varied occupation which had been lucrative enough, despite the ravages of recent tax laws, to bring him to his present idleness, and this one had pleased him the most because Lucy had become part of it and had taken over the garden with an imperious and reckless enthusiasm.

One snag with such an occupation is the necessity to keep moving in order to establish the gain and remain solvent. The property burgeons while the funds dwindle away, but with a little capital left they were content and unwilling to sell up. Otherwise their still-early romance seemed to them both to flow towards an unseen, distant gulf like a stream bubbling with ideas about a river.

As he waited for the kettle to boil, she came through and

slid her arms around him from behind, her face pressed against his shoulder.

"This is cupboard love, my love. How are we fixed for readies at the moment?"

"Um, cautious. I suppose it depends on how much we're talking about."

"I was afraid of that. I suppose I'd better be frank and direct and come straight out with it. Ninety-five pounds."

"Ouch. Come on, Lu, what's it for?"

"A boot."

"One boot?"

"Korrekt, gospodin."

He laughed gently. "And why should one want one boot, pray?"

"Er, because the pair costs an arm and a leg, in which case one would only want one. Wouldn't one?"

He turned round, chuckling at the absurdity and at her sorrowful expression, running his hands inside her hair. "A hundred-and-ninety quid for a pair of boots is pretty damn steep, isn't it?"

"But they're such beautiful boots! I saw them a whole week ago and I didn't mention it then. That was very restrained of me, don't you think?"

"Very. If you want things like that, I'll have to get a job, won't I?"

"Oh, I didn't say that. But just think how much more desirable I could be with some adorable boots."

"No you couldn't. Not possibly more desirable."

"I'd dance for you in just my boots . . ."

"They couldn't make it better. Do you think I need an extra stimulus or something?"

She gazed soulfully at him while he poured from the kettle. He glanced at her, trying not to grin at the appeal of her eyes, amber and green. Back in the drawing-room he noticed that her paper was open at the property section and asked, "Were you looking at the houses?"

"Oh, only for comparisons. I wanted to see if the value of this one had gone up which would mean you were richer than you thought. A little encouragement, perhaps." She looked at him ingenuously and settled back on the carpet with an exaggerated sigh.

Stuart stared rather grimly at the smouldering logs, a token comfort against the dreary weather. But for a loan to an old friend it would have been no problem; whenever he thought about it now, he had a secret guilt and wondered for the hundredth time at his own lunacy in staking a hothead called Rollo to £20,000 more than a year and a half ago and receiving not a word of encouragement since. He decided later that Rollo must have some sixth sense about when people are feeling flush and adventurous. Stuart had just sold his previous house and bought the high old barn for a moderate song. Regret had followed quickly, within a very short time of seeing a fleet figure sprinting down the Bayswater Road and hurling itself with reckless panache on to the platform of an accelerating bus. A very stern black lady conductor had promptly rung the bus to a halt and ordered her off; Stuart caught sight of her face as she turned away crestfallen. He had gasped and braked too sharply so that the tyre-squeal made her jump and glare at him. He had leaned over to open the passenger door and looked up at her.

For a long moment she had stood there puzzled, her head inclined. He hadn't known what to say and finally she asked, "OK, when and where?"

"Sadler's Wells, about four years ago. *The Firebird*, you were sitting behind me and I didn't have the nerve to talk to you."

"Did you enjoy it?"

"No, I was miserable for months. Seriously. I tried to find you through the theatre but the agency kept no records. I thought of making an appeal on television."

His chest had constricted violently as she'd smiled. "I meant the ballet."

"Yes, even though my grandma dragged me there. Where do you want to go?"

"Patagonia."

"Wrong bus then, anyway. Hop in and we'll go and find someone to introduce us. If you say no, I'll run you over."

"Forceful type, huh?"

His determination might have showed on his face since he didn't answer but watched as she slowly lowered herself into the passenger seat, shut the door and held out a slim hand.

"I'm Lucy."

"Always?"

11

She looked surprised. "No, I was *née* Ludmilla Simonova. How did you know?"

"You were speaking Russian to the woman with you."

"My mother. She's from Leningrad, years ago. Do you speak Russian?"

"No, but I recognise it. I'm Stuart Kody. My father was Czech. I ... you're terrifyingly beautiful, it makes me clench." He had blushed then at his own boldness while she watched him quietly and then stunned him.

"Actually, I remember you well. I was hoping you'd talk to me. If my mother hadn't been there I'd probably have prompted you somehow, an ice-cream down your neck maybe."

When he got to know her better he realised it was no exaggeration because she was electrically impulsive and unusually sure-footed. They were married within weeks despite the anxious tears of her mother, now more or less reconciled, if sometimes clucking her disapproval of his contented joblessness.

He hadn't told Lucy about the loan to Rollo, reluctant to admit an obvious flightiness, financing something barely explained, almost certainly dubious, half the world away, and expecting to profit without personal risk or effort. He was now beginning to feel that, if the lions or the Jaapies didn't commit GBH first, he'd do it to Rollo himself on the diminishing off chance that he ever saw him again. To be fair to himself, despite talk of enormous profit, he knew it was far less his own greed than Rollo's bright-eyed enthusiasm which had made him contribute, and he thought ruefully of his brushed-over attempts to suggest a smaller loan. Recently he'd been wondering whether to contact the South African Embassy to see if they could discover any news of him but he'd hesitated in case the enquiry might lead into unspecified trouble. Rollo had promised the return in less than a year.

He looked down at Lucy again, frustrated and annoyed at his own folly and his need to find a new solution aroused a determination to confound the budget. Not only did he love giving her things but parsimony was out of character and only arose from feelings of married responsibility. In this he perhaps underestimated Lucy; he didn't resent her implication that he should get a job, she was probably right, but he was equally determined not to get one. He cherished his self-dependence, it made him feel more alive and imaginative. It also amused both of them that it could make other people suspicious. Sensing, she said, "Do relax. I'm only being unreasonable."

She looked round to smile but he was already up and walking away, leaving his paper lying on the couch. She loved it when he was busy, it put a purpose into his walk and his movements, a single-minded resolution. He had short, dark-brown curly hair which added to his rather boyish expression, itself belying an almost aggressive independence. Had it not been for his three years in the Army she would seriously have doubted his employability and she avoided nagging him even in play. His walk was stocky like a good games player although he didn't seem to favour team sports. He admitted to being a competent skier but they hadn't had any sort of holiday since their honeymoon, being fully occupied with the house. The thought swept her back to that idyllic month cruising the Seychelles on *Sailor V*, a boat belonging to one of Stuart's Army friends, Rollo Runyan. She thought it hilarious that anyone could actually be called Rollo but she had never met him. Stuart had only said that he was a nice guy who lived hazardously somewhere in Africa.

For the next twenty minutes or so she was aware of Stuart moving around the house but she stayed intent on her paper. Outside, Gloucestershire disguised her preparations for autumn through a courage-testing curtain of drizzle. The rain looked set for the whole day and she knew that waiting for it to clear was deceiving herself and betraying her plants. In spite of it she stayed in front of the fire until he came back and sat astride her rump, leaning forward to whisper through her hair.

"Treasure hunt!"

Lucy squealed. "Oh, no, you're all wet! Not outside?"

"It starts in the coldest place in the house but it gets warmer and warmer," he answered, kneading the firm skein of muscles in her back, his thumbs digging.

"Well, let me up then, you cad."

He got off and settled happily back, smoothing out his paper but watching her at the same time because she had so many ways of getting to her feet, some of them quite baffling and often invented. This time she arched her back severely, thrust forward on to straightened arms and floated her feet just above the carpet until they were next to her hands, her body bent double. It was almost unexpected when she simply stood up from there, tucked in her rust-coloured shirt, smiled at him sweetly, and bolted for the kitchen.

Starting from the ice-box she was well into the hunt, howling theatrical anguish when she could extract a clue only by fashioning a probe out of a coat hanger or reaching in to the lavatory cistern for a weighted polythene bag. The last one lay in the fork of a rowan sapling at the end of the garden, a long, wet sprint through the rain to discover that the treasure had been taped to one of the belt loops in the back of her trousers right from the beginning. She came crashing back into the house and hurled herself at the upraised newspaper, seeing it shaking with Stuart's laughter.

"Kody, you're an awful bloody tease and I love you, you sod, it's Sunday and you knew I wouldn't be able to rush straight out and buy them." She panted, waving the crumpled cheque and kissing him with abandon. "Hottest place, indeed!" She pummelled and tickled him, completely wrecking his paper.

"That tree will have to go," he said, struggling.

"The rowan? Why, I've only just stuck it in?"

"They're supposed to keep the witches away and it's not working. Anything that doesn't work round here has got to go, do you hear?" Interpreting her glance his own way, he added, "Except me, that is. Someone's got to be in charge."

"Huh, well, you've got me going now and it's not really all that horrid outside. I must do those wallflowers, I promised them. You know, I think they need a good talking to for being so bourgeois. Have you seen my sou'wester anywhere?"

"Bathroom. You were using it for a shower hat."

"Oh. So I was." She leaned down and kissed him on the forehead. "Thank you, I promise you'll love them."

She was out in the little cedar greenhouse when the call came so she was unaware of the moment when the stone toppled into their quiet pool. The telephone rang, a collect request from the mining town of Kimberley in South Africa; in his surprise, Stuart didn't query and heard a familiar voice almost at once, as if his thoughts had conjured it.

14

"That you, Stuart? How you going?" The accent was more noticeable, somewhere between Australian and Afrikaans, but the inflexion unmistakable.

"Rollo! What the hell have you been doing? I'd almost given up on you."

"No more than I said, but there's a slight snag. I'm holed up and not mobile. Need help. You'll have to come, right away. I've booked you on the Wednesday night Jumbo to Jo'burg. Air taxi will meet you."

"Not mobile? What's the matter?"

"Well, I got a little bit kinda shot, you know."

"Shot? What are you doing, is the law after you?"

"Well, yes and no."

Stuart glanced round to see if he was still alone.

"Rol, I told you, I'm not going in the slammer for anyone, ever. What sort of shot? How long are you immobile?"

"It'll be weeks, bust thigh-bone. Take my word, it must go now and there's only you to trust in a number like this. The haul's terrific. I wouldn't ask you if it wasn't kosh."

"Why were you hit, is that part of it?"

"Not really, and anyway, there'll be no problem for you, my word on it. Just come on your own and don't tell anyone, OK?"

"What have I got to do?"

"Don't be daft, this is a phone, right? Tell you when you get here."

"Look here, Rol, I don't –"

"Sorry, mate, I really am, but there's no other way. Either you come or it's all screwed and your money's thrown out the window."

For agonised moments he hung under a black cloud of foreboding, then with a wrench he thrust it away, swearing viciously. Rollo said a distant "Ouch!" but it didn't make him smile.

In a cold voice he said finally, "All right, damn you, I'm coming. Do you need anything?"

"Bit of money, that's all. I spent every cent. 'Fraid I couldn't pay for your flight even, but don't worry about getting it back. It's all set, man, I tell you. Just don't breathe a word to anyone, not even what's-her-name, Lucy."

"Don't be daft, I've got to tell Lucy."

15

"NO! I said no one, strictly. There's reasons. Just make something up to tell her, at least till it's done, OK?"

"Why? I hate to do that, we're close as fingers."

"It's for her own sake, you pratt. Look, good on yer, I'll see you Thursday morning, bright."

The line clicked dead and he sat in a lengthy daze, the receiver dangling from his hand. He couldn't understand why there might be any possible risk to Lucy, that she had to be ignorant for her own sake. He'd never told her a lie and they were by now so sensitive to each other that he felt she'd know instantly if he was acting. Frowning and nervously angry, he looked at his watch and then went to the kitchen window and whistled. He could see the yellow sou'wester in the greenhouse turning towards him so he made a drinking motion with his thumb and pointed to the village. Lucy nodded back and made a shooing gesture with her hands.

He took a battered umbrella from the stand and went out of the front door. The Horse and Groom was opening late as usual; he could see a group near the door only just being allowed in at ten minutes past midday, their protests audible through the persistent drizzle. Inside the bar they were rewarded with a huge cheering fire, the first of the season, and old Jack was already pulling pints and responding to the surly remarks with some thick-skinned backchat. Stuart was preoccupied and nodded absent replies to the friendly "Owars" from thirsty faces.

"Wot you done wi' your little missus then, Stoort?" said one, but before he could answer, Archie, a red-nosed retired pig-farmer said, "'E don't want to bring 'er in 'ere no more, all you durty boogers allus touchin' 'er oop."

"Ooor, listen to 'im, isn't 'e the wust!" called Jack from beyond the bar. "Fifty year o' starin' at pigs' arses you'd a thought cured 'im, but 'im so randy still, he'd shag a slow puncher!"

There were some gravelly chuckles and Stuart backed up to the fire with his pint, only half his mind trying to decipher the last remark. Seeing him unresponsive and a little distant, they left him alone, but when Fogarty came in, Stuart had a sudden idea. Fogarty was a telephone engineer, unsmiling and very reserved but he'd been friendly with the Kody's ever since their arrival in Carsey. He'd been up the pole outside making their connection when Lucy had called out to offer him a cup of tea. It was so long since anyone had been pleasant to him, he slipped a little and nearly fell off the pole and, in his gratitude, he taught them how to make free calls long-distance, though neither of them had ever remembered to use it.

When he came over to the fire and gave a brief nod, Stuart asked, "Fog, what do you dial when you want to check if your phone's ringing properly?"

"Varies from place to place. Round here it's 1232. Dial that and put 'er straight down, should call you right back. You got a problem, then?"

"I'm not sure, but it's a good way to find out. Thanks."

Fogarty nodded but didn't say anything else, maintaining his usual awkward shyness. The others were ogling the nudes in the Sunday gutters and occasionally calling out the more scurrilous headlines. With great glee, Archie read out hesitantly the tale of a couple caught *in flagrante* on the floor of a jammed elevator, where the engineer was called and solved the problem too rapidly, in front of half the hotel staff and the woman's husband.

Lucy came in the door just at this point, shaking out her hair from the sou'wester; some of the voices hushed at Archie but he ignored them and even raised his own to say, "Don' you worry 'bout our Miss Lucy, she been married more 'n a year, she knows what it's all about b' now, I reckon. Come on, Miss Lucy, tell us the okkedest place you ever 'ad it off, why don't you?"

"Because," Lucy answered in a piping and very superior voice, "it's none of your business, you horrible, filthy old man." She paused to take off her cloak and hang it over the end of a tall bench-back. "If you simply must know, Archie, it was in the car-wash, just off the Oxford by-pass, that big job where you have to go through a sort of tunnel on a conveyor."

There was a concussed silence for about five seconds as the locals digested her remark. Stuart buried his face in his tankard as he heard Lucy ask for a gin-and-tonic in the same over-cultured voice, then the place exploded. He heard a wet snorting beside him and looked round to see Fogarty's eyes full of tears over a huge, disbelieving grin.

"You must've been bloody ready," Archie said when the noise subsided a little. "They don't give you much time."

17

"Nothing like enough," Lucy answered quite seriously. "We had to tell the man that his machine had missed the car and we wanted to go through again. He got frightfully peeved about it. Oh, thank you."

Jack passed her drink over and Archie, unable to speak for wheezing, indrawn laughter, waved a pound note at him before dropping it. Lucy walked over to Stuart with her nose in the air, her face still dead-pan, all the eyes drawn irresistibly to her. In support, he avoided meeting her glance as she stood beside him, proudly it seemed.

At times he found the sheer vigour of her personality alarming, the quicksilver threatening to baffle his more stolid judgements, and at twenty-eight he was laughingly unable to decide whether she would age him prematurely or keep him young for ever. Only that morning he'd gone downstairs and returned to find her exercising on the bedroom floor. She was naked, on her forehead and forearms like a T, her legs stretched and swinging in a horizontal splits; so he had put down the coffee mugs, tiptoed over and planted a kiss right in the soft centre. He expected a shriek and a tumble but instead, after a still pause, the taut-muscled thighs closed soft as chiffon before the real power was turned on and trapped him, stifling his breath. He'd held it as long as he could, frightened that his only escape, when he got no response to nasal moans, was to wrench and possibly hurt her, then relieved to be abruptly freed at the wrestler's double tap of submission.

"You were suffocating me!" he'd protested.

"I'm sorry, my love. I thought it was the milkman, walked right into my trap."

He'd shaken his head and said, "He doesn't come on Sundays."

"Poor chap!" she giggled, pulling him down again and the coffee cooled to room temperature.

Now as he drank his beer the dread of leaving her for the first time began to cloud his feelings like the dreary day outside. His primary instinct was to forget the call and say goodbye to both Rollo and his investment, but deep down he knew he wouldn't be able to ignore his friend's plea for help, certainly not without contacting him and that was apparently impossible. He was further troubled by not knowing either what was required of him, although it certainly

18

sounded less than legal, or how long to tell Lucy he'd be away. Worst of all was the very need for deceit and, more immediately, to cover his concern before she noticed anything.

He put his arm across her shoulders and she responded with a slight *moue* and a wink over her glass. Later, when they were walking home, he told her casually that he'd actually applied to the Ministry of Defence for a job and had been waiting to hear for several weeks.

She stopped and turned to him under the umbrella, reaching up to touch his face. "Hey, you don't need to do that, you know, not for me anyway. I married you unemployed, after all."

"It might be a good idea, especially if I can keep it on a part-time basis."

"Using your Czech? You'll have to brush up, won't you? Hey, I'll tell people you're a cryptomaniac and that I sew transistor buttons on your shirts . . . Look, I'll wait till you hear before going for the boots, OK?"

"No, not OK, you get them tomorrow."

"We'll see," she answered, slipping her arm in his and pulling him to hurry. The house loomed snugly through the soft rain, a converted Cotswold stone barn, its windows deep and at random levels with stone mullions they'd rescued from a ruin. Lucy adored it, although able to laugh at a certain chocolate-box tweeness, since it had acquired so much character; when people stopped to photograph it on bright days she was sometimes hard put not to be "shocking pink", as she called an American gesture.

Half-way through the next morning, Stuart dialled the number Fogarty had given him and promptly replaced the receiver. It ran back immediately and, knowing Lucy was in the kitchen, he called out that he'd get it. After clicking out the subsequent whining noise, he faked a conversation which consisted mainly of Yesses and Nos and Right, I'll be there, then he hung up and went through to her.

"The Ministry," he said, "told me they'd written ages ago and why hadn't I called. I've agreed to go up for an interview this afternoon."

He was aware of keeping the enthusiasm out of his voice and Lucy picked on it immediately.

"*Lyubimy*, you have to be keen, otherwise don't even go –

19

and don't let them talk you into something awful, and nothing dangerous either or they'll have me to reckon with." She brandished a spatula with a threatening gesture but his responsive grin didn't come easily. Everything she did since Rollo's call seemed to take on a new poignancy, spreading a hollow feeling in his stomach, the dread like going back to school, the sense of impending loss.

By the time she'd dropped him at the station her affectionate high spirits had lifted him back into good humour; in the train to London he read *The Times* and wrestled with the crossword as an effective distraction. He went first to South Africa House in Trafalgar Square, struggling past a group of bedraggled demonstrators only to discover he didn't need a visa, then to South African Airways in Regent Street where they had a temporary computer problem. They told him he needn't wait if he had a booking and could collect and pay for his ticket at the airport. Annoyed with a wasted day, he had a solitary beer and a sandwich, bought Lucy a huge, nightie-sized T-shirt with DON'T STOP! daubed all over the front and was home by late afternoon.

Having to suppress his resentment at the need to go at all was a constant irritant, although he was aware that most of the married men he knew would jump at the chance to be away for a while and perhaps find a little adventure.

When Lucy came to pick him up, he wrenched open the car door with unwarranted force, leapt in and growled at her.

"So, you conniving old bat, you finally did it!"

Although fairly sure he was joking, she put on an expression of pained surprise. "Did what, my love?"

"Got rid of me, got them to give me some mysterious bloody job. At least you aren't wearing your new boots, rubbing salt in the wound."

"I said I wouldn't till you heard – I take it you had a nice day at the office, dear? What's the job?"

"They won't tell me, and when they do, I can't tell anyone, including you."

"Oh, that's just great ... You remember when you overheard me at the McKinleys?"

"No, what?"

"Someone asked me, as usual, 'what does your husband do?' and I fluffed back with 'Not a lot'. You weren't too pleased about it. Well, what am I supposed to say now, you do something crypto with the Min. of Sleuth? Anyway, it had nothing to do with me, it was your idea." She drove intently, exaggerating the calm in her voice.

"If it wasn't for you and your unceasing demands for fripperies, I wouldn't need a stupid job."

"Very well, I'll leave."

"When?"

"After breakfast. No, when I've got the boots."

"If you do, I'll pee on your plants."

"NO! You murderer, I'm not leaving then."

"Good ... Luce, the honeymoon's not over, I promise, but I do have to go away for a little while, some sort of refresher course, I don't even know how long."

"Is that what you're upset about, leaving me?"

When he nodded quietly she added, "So am I. But it'll be super when you get back, won't it?"

"It is already, after half a day."

She laughed. "You know, you're hopelessly wife-bound."

"Uxorious."

"That's what I said ... what's the opposite, I mean what am I?"

"I don't know if there's a word – husbound, I suppose."

"Sounds good. I've made a special dinner."

"More blackmail, you're shameless. *Lyuba*, I love you so much it hurts."

"Still?" She smiled at his occasional use of her Russian diminutive.

"It's never still. It gets worse as you get nicer."

Her shoulders rose up as if to hide her cheeks in shyness.

"You're just saying that," she smiled. "Just words."

"It's all we have."

"Really? Huh, you wait, Tarzan."

Stuart managed to sustain a playful innocence, being sure he could justify the lie as soon as it was over. It didn't seem like the first fearful downturn in the spiral of deceit.

With some glee, Lucy telephoned her mother the same evening to tell her the news. Alicia Simonova lived in an apartment in North London, a disciplined lady of severe grace who seemed to consider lack of formal employment a major character defect. Stuart charitably put this down to conditioning. She was not without humour as long as the priorities were observed but Lucy teased her mercilessly.

"*Mamushka*. I told you I can't tell you because Stuart can't tell even me . . . Of course it's real, don't you trust him? . . . Well, I do . . . Oh, not again, I wish I hadn't said anything. Not all Czechs are gypsies, I thought you'd be delighted . . ."

She kept making faces at Stuart as she spoke, sometimes gesturing her mother's remarks about what she considered his fecklessness. Eventually she hung up laughing but affectionate and turned to him, mimicking her mother's accent heavily.

"She says you're not good enough for me, my love."

"So what's new?"

"Nothing. And she didn't go to all the trouble of bringing me here to give me away to some unprincipled capitalist who is probably now going to work against the mother country, her precious *Rodina*. At least she's patriotic to the bitter end. She's only jealous, she loves me being happy but wishes it was all her own doing, certainly not yours."

"It'd be a lot worse if you weren't. If I did anything to spoil it, I think she'd kill me."

He stopped abruptly and turned away wishing he was a more proficient actor, at least until he had time to adjust to his new rôle. Whenever he had the despairing thought that things might not be the same for them again, the apprehension made him feel physically sick, an unwitting defendant on every charge of cruelty and negligence. Compounding it was his inability to ask Lucy's forgiveness in advance; a desire, however craven, that would probably meet with flippant indulgence. He also kept telling himself that it was ridiculous and unnecessary to keep anything from her, so the secret recurred as a constant battle right up to the time of departure.

Tuesday and Wednesday he spent in a guilty rush of small and long-promised jobs: servicing the car and cutting a huge load of firewood. Lucy's encouragement and gratitude were actually galling for the first time, something he was to recall sadly in the days ahead as a bitter prelude to their last night together.

In the bedroom they usually kept a small lamp glowing because they delighted to see each other, watching faces and forms and the reactions to caresses. This once it was he, not

22

Lucy, who broke the spell of their quiet familiarities, simply because he couldn't bear for it to end. All movement ceased. His mouth next to her ear, he began to confide all the most gentle and largely unspoken lovers' thoughts, the nothings often discarded early in a relationship. Because of what he withheld, it began for him as another attempt to substitute for truth. Lucy's reaction completed it and then transformed it into something else entirely.

He was talking quietly and holding very still when she interrupted and began to clutch at his shoulders with her extraordinary wiry strength.

"I'm frightened," she hissed. "Something's happening."

Misunderstanding, he thought she had some premonition about his departure and he tried with a helpless desperation to allay her fears. Her tensions only redoubled and she began to make soft, plaintive keening sounds, gripping with astonishing ferocity. Wildly apprehensive, he could only hold her and mumble platitudes as if to a child while something as latently cataclysmic as a faulty dam or a dormant volcano seemed to be threatening all of their existence. A never-to-be-described, utterly personal drama soared in crescendo like a plea of Gothic tracery and camber, and when he realised what was happening, he tumbled pell-mell with her in the vortex of finale, a manic shuddering which left them aghast and wide-eyed in the low light, aware of nothing at all but themselves and the microcosm of their stage, with no possibility of an encore.

It was her words several minutes later which completed the burning of moment to memory. She spoke in an awed voice, wistfully.

"That must be the ultimate privilege. You talking . . . not even moving . . . loving and being loved as though my spinal fluid was being poured into a centrifuge with yours . . . being surged and spun into honey . . ."

Stuart found nothing more to say and he could only nod a jumble of agreement and disbelief into the warm, damp confluence of her neck and shoulder. He felt nothing could spoil the moment because nothing could lessen her, certainly no small enforced deceit on his part. He felt only a strange wonder and humility.

Two

At Heathrow in the late afternoon, when he went to collect his SAA ticket and check in, Stuart stared in disbelief at the figure he was supposed to endorse.

"Is this with an open return?" he asked. "Isn't it much cheaper in multiples of a week, or some such?"

The girl looked sympathetic and tapped her console keys, eventually shaking her head. "No sir, you have a one-way booking only, our executive Gold Class."

"Well, I don't want it," he protested. "Give me a cheapie near the back." Realising from her expression that he was cornered. She assured him that the tourist section had been fully booked and evidently Rollo, with typical disinterest, had simply booked him into the next section up. He asked for confirmation and waited till the last call but to no avail. He had a strong urge to cancel altogether and would have done so except for the impossibility of contacting Rollo or discussing it with anyone. Furious, he signed on for the executive class and was gingerly fed another apology. The section had suffered a small overbooking and as he was the last to check in he was requested to accept a First Class or Blue Diamond seat instead, for the same fare.

"Why me?" he said with plaintive jocularity and the girl filled in his ticket without further discussion.

"Just beyond gate 31, sir," she said with an envious smile. "The Blue Diamond lounge. Try to enjoy your flight, won't you, sir?"

The lounge was hushed and dignified with a large variety of drinks and canapés of prawns and smoked salmon. A

24

dozen other passengers sat reading newspapers or watching
the television, their own mutual appraisals completed and only
the newcomer with his casual dress and light grip to be
assessed. He helped himself to a *Guardian* and a cup of coffee,
then selected a packet of nuts from the low table in front of
him. The cellophane was extremely tough and gave him a
pyrrhic victory as it burst and scattered its contents on the
carpet. In the certain knowledge that the others wouldn't
have bothered, he picked them all off the floor and recovered
his self-assertion. Blissfully, they were called to the aircraft
only five minutes before taxi-time, given a choice of sparkling
Cape wine or orange juice as soon as they were seated,
followed by handouts of eyeshades, slippers and headphones.
The seat was huge and extravagantly spaced; raising his toes
still left him twelve inches to spare before the one in front.
The steward was good looking without being suspiciously
limp-wristed, and the blond stewardess was like a flower after
the rain, poised, solicitous, groomed to almost plastic perfection but saved in the end by a mole on her upper lip and a
broken finger nail. They were still taxiing to the take-off point
when she came to collect his glass and hand him the dinner
menu. Looking at it started a drooling frenzy coupled with a
strange guilt at the idea of enjoying himself alone. Lucy
seemed to hover permanently around the edge of his awareness.

He was one row from the front of the Springbok 747 where
the fuselage curves to give a half-forward vista; it seemed
unnaturally far off the ground and, when the brakes were
released to the trundle of take-off, the engine noise stayed
well behind and almost inaudible while the chassis rode the
runway bumps like a huge and overburdened lorry. He understood then why the 747 always seemed to hang in the sky
going nowhere, simply because of its size; at what seemed
from his eyrie no more than about 40 mph, the trundling
ceased as the nose was haughtily raised and the three hundred
ton monster performed the unthinkable once again.

Stuart's feeling of unreality persisted as he applied himself
to the finishing stages of a lengthy thriller riddled with sea-
going improbabilities. With almost perfect timing the stewardess renewed his suspension of disbelief with a brain-fuzzing
array of assorted cold appetisers followed by a choice of
caviar or other *hors-d'œuvres*. It stayed painfully difficult to

enjoy without Lucy to share it; her enthusiasm for good food was boundless and her absence felt like a missing limb.

A passenger in the front row was brusque and curtly demanding of the girl, making her work hard just to keep her poise and control. When she next came to Stuart he said, "That's it, don't let him get to you." She answered with a grateful smile but he was aware of the man's head jerking round and that in the super-quiet he must have been overheard.

Some time later the man got up and, on his way past, bent down as if to speak a confidence. His face was broad, tanned and very hard.

"Where are you from, mister?" he started to say in a strong Afrikaans accent but Stuart held up his hand to stop him. He saw the annoyed puzzlement on the bluff face and said quietly, "You and I have nothing to say to each other."

"Then by Hick you better hope we never have to, China," came the hissed and furious answer. He filled his jacket broadly and worked huge, gnarled fists but then, suddenly, his right hand shot out as if to make a grab at Stuart's clothing. He thought better of it and partly withdrew the hand but they were still left in an absurd glaring impasse.

After a few moments, Stuart broke his own tension by chuckling coldly. "Go away, you stupid gorilla, or I'll put something sticky down your neck while you're asleep."

"Where we're going, nobody threatens me, mister. God help you there, that's all."

"Go and sit down," Stuart answered with disdain. "And stop behaving like the school bully."

The big hand flicked out as if to strike him but it was only a feint. Stuart felt his blood pounding again as the anger resurged. The man continued to glare at him so he tightened his mouth and formed a single obscenity. It was assertiveness more than a break of control but its cost was to prove beyond calculation. He looked blithely away after speaking and thus failed to see the look of determined spite that filled the granite face of his antagonist. He simply wanted to be left to resume his meal in fabulously padded and cosseted luxury and indeed he was quickly calmed by meticulous attention. If the stewardess had noticed anything, she refrained from remarking on it although maintaining a particular deference.

For the main course he was faced with a choice of Lobster

Cardinal, pheasant with chanterelle sauce, roast saddle of lamb stuffed with spinach or the Chef's Special of steak, kidney and oyster pie. He knew Lucy would have loved the quiet dignity, the surprise of china and real glass. He chose the lobster and kept to champagne throughout, a Mumm Cordon Rouge which set him aching again because it was her favourite drink of all. To soften the blow and her chagrin, he resolved to tell her about the adventure only after she'd eaten something comparably delightful.

The meal finished with fresh strawberries, mints and coffee and later he watched part of the movie, an American teenage romp which seemed to bypass him altogether. He switched his dial to a programme of classical music and, thinking of the man in front, ordered a righteous cognac, remembering little afterwards except for the brief twitch of awareness when the girl collected his glass from falling fingers, helped to lay his mammoth seat out for sleeping and gave him a blanket and two pillows. He was aware of her attention, a heady perfume and the gentlest touch, but for him she held no physical allure.

Although the shades were down he awoke at dawn aware of some subdued activity which proved to be breakfast being freshly cooked in splendid variety, squeezed juices, every style of egg, turbot, bacon, mushrooms and sausages. The only other sound remained of the airstream over the skin, a hushed and unobtrusive whispering.

Stuart didn't normally bother with breakfast on his own but the treat was irresistible; he ate slowly of almost everything, eyes frequently closed and savouring and finally when the bar closure was announced he rounded it off with more champagne, feeling a thorough hedonist.

The lavatory compartments were also class reserved and stocked with toiletries, without queue or bustle, four of them for about twelve people. It was all such a luxury he could hardly bear to think of future flights in normal circumstances and, slowly, he began to realise it was one of the few times he'd had even a mild hankering for riches, the others being almost exclusively when he'd seen something unaffordable for Lucy. It was also the first time he'd woken without her for over a year; distance brought a detachment sufficient to make him wonder if he was overly obsessed or infatuated by her. Whatever it was he relaxed in the certainty that he was

27

helpless before it, and she seemed to colour his life like a sunrise stopped and captured at its most fulsome moment.

As the door opened to the mobile steps, an American passenger in front of him said to the stewardess, "Honey, I always fly First Class and that's the best yet," hot in his denial when she suggested he said that to all the girls. They filed off without haste or anxiety, another contrast with the usual pointless pressure in tourist sections.

"I wish I could say the same," Stuart said to her, explaining to her puzzled look that he hadn't flown First before and was unlikely to do it again. "I wasn't exactly a paying guest."

When she understood and smiled her goodbye, she added, "My name isn't Lucy, by the way."

With deliberate sheepishness he asked, "I called you that? I trust that's all I did?"

When she laughingly confirmed it, he pointed to the broad back at the bottom of the stairway. "Who's the big rude bull?"

She hesitated a moment for professional discretion but then said quietly, "Thanks for sticking up for me. He's BOSS, State Security. Or so he wanted me to know, which I didn't. Bad news, keep well away. His name's Kobus de Hoek."

He nodded and shrugged that he was unimpressed before mouthing her a light kiss and turning away. He felt refreshed and tingling, and outside, with the city's 6000 feet above sea-level, the air was crisp, dry and invigorating. They went quickly through Immigration and even so the bags for the Blue Diamond passengers were already coming off the conveyor, a source of wonder to Stuart but clearly normal for the expectations of the privileged. De Hoek was nowhere to be seen, however.

After Customs he showed a small hesitation outside the barrier and a tanned young man in an open-necked bush-shirt came over to him.

"Kody?" At Stuart's nod he said, "Follow me, please. I'm afraid you've got another couple of hours airborne. You must be tired, I guess?"

"Not a bit. Slept all night, champagne breakfast. In my next life I'm going to be rich."

"I think Runyan's plan is to have it sooner."

"Huh. Not when I've finished with him. You know him well?"

28

"I should say. Been pissed with old Rol more times than I care to think. Right bloody hell-raiser ... Mind you, he's had to slow down a touch recently, did ya hear?"

"I gathered something. What happened?"

"Big bullet but a long shot. He was lucky, only smashed his thigh-bone without pulverising it. I guess it was something unofficial because he's had to hole up. Me and a few cronies have been laying false trails here and there, no idea what's going on. He said someone would come and sort it all out. Maybe that's you, eh?"

"Maybe not. Maybe I'll just break his other leg and go home."

They re-emerged into brilliant sunlight and a taxi took them a long way round to another section of the airport. Through a low building, they walked out on to a tarmac GA apron and towards a slightly corrugated-looking Cessna twin, a 310N which had seen many a better year, standing frailly on its long oleos like a tentative wader. The engines were still ticking with contractions.

"Just got in?" Stuart asked pleasantly, privately wondering about inspection and maintenance logs. It was real now, the physical exposure, and he wondered whether his constant awareness of Lucy, with himself integral to her happiness, would make him indecisive and perhaps ineffective in a crisis ... a foreign country, with something already seriously wrong, knowing the penalties and daring to continue. Thinking of Rollo's understatement, he decided he probably hadn't heard the worst of it yet. He thrust the thoughts aside as the pilot nodded, climbed on the starboard wing, opened the passenger door, took his bag and tossed it into a second row seat.

"My name's Mike Desouches, by the way," he said, settling himself in the left seat and selecting ON for the Master switch. There was the familiar sound of a gyro spinning up and the VHF came to life at once. Desouches turned to see Stuart already strapped in and double-latching the door.

"You done any o' this?" he asked.

Stuart shook his head. "Not really. Student licence, about fifteen hours, but the cost back home got a bit much."

"Well, that's good, you'll be able to do some straight-and-level for me. The George's on the blink. Give you something to do, eh?"

29

He added a wry grin when Stuart ventured, "Everything else works, I take it?"

"Yiss, more or liss." Desouches played with an exaggeration of Afrikaans. "Don't be nervous, will you?"

"All right," Stuart answered, pretending instant reassurance which made Desouches laugh and shake his head.

"Rollo calls me Mickey Mouse Airlines," he said, thumbing the starter for the Number 1. It came healthily to life, rattling the old airframe severely as he called the tower, through the hand-mike, for his clearance. Stuart asked why there were no headsets and was answered with a quick, "Too sweaty." As soon as the Number 2 was running, Desouches released the brakes, did a rapid left-and-right check and swung on to the southbound taxiway. His fingers spanned dials and switches in a practiced muttered routine which gave some reassurance about professionalism, but Stuart knew it was wrong when they didn't bother to hold for an engine run-up, simply took their clearance at a rapid taxi, swung on to the main runway and opened up. He was only familiar with one type of light single and even the ancient twin was a bewildering and fast sophistication for him. He was leaning over and trying to orientate himself to the panel in front of the left seat where he was more acquainted when he found the airspeed indicator reading 95 knots. At that moment, Desouches eased the column back, the rumbling beneath them ceased, then his right hand snaked out to the gear switch. They could only have been inches from the ground but Stuart decided to remain unimpressed although unsure how to react when Desouches, still accelerating flat out and making no attempt to climb, actually looked across and said something with a broad grin.

"What?" He straightened to hear but the noise and the accent made it difficult, the affirmative sounding like a flying instruction, "Yaw".

"*Ja.* I once had to fly in a movie, the totally incompetent number where the guy has never done it before. It's actually harder than doing it properly."

"Like this, you mean?"

"You mean, which is this? Hah, hah!" They were still streaking along the runway at zero feet, full throttle and 150 knots but the end was in sight and Desouches reluctantly eased back the column into a very high rate of climb, trimmed with an apparent indifference and said carelessly, "She's all yours, mister."

"What?" Stuart said sharply but the other man was already half out of his seat, kneeling on it to rummage behind him. Gingerly he took a grip on the yoke and felt sweat break out on his palms almost at once, then he determined to relax and do as much by the book as his limited knowledge would allow. He pushed forward to ease the sharp rate of climb and, at the same time, drew back the twin throttle levers to reduce power. Desouches turned his head to watch him.

"OK, good. Now trim forward slightly until the pressure comes off the column. The other two levers are the props, ease 'em back to give 2300."

"Sorry, I don't get that."

"Propellor pitch dictates the engine speeds, while the throttle adjusts the power output. It's a kind of compromise, like going into overdrive for cruising."

"So what should I do with the throttles?"

"Ease 'em forward slightly till the manifold pressure shows 22 inches. You'll see them under the rpm gauges ... yeah, that's it. Just hang in, I'm trying to find my sandwiches."

"What's the heading?"

"235°, give or take."

Minutes passed with Stuart concentrating stiffly, Desouches taking nonchalant bites from a curled-up sandwich. "Want a chew?" he asked discouragingly but Stuart shook his head without taking his eyes off the panel.

"You're doing pretty well for a guy with only fifteen hours," Desouches commented after watching quietly for several minutes. "Why don't you relax your fingers, tension only works against you. That's what tension is, useless."

Stuart smiled gratefully, understanding and feeling a delicious and gradual loosening creep through him. After a while he grinned without glancing across, aware of the other's casual scrutiny.

"Is this where I get over-confident and blow it?"

"D'you know, that never happens if you're aware of the possibility. I reckon anyone with the feel of it is as bored as a bolt-hole by a flying school long before he gets his licence, which is when he discovers he's not competent to do anything but go on being a student or a fair-weather flier for

31

ever and ever. At the moment this is taxing for you, concentration, so you're really enjoying yourself, I'll bet?"

"True. Look, will you show me everything that's going on here and not too quick?"

Desouches feigned indifference. " 'Kay, but instructions extra."

"Rollo's paying, isn't he?"

"Huh, in *my* next life, maybe. Let's swop seats, I'll go in the back while you slide over."

Stuart's tension returned the moment he found himself alone at the controls, but Desouches started cackling from behind once he'd flopped into the middle seat and then got his foot stuck. Laughingly he completed the highly unorthodox manœuvre without Stuart having serious height or control loss and for the next hour he was enthralled by the complexities of twin flying. Bumptious as he seemed, Desouches had no time for preciousness or reserve and was an unstintingly good teacher, making him repeat or recite back everything he was shown. It was exhausting and exhilarating at the same time and Stuart realised he hadn't enjoyed himself so much in the air since his first familiarisation flight at a now-defunct Midlands flying club. It was also the first time he'd genuinely wanted to resume lessons since feeling the disillusion of an embittered and none-too-hygienic instructor.

The terrain below was a patchwork of vast farmlands wired with murram roads and distantly bisected by the main highway, dried up by the drought which continued into winter. Desouches pointed silently to their position on his chart, showing where they were leaving the Transvaal for the Orange Free State and the huge stretch of water of the Bloemhof Dam ahead, two-thirds of the way to Kimberley. Imperceptibly the left wing began to dip and the aircraft's heading reduced towards the south.

Desouches waited a while before remarking on it and Stuart came back with a jolt at his muttered query, "Where you goin', min?"

Lucy, always Lucy, not so much intruding as being summoned to join in everything and Stuart gradually dropping what wasn't easy to share. He realised he hadn't thought of resuming flying simply because it was an activity which, in its early stages at least, didn't include her and therefore lacked that essential piquancy. He had a small inkling that it was time to do something about it.

"Sorry," he grinned sheepishly. "First time I . . ." He stopped but Desouches either read his thoughts or spoke from long experience.

"Touch of the LAMMs? That's what I call it, stands for 'Look at me, Mammy.' Lotta people lose concentration because they've got too much going on, like, instead o' being the thing, in this case a twin-engined Cessna with a man attached to it, they get conscious of Self, like 'If they could see me now,' or 'Wish you were here.' It takes them away, really, so they don't achieve anything. That's how you get lousy lovers and good pilots – or vice-versa. Where were you?"

Stuart shrugged. "Doesn't matter. But you're quite right."

"Ha. So you got a small son or a brand new lady, is that it?"

Stuart felt no annoyance, appreciating the word instead of a man-to-man crudity. He glanced quickly to his right and nodded with a slight smile because it remained one of his delights to introduce her to people as before they were married, "This is my lady," – which so often evoked the question, "But I thought you were married?" and he could then confirm it with pride and pleasure. Lucy loved it as well, feeling it to be a much brighter and livelier word than "wife" with its staid implication of a finished adventure.

He was still in a turmoil of mixed emotions, still bewildered by the wrench of parting, still travelling southwards and away; on the brink of something perhaps exciting and uncertain yet still wishing to be finished and heading home. He brought his attention back to the aircraft and all too soon Desouches was pointing at the startled needle of the Automatic Direction Finder, reaching across him for the microphone, changing frequency, calling Kimberley to extend his flight plan "for a small sight-seeing detour". Acknowledged, he turned south abruptly and began a rapid let-down, telling Stuart to follow through on the controls, to lower flaps and undercarriage. Only then did he see their target, a rough dusty strip carved out of the bush which they approached at an alarmingly steep angle yet flared to a delicate touch-down; as soon as they halted, the engines left on tickover, Desouches opened the door, reached in for Stuart's bag and stepped on to the wing, beckoning.

Stuart followed the gesture and got out feeling bewildered, but the other didn't explain, simply clapped him on the shoulder, said, "Be seein' you," and ducked back into the aircraft. He heard the latch snapped from inside so he stepped off the wing and the engines roared up again. Swirling dust, the Cessna took off cleanly using the second half of the strip, banked right and disappeared, its sound receding quickly beyond a low rise. Stuart stood in the gathering silence, his skin growing sticky, looking about him for the eyes of watchers or predators and anger filling the place of puzzlement.

Suddenly, an engine burst into life and a yellow jeep erupted from the nearby bush shedding shrivelled foliage and thorn. The driver had a grinning black face under a coarse woollen cap and swirled up to him, the vehicle bucking; shaking his head, Stuart had to return the grin and got into the front seat feeling some relief: the nonsense could only have been Rollo's doing.

"Ten minutes, master," said the black. "An' I been told not to scare you."

The ancient jeep cantered crazily through the bush, dodging thorn and termite mounds, its engine screaming at the abuse. Eventually the driver pointed down a long over-grown approach path to an old deserted shack, its corrugated iron roof held down with large stones. He stopped then, watching carefully before moving on to some signal unseen to Stuart who was coughing away the enveloping dusty wake. He knew for certain who was waiting there.

Reading herself to sleep alone for the first time in more than a year had been strange enough; waking to reach out an arm into cold empty sheets where there had always been a welcome or, at least, residual warmth, was almost bewildering. There was birdsong and a leafy light-pattern on the ceiling, a distant late cockerel, other comforting country sounds which yet roused her to a feeling of curious isolation. Lucy rolled over, turned her pillow into a hug and kissed him demurely on closed eyelids, smoothing back the hair on his temples. It was far from satisfactory, she decided, an empty gesture for herself, and resolved not to do it again. Throwing back the duvet, she drew her right foot up behind her hip, extended her left leg to the vertical then swung it down strongly past the edge of the bed. Her torso rose in counter-balance and she was instantly on her feet, going straight into a hard sequence of stretches before heading for the shower.

Slim-hipped to the point of boyishness, lithe and quick, she knew well enough how much physical advantage she'd been given to captivate and enthrall. It made her appear elusive which she was not, and also ethereal, a different, subjective joyous quality and, if anyone seemed distressingly in awe of her, she would gently assure them that she was only a person, just another monkey with a different set of tricks. She had few illusions about herself and her one guilty secret was locked away, shared only with her mother, seldom mentioned or even brooded over in her most private thoughts.

Murderess... Only yesterday the thought had surfaced again after a lengthy burial. She wondered if it was because of Stuart being placed in a position of less than total confidence with her – either that or because of an almost desperate quality in his loving and the poignant farewell whisking her fleetingly back to the other relationship, the clawing, despairing destructiveness ending in a brain-spattered horror. The telephone call, then the visit from the Action Police, "Excuse me, are you Mrs –," she didn't even want to remember the name she'd lived under for so short a time, wishing it as buried as an old man's war memory.

Why had she never told him, never even dared ask herself the question? The answer coming simply now under the deluge of hot water, eyes tight shut behind a mantle of streaming hair: because, my love, you are a jewel, and I didn't want to sully your dream, to ask you to share yourself with anything less than wholesome; yet that is what I've done even so by withholding the truth. And I promised Alicia never to tell a soul, she said it was for my sake; well I'm sorry, dear mother, I think I'm going to break that promise at the first opportunity since he is allowed his secrets but I am not... How long? He said he'd call, if not every day, then at least whenever he could, not to speak, just to let me hear one chime to tell me all's well and I'm in his thoughts every day...

In a sombre mood, she finished a breakfast of home-made muesli and then, characteristically, made a prompt decision not to simmer with impatience or brooding but to fill her day with something positive. The first thing that occurred to her was to sharpen the breadknife; Stuart had been trying to make toast from a tetchily flattened loaf, struggling to get a cut started. Faced with an accusing scowl, she'd had to admit to edging the lawn with the knife, and now the memory of his indulgent smile breaking under the eyes-to-heaven look almost made the tears well up. He pretended not to adore the sudden impulses she had to give him unexpected hugs or fluttering fingers, triggered by such affectionate thoughts, but in fact he was wise enough to know that a too-positive reaction might inhibit her from making her exquisite gestures. He pretended not to be completely enchanted by her, whether moving or in repose, naked or clothed, and she loved him for the act, the effort it took him to retain a semblance of control. It was constant proof that he was sufficiently confident of her and secure in himself that he didn't need either to dominate her or to subject himself to her, in that impossible downward spiral of emotional insecurity ... not like that frenzied mess of a Celt who, in his frustration at being unable to accept any reassurance from her, had finally resorted to violence, violation, even attempted degradation ... The suppressed memory, surfacing like a molten bubble, was doused instantly by the grief for the flawed affair and the guilt that he had paid for it with his life. Voicing it, she said to herself, "I am glad for what I have found but I do not rejoice for what has gone, so can I yet be freed and made to feel cleansed? I was guilty of giving him everything of me and there perhaps I failed him – so you were right for him as for yourself, Mr Henry James, 'Our doubt is our passion ...', but not, not for me. My passion is my gratitude."

After a token pass at housework and a shopping list, she paused on a sudden inspiration, looked at her watch, hurriedly changed from jeans to track-suit trousers and ran out to the car. The prep-school children at Langham usually shrieked into the playground at 10.45; sure enough, the small horde was emerging just as she drew up outside. One or two recognised her and waved but when she got out and began to behave strangely, the clamour subsided and the others joined them at the railings to watch her. Clowning, arms outstretched, she wavered along the edge of the kerbstones pretending they were too narrow, then she bent deeply forward and in fluid continuity arced one leg, then the other, right over the top in a walk-over, landing on tiptoe for a perfect split second before another comedy of imbalance. To a bedlam of approval she then made a somersault backwards with more fooling, then went into a series of cartwheels one- and two-handed followed by back-flips, handsprings, a flic-flac and finally, to horrified withdrawal, leapt for the railings and slowly drew herself up until her hips were next to her hands on the flat top bar. She grinned quickly at the upturned faces, then, her head going down and hips rising, she went steadily up into a faultless handstand. There were frightened gasps and more squeals when she couldn't resist a pretended topple, but then she took one hand off and snatched a turn, letting herself stealthily down inside the playground.

After her breathing and the questions subsided ("I thought they only did that on the telly") it was a matter of minutes before she had them organised into ranks of cartwheelers, with the duffers getting special attention. The naturals wanted to learn more, especially somersaults, and had to be refused because of the hard tarmac surface. Then Mrs March, the teacher, emerged, watched out of the corner of Lucy's eye. Had she said something like: "You might have asked me first," Lucy was ready to say sorry and leave. Instead she was given a smile, a hand on her upper arm and a wistfully spoken, "Can you come every day?"

"I expect so," she answered smiling airily. "But we should have a thick mat or some soft grass, for skin and bones' sake."

"You could use my lawn at the back but it's soggy from all the rain, they'd ruin it. Perhaps I can persuade the council to give us some mats – in fact, if you were to come round this evening, you could meet two of them and ask them yourself. You're Mrs Kody, aren't you?"

Later that evening she met two rather stuffy and self-important men, gave them a demonstration, charmed them out of their wits and became promptly employed. They even offered her other schools if all went well and she wished it, and they promised her mats and other equipment.

"Just one thing," she added in parting, "I want you to help me keep it from my husband. A secret, all right?"

They took a grave delight in her conspiracy, and Lucy began to foresee all kinds of possibilities in joyous deceit and pretended wickedness. She saw it as her counter to Stuart's mystery, resolving that he wouldn't keep any secrets from her, at least not without paying in teasing and suspicion.

Three

A diamond is for ever or a million years, whichever comes first.
Rollo Runyan

Even the regular South African Police still referred to them as the Security Police although they had, because of the unfortunate acronym BOSS forced on them by a persistent small error in the *Rand Daily Mail*, restyled themselves The Department of National Intelligence. Brigadier Kobus de Hoek reached his anonymous and temporary office on Wolmarans Street, mid-Johannesburg, still in an evil frame of mind, furious about Stuart Kody's dismissive remark on the aircraft. Shown his wallet insignia, the immigration computer operator had willingly supplied him with a name and a UK address and, as he strode past his secretary, he gave her the print-out and barked at her after a curt greeting.

"Mollie, get on to London and have someone ferret this Anglo, history, record, the lot. Dig me up some dirt, find out what he's doing here."

Like the rest of those under him, Mollie Vrouwer was quick to his bidding. "The Hook" was much feared, ruthless, vindictive and machine-like in his devotion to duty, rooting out espionage and subversion. His sway was by no means limited to his home town; those of the Embassy staff in London who were, in reality, on the Security payroll had recently been given good cause to resent him as well as an added stimulus to co-operate. De Hoek had burst into a quiet summertime lull with a series of screenings and mordant interviews, all threatening worse than dismissal for a recent breach where an Embassy courier had been selling information to both East and West. The fact that all of it was false and issued only to line pockets was beside the point – it

39

had been going on undetected for 17 months. In London they didn't need to speculate on his fate, having seen him escorted to Heathrow for the next Cape-bound flight by two silent heavies.

The response to Mollie's telex was therefore rapid and within three hours they had established that Stuart Kody, although born in England, had a Czech father, had served three years in the British Army, was solvent but not employed and, interestingly, had married the daughter of an expelled Russian diplomat, a victim of the 1971 purge. They had gained two addresses and at once despatched two pairs of operatives, one to Hampstead, one to Gloucestershire. They found both places unoccupied and had to wait three more hours before the first arrival; Alicia Simonova strolled back to her apartment in the evening, loosely tethered to a dainty Yorkshire terrier.

They gave her five minutes before ringing the bell and, meeting with the expected chain, inserted bolt cutters and quietly chopped it in half. Although they were ready with a stifle, the middle-aged woman, dressed in black with her hair drawn severely to a bun, fell back soundlessly and seized a small chair to swing in frail defiance. One of the men put a big hand firmly on the chair while the other shut the door and attempted to catch the frantically yapping terrier.

"Quiet the dog, woman," ordered the first man, "otherwise we do it. There'll be no harm if there's no noise. We're not stealing, we want to talk."

Shaking with fear, Alicia finally nodded and called to the dog, which still refused to be silent until she gathered it to herself and sat down.

"Where is your son-in-law?" asked the first man, watching her eyes carefully. "Why is he in South Africa?"

Alicia was now certain from the accent that they were not Russians speaking English but it was still one she could not place. "I—I do not know."

He clicked his fingers to his colleague who passed him the bolt cutters. "We have to be sure you are telling the truth," he said quietly. "I am going to cut one leg off your dog to show you I mean it, then one more for every lie."

He thrust the open jaws forward but after a look of squeezed terror, Alicia moved the little Yorkie aside and put

40

her index finger in the fork. "I do not know where he is," she repeated firmly, unmoving.

"Who does he work for?"

"Ach, he has had no employment till, since, the Army."

The man picked up her hesitation at once. "And now?" he asked, his eyes narrowing, flexing his grip on the cutter handles.

With a sigh, Alicia answered, "He gets just now a job with the English Government."

"What sort of a job?"

"Secret. Defence something. I don't know anything else, or where he has gone. A course, he said. My daughter didn't . . ." She stopped with a look of pure anguish in Arctic blue eyes. "Please, she has told me all she knows, please leave her –"

"Where is your husband?"

"Oh, I wish I did not know this. Please, why do you ask?"

"Just answer and we'll leave."

"I . . ."

"Otherwise poochy gets a leg off. We doesn't want your finger," chirped the second man, angrily quelled by the first.

"I understand in Belgium," Alicia answered finally.

"Where? Doing what?"

"Just a diamond merchant. Please go now, I am coming sick. Who are you?"

"It doesn't matter. You won't see us again."

In silence he withdrew the cutters and hooked them inside his coat. He glanced round the apartment which was chintzy but brightly cheerful, then turned to her for a last word.

"We could take the dog and let it go at the end of the road, if there's no shouting. Or we could take your word. Give us five minutes, *ja*?"

Swallowing harshly, Alicia nodded and tried to shoo them away. "Just go, quick, quickly, you have all the time. Go, only go."

As the door shut behind them, she held the little terrier up to her face for long moments, her heart pounding, before getting up and going to a little cabinet and pouring a huge measure of Armagnac, a Christmas present from Stuart. She thought of all the Western tales of the sinister "comrades", the dawn intrusions, the third degree of her native land, and couldn't believe it was happening here. She almost choked on the brandy but it quelled the nausea and gradually she began to regain her composure. Apart from Lucy she had no one else to call, since, obviously, the Police had had nothing to do with it, and she herself had had no contact with the Soviet Embassy for several years.

To be certain, she waited a full ten minutes and then checked outside the door before calling her daughter. There was no reply, nor on the subsequent attempts later in the evening.

The two men waiting outside the Kodys' house heard the repeated ringing and relaxed their vigil with a hasty snack in the Horse and Groom. The locals eyed them suspiciously. It wasn't until after 11 pm that Lucy finally swung into the short driveway, leaving the car lights on while she unlocked the front door. When she returned to douse them, one of the men emerged from the cover of a big hydrangea and slipped into the darkened hallway.

The telephone started to ring again as she turned on the hall light and locked the door. Sensitive to her new solitude, she was aware of a presence in the room just as she picked up the receiver, then with an electric motion she leaped sideways as a hand smacked down to cut off the call. Crouching, she faced her intruder, fists extended one behind the other in instinctive reaction before remembering her teacher's instruction for a real situation, not to betray her skill. Quickly she straightened her arms into a more feminine and ignorant warding-off gesture, backing away and looking scared. The man came forward to make a grab for her and the cold, professional determination in his eyes was enough to inform her what she needed to do. He was big and the space was limited by furniture, so a contact skirmish had to be avoided, even the possibility of a grab.

Kiy Chen had given her a fall-back for such a situation and made her practise endlessly, two grape-sized felt markings on the punchbag a hand's breadth apart; her middle finger dipped in a stiff whitewash and the snake-form strike, made so much quicker by the intention, before delivery, of withdrawing the blow afterwards, a kind of reverse follow-through so that the contact had the full whiplash effect . . . There came a time when even moving across the target she never missed the two black dots, always perfectly placing the

42

little dabs of white which she had to pound off after every session.

As the man advanced, her right hand fell back to avoid his grip and he smiled at her apparent resignation. It was the last thing he ever saw clearly since the double shuck-shuck of her middle finger was too fast for him to register. There was only bewilderment and agony and a stream of tears as he slashed out blindly and knocked over a standard lamp. Lucy dropped into her flattest crouch and dived forward out of range, then kicked the coffee table over to cover the sound of replacing the receiver, all the time watching the blinded man's fruitless groping. She felt curiously detached and verging on pity but then gasped at seeing another face at the window. She froze in indecision, at last given enough time to appreciate fear.

Only later was she able to congratulate herself on the cool intelligence of her next move. She slid the telephone out of sight behind the sofa, dialled 999, and sprinted upstairs just as the man outside smashed the window and began to grapple with the catch. He freed it and clambered furiously into the room, took a quick look at his colleague before darting behind the long sofa. He picked up the receiver and heard the operator's irritated voice, "... again, Emergency, which service did you require?"

He slammed the receiver down and turned to his injured partner, not knowing that a small voice above was asking for the Police on the extension after waiting with desperate restraint for the click of the receiver downstairs.

Giving brief and breathless details, Lucy locked the bedroom door, jammed a delicate and favourite chair sadly under the handle and went to the window overlooking the garden. A plastic drainpipe off to one side offered the only fragile escape but pounding feet on the stairs left her with little choice about testing Stuart's workmanship on the pipe-fastenings. He'd told her plastic was best because it was burglar-proof. With a slight hesitation she swung out and shinned rapidly down. It held her until she was five feet from the flower-bed when she felt it sag quietly outwards; she let go and landed softly in the dark wet earth. She listened a moment and moaned to hear a splintering from upstairs but then she was off and running, familiar with her home ground, wildly alarmed but at least confident and free.

There was no pursuit, but a surprisingly few minutes later she heard a powerful V-8 being worked hard through the gears, broad tyres whickering beneath the urgent stabs of a blue rotating beacon. The 3.5S Police Rover scythed to a stop outside the gateway and Lucy felt her shoulders sag in relief as she began to tiptoe cautiously back. By the time she reached the house, one officer had made his way round to the back and she called out to him, shielding her eyes when his torch stabbed out for her face.

"Did they both get inside, miss?"

"Yes."

"Well, they're either still there or they've gone. Any weapons, do you –?"

He stopped at the sound of a car starting and a violent take-off about two hundred yards away, then sprinted round the house to shouts from his colleague. They both leaped into the car and the engine started before either door was shut but when the driver let the clutch in, they heard a hideous thrashing noise from underneath the body. The car jerked forward a few inches as the drive shaft ripped up into the floor and began to shred the upholstery. The driver switched off hastily and they both got out, heaving with unspent adrenalin. A brief examination with a torch was enough and the driver stood up holding a bent piece of metal, his expression one of outraged disgust.

"Must've slipped their jemmy into the universal coupling." he said to his colleague, palming a fist viciously but leaving Lucy no wiser.

"Did you see a car? Any descriptions?" he asked her urgently.

"No, not really, it was all too quick. The one inside was very big, the other was just a crazy face at the window. The first one had black hair, square face. Very unhappy, I poked him in the eyes."

They looked at her with startled admiration then one of them relayed the information over the car's radio while the other suggested a look inside the house.

"I can offer you a cup of tea – or a push," she said giggling, realising she had slight shock. "Or I could tow you with the Golf."

He didn't reply but climbed in through the smashed window and searched around, putting lights on before opening the front door. To their questions, Lucy replied that there was nothing missing, only the capsized lamp and broken window left in evidence. Then she remembered the bedroom door. They found it hanging by one hinge but to her delight the little Queen Anne chair had sprung away and was undamaged. She replaced the telephone receiver and then they accepted her offer of tea while they waited for a tow-truck and the fingerprint man.

While they were in the kitchen, the telephone gave a single long trill. Lucy looked up startled and then quietly relaxed with a slow spreading smile.

To inquisitive looks she explained, "My husband. He's away but he promised to do that every day he could, just one ring to say he's OK and thinking of me."

"And where is he, can you get in touch with him?"

"No, I can't, I don't know. He's not allowed to say."

"Oh, how's that?"

"His work's secret."

"You can tell it to us, ma'am, surely?"

She shook her head impishly, hair swirling. "I can't, I don't know, you see –"

The telephone rang in earnest this time and she ran through to answer it. "Yes, *mamushka*," they heard her say, then an indrawn gasp followed by an exclamation. They went after her when she called out, "Officer, here quickly! My mother was assaulted earlier this evening by two men who threatened poor Harvey, to cut his legs off. They wanted to know where Stuart was, what he was doing."

"Your husband, I take it?"

"Um. They asked why he was in South Africa which is nonsense, he's just gone on a language refresher some-where."

"Who's Harvey?"

"Smith. Her Yorkshire Terrier. My God, they were going to chop his little legs off with a huge pincer if she didn't tell the truth . . . Yes, mama, wait, I'm just talking to the police-men now."

She nodded once or twice at the telephone then explained to the men that her mother had also called for investigators but there was nothing to find. She hung up eventually, prom-ising to call back because the senior Policeman said they should make a check call to the MoD to inform them that one of their employees was being hounded by persons unknown.

"Do you know who to speak to, ma'am?" one asked, but Lucy shrugged helplessly. "Never mind, we'll get HQ on to it. Leave the rest to us. I should think you've had enough for one evening."

The phrase was somehow evocative so Lucy fetched the brandy bottle, poured herself a good measure and then tilted it into the co-driver's cup. He grinned and accepted but when it came to the other he covered his with a hand. Lucy gently prised his fingers apart and poured a measure through them, looking serious.

"You can say I forced you," she said, and his resistance collapsed in helpless disarray.

It was 3 am before she finally got to bed, the window roughly patched and wired and fingerprint powder everywhere. She had called her mother back but it was only a re-hash of events and further speculation and she was coming to stay the following day as previously arranged. Lucy slept in the end comforted by Stuart's single ring and her own feeling of loyal toughness, sure that there must be a simple explanation. She would have tried to find it amusing but for the violence which brought her mind back to her resolution; she found it was reluctant to go back to the terrifying confrontation with the big, dark attacker. At least, she told herself, this time there had been no temper, no fury, nothing even personal, just the sharply cold and confident thrust of an untried weapon. She was strangely pleased to have kept her fingernails trimmed short.

Runyan was slumped in an old frayed hammock, crudely tethered to crumbling veranda posts. The shack looked convincingly abandoned and the termite armies were mobilising for its complete demolition. His right leg was roughly plastered from groin to mid-calf and on the lower part of his thigh there was a brown circle of long-dried blood soiling the grey-white reinforcement. He made no attempt to swat the slow winter flies on it because it kept them away from his face and from the steady grey eyes which observed the approaching jeep. A single crutch and a seven-shell 12-gauge pump-action leaned against the wall within reach. He made no move towards them, the timing was right.

46

The jeep stopped in a half-circle and the driver waited a moment for the dust to clear before getting out and retrieving a box of supplies from the rear well. On the passenger side, Stuart also waited before emerging, expressionless, watching the suppressed grin on Runyan's face, the deep-burnt crow's feet round the eyes producing a quizzical or perhaps mocking effect.

Wooden-faced, Stuart mouthed a soundless oath at him, short and unmistakable, before retrieving his grip from the back and walking up to the crude veranda. The late winter sun warmed palely but there was no wind to exaggerate the chill.

"Does it hurt?" he asked, intoning as much disinterest as possible.

"If I said it did, would it please you, old sport?"

"Try me."

"It hurts."

"Good."

Runyan chuckled. "Mushy," he said. "Marriage has softened you up, obviously . . . Nice flight? What did you think of all my arrangements?"

"I'd like to know what the hell you were doing booking me into Gold Class like some business executive."

"I couldn't help it, there was no choice. The cattle-and-sheep section was full up."

"Maybe, but the Maharaja section wasn't. I refuse to look like someone in employment so I had one of those seats you can get a whole refugee village into. It was peculiar, people fawning and offering fish eggs and fizzy yellow stuff. You know. Nice of you to pay for it, too."

"I was going to say I would, it'll come out of my share, but not the top rate. Forget it."

"Not likely . . . And then Mickey Mouse Airlines was on time, the pilot should be in an institution, and when you send a driver and limousine I'd prefer not to be ambushed."

Rollo grinned back. "The main thing is that you got here without them finding me or connecting us. I'll give you all the gen then you just take off again."

He looked at the driver, who had lit a cigarette and helped himself to a cold beer from the box. "Thanks a lot, Sohrab. Can you come back later on?"

The African took some moments emptying the bottle and then spoke with a twinkled exaggeration.

"Yes, Master. I thank Master for Lion beer." He wiped his mouth and heaved the empty bottle through a frameless window. There was a crash of breaking inside but Sohrab merely shrugged in puzzlement, slouched back to the jeep and grinned at Rollo's protest.

"Show some respect, you damn Dago."

Sohrab joined his fingertips in mocking salaam before driving off in dusty arrogance.

"Help us both to a beer, old son," Rollo said, still narrowly watching the jeep's powdery wake. "You get no respect when you're maimed and broke. He was all right with you. I expect. I told him you were loaded."

"When he called me Master, I didn't realise he was joking. I hate it for real, even Sir."

"Sure, but it's the norm here. Took me a while to break him of the habit, he was very touchy until he realised what I was at. I have to remind him not to presume on other whites, it could get him in a real bind, but for sure he doesn't want the time bomb to go off here any more than the Afrikaners do."

Stuart nodded and then made a wry face. "OK, why don't you tell me what happened instead of waiting for me to ask?"

Rollo's handsome face grinned back mockingly. "Why should I? You won't even shake hands with your old pal, the man who saved your life so often? You wait, inside a month you'll love me to distraction. Put it there, old son, and renew your sense of adventure."

With a final show of reluctance, Stuart took the outstretched hand and smiled into the familiar grey eyes. "Rol, I think you'd better stay a bachelor, otherwise your roustabout character will wither away."

"You mean you're no fun any more? Hell, I warned you. Usually the silly cows fail my boat test and give up after a week at the outside. That's why I told you to use the sloop. Did you get the name, by the way, *Sailor V*?"

Stuart shook his head, puzzled, and Rollo clucked scornfully. "I won her in a poker game off this ignorant Queenslander. He thought that's how you spell *C'est la Vie*!" He chuckled merrily and then grew serious again. "So the little missus passed the boat test and wouldn't sulk at the squalor and discomfort and the lack of attention?"

48

"Not only not, you'd have been mesmerised ... OK, I can't think why you've got a roller-reefing boom that's not round but oblong in section, but anyway, she flopped the mainsail off it, gave it a quarter turn and the next thing you know she's doing beam exercises, handstands, somersaults, flips, flops and splits, you name it, up there on the boom."

"Stark bollock?" asked Rollo, drawing in his breath.

Stuart nodded, his eyes closed and memory glowing.

"Snake-in-the-grass!" Rollo hissed "Fancy pulling a stunt like that to take your mind off her shortcomings ... But don't you worry, old son, soon as I get back I'll make some trouble for you, get you off the hook. Some pass the boat test but none get through the 'You-and-that-disgusting-friend-Runyan' programme."

Stuart only half-heard the banter, his mind far away, surprised at the constant little pulls on the tendrils of his emotions. He now felt ill-equipped for any of the devil-may-care horseplay and adventurousness he used to share with Rollo during their Army days, when creating risk to limbs or life was essential to, if not a statement of, being alive.

"Main thing is not to let her find out you're rich."

Stuart brought his attention back. "What? Oh, how much?"

"Each or all together?"

"How many are we?"

"Just you and me, mainly. We should clear a Big One each."

Stuart waited while Rollo grinned. "Dollars, I take it?" he asked eventually, feeling dubious about the rate of return, £20,000 into $100,000 or, at the going rate £65,000, excellent in terms of an annual return but not when years of freedom were at risk.

"So ... glad you came?"

"Not yet. Give me the bad news, what went wrong?"

"Ah ... Pull up that crate and dock yer bum. Got a cigarette?"

"No, I stopped." Stuart grinned almost contritely before adding, "Condition of marriage."

"Ah-well-no-fine, as they say around here." Rollo looked at him with some disgust. "Pass me a pack from the box of stores ... thanks. So you resent her for that presumably? It's a good start."

" 'Fraid not, I'm delighted. I *love* not smoking. Perhaps I replaced it with another addiction. You were going to say?"

"OK. Well, I made several good trips up the West Coast for the best part of a year and – what's the last thing you'd expect anyone to bring into this great Republic? I'll save you the exhaustion of thinking: Diamonds. Not so easy to get hold of here but up the Coast, much easier, Namibia, Angola, even Sierra Leone. IDBs, illegal diamond buyers, all scarper from there to Europe and no one's on guard for them to smuggle into the south, I mean that's lunacy. IDs crossing domestic borders only carries five years, see, but out of South Africa it's a bit different."

Stuart's eyes narrowed but he said nothing. Rollo went on blithely.

"So I cruised around buying here and there, driving a bakkie, that's a pick-up to you, to keep myself in beer and stuff since all our capital was marked for the goodies. Somehow the mineworkers always manage to get stones out, God knows how with X-rays here and lasers there, probes up their arses, muzzles on their snouts, I don't know. In the Police Museum I saw an X-ray of a guy with a taped package inside him, he must have hammered it in, it contained over eight thousand stones. Another had six thousand in a bicycle tyre . . . They get proper rewards for turning in their finds but still they'd rather sell to people like me, it gives them a kick to beat big brother. Thing is, I hadn't bought any here, and while everyone knows that the diamond smuggler is the biggest brag in the world, I'd kept very quiet and low, yet somehow the word was ahead and I was set up. Patsied. Last week I was up near the local Bophuthatswana when a strange one came in the night with three stones, one of them big, clear-looking, I mean big, should cut to 20, maybe 25 carats and the other two, don't breathe . . . OK, I was in the usual mildly pickled state on the point of sleep 'cos normally I wouldn't touch a stranger but they blinded me. The two rarest, a pink and blue, about the same size, would have cut to maybe 6 or 7 carats each. Staggering. The price was a joke but I was just about cleaned out so I told the Aff to wait in my room. I was going to have to borrow. Too good to pass up, see, but he didn't want me to go. Started shouting. I thought he didn't trust me; anyway, I clobbered him, grabbed the stones so he couldn't change his mind and went to get

50

the loot from a mate who runs a den. It was pitch black outside but I reckon they had some kind of intensifier and obviously the plan was to let the first guy out clear and then nail me with the IDs. I was going for the bakkie when I heard them bust the door down, guess you can't tell black from white, or brown from pink anyway, with a night sight; well, I ran like a cheetah with his tail on fire, putting street corners in the way. Truck was no good, obviously, but I found an unlocked scrambler outside a late bar, kicked it up and lit out of town. I saw there was a car coming after me so I took to the bush where they couldn't follow, Jeez, I must have been nearly a mile away, leaking like a sieve from the thorns. I saw the car stopped and assumed they'd given up then I got hit by the most staggering bloody pile-driver of a Liverpool spanner right here in mid-thighbone. I was unhorsed, you might say. Unconscious as well, don't know for how long, few minutes at the most, impossible shot in the dark, just lucky maybe. Helluva big slug, elephant-stopper, not the sort you'd have in a modern HV with a sniperscope, well you can, I suppose, but you'd need a trailer and two Affs to cart it about . . .

"Anyway, I came round sometime, put a tourney on my leg, gritted a tooth or two and got going again. Starting a stiff bike one-legged is not something you practise for much and I honestly can't tell you how I did it. Sheer courage, I guess, and –"

"Centuries of good breeding!" Stuart joined in their old joke about the upper-crust regiments, but was shaking his head in astonishment at the feat. "I'm feeling prickly, Rol, all of a sudden. What happened then?"

"I holed up and later contacted Mike, your pilot. He flew me in a bent doctor from Potchefstroom and I think he acted all suspicious to let the heat believe he'd got me away. A set-up like that must have been instigated by a company dick, in conjunction with the regular cops, SAPs, so it was risky for Mike but they let him be. Maybe they were hoping for a lead. They'd never think anyone crazy enough to stay around Kimberley of all places . . . Shit, and I was almost there, thinking we were home free. I was going to throw rocks at your windows, man, let you find them yourself in the garden! It was greed, plus I reckon they didn't know I was running out of cash for buying."

51

Stuart nodded slowly, beginning to see the picture more clearly. "And now?"

"Well, yeah. That's where you come in, you're the only straight guy I know, and even you haven't been tested with drooly little things like carbon crystals. Diamonds are not for ever, you know. Everything flows, the philosopher said: every diamond is slowly degenerating into black carbon. Takes about a million years, though, so it isn't all that worrying ... I'll have to stick around until I can walk normally through an airport barrier with my second passport, the other one having served me well for a year. I'll have to be purgative-clean in case I'm recognised or suspected, so the master-plan is for you to drive easy from Jo'burg to Mozambique with our joint futures in your broad Slavic hands."

Stuart blew out his cheeks disgustedly. "That's the border with the different sentence attached, I take it?"

Rollo knew not to dissemble and nodded gravely. He repeated the movement when Stuart added, "And you really expect me to believe you've got a broken leg inside that? And anyway, what's the hurry?"

"The hurry is I'm hot and I'm nervous and Tiki is threatening to split, he wants out, now. Listen, you're just a tourist, an innocent and they couldn't possibly connect you with me. Imagine combing England for people known to have consorted or conspired with one R. Runyan. Missing in Action."

Stuart looked sceptical. "Have you been MIA before this, so to speak? And what about Army records?"

"There, perhaps, a frail familiarity between us, like fighting and getting drunk and locked up together, etcetera."

"You mean, you getting into scrapes and me getting you out."

"Whatever ... I hardly think anyone's likely to piece it all and connect you, do you?"

"I've no idea. Tell me about the plan. I can't tell you how often I've wondered how you managed to persuade me to part with all that loot, a lot of vague waffle, that's all I heard."

Rollo smirked. "It was like Judo, I used your own impetus, your greed ... all right, your enthusiasm, willingness ... Right. The plan. You go back to Jo'burg and to a certain

52

address which I'll give you. There you pick up a Daihatsu Fourtrak which belongs to a man in Mozambique, Maputo, what used to be Lourenço Marques. You then go to the Central Post Office and collect a parcel addressed to you and you take it to a fellow called Tiki Powers who understands how to temper glass for windscreens. He works for an auto assembly plant in Pretoria. He's an old lag who appreciates my sense of humour and honour and who knows that I will kill him slowly if he palms a single stone or breathes a word, but that he will be happily solvent for perhaps the tenth time if he keeps quiet. He will make you a windscreen for the Daihatsu and meld into it the contents of your parcel. It will be quite a thick windscreen and he assures me that all the faces and roughnesses of the stones get cancelled by the molten glass. Invisible to all except polaroid glasses which usually show peculiarities in windscreens anyway."

Stuart's face wrinkled in disbelief. "You mean he's tried it?"

"Sure. Also he said he could lay them out in a pattern, it's the last thing anyone would suspect. I mean sure, tyres, tanks, sumps, chassis beams, hollowed-out bolts, hydraulic reservoirs, batteries, radiators – they caught one guy with a dozen in his whip aerial. You can imagine that's the very last place they looked after reducing his Range Rover to a Lego kit, never mind what they did to his old lady. I heard she went cross-eyed overnight ... Another guy fed his dog with a diamond pastie and tried to sue the government for cruelty when they gave it an enema. The judge was remarkably unimpressed."

"Terrific. And when they take this 'Whatnotsu' apart and find nothing, Kody gets out his spanner, rebuilds it and drives into the sunrise, is that it? Sorry, I won't do it."

"The Fourtrak is dead square and simple, that's why I – but listen, the point is they'd never do that to you, it's only if you're an old hand or if they know you've been buying."

"So how did they catch up with you?"

"I can only guess. De Beers say they've disbanded their own private detective force but I don't believe it. So they could have got one of my sources and given him a little treatment."

"Torture? That too, huh? Listen, Rollo, you'd-better think of something else. I'm going home."

53

"Shut up and listen. It's a degree of suntan, that's all. You're not even a *rooinek*, a redneck. Go pink and look stupid like a tourist, they won't even look at you, it hurts their eyes."

Stuart shivered, wondering if it was simply the breeze stirring the chill, dry air. He shook his head again but Rollo chose to notice only the first reaction.

"Yeah, it gets pretty parky later on. I've been here ten days now, apart from that dart into town to call you and set things up. You may remember from our creepy-crawly days, the one thing I hate is sitting out. Bit later on, when the chill comes, I get into my sleeping bag and stay there till morning. Stops me drinking, too, 'cos I can't be bothered to get out for a leak. Let's have another beer, eh? You hungry?"

Absently Stuart reached into the box for two more bottles.

"No, I feel like I had six breakfasts, swilled down with champers. Suddenly gone sour on me, you and this bullshit."

"Listen, it's a piece of pud. You just drive to Maputo, to a shipping office, book the jeep on to a Europe-bound freighter, preferably Belgium but it doesn't particularly matter, then you go to the airport and fly home to your boring old wife and two veg."

"First Class, I suppose?"

"Well, that's up to you, Getting the taste?"

"And the shipping, I was supposed to pay for that as well?"

Rollo shrugged helplessly. "Who else? You can do it COD. That's the way it goes, chum, I'm sorry, OK, so we put the same amount of cash up front but I've been slumming it for a whole year, all scary stuff, remember? You've just been contract-testing bedsprings and chartering expensive yachts free of charge. Look, you can't just take out the windscreen and post it to Belgium, it wouldn't make sense on a declaration. This way is kosher, you're declaring a car. By the time it gets there I should be free and frisky again so I'll deal with the rest of it. I know a bod who'll handle the IDs, – bit of a touchy subject in the rock world so you've got to peddle softly. So to speak, hah, hah."

"Hah . . . When that Sohrab comes back, I'm off home. I'll tell Lucy I didn't get the job and that's the end of it."

"What job?"

"I told her I had an interview with the MoD and couldn't

54

talk about it. It'll be a relief not to lie any more, you bastard. How are you planning to get out when you're OK?"

"You'll lend me the money, especially when you know the Daihatsu's waiting to be collected in Antwerp."

"Hey, wait a minute, I thought you said it belonged to a man in Mozambique."

"Well, it did really, but he'll have claimed on his insurance by now, I should think."

"Oh, hell, Rollo, it's stealing meanwhile, for God's sake!"

The grey eyes opened wide. "Smuggling stones is not exactly on the level either, you pratt."

"I'm not *doing* either!"

"Listen, we'll see him right as soon as we can afford it. I agree it's a bit different from running stones which is more of a sporting gesture. Like when we lifted that Police dog or the Legionaires' *képis* ... Anyway, we bought the stones, paid for them."

"Rollo, they're still *stolen goods*."

"God, what's happened to you? OK, it's the same in purely legalistic terms but nicking a few diamonds from a huge faceless monopoly isn't a crime against humanity like rape and violence. Thin lines, man, like there are immoral thefts which are quite legal."

"Such as?"

"Sharp practice in business. Or conning, say, getting people to sign over things by persuasion, when you know they wouldn't if you weren't so plausible ... Look, men invented laws like they invented crime; the laws are for society's protection, but society has no great interest in the success or failure of a rock monopoly."

"Really? What about all the miners, sorters and cutters whose livelihoods depend on the monopoly's stability?"

Rollo grinned suddenly. "We can shoot bull like this all day."

"Well, *you* can. I'm off."

"Smugglers create jobs for Customs officers! Anyway, it's only because there's a monopoly that the prices stay high, the jobs remain stable and so it's worthwhile trying to pull off a small scam. I'm told de Beers have whole loft-fulls of stones and if they released them all at once, diamonds would be worthless. Naturally they deny that hotly too and there's no way of getting at the truth. Meanwhile let us be grateful."

"What's the penalty for carrying out of SA?"

Rollo was quick to see the first chink in Stuart's defence: he was challenging his own courage.

"I'm not sure, they made some changes."

"Bollocks, I don't believe you. And why were you so adamant about me not telling Lucy?"

"Because . . . Look, supposing they did somehow make a connection between us, the team in England isn't exactly insignificant, with the Diamond Trading Company, de Beers, right there by Holborn Circus. Let's say they find you gone, they might think to ask your Lucy where you were or what the riotous Runyan is about. As things are, she can't say, even if . . ."

There was a crack as Stuart's sudden tension broke part of the crate's lid. White-faced he said slowly. "You mean someone might think of putting some physical pressure on her?"

"Look, relax, take that expression off. In simple terms, yes, although nowadays they know very early if a person's hiding something. No need to hurt them at all, I mean certainly not if they don't know, see?"

Stuart put a hand over his eyes as if trying to squeeze out some malignancy.

"It was only a precaution, don't worry about a thing," Rollo went on, then chuckled again. "There's another point though; when you fall out with her, you won't want her to know how much you've got!"

Stuart quelled the flash of anger, realising the banter held no malice, but it was a few moments before he was mollified enough to smile when his friend added, "Come to think of it, it's probably better she doesn't know even if you don't fall out with her, in fact it's certain. Everyone loves a little mystique, why not?"

Rollo looked up at Stuart's expression and brightened even more. "You know, that was absolutely brilliant of you, that Secret Service number. Do you realise what you've done?"

He leaned out of the hammock, his eyes alight. "Genius! That's your passport to freedom, and you can never get sacked. Go on the piss with all your old mates, climb rocks in the Andes, ski with the jet set, catch the clap in Kalamazoo – anything! Just fingers to the lips, on with the balaclava and sneakers, and off you go. 'Her Madge's Government needs me, my love,' you utter sadly, shut the door and sprint for the fleshpots. And she'd never be unfaithful, thinking of the dangers you're facing – God, what fun! I'll have to get a wife just so I can do it too, we'll work for the Ministry together, hee-hee . . . Don't look so sad, Stu. It's not like real deceit, the end of your dreams. You'll be bringing home the bread, buying her all sorts of flash gear, fur coats, cashmeres, leathers, silks –"

"Boots," Stuart put in wistfully, his eyes in the distance.

"Sure, boots too. In any case, you can't tell me she hasn't got some secrets of her own, some diabolical fancy hidden away in a pretty little head. She's only human after all – and you can't really believe she still sees you as a prince, the white knight. I know what you smell like after a week's patrol. Anyway, you're so damn straight you put all your cards on her table, I'll bet, and no serious player does that, ever. It means you want to lose, or at least that you're not interested in the game, see?"

"It wouldn't work with Lucy, she'd know I was hiding something."

"Of course she will, you're supposed to have a whole secret life. The caveman used to pick up his club and disappear for a fortnight, then come back with a dead moose over his shoulder and a grunt for a greeting. No explanations. The fact that he'd stolen it from Tom Troglodyte was irrelevant, didn't need admitting."

"How do you know?"

"Stands to reason. Anyway, why should Mrs Caveman have cared? Probably adored her own private life. I'll bet you're a real pain in Lucy's arse, hanging round the house all day. What do you reckon she's doing at the moment, crying into the pillow? Toying with the shower and thinking of you?"

"Shut up, Rollo."

"– Replaying all your home videos? Hey, did you hear about that honeymoon couple in Italy? Viewing finishes early there so most people watch till the bitter end and this couple, sensing bedtime, waited for the screen to go blank before plugging in their VCR. They got into the cable system by mistake and the whole apartment building was treated to their no-holds-barred-happy-hols movies. Imagine the looks next morning, I'll bet they had to leave! How was it, anyway, your honeymoon? When I got to the Seychelles I was told they had the highest rate of VD in the world, centuries of visiting matelots. Wouldn't have bothered you two, I suppose, but it was quite a set-back for me after a month and a half at sea."

Stuart's eyes turned wistful again at the distraction. "I tell you, Rol, if we'd known where to write, we wouldn't have known what to say. We've been bursting to say thanks. With the no-spear-gun law, the islands were still seething with every kind of exotic fish, inquisitive and unfrightened. The only thing we missed on the boat was a compressor for the bottles, we'd have stayed down all day. It was magical beyond description. Just not enough air."

"You were probably trying to do it at ten fathoms, puts up your air-demand to impossible levels, all that puffing."

"Don't pry."

"Sorry – but what's with the shy grin?"

"Huh ... we had good winds too, up and down, all reaching. It was almost too perfect, we both get a big rosy glow just thinking about it. I know Lucy wants to go back again but daren't mention it because of the expense."

"Your new job'll take care of that."

"She also wants to get the business half of a *coco de mer*."

"What do you mean?"

"You must know, the Seychelles double coconut, it's the exact shape, front and back of a female's pelvic –"

Rollo interrupted, frowning, "Yeah, I know *that*," he laughed. "What a marvel, eh? Lovely smooth round buttocks, mons, pussy whiskers and even a very secret entrance ... What's the business half?"

"Our half. She got one of the ladies, the nut, but the male tree is equally weird, didn't you know? At pollination time he sprouts a huge curved catkin exactly like a donkey's dong, the pair are like Disneyland's erotic joke. Lucy wants to wait in the forest and *catch* them!"

Runyan shook his head and laughed delightedly, wincing at the reaction from his wounded leg. "No, I didn't know about that, it wasn't so interesting, I guess. She's quite an earthy lady from the sound of it, perhaps I'd better not meet her."

Stuart said nothing, getting up from the crate and leaning against a rotting roof support.

"Toss me a ham butty or something, will you?" Rollo's

58

voice cut in on his reverie. "Soon as this is over, after pay-day, you'll be able to go sailing again. Meanwhile, you may have heard that South Africa is having a temporary, I hope, state of hostilities with Mozambique, but we can get round that all right ... Stuart, are you listening?"

But Stuart was already moving out of earshot, glad that Rollo couldn't pursue him with more banter. His thoughts were in turmoil and he halted suddenly when he realised what he was doing – giving himself time to think.

It was easy enough to understand Rollo's bland assumption that he'd co-operate because in the old days he would hardly have hesitated, the risks largely unconsidered. His refusal now must make him appear wet and churlish and his thoughts reached inevitably out to the cause of his changed attitude. It was blatantly simple: he didn't want to bring her the slightest unhappiness and he didn't want to spend any part of his life locked away from her. It wasn't even as if, on the return expected, he was going home with a vast fortune to offer her, which she wouldn't have cared about anyway. On the other hand, the idea of going home empty-handed and with the expensive fares wasted was unpalatable and he wasn't even sure, when eventually he could tell her all about the idea and his refusal, if she would be pleased and proud of him. She was still full of youthful mischief and adventure herself.

He strode the dusty earth with his hands deep in his pockets and eventually arrived back at the sagging veranda. Rollo spoke first.

"At least get the stones to Tiki Powers for me, OK? Let him make the windscreen. You examine it and tell me if it's good. If he's right and you can't see a thing, then –"

"This Tiki Powers, how well do you know him? What's he getting out of it, I mean would he get more by denouncing me?"

"'Course not, he'd have to implicate himself anyway. Look, will you do the first bit and see? At least that. I can't do it myself, either now or later. I'm Wanted, and this little world doesn't exactly brim with trustworthy villains. Will you check it out for me, eh?"

"Lieutenant Runyan, you are sitting there Confined to Barracks and trying to dish out Grunt Duty. Hey, why couldn't this Powers person take it over?"

"Good question. Because then he'd want the tiger's share and also because then he's on the outside clear, if you see what I'm getting at. Anyway, he's got form and he does not have guts. This was to be my bit, remember? 'Never order what you're not prepared to do yourself.'"

"Except under fire," Stuart answered grimly. Only an amiable chuckle came back to him yet he knew Rollo too well, knew that underneath he was tense as a snake, hurting from his wound and, far more than that, smarting at being immobilised. For himself, as a last guide, he found he was unable to pinpoint which was the strong-minded decision since it isn't necessarily the harder one. The only certainty was that his friend was dumping him nostril-deep into something highly unpleasant, and not for the first time.

Four

Absence from whom we love is worse than death,
And frustrate hope severer than despair.

Wm. Cowper

"A little assumption," Rollo was saying, "just bear with me a sec, on spec. Um? Being a Brit, you'd have no problem going in, though you need a visa. I couldn't do that for you but I'm told it doesn't take more than a couple of days. Pass me the map, will you?"

He pointed to a satchel and Stuart groaned inwardly at the thought of kicking his heels for any days at all.

"I feel ridiculous," he said, unfolding the map. "Only just got here and I want to go back. That's the effect you have on me."

Rollo ignored the remark and smoothed over the chart to leave the East Transvaal showing. "Here," he said pointing, "that's the main N4, and speed limits are tight. A bit low, though better than they were. A hundred klicks mostly, that's under 65 mph. Middleburg, Nelspruit but not Komatipoort, that's the confrontation border. Lots of growling and nonsense. Right turn here just after Malelane and cut into Swaziland. Nice sleepy border post near Nhohho, no problem, just another half day or so to drive across Swaziland and into Mozambique from there. Roads are ropey and it's all mountain, probably why the Jaapies didn't want it. Also it's somewhere to go to see what nipples look like, you'll be stunned, they're still blanking them out here . . . Main drags only, go to Mbabane then east, say two or three hundred miles. Give us a ring when you get across, 'kay?"

"How?"

"Eh? Oh, call Tiki. I'll be in touch with him."

"A question: the last three stones, the set-up ones, isn't somebody wanting them back?"

"I doubt it."

"Rollo . . ." Stuart said on an uprising note of warning.

"OK, there's a reason. I told you de Beers have officially disbanded the IDSO but naturally there's people in the trade who do freelance security work. Private dicks, bounty hunting. This was one such, so only he would have known who he was chasing, chances are, and which stones he'd planted. In the confusion that night a Police marksman shot him by mistake for me. The sod tried to borrow my bakkie to give chase. His name was Otis and no regrets, miss. Satisfied?"

Stuart looked back at him for a long moment. "As long as there's no murder hunt. I'm feeling very nervous about my freedom, everything screaming at me not to go through with this nonsense. Any chance we're being observed at the moment?"

"None at all. They'd grab me straight away, wouldn't they?"

"I've no idea . . . You haven't actually done anything wrong yet, not in SA, except perhaps for shoving off when someone told you to stop and tried to convince you with a heavy musket that they meant it. The bit I don't like is that the only crime will be committed by me, you bastard."

"Not even that, Stu, if you consider that the stash isn't SA-mined stones in the first place. Admittedly they wouldn't see it that way. But in the glass! That's got to be genius, eh? Never think of looking into something you can see through. It's brilliant."

Rollo looked up and pointed. "Here's Sohrab coming back now. He'll take you up to Warrenton and you can get a car from there. Avoid Kimberley, it's just a dump round the biggest hole in the ground you ever saw, half a mile deep and all of it grovelled for. I think of it as a sort of inverted monument to greed. You're not much of a sightseer anyway, if I remember."

Stuart said nothing, watching the jeep swirl to a stop. He turned and looked Rollo straight in the eyes, feeling no avoidance or untruth which would have been his excuse to duck out and run. The old camaraderie was unfaded, he realised almost with regret.

"How many years does it carry, Rol, smuggling out?"

The answer was flat. "Twenty-five. It went up from fifteen."

"It isn't worth it."

"Not put like that, maybe, though it's a lot of loaf. But this is so perfect I could almost give you a written guarantee. I'd have done it without a qualm, the only reason I'm not is because I don't rate my chances, not after what happened. For you it'll be a breeze. Anyway, me and Tiki would always come and spring you, don't worry." He finished, smiling, "And you'll help, won't you, Sohrab?"

"Whatever you say, Master," the black grinned merrily.

Stuart felt and partly quelled a surge of anger at their flippancy, picked up his grip and went to the jeep.

"Let's get it over," he said curtly, raising a hand. "I'll see you, Rol. I hope the windscreen's no good, that's all."

Runyan nodded back, the smile fading as their eyes met again. If it really came to springing him, Stuart had a strange feeling that he meant it, even if a small army had to be raised and trained to storm a prison. Rollo had always shown a dangerous tendency to stand by his word, a good enough reason for liking him, but for the moment the anger stayed alive for many miles. The sun sinking in the far north-west was disconcerting as he tried to orientate himself to their direction and, later, it made driving into it very trying in the crystalline air. The jeep was too cold and noisy for conversation with Sohrab and he was glad when they at last arrived in Warrenton and he could find a closed saloon for the rest of the journey, some 400 kms to Johannesburg.

Even in the southern winter the country shimmered in arid vastness, ranges and plains alternating endlessly. Stuart tried to set his task aside and thought of the hard courage and persistence of the early explorers compared with his own speed and comfort, daily facing twenty or thirty miles of flat trek followed by a climb and yet another flat panorama of despair for El Dorado.

That some had found it became all too evident later in the seething affluence of Johannesburg. He found a motel on the outskirts after passing signs to Soweto, the name of the huge and notorious black township reminding him he yet knew nothing factual about the turmoil of social life and democracy in this troubled and fearsome land, beyond the rest of the world's news reports and universal condemnation. It didn't stop him wishing he was out of it, and he had no trouble remembering to call his home number, one single ring.

63

The following day he went first for his visa and was pleasantly surprised to have no wait or difficulty since the traffic for South Africans into Mozambique had virtually dried up because of the hostilities. He delivered the hire car, picked up the almost new Daihatsu and went to the main Post Office. He was surprised to see blacks and whites in the same queues and asked an African girl next to him how long it had been so. She was too shy to answer him and too taken aback to be so casually addressed. He wanted to put her at ease but had to spare her the embarrassment. The media would have instantly reported a ban, he reflected, but good news or a softening of rules made poor copy – and perhaps just as well, since complacency has worked some lethal spells.

Asking for a parcel made him suddenly nervous about a stake-out or a trap, and he drove away feeling exposed even with it jammed out of sight between the seats. He had to persuade himself to be completely casual, knowing that furtiveness stands out to a trained hunter's eye.

He headed north out of the city in search of Tiki Powers, again in crisp bright air. It seemed to reflect the apparent sanitised atmosphere of a well-to-do city but as he got clear he saw a smoke overcast to the west which he learned later was the black area of Alexandria where they had no electricity. Stuart had resolved not to share the universal and ignorant condemnation but simply to observe and wait for his own judgements to form. There's a righteous self-indulgence in condemnation which falsely fuels self-esteem, and Lucy's reaction to hypocrisy was as quick and cutting as a noose-wire. He thought about her all the way to Pretoria.

At Powers' home address in Winternest a rather blowsy woman answered with an off-putting midday lasciviousness odorously fuelled by gin. With some reluctance she redirected him to the factory in Rosslyn where her husband retreated to work. Stuart arrived during the lunch break and was relayed to an open space with dried-up grass and stone benches. Carrying the parcel, he found Powers from a description, disconsolate and alone, with sandwiches and a beer, a short, rotund little man caricatured with two smears of hair flattened across his bare skull.

Stuart coughed and said, "I'm from Runyan. Did he call you?"

"Yeer. You got 'em?" The sad eyes came alight as Stuart

patted the small parcel. "Good. Can't do a thing now except shape up, so come back this evening after we close, say quarter-past five. You got somewhere to go meantime?"

When Stuart shook his head, he said, "Stay with us, then – but not during the day, the old bat'll have your breeks off quick as a dipper. If she hasn't already."

Stuart grinned palely and reassured him, getting up to go.

"Right, we'll meet up later. What's your fancy, cheetahs and crocs or monuments and museums?"

"That's easy, the first."

"West from here, take the 513 towards Silkaatsnek. Did Runyan tell you it was my idea?" Disillusion seemed to sour the question and he scrutinised the answering nod carefully.

"My mum always said I'd outsmart myself one day. I guess I've waited long enough. Drive carefully, won't you?" he added pointedly. "And don't get eaten, not with that."

Stuart left him and went back to the car. Feeling awkward with the parcel, he removed and discarded the wrapping. Inside was a soft leather bag which moved with a slippery brittleness. He put it quickly in his pocket and was glad of distraction to help him forget its ominous presence.

He spent a blissful afternoon at the de Wildt cheetah research and breeding station, convinced that the cheetah was the handsomest and most dignified of all animals, and thinking of how Lucy would have been stock-still, enthralled by the cubs. He was told they make good pets because of a bias towards dog rather than cat characteristics, but their beauty was matchless in the haughty feline grace.

The crocodiles were a sombre, chilling contrast, fascinating for sheer reptilian evil, yet even watching them he was again beset by her unaccustomed absence. He tried to shake off the feeling, churlishly wondering if he was submerging his personality beyond reasonable limits. He remembered a contemporary in his first year at university who lost his heart to a lively young student nurse. Asked what it was like to be in love, the youth looked bewildered and answered simply, "I just can't stick it when she's not there."

Back early at Powers' factory he had to wait until all the staff had left before he was led into a small untidy office, the desk covered with orders, ashtrays and dirty cups. Powers closed the door and said, almost reverently, "Let's see what freedom looks like, then. Is it pretty?"

65

Stuart glanced at him quickly and then smiled. "I haven't looked yet."

"What? How could you resist it, man? Come on, warm a cold heart."

"All right. But I don't really want to, it's like counting chickens."

"Turkeys, more like."

"And if I don't get a move on, I'll stiffen up solid with sheer fright."

He drew the little yellow bag from his pocket, loosened the draw-string and spilled the contents on to the desk where Powers had cleared a space with a sweep of his hand.

"Oh Martha and Mary," breathed Powers as the cupful of stones gleamed palely on the black rexine. They looked dull and unremarkable except for a luminous uniformity of opaque colour, but when Stuart stirred the little pile with his finger they both peered curiously at three oddities held together in a twist of polythene. Stuart opened it and eased out three heart-stopping rarities: an octahedron of perfect sea-on-coral-sand blue, a cleavage of pink, both running in the rough to ten or twelve carats and a great big white, which Rollo had estimated as over 40 carats. It seemed a ridiculously large bait to trap Rollo, they must have felt supremely confident about its return. Powers picked up the big stone first and held it up to the light. Its surface was rough to look at but oily to the touch, warm and unmistakably genuine.

"Can't see any inclusions though it's hard to say in this state. The colour seems real fine. But it's too big. The glass won't hide a thing this size. Those fancy colours neither. And they're probably worth about as much as the rest put together."

"Why?" Stuart asked.

"Rarity. You can't price a good pink, nor a blue really. It's a question of who wants it. They're breathtaking when they're cut, I saw some in an exhibition once. But look at these others . . . He's been very selective, can't see any dross." He stirred the pile with his forefinger. "No smalls, and all good whitish colours. Certainly no Capes."

"What's your deal with Rollo?"

"Ten per cent. Of what, I don't know yet, but it'll be a good stack if they're sold properly. He'll know what to do . . . Put 'em away quick. I'll see you later. You'll have to think of something else with the three, I should have a good think about it, if I were you. Don't be tempted."

"To what?"

"To take a chance, like up your arse or somewhere else in the car. This has to be beyond chance, for all of us."

"Tell me," Stuart said slowly, "if you knew about it, why couldn't you have taken them out yourself? Why did Rollo have to send for me?"

"I've got a record. I tried it before and I got three years. For nothing. Sellotaped in a casual newspaper . . . Now, you better let me get on with this. Bring the Daihatsu inside, then go and beat your brains out making a plan for the three fancies."

"All right. How do you make a windscreen, anyway?"

"Toughened? You get a piece of glass and shape it to a template then you bake it in an oven, bend it to shape and cool it on the outside, selectively for zoning. The different rates of cooling create a tension in the material so that it pebbles on impact rather than splinters. It's a bit like case-hardening steel, creating a brittleness. I can't show you, it all happens in the ovens and coolers. Were you worrying about your stones falling in the furnace?"

"I'd almost prefer it if they did. Diamonds burn up at high temperatures, don't they? You can deal with it, I'm sure. Can you lend me a car while you're doing it?"

As he drove back into Pretoria in Powers' old Ford he felt a half-hearted disgust, half-hearted only because of the apparent quality and rarity value of the two coloured stones and the big one, the delicacy for Rollo's own greed, the ones which made him bend a golden rule and agree to buy IDs from a stranger. In the end the problem had seemed to clarify itself. It was a note on the back of a cheque-book which first gave him the idea, the prescription reference for Alicia's reading-glasses. These he was able to buy from an optician in Pretoria, very expensive because of a premium for immediate service and, he suspected, for keeping them open late. Under pretext of including a note, he tucked the two coloured stones into the case, sealed up the jiffy-bag and asked the optician to send them Registered Post, complete with Customs declaration, to Alicia, care of his lawyer in Oxford. As the Post Office was closed, they promised to do it first thing in the morning.

He felt defiant about any recrimination from Rollo but not enough to make him despatch the very valuable big stone in the same way. Back at Rosslyn he told Powers what he'd done but the little man only shrugged.

"They make it or they don't."

"But this big one, what's it worth?"

"Stab in the dark? Half a million rand, maybe." The answer shook Stuart visibly, since the mathematics of the whole thing seemed crazy.

"I did have an idea for all of them," Powers said, "I bought some stuff. Much better with the singleton. Here, see what you think."

He held out his hand and Stuart gave it to him quickly. Powers had made a small cubic mould in some silica sand and he mixed two tubes of rapid epoxy and spooned it in. Stuart watched him as he pressed the diamond into the middle of it and smoothed away the excess. Finally he fed in the end of a cheap key-chain and then answered Stuart's puzzled frown.

"If they stop the car, the first thing they do is take the keys off you, right? Then they rummage the car. Then they give you the keys back."

Stuart digested the logic as Powers led him through the workshop to the Daihatsu. It had been cleaned and the new windscreen gleamed under the bright striplight. It was clear and apparently perfect.

"No one saw you? Isn't there a night-watchman?"

"No, not needed. Glass is too cheap, except the big plates which are a bit difficult to run off with. Let's go and have a drink, face the Margie. I told her you'd be joining us for dinner. She sounded pleased . . ."

They left as soon as the epoxy had hardened and Powers tossed him an opaque amber cube and key-chain with a nervous grin. Stuart clipped it to the keys and backed the Fourtrak outside while Powers locked up. The man seemed very nervous, his glances seldom connecting, his driving jerky and agitated as he led the way.

It was quite dark but Stuart was able to see through a pristine shining windscreen without blur or blemish. He was frankly astonished and kept looking for flaws every time oncoming lights shone through it. A scheme so simple and so perfect, it began to resolve all his doubts, although a nervous

68

twitch which had begun to affect his right shoulder didn't disappear until the second large whisky in Tiki's house half an hour later. Margie served them a passable meal but was rather glassy-eyed on gin, blaming the men for being late and so extending her cocktail hour. The house was untidy but contained expensive items like a large remote-controlled television and video, and a multi-function stereo. Feeling awkward in her company, Stuart decided there was no need to wait for contact with Rollo; he resolved to sleep early and leave for the east at first light. Before going upstairs to his room he asked to use the telephone. Powers agreed instinctively but raised his eyebrows at the mounting number of digits being dialled until he was on the edge of his chair with alarm.

Stuart heard the distant solitary tone, mouthed a secret kiss and immediately broke the connection.

"Glad you changed your mind about that," Powers grumbled, "or was it engaged?"

Stuart shook his head. "No need, after all. I suppose the car's OK outside?"

"I'll tie a string from it to your toe, so if someone steals it you'll wake up."

"Bloody thing's stolen anyway. Runyan's got no principles."

Margie appeared to have fallen asleep but now suddenly jerked awake and stumbled off to bed with a muttered goodnight. In the doorway she turned and gave him a knowing look which was quite unmistakable but Stuart contrived to glaze his return focus. He had the distinct feeling that the slightest response would have her sneaking into his room while Powers slept, the last situation relished by a man in love.

Powers raised his eyes to the ceiling as they heard her attempt to close the door and stumble upstairs. "If you do your stuff," he said quietly, "I'll be away before the bill comes in."

Stuart had no wish to discuss the problems surrounding a soured marriage so he said, "Otherwise, what's it like living here?"

"Uneasy, it's like something's going to happen but everyone hopes it isn't. You hardly meet a soul who isn't certain that things will change, apartheid will go, is already going in

69

fact, there'll be radical upheaval but really they're all holding off, saying not yet. Putting off the discomfort. Keeping a tight censorship on the press, too. See, the Afrikaners are very defensive because of the pressure from outside and they also realise they mustn't move too quickly. Still, without the pressure they wouldn't move at all. As it is, the blacks'll be getting a limited representation. Well, it's a start I suppose, but there's such a tremendous affluence gap."

"But I've seen quite a few blacks in some very expensive cars."

"Oh, sure, it can be done if they're smart enough, and actually you only have to take a brief look into some of the neighbouring countries and you'll see a huge drop in black living standards."

"So where does apartheid still apply?" Stuart asked, remembering the Post Office.

"Buses, housing areas and schools. But they're building up decades of resentment and the Jaapies still think everyone's bullying them unfairly. The cops are one of the worst aspects, just thugs." Powers yawned and smoothed the thin strands across his shining scalp. "Anyway, I want to go and not just for personal reasons. These people don't laugh at the same things we do, if they laugh at anything. Peculiar bunch. And the affluence creates, seethes with nouveau smarts, false friendships."

"But your ten per cent, that won't be much of a new start, will it?"

Powers looked surprised. "I could get by on a lot less, don't you worry, and this way I'm not risking any more time inside. You want to leave early?"

Stuart nodded and stood up. Powers showed him where the coffee was kept for the morning and then took him up to his room. Once alone he was beset by an enormous loneliness and a physical craving; the expected remainder of days seemed to stretch ahead interminably and the more he tried to shrink them, the more the flickering tendrils of fear returned.

De Hoek was puzzled that they had turned up no trace of Kody since he had felt a hardness of character from their brief exchange which told him something as a professional man-hunter. However, it had only been a couple of days and the check was still running. He'd had a brief report about the questioning of Alicia and the bungled attempt on Lucy Kody, but at least the intruders had managed to leave a short-range bug in the house so that conversations picked up the next day showed clearly that they knew nothing useful.

Later, his vindictiveness unassuaged, he ordered his ferrets to dig up some friends, local gossip, anything for a lead, and through illegally-perused Army records they found eventually a Sergeant Tony Callum, a tough cynical old soldier who had served under Kody in Nothern Ireland.

"Aye, the Corporal's War," he said over a free pint and a large Bushmills. "And I was a corporal then. Off'cers only got in the way of running things, we used to send them off fishing or the golf. Fooking nuisance, off'cers. Kody, well, he were all right, kept to himself a lot, except for a wild one called Runyan, Rollo, another Lieutenant. 'E had Sticky End written all over 'im. But they made us laugh all right."

"Do you know where this Runyan is now?" asked the interrogator.

Callum had shaken his head. "You could try among the mercenaries, Mad Mike or that Seychelles thing, that was up his street, if you could get him past the tarts. Yeah, I'd try East Africa if I was looking, Rhodesia, Mozambique. He'd be too fussy for the west, 'ot and 'orrible. He didn't like fighting, he liked horsing about and scheming. Like I said, Sticky End, mark my words."

This information was relayed back to Johannesburg and with some forced co-operation from the regular SA Police, de Hoek was routinely informed about the attempted plant of stones on Runyan who was now actively sought for robbery and assault. De Hoek felt a professional quickening; it was all the connection he required and he put out an immediate all-points multelex for Kody as well, thus effectively sealing off millions of square miles for wherever there were ports, posts and patrols covering legitimate exits. With the knowledge that Runyan had been buying IDs and also, from blood traces found where he'd been shot off the scrambler, perhaps severely wounded, de Hoek felt he knew exactly what he was after in Kody and could therefore count on full police co-operation.

Stuart drove with conscious care, wary of the speed limits,

and glad to be driving on the left to minimise the chance of error. The small square vehicle was buoyant if robust; although not built for speed, it's high-backed seats were very comfortable. As the morning progressed and the miles eastward reeled off, he felt constantly worried and disorientated by having the sun on his left; it seemed to be telling him he was going the wrong way, like a pigeon with its homing devices scrambled. He stopped in Middelburg for fuel, coffee and a sandwich and then resumed his journey almost at once. Intermittently, the big amber cube dangling from the ignition switch rattled uncomfortably against some interior projection, itself a constant reminder of his mission even though the windscreen, slowly blurring with insects, betrayed nothing of its invisible fortune.

Hundreds of square miles of prairie farms unravelled as the altitude reduced, while active mineworkings showed their ceaseless contributions to the country's wealth in minerals. Slowly the terrain became more lush, the trees gathered in and the fields grew green with the elephant-high and densely-waving cane.

It was very beautiful, especially with the seasonal cool air and its glorious distant clarity. He could see himself at another time, full of hope and boldly arriving, staking a claim, putting down roots, building a house and a spread and security, though for him entirely coloured by the notion of Lucy beside him and her gusto to inspire.

And then, he thought, having reached this state of temporal grace, gradually facing up to the possibility that another race of different education, privilege, colour and custom might one day come and take it all away, simply by an over-powering right of numbers. He fancied he would have joined with those stubborn, reactionary Boers and suppressed a few principles in favour of self-preservation. The righteous world and the media's downgrading bias had together produced some harsh if unanswerable judgements.

Reaching Nelspruit in the early afternoon, he felt a nagging urge to cut off into the Kruger National Park for a glimpse of the game, it seemed absurd not to visit one of the world's special places while he was there, but he knew he was really trying to postpone his point of dread, the turn-off to Jeppe's Reef and the Swazi border. In the end, he stopped off the road, locked the car and simply walked for a couple of hours, trying in a brief interlude to absorb some of the feel of a still primitive and vibrant land. Its winter time was lit by flame trees, poinsettia and bougainvillaea, while the "half-man" cacti-lined random hillsides like scattered soldiers on manœuvres, with fiery orange plumage, standing easy.

The sun was low behind him as he left the N4 and turned south, his dread increasing. It was lightened momentarily by a sign to "Laughing Waters", an imaginary throaty chuckle from Lucy because it was on the road to Nhohho, but then suddenly he rounded a bend and saw the barrier across the road, huts and small houses, uniforms and rifles and all the brooding looks to start a hidden thumping in the hearts of guilty men.

He put the Fourtrak in the "parkering" slot indicated, got out and went into the office. He was only just in time, for they closed at 4 pm. The Swazi barrier crossed the road a hundred yards farther on, manned by different uniforms. He filled in the blue SA exit form, showed his passport and was given a little square release card for the car and then as easily dismissed. Blacks waiting in a separate queue watched him curiously as he went back out to the Daihatsu, started it, backed out of the slot and approached the barrier. An ancient African in an old trench coat was about to lift it but jerked in response to some order from the office. Stuart followed his glance and saw two white soldiers in spread stance, each with an R1 trained at his head. The sweat seemed to freeze on his scalp as he switched off and stepped out, hands high and his best attempt at a look of puzzled innocence.

"Against de carr an' sprread, man!" one of the soldiers barked, the meaning if not the words only too clear. Another man came out of the building casually doing up buttons on his BD blouse, waiting while the first soldier searched Stuart very thoroughly before pronouncing him clean. The rifles were lowered and safety catches clicked and then they ordered him towards another building close behind the main one. He found himself in a round concrete cell about six feet in diameter, empty, dirty and windowless. A heavy door slammed shut without excessive force but it seemed like the judge's gavel emphasising orders for the hangman.

The multelex from Wolmarans Street had only been issued at midday and de Hoek was pleasantly surprised when Mollie

Vrouwer handed him the reply slip from the Northern Swazi border post: "S. Kody held await instrs 1650".

Mollie was taken aback by his rare smile until she saw the ice in it. "Send back to hold him for us as well as SAP," he said. "I'll fly up tomorrow." He didn't bother to look at her expression. She clicked out while he mused about the prisoner's origins, and those of his wife, and found great satisfaction in the smell of Soviet meddling and a legitimate excuse to bring the agent in without fear of reprimand. He was even more convinced later when a surveillance report came from London that the local Police had returned to Kody's house and questioned wife and mother-in-law further since they had failed to find him through the Ministry of Defence, the Foreign Office, MI5 and 6, or any civil service list. De Hoek saw an interesting puzzle to unravel in the course of his revenge and anticipated it brightly.

Lucy remained cheerfully baffled. She was certain Stuart had said the Ministry of Defence but on top of the Police enquiries her own calls had also proved fruitless.

With her still-shaken mother come to visit and be heard, she was at least partially distracted and between them they had a feast of speculation. When the call had come again on the Friday evening, the single startling ring, Lucy smiled and relaxed but Alicia grew more agitated, her mood communicating itself to her little terrier.

"What's *paranoia* in English?" she asked.

"Same word. Why?"

"Conspiracy again, I feel it," Alicia said. "Because of you and of me and, of course, your father. As though to spy was in the family."

"He's not a spy, don't be silly," Lucy answered but with a feeling of unreality. The Police had told her there was no chance of tracing a single ring but at least the calls meant that Stuart was all right and that everything was normal as far as he was concerned.

"I suppose I should be pleased now about your training," her mother said, secretly gratified that one of the intruders had been damaged. Her heart still missed beats when she thought of the little leg in the huge jaws of the bolt cutters. "Do you think it's possible they have a department not listed anywhere, really secret?"

74

"Mama, he's just probably not registered anywhere yet, sort of still on approval."

"They must know ... Alexei would know better than anyone, I expect." She gave a guilty smile. "I could call him and ask."

Lucy only chuckled at first, although there was still an element of mystery and excitement about her long-absent father. Alicia pressed the point until Lucy realised she was serious, when, to her mother's surprise, she said, "Why not?"

Alicia almost leaped for the telephone and punched out the code from memory. She held on in growing disappointment at receiving no reply, turning her mouth down and looking at the clock.

"Some Belgian whore is having a good dinner," she said with some bitterness. "I'll try again tomorrow."

The next day, Saturday, there was still no answer, and Lucy began to have her doubts about the wisdom of making the call, feeling it might be some kind of betrayal. They had two visits from a local constable in an unmarked van. He had a big woolly Alsatian called Banjo which Lucy knew was a Parachute Regiment expression meaning to obliterate or flatten. Getting familiar over a cup of tea laced with whisky, Constable Stubbs described how he would let Banjo chase "villains" and sometimes act a bit slow in calling him off, so "the boy can have a bit of a chew, keeps him up to the mark, see?"

Lucy didn't find him very easygoing despite his frankness. Alicia felt that owning a large chewy dog marked one out as either inadequate or distinctly right-wing so they had a measure of agreement. Harvey Smith was particularly circumspect when Banjo was around, which Alicia resented.

They stayed in all that evening but this time the telephone remained silent, giving them an air of tension throughout dinner and long afterwards. Alicia watched the little television while Lucy read, interrupted once by her mother's query about the grammar in an interval song in a chat show:

I won't dance for you but I'll dance for a diamond,
So I heard my lady say,
But when I dared the Law and I stole a diamond,
She said she would have loved me anyway.

75

The real reason for her enquiry, it appeared, was more maudlin. "Your father was always so naughty, even in the commercial section. That's how he got this." She held out her left hand to show her diamond ring. "Two and half carats and little ones all round. From Siberia. He made me dance for it, I remember."

Lucy nodded sympathetically but joined in the chorus as a distraction, having heard the song before.

And now she calls me her darling,
And says she, she says she would,
She says she would have loved me,
She says she would have loved me – Anyway!

The whimsy made her feel thoughtful and, before going to bed, she voiced something that had been troubling her vaguely since Stuart had gone away.

"*Mamushka*, I want you to release me from my promise. When Stuart gets back, I think I must tell him about Patrick."

Alicia gazed at her seriously for some moments. "Why? Do you think it wise to tell all? Such a bad business."

"I think it's vital, if only for me. Because of my promise to you, I have something I can't tell him and I feel it's in the way."

"And you want confession?"

"I suppose so, something like that. Openness."

"But you don't need it, *lyubimy*, you know how I feel. I thought it against you to have it known. You should have no guilt . . . Does it stay with you?"

Lucy nodded and her mother touched her cheek softly.

"Do as you wish, my child. I don't want anything to take your happiness, even if he is only a Bohemian."

"Oh, Mama, don't be silly, he's a lovely man, whatever your prejudices. Nothing can spoil it for us, I promise."

"Don't say that! You never tell with people . . . What about if he knew your father was Jewish, did you tell him that?"

"Goodnight, Mama," Lucy said laughingly, arm around her shoulders. Alicia kissed her and added, "Your father also lived secrets but I had none from him. Perhaps I should have, for the mystery, to hold him, do you think?"

Lucy only smiled archly and didn't answer beyond a small

76

shake of her head. She had her own ideas about allure, and deception was only for short-term fun and mischief, not for a rôle in life.

Still, she had dark feelings that night, uneasy at receiving no call and wondering why Stuart couldn't at least get Saturday off if it was a harmless language course. Maybe there's more to it than that, she thought, since he was tough and resourceful. She never thought to doubt him though, because of his straightforward approach unsuited to skullduggery. Such a funny word, it seemed to resound in her head, keeping sleep away for a long time.

Five

... and it had only just begun. I stood like the cricketer
who is out for a duck.

H. M. Tomlinson
(The Sea and the Jungle)

The tiny cell had enclosed him for over five hours and no
one had come near. His breathing felt dry and shallow since
the only circulation came from an air-brick up near the
ceiling, way out of reach. He alternated sitting and standing,
sometimes stretching, hearing nothing outside beyond the
occasional dog barking and distant engine noises. Nothing
seemed to pass through the border post. He brooded that he
could so easily have been waved through without a question
or a cursory glance and back home he would by now have
been given an explanation, questioning or at least a formal
charge, something to eat or drink if only water, somewhere
to urinate. His cell apparently contained nothing at all, not
one single concession. No one had asked or told him anything
and from time to time he had to work hard to control his
thoughts or else a bout of shaking seized him, threatening
panic. He was acutely aware of being still in South Africa
where you could be held without trial for ninety days, where
stealing diamonds was virtually a crime against the state, and
where defensive feelings about the whole world's indictment
made conservatives viciously over-reactive.

He had known fear before but in a different guise, the
snick of a passing bullet twice outpacing the speed of its own
sound, burning gasoline from an Irish milk-bottle bomb
whooshing into the Ferret scout car, the sounds of shocked
despair from an injured comrade – combat hazards which a
soldier's toughness and training conditioned him to handle,
not this isolation and acute terror that he had thrown away
his liberty, in effect his life, to an endless stretch of im-

78

prisonment and Lucy, always Lucy in his thoughts, burning in his head, ice in his midriff, eyes closed in the blackness, teeth clenched to stifle the involuntary chokings of his dread.

There was one chance, he thought, that the diamonds were cleverly enough concealed never to be found and that with sustained and righteous denial he might eventually be freed. But they had known something in advance, his name was on a list so someone had to have given a tip-off. He wondered if Powers had been paid more than Rollo's sorry percentage to betray him or whether Rollo himself had been caught and forced to talk.

As the waiting stretched out, he felt more able to dismiss the speculations, he had a feeling about Powers who anyway knew what Rollo would do to him. That Rollo himself was the informant was unthinkable except that they could easily have tortured him, and Stuart was well aware that there was no longer any question of gritting teeth and being the last tough hero. Interrogation, he knew, had been finely modernised; with the very tough, bolshie or idealist specimens, pain would never prevail but the new drugs were not so much irresistible as that they simply destroyed the very mechanisms of resistance.

Strangely, his self-control improved with the passage of time and when he finally thumped on the door it was more in anger than anything abject. After several tries he heard a distant voice ask him what he wanted.

"A drink and a piss, what else?" he shouted back. In a minute or two he heard footsteps and the door was opened very cautiously. One of the soldiers stood there, out of the beam of light from a doorway in the main blockhouse, and pointed to a large tin of water and an empty plastic bucket at his feet.

"Room service," he said, seeming bright and friendly.

Stuart blinked in the light. "Why am I being held, did anyone tell you?"

"Orders, China, all they give me. Some cops coming to talk to you and a man from the flying school."

"What? How do you mean?"

"Everyone knows, min, the thirty-fifth floor, BOSS. When you've talked enough they shove you out, see if you can fly. Or even if you don't talk. And funny thing, you're just as dead if it's the ground floor."

79

"I see, thanks. When?"

"Cops tonight, BOSS tomorrow. Stay back." He lowered his voice. "I wouldn't try anything. Vinny's as mean as a green mamba, he thinks it's one of his perks to cut loose if he sees you so much as scratch yaw bites. You'll get a tin of corned beef shortly, it's to make you firsty. What did you do?"

"Nothing."

"'Course not, thet's the spirrit. See you later."

After another two hours the corned beef arrived, the tin sliced jaggedly in half and passed in on the point of the bayonet which had opened it. A different voice from outside called roughly.

"Police aren't coming till tomorrow. Inspector's got a bunfight. Says to me, 'Ask Kody if he's going to tell us where the rocks are before we take his jeep to bits.' What do you say, *rooinek*?"

"Nothing. I don't know what he's talking about."

"Right. Second question. 'Is he going to tell us before we put his bollocks in the vice, or after?' He says he knows you got 'em, he knows he's going to find them, it's a question of how much squeezing and such you fancies before he gets his hands on them. The rocks, that is."

"Ask him, do I have any rights to phone lawyers or Consuls or a senior police officer, since he has no business holding an innocent man in this rat-hole."

The soldier chuckled harshly. "Did you want his answer now or after I'm telling him? Inspector Strijdom is going to have a *lekker barbie*, a fine hangover, and the chopper-ride won't improve it. Why doesn't you save yourself the trouble, tell him where they's hidden and get on with your twenty-five years? Or you could make a break for it and I puts you out of misery with a magful of this lot? No, I don't think Strij would like that, but you can be telling *me*, hey?" The voice had gone low and conspiratorial. "If you've got a big stash we could split from here and leave him scratching – what do you say, *rooinek*?"

Stuart looked up sharply but couldn't see the features, only the silhouette. "Soldier," he said after a few moments, "I'd pay you a fortune to be out of here and on my way but somehow I think you'd want it in advance."

"That's dead rright. How much, min? I mean, what's twenty-five years worth, your life or mine? You married?"

Stuart shuddered uncontrollably in an overwhelm of tension, his fear and remorse now confused by the glimmer of hope.

"You can have the lot," he said quietly. "Everything I own. Obviously I don't have it here, but I know you'd kill me if I didn't deliver so you can be quite sure."

"Rright, unless you got me first – no, you wouldn't know where to look. But come on, man! It's obvious you're carrying and the stuff has to be in the jeep, right? Half a million rand, you got that much?"

"Yes."

"OK, step out here gently." The voice went down to a whisper. "You walks ahead of me, down the light towards the doorway. And quiet."

As they emerged into the lighted room, he saw the back of the other soldier's head; he was sitting at a table reading a newspaper and he was black. The head started to turn as Stuart heard a click behind him, followed by a numbing explosion just down by his waist. It seemed the film ran in reverse as he saw the far side of the head spray against the wall, taking the newspaper with it, then the little red mark of the bullet's entry just behind the ear. The R1's round was a copper jacket streamlining a soft-nosed centre, needlessly devastating.

He whirled furiously, shouting. "You stupid bastard, what the hell did you do that for?"

The white soldier just smirked at him. "I just burnt your boat, *rooinek*. You are now wanted for murder, plus you won't be thinking I'm just being tricky for the brasshats. Where are the goods?"

Stuart could only stare, feeling the walls close in and unable to comprehend such indifferent callousness. He saw a darting, rat-like face under a pulled-down forage-cap.

"Agh move, man! The stones for you freedom, come on!"

In the cell, Stuart had already written the diamonds out of his consideration, the only thought being liberty. Now they had redeemed themselves and become the price of his life. He shook himself, realising he was too dazed to think clearly. His first rational idea was that, once given the information, the soldier would be certain to kill him as well. He could then bury the stones, set fire to the Fourtrak and deny they ever existed.

He held up his hand deliberately slowly and put an edge of command in his voice. "Wait a moment. I want no bargain with you, but this is the way we'll do it. The stones are there but you'll never find them if I don't tell you."

"But you arre gonna tell me, you've been given to me, you're the one I've waited months for, putting up with that dripping Kaffir there, and today no SAP around, no MPs, I've got a rebuild bakkie they'll never know to look for, another passport, I'm on my way, *rooinek*. Now, where's they, an' quick, before I blow some bits off you . . ."

He snatched up a half-full mug of coffee and drained it quickly, still keeping his rifle at the trail, pointing at Stuart's belt buckle.

"If you do anything to me, it's finished. Be sure." Stuart's voice was tight and carried his total conviction but he felt a dizzying fury at the callous murder. "I'm going to tell you where they are, but only where you can't shoot me. Is that clear?"

The soldier looked at him suspiciously for long seconds, as if for a sign of weakness. Seeing none, he suddenly made up his mind, thumbed on the safety catch and propped his rifle in the corner, standing in front of it.

"Rright, outside make a move!" He thrust with his arm and propelled Stuart towards the door. Stuart allowed him the gesture and they went round to the front of the building where he had first arrived. The barrier was still down, the Daihatsu parked off to one side. The soldier leaned into it, slipped off the handbrake and pushed it easily back a few feet in the circle of its locked steering, turning it until it pointed at the barrier. He rummaged a moment and the headlights came on.

"That way!" the voice barked, pointing at the barrier. "There's no one on the other side, the Swazis've knocked off for the night, I'm in charge of both sides, see? We go a bit over there, then you go a pitch further and do some fast talking. Then I go back for the goodies and you wait for me in the road. Don't leave it, the edges are mined on both sides. For real. If it was light you'd see the odd *donga* where a kaffir-dog tripped one off."

"Which kind of mine?"

"Anti-kaffirs. Springers. How long to remove the stash?"

"Seconds only . . . Are you coming back this way?"

"What do you think? I want you here in the lights where I can see you, I don't want you crreeping up while I gets rready. Stay on the road and trust me."

Stuart said nothing to this absurdity and they went on at a quick march. After a few hundred paces the road started to curve and the soldier slowed and stopped.

"This does it. You go on a bit more, twenty, thirty metres, just so's I can beat you back to the gat, not so far that I doesn't hearr you."

Stuart complied, the back of his neck prickling even though the soldier was unarmed. He stopped and turned when the voice called again and he could make out a dark silhouette standing in the middle of the road.

"Rright, my China, now you give!" the voice said, its excitement undisguised.

When Stuart told him he didn't at first believe it but something in the resigned, defeated tone must have convinced him.

"You're meaning, they're in the glass, moulded? In the *glass?* How do you get 'em out?"

"Break it. It'll fragment."

"You'll need an X-ray machine to find them in the pieces."

"Maybe. I don't know. Get on with it."

Without another word the soldier spun and trotted away, stopping suddenly two or three times to hear if he was being followed.

When he was half-way back to the barrier. Stuart turned the other way and began to run on the ribbon of dusty tarmac as fast and as quietly as he could, running from the complete certainty that the soldier would return to track and kill him. That way his word would stand and there'd be no need to flee, fearing nothing except disciplinary action for allowing the prisoner to escape and he would certainly put the blame for that on his dead comrade.

He'd had little recent exercise and fear is exhausting in itself but he felt he was running for more than his life. The empty chasm he'd seen before him in the cell, the endless dead, stretching, black years without Lucy, had given him a foretaste of something totally unthinkable. It dragged extra energy from some deep resource and he ran at what seemed, in the dark's exaggeration, quarter-mile speed for six or seven minutes, wondering how far the mine-field stretched, until he heared the sound of a car accelerating distantly behind him, over a mile way. The terrain was a complete unknown, even with the low half-moon. He had one thought that the anti-personnel mines weren't so thickly strewn away from the border-post area and long before the approaching headlights could pick him up he left the road, preferring his chances.

His chest heaving stertorously, he walked into a single strand of barbed wire, unsnagged himself and ducked under it, darting quickly but gingerly away in search of cover. He made a point of stepping on the darker patches, hopefully clumps where mines might not be sown.

The vehicle approached very nosily, certainly not the Daihatsu, but also quite slowly, its lights weaving from side to side, searching. His heart still pounded, it seemed, with a massive noise and he tried pointlessly to stifle his lungs' furious gasping. He watched as the car went past another half mile up over a slight rise then in a few minutes it came back and retraced the whole route. He could sense the soldier's desperate dilemma, whether to return to his post and hope the escaped prisoner was never found or whether to cut out for instant riches but with the doom of a fugitive existence.

On the next pass to the south, a powerful torch swung to and fro across the minefield from the creeping car and Stuart pressed himself flat into the dry earth. He kept absolutely still, fearing to chance his luck any more but wishing he was further from the road. He realised he was well within range of the strong white beam and as the car came near he felt himself tensing, tensing uselessly but inevitably against something that he would probably not hear or feel except from some fleeting border of eternity.

The car growled along right opposite his position but he closed his eyes and pressed down, unaware of the light passing right over his body. There was no pause; the car kept going slowly by, its exhaust crackling in the stillness even at low rpm. Finally the soldier gave up and Stuart tensed to hear the engine kicked down a gear and gunned up to maximum acceleration. There was no pause in its southward flight yet he stayed still, listening until long after the sound had faded, recurred and finally ceased altogether. Then he heard a rustling nearby and went rigid again, realising suddenly he was in a lethal part of the world even without the dangers posed by desperate men.

He waited a full hour, punctuated by noises real and imagined, cramped and chill, the sweat only half-drying on his clothes, and then a snake, spider or land mine prickled every nerve-ending for every inch he crawled back to the road. At last he stood up and walked slowly back to the border crossing. The headlights on the Daihatsu were on high beam and getting weak but the blockhouse door was closed, interior lights extinguished. He assumed the soldier had wanted to delay discovery as long as possible.

Stuart turned off the Fourtrak's lights, noticing that the key was not in the ignition. He wondered if the soldier had taken it with him and whether he'd one day discover the treasure it contained in addition to the one in the fragmented glass. A few stray shards protruded from the rubber flange to show where he must have broken it carefully, crazing without shattering it, and lifting it out like piecemeal sugar frost. There were one or two remnants on the floor gleaming palely in the star and waning moonlight. He supposed they could be diamonds but found he was totally uninterested. The door at the back of the blockhouse was unlocked and, switching on the light, he found everything as before, the other soldier still slumped where he died, his rifle alongside him but the telephone thoughtfully taken off its rest. He kept his eyes away from the spattered wall.

He felt utterly weary, thirsty, dirty and confused. In a desk drawer he found a bottle of whisky and, in a small kitchen, a fridge with iced water. He poured himself four fingers of Scotch, topped it with water and drank half straight off. For the first time in a year he felt like a cigarette but a moment's thought of Lucy and further betrayal dismissed it immediately. He finished the drink and built another, all the time listening with an intensity that seemed to stretch the very skin of his eardrums.

He picked up the dead soldier's R1 and saw that the magazine had been taken, but he worked the action and a live round clicked out of the breech. He replaced it, found another torch, and went outside, swaying with weariness but deciding it was impossible to wait in the building. Round the back among several dismantled vehicles he found a body-shell with a reasonable seat in it. He crouched there with the rifle across his knees, the glass and the torch in his hands but, in less than a minute, he was slumped in exhausted sleep.

Several hours later he struggled out of the grave of unconsciousness to the deep thrashing of a helicopter as it settled in another part of the yard and sent up a massive, choking dust cloud. He waited for it to clear before getting out and walking towards it, carrying the rifle by its strap, muzzle down.

Two uniformed policemen emerged, one with pips on his shoulders, followed by two men dressed in mechanics' overalls carrying tool boxes. At the sight of him the inspector came stiffly to a halt and looked around with alert suspicion.

"Who are you? What are you doing here?" he barked sharply. His face was curiously oblong and under his eyes were deep folds, of dissipation rather than kindliness.

"Take this off me, will you?" Stuart answered. The whole group stopped, crouching under the slowing rotors as he proffered the R1. On a sign from the inspector, the second policeman took it carefully. "There's been a cock-up. One of your men shot the other, thinking to get something from me. He's gone now, into Swaziland. The one inside is dead, a head shot. I didn't do it and nor did that rifle, unless he swopped them. The one who's gone is called Vinny, I think."

"What did he take?"

"Nothing, far as I know. Bloody psychopath. I slipped away from him and I suppose he panicked. He hunted me for an hour or two and then took off. My name's Kody."

"*Ja*, got it. He wanted your diamonds, hey?"

"That's what he said, yes."

"Well, so do we. Let's go inside. Piet, ask the pilot if he's got a body-bag, will you?"

As they walked round to the front of the building, the inspector said casually, "That's your jeep there, isn't it? The screen's gone, did he shoot at you?"

Stuart said nothing, just shook his head once.

"Why didn't you take off yourself, after he'd gone?"

"For a murder hunt? No thanks. It was a decent boy in there, too."

"*Ja*. Lead on. And keep off the sanctimonious crepp, it's too early for me."

Inside, with a look of extreme distaste, he took a cursory look at the body and then made a quick tour of the building. Stuart stayed with the constable but, when the inspector returned, he was pushed into a high-backed chair. One of the technicians came in with a square metal box which he opened and plugged into a wall socket.

"Check the voltage first," said the inspector. "Make sure of it. I can't stand it if it's not working properly."

The fourth man came in then with a folded black bag of thick polythene. They laid the dead soldier on the floor and then zipped him into it, faces creased with revulsion.

"Put him in another room till the van gets here." He turned to Stuart looking mean and dour. "Now, Mr Kody, take your jacket and shirt off. We're going to plug you in and you are going to tell the truth, otherwise you are going to regret not using that last round on yourself. Set it where he can see the trace, Leyden, in case he disagrees."

When the sensors were attached to Stuart's arms and chest, the inspector took a small recorder from the technician, thumbed on the Record button and kept it in his hand between them. He read the details out of Stuart's passport, gave the date, time and location and then pressed the pause.

"In the SAP we don't use lie-detectors, they are held to be unreliable and inadmissible by the courts. I don't agree and I've borrowed this one from de Beers. They use them in the mines quite effectively. For now, I'm your court. Try convincing me."

Releasing the pause he began formally. "Trace running. Inspector Jan Strijdom questioning. Mr Kody, please tell me a lie."

"What? Oh . . . My name is not Stuart Kody."

The trace jumped. "Thank you. Lie recorded. Mr Kody, since you came to South Africa have you seen a Mr Roland Runyan?"

"Yes."

"Thank you. Did he give you any diamonds?"

"No."

The inspector hesitated with evident surprise and looked at the needle trace on the polygraph. "Hmph. True, apparently. Are you carrying diamonds now, or are there diamonds in your vehicle?"

"No."

"True. Did you give them to a soldier, Corporal Vincent Cornelius?"

"No."

"Says it's true . . . why then did Corporal Cornelius abscond?"

"Because he shot the other soldier. I saw him do it."

"True . . . And you got away from him before he could do the same to you?"

"Yes."

"How did you do it?"

"In the dark. I ran across into Swaziland as far as I could and hid in the minefield. When he couldn't find me, he took off."

"True, except that there's no minefield . . . Ah! Mark the trace showing prisoner's sharp reaction to this statement. Mr Kody, Corporal Cornelius thought he could do a deal with you, why?"

"He had the idea I was carrying diamonds."

"And were you carrying diamonds?"

There was a long pause, the trace flickering steadily as the paper-roll turned. "Note that the prisoner did not answer this question. Trace unsteady."

"I wasn't sure how it would react," Stuart said carefully. He was sweating and unable to wipe his forehead because of the wires on his wrists. "The corporal demanded diamonds. I told him they were part of the windscreen. He smashed it and took the pieces."

"True." Strijdom stopped the tape-recorder in slow surprise and said sharply, "Al, see if there's any loose fragments and X-ray them." He pressed the record button again.

"Mr Kody, are you in possession of Illegal Diamonds?"

"No."

"It agrees with you. Have you been in possession of Illegal Diamonds?"

Stuart's mind found the immediate loophole to this question, diverting possession to the Fourtrak's windscreen. He decided it was worth a try and concentrated on the notion, quickly, before the pause betrayed him.

"No."

"True." The inspector sounded weary and frustrated. "But Cornelius believes he has diamonds in glass fragments?"

"Yes."

"True. Mr Kody, why are you in South Africa and trying to cross into Swaziland?"

Stuart realised that he might have survived the vital questions and need answer no more but he couldn't dismiss the feeling that he was fighting for his life. He switched his mind to a new set of facts, creasing a new truth out of a new decision.

"The Daihatsu has to be returned to its rightful owner and Mr Runyan was not in a position to deliver it."

"True. Why was he not?"

Pause. "This question not answered. No compulsion. Is Mr Runyan still in South Africa?"

"No."

"That's untrue!" Strijdom's voice rose. "Where is he?"

Pause. "This question not answered. We cannot justly accuse prisoner of harbouring a fugitive." He thumbed off the recorder again. "We can however beat the shit out of him until he tells us."

"It wouldn't do you much good, he'll have moved by now anyway. Might even have left the country."

"He was injured?"

"Yes."

Strijdom switched on the recorder again. "Prisoner Kody stated off the tape that Runyan is injured, whereabouts not admitted ... Kody, are you certain that Runyan did not conceal IDs in your vehicle, even in deceit of you?"

"I'm quite certain. I am not in possession nor are there any in the vehicle."

"Not a flicker. All true as recorded. Mr Kody, you will then have no objection if we destroy the vehicle entirely, compensate the owner and return you to Johannesburg?"

"None whatsoever. It would save me a lot of trouble."

"True, bloody true, Mr Kody."

Just then one of the technicians came in from another room. He had a saucerful of glass fragments and Stuart found himself quaking violently for a moment before the man said, "Nothing there, sir. No phosphorescence. Blank. The car is virtually new, it has not been resprayed or dismantled and there are no immediate signs of tampering except a couple of marks where someone might have tried to remove the windscreen whole. Not so easy as you'd think. Obviously hollows and reservoirs would have to be examined properly. Do you want us to do it?"

The inspector passed a hand over his face. "Bring us some coffee from the flask. What time's that gorilla de Hoek arriving?"

"About an hour, sir."

"Tell me we haven't missed something: is it acually possible to conceal diamonds in window glass?"

The technician named Al looked surprised for a moment before shaking his head with conviction. "Absolutely not," sir, you'd see lumps like bubbles. Diamond's refractive index is 2.4 while glass is only about 1.6. Even lead glass isn't more than 1.8. Of course, there's cubic zirconia at 2.2, but even then it would still show lumps. Anyway, come to think of it, you couldn't make glass out of it, the crystals go opaque with temperature even if we had the technology to do it, which I'm sure we haven't."

He paused, realising his speculation had carried him away. "Er, anyway, this is ordinary, frangible, toughened vehicle glass. Sorry."

The trace was still running but Stuart didn't dare look at it. His mind was in a ferment at the discovery that it had all been for nothing and that Tiki Powers had pulled off as neat a double-cross as his own gullibility would allow. A murder had been committed and ex-Corporal Cornelius would have another in his heart when he too discovered the deception. There was also something familiar and ominous about the name de Hoek, but before he could recall it, Strijdom turned to him again and switched on the recorder.

"Right. Mr Kody, will you state for the record and for the polygraph that you are not and have not been carrying or conveying illicit diamonds on your person or in your vehicle?"

Stuart realised almost joyfully that he was now able to give a truthful affirmative but then he suddenly remembered the big stone concealed in the epoxy cube on the key-ring. He wondered desperately where it was but even so the short pause was enough to gain Strijdom's full attention. And Powers had had the gall to be helpful about the cube, so that Stuart was entirely confused about Powers' motives and whether to feel grateful or murderous towards him. Either way he realised that only the truth could save his freedom. Looking up beyond Strijdom's head he glimpsed the key ring hanging on a board with several others.

"I have to confess," he said slowly, "I thought I was carrying clear gem-stones in the windscreen glass ... Evidently I was not."

"True," Strijdom intoned, watching the polygraph. "You admit criminal intent?"

"Conspiracy, yes. Fact, no."

"This interview closed. Tape counter 124. Stick him in one of the Rondos."

"Are you charging me with anything?" Stuart asked as they peeled off the pads.

"Hope I don't need to. The Hook'll get you for something, let him do the paperwork."

He looked away disinterestedly and said to the assistants, "I think you'd better give the car a proper going over, just in case. The full works, but use your judgement. I don't want to stay too long."

"Listen, I'm not going to break for it, am I? At least don't put me back in that hole," Stuart managed to say without pleading.

The inspector's expression stayed completely blank as if he hadn't heard, and he concentrated on pouring coffee from the thermos. He saw the bottle of whisky and casually laced his mug with a couple of lidfuls.

The constable returned Stuart's shirt and jacket before ushering him out to the tiny dark cell. He locked him in without a word. There was a smell of stale urine and he kept still, trying to adjust his eyes to the very faint light, to avoid knocking over the container.

He felt as though he'd been through the wringer, baffled and tormented, all for nothing. He'd driven those long miles staring through a clear and innocent windscreen and too trusting even to check with Polaroid glasses. And yet Tiki Powers, he decided, must have been totally crazy to pull a stunt like that and was presumably now on his way out of the country by a different route with yet another supposedly foolproof scheme for concealment. Time would be on his side with Stuart safely locked up or at least in Mozambique and Rollo unreachable and still in ignorance. And the only reason Stuart was in South Africa at all was because Rollo couldn't trust anyone else with his precious hoard.

He felt a huge wave of despair engulf and up-end him and

he slithered down the dank wall into a foetal crouch. The inspector's remark about sanctimoniousness had stung, the young soldier had been reasonably decent and Stuart had his own brand of toughness which found self-pity repellent. It was the thought of Lucy and what his imprisonment would do to her which jellified his thinking and made insignificant to him the thought of his own fate and deprivation.

If the problem was purely his own he felt he could cope with it; it wasn't even the tie of marriage complicating his independent fate, it was simply love, what he genuinely felt was a completely devoted, lifelong love, insoluble, irresistible, as unshakeable as a fishhook in a ganglion. The thought of her cleared away the discomfort of his empty stomach but replaced it with a hollow, churned longing. He had once or twice in the past let his mind stray to the idea of losing her, causing such acute poignancy that he had to dismiss the thought in haste; now that it was no longer an idea but a real possibility, he had the impression of impending heartbreak, the pointless voyage of dark, face-squeezing despair on which he had embarked once before when his mother died; but then he had had a child's resilience and his grandmother's skill at distraction, exhausting him so that the excruciating moments of sadness alone in his bed were mercifully curtailed.

The loss facing him now like a black and slimy wraith was perhaps worse for being imaginary, a probability but not yet a conviction. He groaned aloud as her face filled his vision, smiling impudence, hair tossed in defiance, the wiry strength giving such feather lightness to her movements, a tiny sweep of finger across his temple leaving him trembling and wondering if she had any idea what such a gesture could do to a lover's emotions. And laughter, always so much gaiety and laughter . . . a dinner party where another couple had stunted the conversation with endless platitudes and Lucy had suddenly thrown the spanner: "Of course, the proof of the pudding is in the pulling," said quite seriously and without looking up, and after a short silence the whole table breaking up in hilarity, Stuart compounding it by trying to hide his mirth behind a napkin. And Lucy, perfect Lucy, looking up then in pretended startlement, shoulders back and head typically high and poised, and no one sure if the malapropism was intended . . . Lucy terrifying him almost to fury when she disappeared from *Sailor V* on the windsurfer in the moonlight, its blue sail invisible until she crossed the moon's path and then swished down the beam and back to him like the real Venus on the water, so much more beautiful and lithe and real than Botticelli's flaccid pink goddess . . . The physical vision its own agony, so taut and high in the rump, deep cleft of back muscles, thighs toned and ash-hard beneath silky skin, little cords standing out behind the knees, tiny bony feet misshapen by ballet shoes, breasts high and almost integral with pectoral muscles, the fine poise and dignity of her trained bearing. She was beyond loving, he felt he didn't possess the equipment of words, gestures or caresses ever to express the extent of his feelings and his intoxication without descending into an impossible cloy of sentiment.

As the tears began to well up and then overflow, he forced his mind into a blanket-fog like cottonwool over the eyes, the reality finally grasped and a dumb realisation that the pain would be unbearable and the only respite lay in an extinguished mind. He understood then how some prison cases might curl up into mute catatonia and never again in even fifty years acknowledge another human being or express any emotion whatsoever.

He didn't hear the second helicopter arrive and when the cell door opened and a voice ordered him out, he stayed where he was, feeling engrossed in practice for a new existence, one without hope or fear, joy or sadness, pain or pleasure. He was pulled roughly into the light, propelled over to the main building and smartly back to reality when he recognised the big, brutal and ill-mannered passenger on the 747 from London.

De Hoek stood in front of him, three or four inches taller, formidable, broad and scowling. Before Stuart could express a reaction, one huge fist smashed out towards his left eye. He had a microsecond to tilt his head and take the blow on the edge of his brow, feeling himself plucked clean off his feet and sprawled painfully across a flattened tin waste bucket. Blood ran freely from a split and he heard Strijdom say something in mild remonstration.

De Hoek's clipped voice cut him off. "That was personal and nothing to do with business . . . Goddamn it, I think I broke my fokking hand!"

Stuart found he couldn't focus properly and there was a mighty throbbing over his eye. He was pulled roughly to his feet and dumped in a chair, still unable to see anything but vaguely aware of questions.

"Kody, I said, who do you work for?"

"No one. I don't work for anyone."

"Well, I happen to know you do – and I also know how to make you tell me so why not make it easy so I don't have the chore of sticking things in you."

"It's true. I don't work for anyone."

"Hey, don't play games with me. I mean for the British Government, which department? What are you doing on my pitch? Or are you doubling for the Soviets?"

Stuart tried to register an amazed expression but either he failed because of his bloodstained face or de Hoek impassively ignored it. Strijdom went outside and left them alone, apparently in response to the merest eye movement from the Security Chief.

He tried to wipe the blood away with the back of his hand, feeling it drying stickily. "It's rubbish. You're making it up for some reason, something else to nail me with."

"You're nailed already, by Strijdom. I want my own answers and when I get them I'll decide what to do with you."

"Is he charging me then?"

"He'll do what I tell him, but I'm not here to mess around. Talk now, or I'll get the needle to do it and that can damage you. I know you're in clandestine ops. of some kind and I need to know all about it."

Stuart shook his head dumbly; de Hoek stood with a decisive movement, pulled out a small tape-recorder and waved it in Stuart's face.

"A bit crackly. It came down the phone line this morning, on the high speed. Listen."

He pressed the play button and at once a jolt of alarm went through Stuart like 500 volts. Lucy's voice, a man's questions.

". . . his work's secret."

"You can tell it to us, ma'am, surely?"

There followed more of her conversation with the Police interrupted by the phone call from her mother. Much was edited out in squeaks and crackling, then he heard, *"when Stuart gets back, I'm going to tell him about Patrick,"* then Alicia's accented reply, *"Do you think it's wise to tell all?*

Such a bad business... What about if he knew your father was Jewish?" followed achingly by Lucy's carefree laughter.

While Stuart stared at him in bewilderment, de Hoek explained casually. "It seems she had intruders in the house and wanted to get in touch with you. The reason she didn't know how to is because you're in some secret service, not because you're estranged. For some reason she's well-disposed towards you – you want to hear the sloppy bits?"

Stuart shook his head. "Is she all right? What's that about intruders, how did you get that stuff?"

"Because *we* did the intruding, because *I* was after *you*, because I am a vengeful man and you find some very nasty little things when you start turning over stones. So look what I found, and all because of your superior horseshit over some tart on a plane, what you *rooineks* call 'hoighty', isn't it? Well, now I know you are no fokking Brit even, you're a slimy Slav, on the make in my country, a quick in-and-out, something for nothing. *Ja*, well let me tell you, I *worked* for my First Class seat, worked bleddy hard and no hand-outs." He lowered his voice. "You know about truth juices, don't you? That I'd not only find out who you work for, you'd even give me the scam about the diamonds, maybe about handing them over to me, would you not now, my China?"

"You can put me on the polygraph if you like, I won't limit to Yes and No, I can tell it all now except –"

"*Ja*? Except what? I know: you want to do a little deal with me but you don't know if I'll keep my end of it? You must have been cunning as a Cape rat, 'cos if you could see out the back window, you'd see Strijdom's boys doing a fair jobbie on your wheels. If it's there, they'll find it, believe me, so what have you got to say to me, hey?"

Stuart wanted desperately to ask a childish: "Then you'll let me go?" but by an effort he resisted. "There's a forty-odd carat white which they won't find. You can have it for my freedom. I have no other stones, I've been very neatly ripped off."

"*Ja*, I heard it. Tough ... OK, so when they get through out there and find nothing, they'll maybe let you go, it depends on what I say. You best hope they find nothing. So where's the big one, the one for me?"

Stuart looked at him for a long, long pause, wiping his eye once or twice. He felt coldly furious to be in the supplicant's

95

position with this big brute of an Afrikaner. He said stubbornly, "I'd like to know why you were so high-handed with the stewardess."

"Christ, you've got a fokking gall!" de Hoek shouted, springing to his feet, smashing his fist into his left hand and then gargling at the pain of his forgotten injury.

"All right," he growled after an interval of simmering down. "I'll give you your little victory. I decided you were maybe right. I don't appreciate other shits like you pointing it out. All right, Slav?"

Stuart nodded in some surprise then he too stood up.

He went over to the board on the wall which was covered with numbered hooks and took down the key-ring with the big amber cube.

"It's in there," he said swinging it like a hypnotist's lure. "All yours."

De Hoek took it away from him gently enough, nodding with a slight grin of triumph and trying to look into the hazed epoxy. "How much?"

"I've no idea, but I'm told it's massive. The diamond detective supplied it for a lure."

"Otis? He was shot trying to trap your mate Runyan."

"Yes."

"All right. I'm not after him – they are." He pointed outside and made an abrupt decision. "You keep this for me, you can run it. You take it and sell it and put the proceeds into an account for me in Switzerland and at some stage I'll telephone you for details. I can't talk to you any more now about what else I want, I'll be in touch when you get home. Maybe you're not important and you're only here for this. I'll find out, by and by. I don't need to tell you what'll happen if you don't oblige me but it'll start with your old lady, however young and loving she is, right? You'll be free to go if the car's really clean, but on south, not back. Don't ever come back, unless you check with me first, right?"

Stuart nodded and said quietly, "Thanks."

"*Ja*. Go wash your face. Yaw head's too hard but I guess you got guts. You want some coffee?"

Tikki Powers had spent too little time with Stuart to reveal an essential character weakness, an almost craven fear of disapproval. He spent a very anxious day and night waiting for the call that would ease his mind at least temporarily, since he was a man filled with dreams and schemes that were rarely successful. When the telephone finally rang on the Sunday morning, his tone betrayed evident relief as he shouted to Margie that he'd answer it, but he heard Rollo calling instead of Stuart.

"Tikki, how did it go?"

"He went off all right but I haven't heard. He left twenty-four hours ago, more."

There was puzzlement in Rollo's voice which he brightened with optimism. "Oh . . . well, maybe he couldn't get a call through. But it worked, eh, did it? I still can't believe the simplicity. You're a genius, Tik, I mean it. We can do it again and again!"

Powers' nerve failed him doubly and he found himself shaking his head at the instrument before Rollo's insistence forced an answer.

"Listen," he said eventually, "I only tried it out with glass and pebbles. I found out in time that it's the index that's crucial and it wouldn't work with –"

"Tiki, what the hell have you done, put them in some stupid place where they'll be found? DAMMIT, that's my best mate – what about my other suggestion, round the rim, did you –?"

Powers' face was screwed up against Rollo's anger. "Yes, right," he said quickly. "In the edge, hidden by the rubber and a bit of compound. Probably better that way, anyhow."

After a long interval, Rollo said in an icy voice, "Tik, how long have you known it wouldn't work? Why didn't you tell me? We've had a whole year, dammit."

There was another silence until Powers dropped his voice against Margie's eavesdropping and said with some self-pity, "I can't wait any more and you'd have done it without me if it hadn't been for my idea. My freedom, remember, two hundred thousand dollars? How're you, how's the leg?"

"Limp . . . Tiki, I think I'll kill you if they've got him."

"No, they can't have done."

"Well, he should have been clear easily by now." Rollo swore viciously and promised to call back later, while Powers put down the phone in utter dejection.

De Hoek finished his coffee and looked out of the window.

There were sounds of conversation and normal border traffic from the front of the building but the work on the Daihatsu was discreetly out of sight.

"If I were you," he said, "I'd ask them to lend you a set of tools and an air pump, otherwise you'll be a bit stuck. When they do a car, they're usually sure enough the owner's a scoundrel to let him put it together himself, even if they find nothing. Some of them can't do it. Are you handy?"

At Stuart's nod, he added, "I'll put in a word because I want you out of here, maybe they'll help, I don't know. Anyway, I'll give the nod to Strijdom that you're clear if he doesn't find anything. I take it he won't?"

Stuart nodded and suddenly trembled to think that Powers might have put the stones somewhere else in the vehicle.

De Hoek didn't notice anything and eyed him levelly. "One question: who paid for your ticket if you're not on government business?"

"I'd no choice, the aircraft was full."

"Mm ... better hope that checks out. Meddling ... the Brits started all the damage here and by Christ do we resent you for it! Now everyone's meddling including the Russians, but don't worry, we're on top of all that. It's what makes us so hard, see?" He stood up with sudden finality. "I trust we won't meet again," he said curtly and went outside.

Stuart saw him walk over to the inspector who was watching his men working. They exchanged a few words and then de Hoek strode off out of sight. Two minutes later he heard a light turbine helicopter wind up slowly, steady in the hover, and bank away sharply to the west.

The Daihatsu was up on blocks, all the tyres were off the wheels, the petrol tank out, exhaust pipe in sections and door locks hanging out of their sockets. They had a whole series of stalked mirrors and one of the men was measuring the tank inside and out with a special caliper. The other probed in the engine compartment. The sump was off and lay in a black dusty pool of oil, while water dripped steadily from the various loosened hose connections.

Stuart wandered outside feeling an odd kind of relieved detachment and the unreal effects of a short and restless night. Strijdom saw him coming and waved him back inside, but a few minutes later he came over.

Stuart said, "I was hoping I could have a go at putting things back while there're still some tools knocking about."

"Well, could be that shows a certain confidence." Strijdom spoke affably enough and Stuart felt he detected a note of pity that he had been so sadly duped. "I think we'll be wrapped up in an hour or so – you can go and put the tyres back on if you like but stay away from the car itself. The lads'll take care of any two-handed jobs like putting the tank back and bleeding the brakes. You'll have to scrounge among the wrecks for oil, they kicked your sump over by accident. Your filters will be OK, we just X-ray them."

Stuart found a couple of tyre irons and started work, finding it a lot more difficult than the display of practised fitters. From close up, the almost new Fourtrack looked ravished, especially with everything gaping open and the windshield missing. The rubber surround lay like a twisted snake in the yard among a pile of mats, plastic facia covers and neatly sliced upholstery, but he didn't care about any of the damage. He just wanted to get going, to make the final conviction that his ridiculous ordeal was really over.

He was perspiring heavily by the time he'd replaced and inflated all five tyres, then he got very filthy in the process of finding enough oil from four different wrecks.

As he passed the blockhouse with the last container, Strijdom called out to him from an open window. "That's about it, unless you want to do the whole coachwork bit. They just piled the seats in and refilled your tank. Which was your ignition key?"

Stuart answered levelly, "The one with the amber cube."

"Come and get it when you've put that oil in."

Too tired to speculate, he filled the sump, checked the hose connections and the wiring and closed up. The men were still refitting the exhaust pipe so Stuart left them and went back to the office. He could hear the normal traffic of the free and innocent on the other side, very light because it was Sunday.

Inside, Strijdom seemed almost affable. "It's fascinating how ingenious people get, you know. Wouldn't that have been something to have had it in the glass? Of course, if you think about it, the key-ring's a good place to beat a search, it's neither on you nor in the car, but it takes a bright one to think of it. One guy tried it with a miniature brandy barrel on the key chain but he was greedy, the barrel was too big and heavy. There's one last thing, I'm afraid, we'll have to give you a proper body search."

After this unpleasant indignity, Stuart was given space to wash and dress and then Strijdom gave him back his passport, wallet and grip. Finally he held up the key-ring and spun the amber cube briskly round in front of Stuart's face. He seemed to have recovered completely from his morning dudgeon, the bags under his eyes appearing less pronounced, but Stuart was trying to stop a leafy trembling from affecting his own legs. He had a strong and infuriating feeling that he was being teased and he couldn't help wondering if de Hoek had given him away and hit upon a finely cruel revenge.

"On your way, then," Strijdom said. "I don't expect you'll be back." Even then Stuart found himself disbelieving, holding himself from reaching for the key. Strijdom casually dropped it into his hand and turned for the door.

Outside, the men were putting their equipment away. Feeling close to vomiting, Stuart walked over, flung his bag into the passenger space, put the key into the ignition and turned it. The battery was very low from the long discharge of headlights so the engine turned only sluggishly and refused to fire.

"Hold on," one of the men said and they both leaned shoulders behind the car. Stuart helped gratefully, leaped in and declutched. The engine caught at once but he was puffing and hypertense as he pulled the door shut, wanting desperately to put his foot down and swirl out of the yard at full speed. Somehow maintaining his control, he began to move off slowly and casually, but as he approached the compound gate a voice called out harshly. Turning his head, he saw Strijdom pointing to a pile of bits and pieces lying neglected to one side. Almost snarling with impatience, he reversed back to the pile and the inspector leaned in the nearside window, grinning.

"You'd better get this lot or I'll have you flogged for littering."

The rear door was pulled open and the loose bits of trim were tossed randomly inside, plastic covers, an ashtray, the handbook and, among the last, the now redundant windscreen surround, still with a few chips of fractured glass sticking out of the rubber.

Trembling with forced control, Stuart got out and walked

right round the car to make sure everything was loaded. He was very close to breaking point when he got back in, accepted a square blue crossing card from Strijdom and drove gently out of the yard. The same black in the trench coat took the card with unnecessary scrutiny and finally raised the barrier. He gave a casual wave. One hundred yards further on, the now active Swazi Customs and Immigration required more form-filling and even a fifty cent road tax. Finally as he stumbled out of their offices with his clearance it still wasn't over for him, since he kept expecting recall or another surprise. The engine stopped abruptly after about fifteen miles when he was beginning to relax but he found the fault – the HT lead loosened from the coil – fairly quickly, and by that stage there was enough charge to restart.

He had put out of his mind completely the additional torture of finding the first mile of Swazi territory just a normal, petering-out village, with children and dogs roaming happily where he had quivered and crawled among deadly snakes in a minefield. Just after Pigg's Peak, a little town halfway to Mbabane which seemed to have six supermarkets for each inhabitant, his eyes began to faze and he pulled off the road to doze. He was woken an hour later by rain slanting through the open windscreen so he blearily set off again, stopping once to retrieve a tattered sheet of polythene to cover himself. The rain increased steadily until the interior of the car was sodden and his speed reduced to what his streaming eyes could handle.

He only made it the few miles to Forbes' Reef, reeling with tiredness and hunger. Four cold beers in an earthen-floor bar followed by some fried yams and a long skewer of un-identifiable meats brought restoration and then helpless drowsiness. He received some solicitous remarks about the state of his face where de Hoek had struck him, accentuated by unshavenness and obvious exhaustion. He was assured of gasoline the next morning and a telephone as well but in the meantime there was nothing to do but sleep. He didn't care that the bed he was given had a smell not to his liking, it was a bed in a place of freedom. There was a big yellow dog to guard the car which looked like fair game for small collectors once the rain stopped. He slept for fourteen hours.

In the morning, after a delightful breakfast of papaya and green tea, he eventually found the sole working telephone and had to wait half an hour for his turn. The little black lady operator took his rands and very studiously provided the Johannesburg code but a sleepy Margie had to give him the factory number for Powers, who had gone to work as for a normal Monday. Stuart kept his voice quite bland.

"Sure I made it, Tiki, but the car broke down, back end of nowhere. All right now . . . Yippee, nothing, we're only half way. Listen, I've got to speak to Rollo about something else, it's very important. Will he be calling you today? . . . Good. Get him to leave a number with you so I can get to him, say this evening, between nine and midnight . . . OK, later then, Bye."

More than anything he wanted to call Lucy but was put off by the queue forming behind him and she wouldn't necessarily be home in the morning. Outside the building, children were vandalising the car since it now looked like a play-pen. They even had the back open and were rifling the contents. Stuart grinned to see two boys twirling the rubber strip for a third to skip over; they were big-eyed, grinning and innocent and he would have left it with them except that one suddenly squealed and dropped his end, his finger bleeding.

"Better put it back," Stuart said mildly. "There's glass in it. You're all little thieves, now get off."

As they scattered he tossed the rubber and a few other loose pieces inside and set off with a scampering entourage, leaving them quickly behind and waving happily. He drove all day, via the scruffy little capital Mbabane, hundreds of weary, steep and twisting miles, a problem-free border crossing into Mozambique and by the evening he was wearily delighted to see the lights of Maputo. Nearly there, nearly there, he told himself, then the first flight out. Rollo with a lost year, himself barely with his liberty, both of them with a fortune down the drain and still even the spectre of de Hoek if he didn't obey instructions for the heavy treasure on the key-ring.

He found a small hotel easily enough and was grateful to leave the car to the concierge after detaching the key from the cube and chain. He rang Powers again and found him curiously strained, almost dismal, as if the fun were all over. His questions about the journey and a freighter booking for the car seemed vague and uninterested and Stuart found he didn't have to make any big pretence to be exultant. He glanced up from the dark little booth as the concierge came back in, but the old man was taking no notice.

"Listen, Tiki, did you hear from Rollo?"

"Yes, here's the number."

"OK, I'll be in touch when it's all settled."

Rollo was still somewhere near Kimberley, in the backroom of a bar to judge by the noises and the waiting. Eventually he heard a gleeful roar and echoing congratulation and he had to shout very loud to interrupt.

"Rol, will you bloody listen! Powers has ripped us off. I got stopped. They knew I was coming. I did a deal with a soldier, I gave him the windscreen to let me go but there was a killing and I had to tell the cops all about it. I mean, including the stash. They were a bit surprised and then told me it couldn't be done, you can't hide them in glass and ... What!"

Rollo's voice was still highly excited. "I said I KNOW! ... Powers knew that. Jeez, you gave away the screen, Stuart, NO! How *could* you?"

"What in creation do you mean, how could I?" Stuart's voice rose to a fury and the old black concierge looked full of alarm. "You say Powers knew, so they weren't there at all, and now you're screaming at me for giving it away! I saved myself, dammit, what would you have done?"

"They WERE there! They were round the edge, that's all! In the rubber, you crap-head!"

Stuart said breathlessly, "Wait, Rollo, two minutes."

He hurled himself out of the booth and almost wrestled with the concierge. "My car, where did you put it?"

"In the parking, at the back, sir. It's all right, sure-sure, and the key is here."

"It's not locked. I've got to check something, quick, show me!"

The old man had a close-cropped greying head and a shambling walk. Reluctantly sighing, he led down the steps and round to the back of the building. Stuart ran ahead and found the Fourtrak there with its gaping empty front and the pile of miscellaneous fittings in the back. He couldn't see inside as the interior light hadn't been replaced and he rummaged around frantically for the heavy rubber strip. A sliver of glass nicked his finger as he found it and pulled it out, his chest heaving with relief and his thoughts in ferment.

The concierge had just caught up and his grizzled head shook in mystification as Stuart shut the rear door and sprinted round to the hall with a breathless thanks. He threw himself back into the booth but there was a smacking noise in the receiver as he called, "Rollo, are you there? ROLLO!"

He imagined his friend was probably banging the receiver into his hand or on to his leg-plaster in impatience and frustration. Finally he heard a snarled, "Hello!"

"I've got it," he said almost quietly, noticing the curious stare of the returning concierge.

"Got what, you turd-brained Polack?"

"The outside strip, the flange. It's got all the bits in it. Powers must've used some sticky stuff so they didn't fall out . . . Rollo? Rollo? . . . Yes, dear, I love you too . . . What the hell do I do now? The car's a shambles, it was rummaged, plus it's nicked . . . No, don't tell me, I've had enough. This is what I'm going to do, I'm going to shove the flange in my grip and get the first plane out. I'll just keep the stuff till you get back. No hurry . . . Tiki, yes, but he's lucky too. If he'd told me where they were we'd have lost them, I'd have failed the lie-detector. Not knowing, I was still a mule, that saved me. No, there's more to it, I'll tell you when I see you . . . That's what I mean, the other three. Some other time, Rol. Get well soon. Bye."

He hung up without waiting for more, paying a large phone bill and having to change a traveller's cheque. He also called Lucy, somehow resisting more than a single ring. It was midnight before he had eaten and fallen into an uneasy sleep but the next day everything went with almost graceful ease. He abandoned the car down a side street. It gave him a strangely light-hearted feeling to leave it and having found the offices of Lineas Aereas Moçambique and discovered they took credit cards, he got a later flight to London via Lisbon. Second-class, he decided almost ruefully, yet glowing with wonder and gratitude for a sorely earned and undeserved freedom.

Six

Guilt is the aphrodisiac of our mothers' fondest hopes.
                    C. Randolph Parker

When the papers arrived, fed singly through the letter-box by
a small boy making *Oompah-Oompah* in a marching private
world, Lucy came from the kitchen and remembered wistfully
the happy Sunday morning of a week ago. It seemed much
more remote because of wanting so badly to talk to Stuart
and not hearing any single ring the previous day. She worried
about being out and missing it and she had a distinct hollow
feeling which she put down to randiness; in her head she
invented conversations for his return, variously accusatory,
seductive, inquisitive and playfully trying to conceal her
anticipation and delight.

She hugged the bundle of papers and went back to take up
her mother's tea. From the kitchen window she saw
movement in blue: Stubbs the dog-handler again, who had
clearly taken to her and was going beyond his duty. Lucy
was seldom disturbed by people staring at her because of the
detachment in her self-awareness. She could be quite un-
abashed, although easily disconcerting, with a pointedly
cocked hip or a jaunty agreement, in reference to her
physique, "Nice, isn't it?" It was surprisingly effective in
disarming lechery or suggestive remarks and the lies would
disappear from profligate eyes.

She saw some activity up near the edge of Simon's Wood,
a figure turning. With a more concentrated look, she realised
she was seeing a brown dog jerking on the end of a man's
arm and then the two went down out of sight. Not far away,
the blue figure of the constable was approaching without
apparent haste, in fact he seemed to be casually strolling.

Lucy took the tea-tray upstairs and her mother thanked her sleepily. She said nothing about what she'd seen but a little later went outside and met Stubbs returning, handcuffed to a burly figure who wore a muddied and torn green raincoat but was otherwise not dressed for the country. He was seriously in need of medical attention for a mauled right arm.

Stubbs carried in his other hand a polythene-wrapped device which he said was receiver/recorder. Banjo, he explained, had sniffed it out and then followed back on a scent. Banjo looked bright-eyed and alert, glancing up quickly on hearing his name. The man wasn't armed but Stubbs bluntly stated that Banjo didn't like to take chances on that score and was simply doing his job. It sounded like an explanation he'd given before.

When they reached the house another car, summoned by radio, arrived to take the man away for questioning. Lucy wanted to bandage his arm but Stubbs didn't share her feelings and kept her away. She didn't recognise the man and could offer no explanation.

The Police found a car with CD plates some distance away and after that everything went silent. There were no more visits from Stubbs, simply one more call to reassure her that she wouldn't be bothered again.

Lucy was determined to take it all calmly, especially since, with the weekend in Whitehall, there were no more enquiries she could make. Alicia was further intrigued and alarmed but Lucy steered her firmly away from further speculation and more attempts to contact her father.

They walked the afternoon away and Alicia gradually relaxed, the TV was in the open and there was the prospect of Cary Grant in *To Catch a Thief*. Lucy decided that Grace Kelly didn't look strong enough to be a cat-burglar. She refrained from saying so because she knew it would spoil her mother's rapture with the tale; Alicia hadn't acquired a Western cynicism and was romantic enough to involve herself completely. For her, a movie could still be a complete reality, not something made on a set or location, and in one way Lucy could envy her the ecstasy of total belief. She couldn't concentrate well herself anyway, she made a wan attempt to tell herself that she was involved in a thrilling romance with a man of mystery but it didn't work for her. She knew about the lies thrown up so easily by girlish imagination and the unhappiness it could cause. She was in bed early and reading when the telephone startled her; it gave one single ring and a fraction of a second one before cutting off. Lucy closed her eyes with a sigh, never so aware of her craving for affection and two single tears squeezed out. She felt meltingly grateful, turning out the light and hugging the pillow quietly to sleep.

The mystery was compounded early the next morning by the arrival of two serious-looking men in plain clothes with a van full of equipment. They showed CID identification and proceeded to scan the interior of the house with strange electronic detectors and, after a few minutes, they located one small suction bug high on the outside of the drawing-room window. They checked the rest of the house thoroughly but found nothing else.

Lucy demanded then to know what was happening but they told her no more than that the device was on the same wavelength as the receiver taken in by Stubbs, and that the man who'd been Banjo'd had certainly been given attention for his arm and then returned to his embassy.

"Which embassy?" she'd cried, but they shook their heads, claiming ignorance and promising to let her know. They thanked her for the coffee and left.

"Mamuschka," she complained, "I feel like a waitress, making nothing but cups for cops, one after another – I'm surprised we've anything left. They'll turn me into a tea-bag."

"It's time this husband came home and got a proper job," Alicia answered with some asperity.

"Well, I've got one myself now and I'll be late if I don't go at once. Want to come and watch? You can, but you're not to interfere."

Alicia duly stayed in the car and watched through the railings; Harvey Smith yapped twice from the parcel shelf and she hushed him curtly. She noticed how seriously the children took the lessons but unlike the formal classes of Lucy's girlhood, there were frequent outbreaks of laughter and delight which Lucy tended to focus on herself so as to control them. She also had a light-hearted informer system going against wiping dirty hands on clothes since the ground was wet from a morning drizzle. At the end of the session there was a competition for the slowest cartwheel with the

107

whole class judging. A beautiful eight-year-old blonde called Vanessa got the vote but then Lucy took the onus off her with an agonisingly controlled demonstration, giving them a nearly impossible target. Her fondness and lack of severity brought total co-operation even from the hopeless cases and Alicia saw with surprise how cleverly she held continuous attention with unexpected and zany stunts, despite the chilly weather.

Back in the car and slightly breathless, Lucy was startled with a sudden hug from her mother, a quick but fierce clasp of affection, and again saw herself momentarily through other eyes.

"Those who can't do it, teach it," she said smiling. "Actually, I always thought that was unfair and untrue."

"Well, you can't be winning competitions with a broken neck, can you?"

"Yes, that's been my excuse. But I wasn't a winner, I wasn't serious enough. And I'd put it another way, if you can't love what you teach, do something else."

"Why didn't you do this long before? I was never thinking of it. That man kept you at home."

"No he didn't, I did it myself. And he's not 'that man', don't be horrid. I wish he'd come home. My bed's cold and empty – and he's always nice to you."

Alicia glanced quickly at her then kept her gaze ahead as Lucy drove home. "I hope he doesn't deceive you. I don't like this secrets business, Alexei was in it more than I knew. Such a deceiver."

"Mama, you're not to start another tirade against him and men in general. I've heard it a few times already and you're not fair."

"How not fair?"

"I saw pictures of you when you were married, you were so pretty, so enchanting and demure. I bet you nearly tore his heart out. I bet you didn't say much; he would have taken that for dignity and reticence, whereas in truth you didn't have the experience or education to have anything to say. Alexei was much travelled already, very cosmopolitan, probably did all the talking for both of you, yes?"

Alicia continued to look rather stonily forward but Lucy sensed a faint nod.

"So he loved you like a beaver and . . . I never asked you if you enjoyed it, did I?"

Alicia said nothing for a moment, looking confused. "I'm not sure if we changed the subject. Child, you have to understand, we did not talk much about such things, even now in Russia they try to make it a small matter. And girls then could not be seen to know much, to seem to want . . . I loved it, he was everything to me, but I used to make it hard for him, I would refuse, I would pretend to need more words, more time, more trouble –"

"More wooing?"

"Yes, so all that happened, we didn't love so much which was not enough for him. I could not hold him interested." Plaintively she added, "There was not enough for me either. I wanted to be really wild, but I could not to show him that side, could I?"

Lucy was about to make a scathing remark but she checked it and put her hand on her mother's arm. "Maybe not then, no. A lot has changed."

"You do not have to be nice to me," Alicia said stiffly. "Anyway, those are excuses all. The fact is I was boring for him at last, like a silly bourgeoise provincial. The things we were taught, so dull and childish, which I tried to teach also you. But you had his naughtiness and sense to not listen. And now I really think men have more to lose by marrying than we women."

"Oh, nonsense, Mama, it's roundabouts and swings."

"What?"

"They do it because they want to, same as we do."

"No, no, it's for what they think they want, most of them are wrong. Women know what they want, that's why men find it so dull when they find out. Late."

"You mean impregnation in security? Well, it *is* the bottom line, for evolution."

"No, I mean that a woman marrying wants children, but the man doesn't, he wants just the woman. Why else would he marry, lose his freedom."

Lucy said nothing for a few moments, wondering how her mother's thinking had got so jaundiced and also whether she wasn't so inaccurate. "Mama," she said eventually, "I married Stuart because he filled me with big, warm feelings. I had an idea of total trust. I wasn't thinking about children, but he says to me now that the idea of having a child with me makes him, well, let's say very emotional."

"Only because he likes doing it, the making bit of the business. Nappies and screaming and no sleep is different."

"Did you want to have me?"

"Yes, of course. I said, the base urge."

"Basic. And Papa, did he want me?"

"That's what I mean, he wasn't ahead thinking. He wanted to have me all day long, like a *zayetz*."

"Rabbit. Or maybe." Lucy said quietly, "he wanted just to love you, trying to find in sex the reassurance that you loved him back. And he never got it, did he, because you didn't think it right to give it, to throw away all your bargaining power?"

"Don't be so hard. I try to think, not to cry any more. Do you think *you* have it right?"

"I'm sorry . . . I've no idea. I want to be honest, so if I'm not, it's by accident or ignorance and friends will tell me, I hope. I'm happy, I've a lovely man, I daren't question it too much. He rang me last night, so he's all right."

"What did he say? Where is he?"

"Nothing. Just one ring, it's enough. I wish I could do it back, that's all."

"And loving Patrick, that was different feeling?"

"Yes, I'm sure you realise that. There's an English expression, to have the silver tongue. He had it, the poetry, he stirred me and I fell headlong. It's only now that I can see my own dishonesty, not deliberate, just not recognising what my feelings told me. Marrying him really worried me, but I put it aside, I suppose because I'd said Yes and felt I had to keep to it. Funny, isn't it, it's still talked about the same way, the man providing the big romantic setting for the question, softening her up with champagne and all the gear, getting her in the mood to say the big-eyed OK. We spiders have the whole thing planned, our decision was made long before, but if we don't give him a good run for his money, he might think it wasn't worth it. It's gotta be hard to be good."

"What?"

"Nothing." Lucy grinned, looking both ways as she turned into their lane. She saw an electricity van stopping outside the house. She slowed right down as Alicia asked finally, with a smile, "And children, what's about my *vnoutchki*?"

"Well, Mama, you'll have to be patient a little longer, I'm not ready to make you a *babuschka*. Every time Stuart loves me, he thinks it's possible I could conceive, and you may be right, it's the doing it they like, or love, rather, if they're in love. So I take him to heaven and I go as well and I bide my time. When I'm ready, I'll ask him if he's sure but I already know the answer. He never has the *tristesse*, the sadness after loving, and as for me, I feel like a ripening grape, a muscatel almost at the turning point, waiting for the last urge from the earth, for when the sugar comes in."

Alicia had to choke on her reaction because they'd reached the house and turned in, and she held it un-Russian to show emotion before strangers. There was just one man come to read the meter and Lucy felt grateful, knowing the converse, that it's typical to be over-emotional with intimates. However, as soon as the man had done his job and left. Alicia suddenly sobbed and threw her arms round her daughter in a great surge of emotion. Lucy patted her head while Harvey scratched at both their ankles.

"The pooch wants a piece of the action," Lucy said eventually, knowing Alicia wouldn't understand and might stop to ask. She answered the question by pointing at the neatly combed terrier.

"*Mamuschka*, I wish you'd try not to behave like a bear, it's not British. Come and have a large sherry and compose yourself. When in Rome . . ." she added and could have bitten her tongue; explaining that you should do as the Romans do even in Gloucestershire wasn't easy and by the time she'd reverted to Russian, Alicia's eyes were glassy with disinterest. Lucy then recognised it as a good defusing device since her mother would rather have prolonged her emotional state, a not very honest indulgence. She took refuge in the garden, seeing her mother starting to prepare vegetables, more or less composed.

Once Lucy was outside, Alicia remembered her private determination, checked through the kitchen window and went to the telephone. She dialled the same Belgian number and fidgeted nervously, waiting for her requested connection. Eventually he came on the line, full of affable charm, the deep Russian voice dearly familiar.

"Alicia, what a surprise! How are you? Is anything wrong?"

"Sasha, I'm puzzled. I wondered if there's something dirty going on again, do you know? Ludmilla's husband is away, we don't know where, there have been intruders, violence, she fought one of them. Now he's working for Defence, we know only that."

"Well, well, how fascinating. You know we –" He stopped himself and asked, "Why are you asking me, Alicia?"

"Because you know where to find these people. Who should we ask, even the Police can't find him."

"Ah, well this one's half Czech, isn't he? Try the Czech section, DI6, Carlton House. I'll get you the number. The chief is, er, Stayres. Adrian Stayres. Surely they should be able to find him unless he's gone across. Why didn't we know about him, you never said? – it must be urgent if you have to call me."

"No, I wouldn't have, well, he's only supposed to be on a language refreshment course."

"Ah, but you don't know for sure? Well, if Stayres can't help you and no one else knows, I'm as baffled as you, unless . . . it could be the new W section, it's completely secret, we've got nothing on it at all except that recruits are mostly outsiders, unplantable. It's a moletrap, a watchdog section, answers to Downing Street, access to every department. Very sneaky. But anything Czech, Stayres will know, I'm sure. Here." He gave the number and after a few nervous pleasantries, Alicia rang off, looking over her shoulder.

She surveyed the garden again before dialling the London number and was quickly put through to Stayres' secretary. She told Alicia she was sure they had no one called Kody in the department but relented to insistence and put her through to the section head. He too was adamant but showed a gratifyingly definite interest.

"Czech, you say, your son-in-law? Fluent speaker, is he?"

"Oh, yes, his grandmother brought him up, with his father. In England."

"Really. And you, madam, from where is your own accent, may I ask?"

"But that's not to do with this."

"Ah . . . can I call you back?" Stayres asked smoothly. Alicia gave him the number obligingly before realising what she'd done. She had a feeling as though she had opened a tin of maggots.

Stayres continued quietly, "If I'm not mistaken, you have the flavour of Leningrad, is that right?"

"I ... yes, I have lived here a long time, I'm a British person."

"Ah, so you married an Englishman?"

"Why do you ask these questions? I'm trying to find my son-in-law. My daughter is so worried, you see."

"Madam, I'm sure that is the case. However, to find someone, one needs a little background and I'm sure you have nothing to hide."

"Oh ... my husband went away. He was already away from me, then your people forced him out. In 1971, from the Embassy, but he was just a commercial attaché."

"Ah, I see. And your son-in-law didn't say where he was going?"

"No, he is not permitted to talk about his work, that's why he didn't say if he was in your section and the Police couldn't find him for us. Perhaps this W section might give something, if I can call them? Men came asking me, threatening, they wanted to know why he was in South Africa. I – "

"Who's that, Mama?" Lucy asked from behind her, making her jump. Alicia covered the mouthpiece and said hurriedly, "Czech, I – wait a moment."

In answer to a question from the phone she gave her name and then said. "Yes, of course you may call again. Thank you."

She hung up and looked directly at Lucy as if to proclaim her truthfulness. "Perhaps the Police asked him to call us. The head of Czech section, he will try to find out ..."

Lucy regarded her balefully for a few moments and decided not to probe and start an argument. Instead she nodded equably and went into the kitchen, trying to quell her suspicions.

Stayres buzzed his secretary and summoned her abruptly.

"Sylvia! I want you to do some rummaging for me. Anyone called K-O-D-Y- been to South Africa recently, find out. Get me the file on one Simonov, he was ponged in '71, that big purge it must have been. Relatives, ex-wife and daughter living here, naturalised. This is their phone number, find out where it is and then get on to the local Police and see what's been going on. Sleeping dogs I smell ... Right, I'll be back at two o-clock."

* * *

"Moles," he said on his return, his voice sepulchral. "Can't be too careful these days, um? Let's have a look."

As he took the files and handed her his brolly, he thanked her silently so as not to expel a pocket of wind. With uncharacteristic gluttony, after a large portion of chili con carne, he'd had two helpings of blackberry cheesecake and was now suffering.

He smoothed back his iron-grey hair and adjusted half-moon glasses. Adrian Stayres was impeccably mannered and attired, arranging himself with a cultivated stillness and dignity. He opened a buff folder and peered into it while asking, "Anything on South Africa?"

"Yes, sir. A Kody flew to Johannesburg last Wednesday evening on an SAA 747, flight number . . . here we are –"

"Sylvia, I don't need the engine serial numbers either."

"I'm sorry. But he went First Class."

"Did he now? Do we smell corruption? It says here he's self-employed. What at? Ask SA section if they've heard of him, will you? If he's any good we'll have to steal him. Now then, let's see."

He began again to read sonorously from the file as she went out. "Kody, Stuart. Born 1955. Father Karel, Czech, Naturalised, RAF Pilot Officer, DFC., married Kathryn Stuart, Brit, in 1953. She killed in road accident in '61, during visit of Karel's mother from Prague, Grandma stayed on, died in '79. Father died in '77. Kody junior did two years London University, dropped it and joined the army on a short service commission. Curious . . . Not employed since. Married Lucy, *née* Ludmilla Simonova, just over a year ago. Hmph . . ."

"Now then." He picked up a cherry-coloured file. "Alexei Abramovich Simonov, a commercial attaché Soviet Embassy London till exp. 1971. Prior diplomatic experience, blah-blah, all over the place, USA, Bangkok, SA, oh yes? Iran, etc. Red 2, 46b '71 (Oleg Lyalin statements) refers London expulsions, nothing specific on Simonov. Wife Alicia, half-Finnish, half-Russian, married 1958. Daughter Ludmilla born Leningrad 1959. Ah! Why this, I wonder? Mother and daughter *both* allowed to come with him to UK in 1965, '67, and '69 in which year they separated. Child accepted 1970 Elmhurst Ballet School, Camberley. Several appeals for visa extensions before mother and daughter granted political asylum.

114

Ludmilla, *aka* Lucy, married Patrick Grady in 1980. Blimey! Grady committed suicide in 1981. Sounds a rather hasty fellow. Sylvia! This Red 2 file, Hawkins signature, could you get him on the house-phone please? – Thank you. Ah, Dickie, this file on the Simonovs, doesn't say what he did to get ponged? Oh, just sort of word behind cupped hand? . . . But now Antwerp, turns up like a bad penny. Russalmaz, what's that?"

"Diamonds, Adrian," came the disembodied voice. "They mine diamonds in Siberia, you know. Staggeringly difficult conditions, working through the permafrost. Russalmaz is their Western outlet, in Antwerp's Lange-Herrenstraat. It's a front, because about 25 Belgian firms buy most of the Russian diamonds in Moscow. The Antwerp thing's a sort of advance listening post under a trade banner. And that's where the KGB sent our Alexei after we ponged him."

"Persona non grata." Stayres echoed weightily, "but not to the Flems . . . Smells a bit, wouldn't you say?"

"What doesn't, but we do keep a weather eye on them."

"In that case you must be many-headed Hydras since they outnumber you about two hundred to one. Anything smelly about the daughter? Fluent Russian?"

"No and yes. She was front-rank material and the Grady number was all set up for pipelining to the Auld Country. I confess to some surprise if Husband Two is finagling for someone. One had the feeling she was not prepared to bat."

"No *Rodina*-sickness?"

"No, just a happy tumbler. Very bonnie."

"Otherwise you'd be after her yourselves, no doubt?"

"Well, we realised that was probably what the Sovs had in mind, so we let it go. Bit moley on the face of it, but we had a job persuading the Cousins."

"All right, Dickie. Many thanks. Let me have any updates, won't you? I'll do the same."

Stayres closed the file and sat for many minutes with his fingers bridged, his mind following mazes of its own making. His low budget and lack of good Czech speakers was a constant thorn, for it is one of the hardest accents to acquire convincingly.

Seven

... Earth's the right place for love:
I don't know where it's likely to get better.

Robert Frost

The flight from Maputo was very long and made fraught
with turbulence and they landed in Lisbon in a freak summer
thunderstorm. He waited several hours in transit and by the
time he reached Heathrow he was pretty well exhausted
again. Blearily he went from the baggage area and out into
the main concourse where people thronged and held up
messages, their faces eager, impatient or resigned. "What
about Customs?" he thought anxiously and suddenly realised
he must have gone with the flow through the Green, certainly
with the downcast eyes of a weary traveller, without a furtive
glance or a beaded brow to invite a serious question. He
stood uncertainly for a moment and suddenly "hrumphed"
at his own foolishness that he could even think to go back
and then through the Green again deliberately, to make it
seem that the bag hanging from his shoulder with its fortune
in rough stones had been fully earned. Behind the barrier a
slurred voice said, "You're in Fairbanks, Alaska, mate.
Brought yer willy-warmer?" Stuart gave a sheepish grin,
turned and strode deliberately away.

Sharing a taxi into London with an affected TV producer
and his frizzy secretary just back from Majorca, he was asked
not very interestedly where he'd been. They fell peevishly
silent when Stuart said he'd been smuggling diamonds out of
South Africa. At Paddington he had less than five minutes to
catch the last train to Oxford, not enough time to call Lucy,
but as he ran for the barrier after waiting agitatedly for his
ticket, he pulled up in astonishment to see his mother-in-law
squeezing off the platform with a small white suitcase in one

116

hand, a bag and a Harvey Smith in the other. He was about to avoid her when she suddenly looked up and saw him with equal surprise and a quick flash of suspicion.

He kissed her quickly on both cheeks. "Alicia, how extraordinary! I'm just on my way home, no time to call Lucy. Will you phone for me and tell her? Not to come to the station, twice is too much, I'll get a cab, tell her I'll be home about eleven, can you do that? This is the last train. How are you? Is everything all right?"

He could see she was struggling to say something but he had no time to get involved. He nodded quickly, blew her a kiss and ran for the train, feeling slightly embarrassed when it didn't leave for another three or four minutes.

Imperceptibly at first he saw the kiosks and the posters slide past and only then did the accumulated tension overwhelm him like the flood tide over a sandcastle. Surprisingly, there were very few others in the carriage, just a group of animated undergraduates in the smoking section at the other end and, near to him, two teenagers with a very large cassette player, temporarily out of action as they tried to re-thread a tangled tape. Stuart found himself grinning broadly, his triumph and relief at the finished ordeal overshone in his mind by Lucy's smiling face and the thought of her expecting him. He began to conjure up conversations with her, knowing it was a mistake because she was seldom predictable, to think of amazing places to go, treasures to buy her, things to do. She'd had a faraway look one day and he'd asked her what she was thinking, his jaw dropping at the answer: "I want to swim with whales."

He had an urge to shout and dance and leap like a Cossack, slamming back the vodka and smashing the glasses, at the same time furious with the exultation for coming too soon. He could only sit there grinning quietly to himself, seeing with trepidation that the tape would be back in action any moment and wanting to preserve his primitive jubilation.

It was garbled at first but still a surprise because he was expecting something loud and heavy; instead he heard a melody with distant harmonies. He could even hear the words:

> *. . . be mine if I would cancel winter*
> *So our life is following the sun,*
> *I lie her on the beach then I lie to the banker,*

How can I stop what I've begun.
It's the way she calls me her darling
And says she, she said she would,
She said she would have loved me,
She said she would have loved me anyway.
How do I know that I know my lady,
How do I know she'll always stay?
With a hundred stones to burden her bones,
Would she – or could she – run away?

After the last chorus, Stuart smiled at the couple. "That's OK," he said. "What's it called?"

The girl was slightly embarrassed but the youth clearly delighted. "You missed the beginning, the tape's chewed." He pressed buttons and fiddled so the girl said shyly, "That's not what he asked, Col." To Stuart she said, "This girl's saying she won't dance for him unless he gives her a diamond, see? So he nicks one and . . ."

The tape garbled and began again:

. . . dared the Law and I stole a diamond,
She said she would have loved me anyway.

Stuart's brain reeled and he sensed abruptly that he was staring at the machine and that they were looking worriedly back at him as if he were a simpleton or worse; then the tape snagged again and refocused their attention.

Exhaustion claimed him then, quite suddenly. He put his head against the side panel and slept, lolling to the rhythm but his right hand stayed firmly on the grip beside him. He couldn't tell why the dreams began or how long they lasted but they took him back into terror, more claustrophobic even than the tiny cell, the door banging resoundingly, darkness, dripping, then wandering in stricken loneliness, free to travel ways that were completely uninviting, then illogically, travelling on a train, the old kind with diddly-dock rails, the train not stopping in the right places and when it did there were too many people pressing, he couldn't get off, shouting at them to move, panic rising, leaping for the communication cord.

Determination carried the day and he awoke too late by a split second. It had already happened, the teenagers shouting, calling him a mad bastard, the undergrads yelling as their beercans and cards were hurled forward by the emergency braking, and Stuart looking up aghast to see his hand still gripping the handle above the placard which assured him of a £50 fine. He slumped down in a daze as the train shuddered to a halt, mortified to see the two youngsters grinning at his ludicrous situation.

Lucy was propped up in bed reading but not concentrating properly. With the intense physical self-awareness that often comes with solitude, she could feel her limbs stirring involuntarily, stretching and twisting. She wanted to touch herself and swept her hands down the long, taut muscles of her thighs, across her stomach, smoothing. The house was absolutely silent; since she'd come back from taking her mother to the station, she'd felt restless and nervy, annoyed to feel unsure what to do with the evening; with nothing worth watching on the television, she even had a notion of a quick visit to the pub for a few laughs but by late evening the tobacco smoke would be overwhelming.

Her novel had really begun to bore her and she tossed it aside, got up and ran naked downstairs, not chancing the jump without shoes. She remembered then a bargain she'd picked up in the Hungerford market, a beautiful leather-bound set of the *Thousand and One Nights*, returning home in overloaded triumph.

"Why so cheap?" Stuart had asked, looking slightly crestfallen when she told him it was the Spanish translation.

She slipped out a volume from the middle of the stack and hurried back up to bed, opening it at random and becoming immediately immersed in the Sultan Zain's search for the perfect, untouched bride in the tale of the Mirror of the Virgins. Zain's commission gave her delighted amusement, as the series of fifteen-year-olds are brought to him for assessment, eyes cast demurely down but the magic mirror gives them all away in intimate revelations, steaming up for those tampered even by eye contact and remaining clear for the genuine specimen. The search was taking a lot of travel and time for lack of verifiable virgins so Lucy skipped a little and missed the point before being brought up short by the inverted Spanish exclamation mark. *¡Pero si, por el contrario, quisiera Ala que la joven haya permanecido virgen, verás aparecer una historia no mayor que una almendra moncada, y*

119

el espejo se conservará claro, puro y limpio todo vaho! . . . "But if, on the other hand, Allah should will that the young girl remains a virgin, you will see appear (in the mirror) a *historia* no bigger than a peeled almond, and the mirror will stay clear, pure and completely clean . . ."

Historia . . . Lucy had to get up and find her big dictionary, not really believing the synonym, but the dictionary gave no hint, *historia* was just history or story and as a coy euphemism quite hilarious. She riffled back a few pages in the Nights and sure enough found a more specific reference . . . *Sus organos mas delicados.*

"I'll bet mine can steam one up," she giggled to herself, laying the tome aside and fetching a small shaving mirror from the bathroom. She sat on the edge of the bed, quizzical at the uncertain outcome; she felt excited and wanted to prolong the moment so she gave the mirror a good polish with the corner of the pillow-case. Then she thought not to do it until Stuart was there but decided that was chancy as she couldn't be sure of the result. She would cheat a little, she decided, and re-enact the scene for him – when he finally came home. There'd been a call the previous day but nothing since, and her sigh had a touch of irritation.

Tentatively she advanced the mirror nearer and decided that if it steamed up, she would heat it next time in hot water or get the tin of demisting fluid from the car. What actually happened distracted her with a jolt of surprise and revelation, raising her eyebrows so far that she felt conscious of her facial reaction. She was open slightly because of her position on the edge of the bed and in the mirror she realised she was seeing what the artist had seen and portrayed for thousands of years, whether inadvertently or not she couldn't say. She forgot about looking for peeled almonds, the shape was unmistakable; it had been used a myriad times even in the most ecclesiastical paintings, in ikons and statues, shrines, cribs and even monstrances, the madonna with the veil sweeping out in folds to rounded shoulders then tapering down with the cloak, and even the cupped hands held open just above the centre, why? when a more natural attitude for prayer or supplication brings the palms flat together?

Although she understood it could hardly be a new notion, Lucy was absolutely thrilled with her discovery; she leapt up and hunted in her bag for a red felt pen then resumed her

120

position with the mirror. Accurately and life-size she traced herself within the frame, thinking how well the Spanish sounded, *"Órganos más delicados"* except for the curious continental habit of giving female parts the masculine gender and vice-versa . . . When she'd finished, she held up the mirror and saw it as the other portrayal, the Hindu *yoni* and in it variously the reverence or despair, the longing or defiance of centuries. She propped it on the dressing table where she could see it and got back into bed.

She was still looking at it and pondering when the telephone rang. She screwed up her eyes in anticipation of silence but the second and third rings continued boldly. When she answered and realised it was her mother, she had to make a deliberate effort not to blurt out her discovery inappropriately but then screeched at the news of the encounter with Stuart at the station barrier.

She burst wide awake with elation and began bubbling with ideas for pranks, suppressing them because Alicia had said he looked exhausted. She took a shower, dressed, and went downstairs for coffee, tidied the kitchen, hid the television in the pile of firewood, put on a record and then remembered his parting present. Frantically she dashed upstairs, listening for the sound of a car, undressed and came down again wearing only a bedspread and the long, shiny crimson boots. She spent time choosing records and stacking them. She tried to read a magazine, waited, stared and listened and finally went back to bed with her *Mil Noches y Una Noche*. This time it failed to keep her attention and by the time the second record had changed she was baffled at Stuart taking so long.

Her mother was sure he'd have caught the train and thinking of trains, night trains, sleepers, rocking to the endless rhythm, was her fail-safe method of finding sleep.

By the time they released him, Oxford station was silent and deserted and there were no more taxis. In a thin drizzle he had to walk all the way into town, through the pedestrian centre and out to the thin traffic on the far side of the Randolph Hotel. He would have run if his thoughts hadn't been so busy and anyway he had to wait another twenty minutes for a cab, being twice refused the half-hour fare to Carsey.

121

He would acknowledge much later, long after his chagrin had disappeared, that the delay had given him just the right interval to change his thinking and thus his entire future. A chance remark made by the railway inspector started it, after his halting explanation and the subsequent laughter.

The inspector was a thin man with gentle eyes in a stern face. "As a married man who is presumably late home," he said, his hand on Stuart's shoulder, "I think you ought to keep it to yourself. I mean, it sounds a lame excuse. doesn't it, pulling the chain? If I were you, son, I'd make something up, preferably something heroic. I've long since concluded that just about everything is bull and is simply a matter of how each person looks at it. I reckon you only need about a five per cent possibility of an excuse being true to make it work, it doesn't even have to be believed. And it's what you don't say that's just as, or more important than what you do. Wouldn't you say?"

Stuart nodded in silence, thinking about something else entirely.

"Ah, well, I suppose you'd best be off. Don't do it again, will you? Next time sit far away from it or tie your thumbs together."

"Thanks. I think I'll get rich and have a helicopter."

Tired as he was, he had expected to be awake half the night sharing his adventures and jubilation with Lucy. The effect of his idiotic mistake was to sober his exuberance and to recall Rollo's bantering suggestions, and by the time he'd paid off a mercifully untalkative driver about a hundred yards from the house, his mood had changed to one of rarified uplift, an enthusiasm as unbridled as boyhood.

In case Lucy decided to unpack his travel grip for him, he crept into the garage and took out the heavy rubber windscreen flange, leaving it coiled roughly on a shelf.

Music came from downstairs and there was a light on in the bedroom; with his heart pounding like a panel hammer he tried the front door. It opened silently as he tiptoed inside, put down his bag and crept up the stairs.

From the bedroom doorway he could see the big leather-bound tome rising and falling steadily from the breathing beneath it and beyond, half-buried in the pillow, was that beloved spray of tawny hair. There was no face visible and, except for the breathing, he would have been ready for a prank. He moved into the room, lifted the book and closed it, bent down to move some hair aside and softly kissed the exposed temple. With her scent in his nostrils and certain knowledge of her presence, he experienced a flooding rush of emotion which felt like all the finest, sweetest aspects of creation flowing together like a slow and golden river.

One eye opened slowly and he watched the iris closing against the light, extending the pupil of gold and green.

"Don't do it again," she whispered, perfectly still.

"What?"

"Whatever it was that made you late."

"It cost me fifty quid. I pulled the chain in my sleep. I was tired, I guess."

"I don't believe a word of it. You didn't want to come home and stayed on the train. You look shattered. And you've been fighting, there's a cut over your eye. I don't love you any more."

"Why not?"

"Because you smell – and because I absolutely adore you instead. Get into bed, smelly, I've got something to show you."

"Not till I've had a wash and a shave. Let me look at you though, in case you've gone off."

He slipped away the duvet and suddenly burst out laughing. Lucy had a moment's consternation before she remembered she was still wearing her new crimson boots. With a delighted toss of hair, she bounced up, leapt off the bed in a flying splits, tried to do a spin on the floor but accelerated out of control and collapsed giggling into the slam of the wardrobe door. When Stuart bent to help her up he felt his knees turn to jelly and he could only subside down next to her.

He groaned his feelings and when she asked what was the matter, her voice mocking as she stroked his head, he said quietly, "How will I find you in my next life? I have to be sure. There's nobody else."

"Nonsense! Women are like buses, remember that's what you said, the first ever tease when the big black lady threw me off the platform? 'If you miss one, there's always another one coming.'"

"No, not true. That's how I explained it, but I told you you were the last bus. The only bus ... give us a buss, bus."

123

"I ... am ... the ... last ... bus," she said very proudly and seriously, leaning over him with her hair falling down, unbuttoning his shirt and trousers. She vroomed like a diesel engine going through the gears, interspersed with the conductor's signal-bell. "You, smelly, are now going to discover what being run over by a steaming great double-decker bus is all about ... Ugh, that's better ... How do I find First on this thing, anyway? Vroom, vroom."

"Vroom."

"Everyone," Lucy said, munching a piece of toast and sitting cross-legged on her pillow, still rosy from the shower, "every woman, that is, ought to marry a truck driver or a sailor or an astronaut. I can't believe that even you and I could have been getting in a rut and maybe not appreciating properly. I mean, it really must be a fantastic pleasure to have you back if I'm prepared to bring you breakfast in bed. I want to throw open the window and crow so loud that every damn cockerel for miles will cower and sulk."

"You're dropping crumbs in the bed. This is apricot jam, not marmalade. And it's not British to talk at breakfast. But you're allowed because you're nice."

"And a foreigner. I'm only pretending to be nice. Today when I get back from shopping, I have something to tell you. Will you do a swap, of secrets?"

Stuart stopped munching and looked at her gravely. He shook his head as he swallowed. "You mean about my work?"

To her nod, he said, "No, I mustn't. I could get put inside for it."

"Could you really? Only if they heard, surely – I didn't tell you last night because we had things to see to, but while you were away somebody bugged this house. Mother and I both had intruders, separately."

Stuart sat up in alarm as she told him the full story, omitting only the jabbing of the big man's eyes.

"And you don't know who they were?"

Even before she spoke, Stuart remembered de Hoek and the tape-recording. He waited, wondering about further complications as well as a name ... Patrick. He had refused at the time to entertain any suspicions, yet now plainly he couldn't mention it.

"In the Secret Service, what do you call a man who bugs people, without the obvious? No, let me guess . . . I know, a Gomorrah! Right?" She looked at him archly for approval but he took a moment to work it out. He didn't chuckle because she went straight on with the rest of her story.

"This Gomorrah had a car with CD plates and was from some embassy. We tried to find out more but I think it was all hushed up and diplomatic. The only clue is that one of the other two asked Mama what you were doing in South Africa."

Stuart looked at her for a long time without expression but the temptation to tell the whole story was nearly overwhelming. He managed to meet her gaze as if thoughtfully, but the memory of the blessed intimacy of the night, the incredible, almost frightening pleasure of again simply sharing a bed with her began to make him question the wisdom of his decision. The spiral of deception kept hold of him since he was sure it wasn't over, and he was still scared and ashamed of the risks he had taken with his freedom.

"OK," she said finally, without rancour, "I thought you did deals in your business."

"Well, yes. You can have my body."

"Thanks, I thought it was worn out."

"Appearances . . . it needs some intensive care, that's all. I think if I could find a way to express my feelings I'd go up in a megaton mushroom cloud."

"You're quite fond of me, then? Is there anything which might disgust you, anything you can imagine which you couldn't forgive me?"

"No, to both."

"Sure?"

He paused, grinning happily. "This sounds like a bad one. Are you going to ask for a written guarantee?"

"Well, it would be nice, but I'll take your word for it. You've never been cross with me, have you?"

"Yes, I have. I'm often cross with you, when you take risks."

"But that's out of fear, not irritation. Look, it's late, there's something I have to go and do, I'll be back in half an hour."

"Where to?"

"Secret." She smiled sweetly, uncurled and dressed hurriedly in a track suit and light pumps. Stuart didn't move as

125

she waved and dashed out of the room but endured his usual terror for her ankles as she took the stairs in two clear leaps. She'd marked the middle stair with a piece of ribbon and normally launched off the top with a slight rotation so as to land on her toes facing the staircase. She used to back-somersault the second half but it was now forbidden since she'd once overbalanced on landing, reeling backwards into the stand; she'd demolished two umbrellas and a longbow and launched through the house the scattered heads of a dozen stalks of pampas grass.

When she got back he was downstairs and dressed, sorting through his mail. He saw she was slightly flushed and raised an eyebrow.

"Been running?"

"Warming up."

"What for?"

"In case I have to run for it. First, I've found employment. At the moment it's only twenty minutes a day but I'm naturally ambitious for promotion and I hope to extend it to an hour by the end of the month when I get some more clients. My body was under-used, you see. I felt restless and unwanted, I thought that if you were prepared to go away and leave me, then there were others who could benefit from my physical attributes. It's true that you are back but I feel a deep compulsion to honour my commitments. I knew you'd understand. Thank you."

She turned and ran out of the room, leaving him staring open-mouthed. He was amused by the speech but naturally curious; he followed somewhat nervously and when he saw her at the end of the garden she was clowning again, pretending to hide, standing sideways behind the tiny rowan sapling.

He took his time walking up to her, noticing her tension.

"What is it, Lu? Tell me."

"It's the second thing, the one you won't like."

He waited, saying nothing, and finally she took encouragement from the affection in his eyes. She began haltingly.

"I . . . tried rehearsing this but I really don't want to think about it any more. I'll just get it said. I was married before."

"What?!"

"Not for very long. He was Irish, name of Grady. He was

126

a dazzler but very up and down, wrong for me, a drinker too, and it shamed him or something, anyway he'd turn aggressive and accusing. There was nothing to do or say to it so I learned to keep quiet but then he began to get violent. You know I'm quick and mostly I could ger away from him but I'd have to walk half the night away sometimes. He got me though, once while I was cooking, broke my nose and my cheekbone. I lied to you about this little scar. And something else I didn't tell you, I did Kung Fu for nearly four years which should have been enough but I betrayed it."

She paused, a little breathless, her eyes round. He was numbed by the appeal in them.

"Go on, don't worry," he said gently.

"Yes. I think it made me begin to hate him, oh, that's a terrible, terrible feeling . . . but anyway, the next time he went for me, I just lost my control and I came out of defensive. The whole principle, you know, we should just parry calmly, back away or counter without striking, but I got furious, I went for him, I was vicious and ugly and full of hate. Anyway, I messed him up, I just more or less wrecked his face, the only thing I didn't do was what I did to the Gomorrah."

Stuart was watching her, very still. "If I find out where he is, I'll do worse than anything, I promise you."

Lucy shook her head. "He couldn't handle it. I should have known he couldn't, maybe I did, I don't know. Anyway, after a week of silent brooding he got a sawn-off shotgun from some Mick friend, he went into the middle of Acton cemetery and put the barrels in his mouth. The Police said it was a special cartridge, I think they call it a chopper. It took his head clean off. I identified him by his clothes, his hands and the ring."

Her voice cracked and Stuart put his arms round her with the little tree between them. "I hope it has berries next year."

"Yes . . . Jelly. You make it with apples or crab apples, very subtle. I feel I cheated you; if you'd known at first, you wouldn't have loved me."

"Yes I would. I always have. You did no wrong anyway."

"I did. I lost my temper, it's the one thing that's not permissible. I gave it up then, I never did any more training. I couldn't face my teacher. With the Gomorrah it was different."

127

More lightly, she told him about the intruder's eyes and her escape and he was almost reeling by the time she got to the description of the Police dog Banjo and the chewing. Stronger than ever was the urge to be truthful and he was mystified later at the strength of his resistance since he had no special stubbornness about changing decisions.

Lucy cleared her throat and begin to sing quietly. "And said he, he said he would, he said he would have loved me, he said he would have loved me anyway."

He put his head back and smiled at her. "I heard it in the train, a bit of it anyway . . . you can't earn this, this feeling, nobody on earth deserves it. It's like a miracle. You see why I'm so terrified for you? And it's probably all selfishness."

"Sure, but I have it too so that makes it all right." She looked up with soft gratitude; distantly they heard the telephone. "Thank you for the calls, it was such a comfort. You missed two days, you rotter. Come on, I'll race you."

She ran light and fluid across the lawn and Stuart followed slowly, lost in his dazed reaction. When he reached the kitchen door, Lucy came out again exclaiming, "It was your friend Rollo, wanting to know if you were back. I . . . I was very naughty, I said, 'Yes, where from?' but he rang off. Is he in it with you or shouldn't I ask?"

"Probably not. He's the son of Trouble."

"Oh . . . but I can ask if you enjoyed it, surely? Did you have a good time, that sort of question, um?"

"Well, I hope it'll get better."

"How often will they . . .?"

"I don't know yet. It depends. I don't want a desk job. But I'm home now and I love it. Do you feel like a holiday?"

She put her hands behind his neck and shook her head firmly. "I've only been working for a week, and there's nothing I could possibly want for now, more than I have . . . How was your Czech?"

"Blank."

"Groan! Oh, boy that'll cost you. The drainpipe needs fixing, plus the bedroom door, did you see? And the lawn mower needs you, it doesn't seem to go for anyone else."

"Like you?"

"*Da*. Just like me. Hard life, isn't it?"

128

Eight

The nakedness of woman is the work of God.
William Blake

Mollie Vrouwer didn't feel she was a traitor in the real sense, rather the opposite since Moscow never asked her for specific or classified information, merely to report whatever Soviet activites came to the notice of her chief. She had been easily persuaded that his function went some way towards defusing tensions or "misunderstandings" long before they became critical. She was intelligent and efficient, and for de Hoek a real asset as a secretarial, filing and sorting machine without any of the drawbacks of being either alluring or, as in some less favoured by nature, resentful.

She was handsome and very disciplined in spite of her predilections. Physically she abhorred men but she was a sensualist herself and, in order to indulge her tastes and entertain the young and pretty, she needed to supplement her income. Moscow had approached her through this channel and their capitalist reasoning was quite acceptable. She had a very luxurious apartment in town as well as a rambling, secluded beach house north of Durban. She ate and drank with fair moderation but only of the highest quality and she would invite to the beach house, singly, the brightest of the young generation. In particular, she favoured girl musicians who would entertain her in return; being female helped her to recognise that a girl is at her most innocently beautiful when she is unselfconscious, as when a musical or other skill can claim her full attention. Mollie adored seduction, particularly if it was very difficult and above all she loved, almost lived for, that startled, breathless expression on a partner's face in the moment of awareness of her desire.

When a later report came through with more detail about Kody's background, following the eye injuries suffered by their London embassy staffer, Mollie wondered why de Hoek had not already mentioned Kody's original nationality and that of his intriguingly dangerous wife, but then she had no indication from her chief that his enquiry inferred any Eastern bloc interest.

The information went into an envelope and was with her contact in Pretoria the following morning, by which time de Hoek was back in Johannesburg and told her to close the Kody file. To her surprise, when she mentioned the nationalities, he merely shrugged and assured her it wasn't relevant; this information she passed on similarly the same evening. She was paid on such results which made her naturally assiduous.

The Pretoria resident lost no time in passing his information back to Moscow; the file on Ludmilla Simonova which had been morgued by the KGB, was resurrected and instructions forwarded at once to London for possible revival along with an enquiry to Alexei Simonov in Antwerp. Simonov replied that he had not been in contact with his daughter for more than eight years but usually received news of her through his ex-wife once or twice a year. Referring to the unconfirmed report about Stuart, he said he had no reason to imagine that his daughter's status had changed, nor unfortunately her attitude to him and his masters.

Simonov had been delighted to hear she had remarried. As a child and early teenager he had loved her dearly in his way. Even after his expulsion had been able to monitor her education, perhaps only half realising the strings attached: proficiency in any of the arts of unarmed combat not being acquired in less than several years, they had made it a condition of her education from seventeen onwards. Ludmilla, he knew, enjoyed disciplines not only because she loved physical skills but also because she was a natural rule-breaker and had discovered, partly from him in early childhood, that you can only be really inventive about breaking or overstepping rules if you've absorbed them to the point of instinct.

They had singled her out for a life in the West and one of the first requirements was to individualise her; the stereotyping of pupils and students for moulding to the Soviet system would be a handicap for her in the West. Accordingly she was sent to an exclusive school which was believed to understand, and have a sufficiently large and varied staff to cope with, difficult or unusual characters and to give them as much attention as they required. It also had to be one which could extend her obvious physical talents. After the separation, her mother was requested not to improve her rather poor English so that Lucy would keep a fluency in her Russian conversation. Along with her chosen modern language of Spanish, the Russian studies continued through her three years at Bristol University, during which she twice went on exchange student visits to the USSR. She wasn't approached during this period but one day, some time after graduation, she was invited with her mother to a reception at the Soviet Embassy and received her first semi-official overture. It was also the first inkling she was given of the career they had mapped out for her and her response had been instant and unequivocal.

Alexei still remembered hearing about it with a certain wry delight; she had been taken aside for the short interview with the second secretary and her reply had been delivered in a high, clear voice giving rise to a conversational lull of cathedral proportions.

"I never learnt the Russian for 'Fuck off!', isn't that strange?"

They tried again, naturally, not wishing to waste their investment, but the later replies were less equivocal still since her old tutor had laughingly obliged her with that specific and a few other handy obscenities. When they finally got around to a harder line of personal threats including exiled disgrace for her faintly remembered father, she went in person to the Soviet Ambassador, apologised, and then gave a semi-rehearsed speech. Alexei had heard the recording with a feeling of confused pride.

"Mr Ambassador, I was an innocent about all this so I cannot feel that I owe any special debt, nor do I believe that children should be forced to feel or show gratitude to their parents for their upbringing, no matter what it costs. Seeking gratitude for parenthood means you're an unsuitable parent, and certainly deserve the resentment you cause."

"It sounds very wise, my dear. However, we are really concerned about matters of global security and what can be done now."

131

"Yes. There's a lot of talk about de-escalation, disarmament and all the nationalist claptrap that never changes, well I feel there's a new mood, a big change coming and I rejoice for it. In the meantime, cold wars need cold warriors and I won't be one of them, especially since there can be no victory, everyone should realise that. Does Russia want to own more of the West, or are the creeping gains purely defensive, against an attack which will not come, since the West doesn't want to own or occupy Russia? Hitler and Napoleon were crazed exceptions. So ... I think about it all in my perhaps silly way and I see two stout fellows in suits of armour swinging at each other and grunting a lot, then one of them takes off his breastplate and says, 'Sod this, I'd rather buy you a drink, come on.' What's going to happen, with the defensive threat removed? I'm assuming of course that neither side wants actually to exterminate the other ..."

The Ambassador had chuckled and asked, "Which of them is going to do it first?"

"That's easy: the one with the most courage and vigour and the best sense of priorities, the most noble and farsighted. Suppose *Rodina* did it first: you'll tell me the Americans will invade and push us around. But what for? And, more to the point, what with? Doesn't anybody realise you can't threaten half the world with an H-bomb, and you've got fourteen times as many tanks and guns."

"How not threaten with a nuclear bomb?"

"Well, it's got to be bluff, hasn't it?"

"You mean like Hiroshima was bluff?"

After a pause, Lucy asked, "How have I earned your disrespect?"

"You haven't at all. What do you mean?"

"It was a silly thing for you to say. You know your history."

"You can't talk to me like that."

"My opinion of you is not important, surely?"

After a short pause, there was another staccato chuckle before Lucy went on, seeming to mock her own earnestness.

"Soviet Russia presents herself to the West as a huge ogre fearsomely flexing its muscles for the great invasion, and you know how dour and unemotional the unfamiliar Russian presents himself. I certainly don't need to mention his ruthlessness, do I? For my part, I couldn't see myself doing other than explaining their character and living the life of this one, my own character – which I'm afraid is no longer that of my childhood, of the Young Pioneers: *A Pioneer holds the memory of the fallen fighters and prepares to become a defender of the Motherland . . .*"

The ambassador's tone was still patronising. "So you're saying that if we disarmed our nuclear component, the Americans would follow suit with relief and lie back on the beach? It's unthinkable, child. If they did it first, that would be different."

Lucy had shaken her head sadly. "Unfortunately, the Russian is still a typical bully, when he gets the chance, from aeons of being underdog. He doesn't have quite the same silly notion of fair play, nor a free press to impress it. And you're still teaching him to enjoy being big-booted and powerful, you're still telling him Great Patriotic War stories, stirring his blood with sickening displays of heavy armour and slogans of 'We are the greatest'. It's the only unction you allow him."

"I'm an ambassador for peace, and you make me sound like a warmonger."

Lucy snorted. "Come on, you're employed by one Master, as you wanted to employ me."

He cut it short then, almost abruptly, "I'll see to it that you can stay here with your mother." He had chuckled then and added, perhaps for her father's benefit, "Alexei Abramovich should be proud of you, you are indeed a fine lady. He was also acting under orders, please think well of him."

"I'll try. Is he actually with the KGB?"

"Good day, Ludmilla Simonova. Enjoy your marriage to the Irishman."

"Oh. Thank you. How did you know?"

"Necessarily. For us, the Irish Republic, you know . . ."

"What about it?"

There'd been no answer on the tape although perhaps the sound of a door closing before it ended.

Lucy was out teaching the next morning when a post van arrived bearing a telegram. Puzzled, Stuart signed for it and ripped it open, but the moment he saw the point of origin he felt furtive once more, back in his awkward role of deceit.

The message read tersely: "ROLLCALL KIMBERLEY

9201 URGENT". He called the number straight away but there was a long and infuriating wait before Rollo was summoned to take the call. It was only then he understood the reason for the expensive delay, the unlocking of a series of doors.

"Good lad. They allowed me one telegram and one outgoing call, that's the reason for you calling me."

"What for, what's going on?"

"I'm inside, they got me. I need some heavy bail."

Stuart blew out his cheeks. "Oh God, what's the charge?"

"IDB and GBH. I've got a lawyer who thinks he can clear me but I need 150,000 Rand, that's about 75 grand sterling."

"I don't have it, Rollo."

"Go and get it. Got a pen? Albrecht Grobelaar, 74 Vestingstraat, Antwerp. He'll need a couple of days to check things over, and then you can let me have a chunk. Don't take less than two million dollars, two and a half it should be."

"*Million?* I thought you said 200,000!"

"No, I said two big – you dumb Slav, do you think we went through all that for *peanuts?*"

"Oh, crazy heaven, I'd no idea!"

"God, I don't believe you're so simple ... Have you still got my Crédit Suisse number? ... Stuart, are you still there?"

"Yes. Sort of."

"Well, cheer up, it could be worse. I can beat it, I'm sure, but I need the bail. Belgium's no problem, they love trinkets. Don't be sore, old son, I know it was supposed to be my bit, I can't help it. You haven't even been shot yet."

"Just shat myself, that's all, waiting in a minefield for a bullet."

"Tough. We know the feeling, eh? I'll give you lots of sympathy when I see you. What about the other three?"

"The big one I traded for my freedom. The others may be lost in the post. If not, what do I do with them?"

"Hoard, don't sell, you'll only get robbed. No way to price them. We'll have one each. Your choice. When will you go, soonest?"

"Tomorrow if I can."

"'Kay. Good on yer."

"Bye."

Stuart's mouth felt dry and his mind was still reeling with unimagined riches when he got a call from London a few minutes later. A woman calling herself Sylvia Warren, secretary to Mr Adrian Stayres, asked him to come to London for an interview as soon as possible "in his own interest and that of security." He agreed to an appointment in the following week. Finally, after enquiries, he got through to the makers of both Bostik and Araldite to find out their respective solvents and neither would tell him. He had to ring his old tutor for the name of a practical physicist and secured his answers that way.

He was almost visibly shaking with puzzlement and excitement when Lucy came home. The urge to brake the spiral was now stronger than ever but he forced himself to quell it since the mission had restarted itself and he didn't even want to give himself false hopes. She sensed his mood change the moment she came through the door.

"What is it, my love?"

"I've got to go off again, Only a couple of days, though."

"Oh no! When?"

"Tomorrow."

"But the Horrocks was coming to dinner."

"He won't mind, and I'll get him to give me a lift to town in the morning. I suppose we'd better get another car, don't you? Which kind would you like?"

She seemed distracted. "What? Oh, the one we've got. It's perfect. You're sounding rather extravagant – are they paying you very well?"

He tried to shrug off the huge figures dancing in his head. "So-so. I won't have to pay for it myself."

"Oh good. Otherwise I'll have to ask for your wage-packet – you know Mama suggested I do just that?" She giggled and hugged him, saying into his shoulder, "I have to share it, tell you what I'm doing."

"I thought Russians were the best secret-keepers."

"That's true. Maybe not when they're in love. But you're right, I'll save it."

She wanted to tell him about the classes, and to rejoice that she'd got her first handspring that morning, and from the prettiest girl. She thought how gifts and talents are quite random, even the special ability to concentrate with real

135

exclusion which little Vanessa had in addition to a palpable bond between them. Lucy had said, "All right, who's jealous of Vanessa?" There was no answer, of course, so she added, "I bet some of you want to be horrid to her when I'm not looking. How many of you think that life should be fair?"

There were calls and many hands raised but Lucy had sensibly decided to leave it at that, after a little mocking smile. The children had seemed thrilled not to get a lecture.

"How many nights will you be gone?" she asked Stuart.

"Only one, I hope. Maybe two."

"And then you'll be back for ages? Say yes, *please*, or I'll ask you to give it up."

"I shouldn't. When I start getting paid we can crack the budget and you can have a lump of capital to do whatever you want with." When he saw her slow smile spreading, he added, "You've got something in mind, haven't you? Tell me."

"Top Secret," she answered, shaking her hair vigorously. "I'll only tell you if it comes off."

"OK, just invest in a boot factory or something. Anything, so long as it's not dangerous."

He wasn't certain about the familiar little flash in her glance and decided it was no use enquiring. He was surprised when with a brisk movement of her hands she slid off her tracksuit trousers and let them fall to her ankles. She stood still and looked at him, deliberately expressionless. She gave a quick smile when he said, "If it comes off, huh?" He faced her, stock still, his eyes not leaving hers but peripherally aware of the grey top not quite covering her little dark triangle. Whenever he experienced her desire as a spontaneous emotion rather than as a reaction to his own, a flame seemed to course up his spine, darting little shocks to a myriad nerve endings. Sometimes it was almost incapacitating, like a paralysing drug.

"I daren't move," he whispered, "in case I'm clumsy."

Lucy waddled towards him without clowning, unaware of anything except the charge she had generated. Deftly she unbuckled his belt, then slipped the button and the zip, firmly but without hurry. She stopped then and hopped away, kicking off her gymshoes and the trousers.

She gave him a chin-up, mocking smile and went into a series of languid ballet poses, using the back of the couch for a bar, the entire emphasis on her legs and hips because she still wore the tracksuit top. His own clothes now in a pile, Stuart went to her and seized her just below the waist, starting to crouch for a lift. Lucy anticipated him and leaped quickly upwards, making it so easy he almost overbalanced. Then she was overhead, back arched and legs straight out and rigid, arms spread and the hands trailing backwards as if in forward motion. Keeping horizontal, she slipped off her top and sent it floating away, showing the tautness of her breasts and the marvellous lines of muscle definition in her shoulders.

"This is called Airstrip," she announced, her chin out like a swimming naiad. Stuart chuckled and tried to hold her steadily, feeling an increase of power just because of her, the slender figure rotating slowly as he turned.

"Fly, little bird," he said, then bent his arms and ran his lips and tongue wetly across the skin of her stomach. There was the familiar and almost intoxicating reaction brought on by the natural scent of her. At times he felt an inner warning not to adore her so helplessly but he could never heed it.

"Clear to land," he said, his arms tiring.

"All right, I mean Roger. Bounce me up, once, and let go clean."

He obeyed, ready for almost anything but what happened. She put her hands on top of his head as he thrust upwards and on release her legs whipped down and round and on to his shoulders. He stumbled but held his balance, unsighted by her stomach pressed against his face. He felt her ruffle his hair.

"That was a super invention," she said, then she jogged a few times and ordered in a riding-school voice: "Trot on!"

"Can't see," Stuart mumbled.

"Never mind that. Go. I'll hold your ears and steer."

He reached up and squeezed her breast like a bulb-horn, making honking noises to go with it. Lucy laughed and tossed her head. "Yeah, out of the way proles, this is a Rolls ... That's it, stairs coming, one ... two ... and I love you. Let's look in the mirror at the top."

He grunted up the last few steps and turned so they could look sideways at their reflection. Stuart felt coarsely solid under her lissom grace but Lucy hugged his head and said, "Is beauty intrinsic? I mean, would a Martian see it in us? I think he'd just see an underemployed computer with a crude

137

fuel and exhaust system. A maze of one-way hydraulic motors all covered with pimply insulation ... I think it's probably all subjective, imaginary. I think we were in love before we ever met and just happened to fit each others' blue-prints. That's how I feel about you, stocky, strong, quiet. It's how I know you're perfect. Am I talking too much?"

"Not yet."

"Bodies are miracles, not just what they do, such endless variety of curves and lines, it's breathtaking sometimes ... Come on, take me to your lair ... let's pretend I'm a fly and you're a spider, you know what they do, horrible things, they suck their victims and eat them alive, what do you think of that?"

Stuart squeezed her rump with both arms and buried his eyes again, nodding silently.

A distant spool turned in response to every word and every sound. A slab-faced monitor, long-accustomed to lascivious tracts from scenes of compromise, this time was reluctantly moved by the tones of obvious loving and delight interspersed with hilarity, for the world in which he lurked, like a reptile under stones, had few associations with real and perfect tenderness.

His reaction didn't prevent him passing on the information that Stuart had not yet encountered Stayres of SIS and now had a destination on the Continent where they could be waiting for him. With typical paranoid suspicion he even wondered if someone was making it just too easy for them.

Nine

I cannot forecast to you the action of Russia. It is a riddle
wrapped in a mystery inside an enigma.

W. S. Churchill

Dressed and ready very early the next morning, Stuart had a
quick coffee and then took a glass of orange juice up to Lucy.
The delicious drowsy warmth of her in the bed almost overcame
him and even when Horrocks tapped his horn a second time
he had to tear himself away from her tugging, sleepy embrace.
He grabbed his overnight bag and hurried outside, waved at
the car and nodded. Then he ducked into the garage and
reached up on to the shelf for the rubber windscreen flange.

With a horrible, crawling spasm of chill terror, he realised
it wasn't there. He switched on the light and looked frantically everywhere but there was no sign of it. He stood for a
moment stunned, not understanding why anyone should have
bothered to steal such a nondescript item when there were
some expensive tools lying about.

He ran to Horrocks' car and said, "Give me two,
Humphrey, I've mislaid something."

"Not your lady, I hope?"

"No. Are you pushed?"

Horrocks' pink moon face beamed back at him. "No problem."

Stuart dashed back into the house and up the stairs,
wanting to yell out loud and having to steady himself.

"Lu!" he said urgently, tugging at her, "Lu, did you move
that rubber thing from the garage?"

"What?" she asked in sleepy alarm. "What's the matter, I
thought you'd gone?"

"The black rubber thing, it was in the garage. Did you
move it?"

139

"Oh . . . You won't be cross will you, please?"

"What did you do with it?" There was an edge to his voice which he couldn't conceal.

"You are, aren't you? I didn't know it was important, honestly. It had bits in it, glass. I'll get you another one."

"Lucy, what did you do with it, just tell me, did you put it in the dustbin or what? Come on!"

"No . . . You see, the washing line broke and it wasn't long enough and I couldn't find anything else. Please don't be cross, I'm sorry, I'll get you another today, I promise."

"No," he said quietly, feeling his clean shirt sticking to the sweat drying on his skin. "Don't worry about a thing. I need to take it, that's all. For the size. Get a new washing line instead."

"You're not angry?"

"No." He swallowed hard and realised he was shaking. "No, not at all. I love you, all the time, all my heart. You didn't cut yourself?"

"No. I tried to dig the glass out but it was too stuck. Is it a secret?"

"Yes. Please be careful. I'll ping you."

"All right, good. And no fighting."

With the kitchen scissors he cut down the washing line and removed the rubber extension. He looked on the grass for fragments but with the morning dew it was difficult to spot anything and the groove seemed undisturbed. He stuffed it into his bag and ran round to the waiting car.

Horrocks raised a mocking, patient eyebrow as he slipped into gear. He was a brewery executive with a gargantuan capacity, resulting in a huge gut and a red blotched face.

"You're puffing," he said kindly "There was no need to get frantic. Does no good, you know. Strains the heart."

"I expect you're right." Stuart stayed rigid for several minutes before he could begin to relax. More than ever he wanted the business complete, to be free of all the anguish and tension that went with it. He was even optimistic that the reason for contact by the man Stayres might evaporate in the next day or two, but just thinking about Rollo made his lips stiffen, like a doctor faced with an incurable.

He found it hugely annoying that the Antwerp flights are

almost exclusively business and cost as much as flying to Italy or Southern Spain. The other passengers were largely Hasidic Jews notable for their dignity and punctilious dress; most had a self-contained demeanor, with black beards and tall hats hiding skull caps.

At Deurne, an airport of no pretensions, in fact ramshackle and underdeveloped, he breezed casually through customs with hand-luggage only and caught a cab at once. The driver spoke English until he realised Stuart spoke French but then Stuart had trouble with his vile accent. They turned off the Diksmuidelaan and continued down the broad dual car-riageway of the Nitbreidinguts until stopped at the lights half-way down. The traffic built up around them, the lights seeming to take a long time. Someone revved his engine with stupid impatience, then the taxi seemed to sag slightly, a split moment before the left rear door was wrenched open. With cobra speed an arm reached in and snatched the bag off the seat beside him. He kept his grip on one of the handles but it snapped off in the violence of movement.

He dived after it, scrabbled and missed. His head connected brutally with the window lever as the door was heaved shut, the blow not solid enough to stun him. To guttural shouts from the driver, he exploded out of the taxi and saw a raincoated figure just getting into the back of a large grey estate. The lights must have changed at that moment as there was more honking and cars began to move off. Absolutely frantic, Stuart charged at the estate, seeing a leg still outside just being raised from the ground. He dived horizontally and hit the door with his shoulder as it began to move away, the rear wheels compressed and smoking. The door didn't close and there was a loud scream as bone fractured. Rolling, he grabbed at the trailing foot and clung on with all his strength, bunching his legs to avoid the rear wheels. There was a bedlam of horns blaring all round and he was dragged about twenty accelerating yards before he was forced to let go and roll away from a violent fishtailing. The car sped away while others bore down on him relentlessly, blaring horns at the stalled taxi and the unforgivable nuisance of a body in the road. Painfully he dragged himself towards the baffled and agitated driver, seeing the rear wheel flattened, presumably shot out with a silenced pistol to thwart pursuit.

The driver shook his head ruefully when Stuart asked him

in gasps if he'd got the number. He helped him into the back seat where he slumped in a confusion of fury and despair. Rollo's disgusted expression and language filled his thoughts with a terrible chagrin. Muttering local curses, the driver took five minutes to change the wheel, the horns still blaring their annoyance, while Stuart wrestled helplessly for a course of action.

His task completed, the driver got back in and voiced the obvious.

"Je pense que vous deviez transporter des diamants, n'est-ce pas? Pourquoi ce désordre, autrement?"

Stuart didn't want to discuss it with him. "They must have got the wrong guy. *Ils ont manqué leur coup.*"

"Vraiment? Peut-être ont-ils entendu votre destination, Vestingstraat, dans le quartier des diamantaires? Aussi, vous vous êtes battu comme un tigre pour le petit sac."

"Continuez tout droit, s'il vous plaît."

Mercifully he complied, sulking and silent, as they went on into town and finally under the great arch of the raised railway station, a long and elaborate edifice of old-fashioned riveted iron and glass. From the wide main boulevard they turned left into one-way Vestingstraat and down to the far end.

Outside 74, the driver was relieved to see Stuart take out his wallet. They haggled briefly over the cost of the tyre and settled at 500 francs. Stuart hobbled into the building and up two flights of stairs until he came to a door marked A. Grobelaar. He rang and after hushed footsteps and obvious but hidden scrutiny, he was admitted in deep suspicion by a hugely muscled bouncer. Once he'd given his name he was admitted into a quiet sanctuary where a small, pale bespectacled man stood to greet him, looking concerned or embarrassed at his torn clothes.

"Albrecht Grobelaar ... You are Kody, yes? From Runyan? What happened to you, a fall?"

While Stuart explained, Grobelaar set him down in a chair and brought him a large cognac. He tutted at the story but with a quizzical expression, as if there must be some reasonable explanation.

"You can't call the police in, obviously, but this is a very close community here, you know. I would not be at all surprised to hear rumours in a day or two. Who knows?"

"You knew I was coming?" Stuart asked pointedly.

"Some time in the next few weeks, certainly. But didn't Runyan tell you about bringing diamonds here? It's so straightforward. You declare your stones at the airport and they come to me in an armoured van. The only stipulation is for the consignee to be licensed and that's the official barrier. There's no duty payable."

"He didn't tell me, perhaps because the packaging wasn't exactly orthodox." Stuart told him about the rubber flange and some of the torments he'd been through getting it to Europe.

"So . . . you're empty-handed and in despair . . . I'm sorry, very sorry, for both of us, but I will put the word out, you can be sure."

"I've got this one only." Stuart took the amber cube out of his pocket. "Unfortunately, its proceeds I've bargained away already, for my freedom. You'll need some nitric acid to remove it."

Grobelaar rang a bell and then rattled a brief order in Flemish to the big man who was called Rolfe. He went out at once, buttoning his bulges.

"He'll get it from the cleaners." While they waited, Grobelaar explained that finished pieces went to be scoured clean in acids by a man who worked in an open booth, issued no receipt and was implicitly trusted. When Rolfe returned, they put the cube in a mug with the acid and watched it fuming. Grobelaar was plainly impatient and when at last the reaction began to slow, he reached into the mug with a pair of tweezers and extracted the big stone, rinsing and wiping it before scraping off some remnants of epoxy. He was absorbed and totally professional, examining the stone minutely through a loupe in reverent silence.

He pressed a buzzer and another small, bespectacled man came in from the next room.

"Hector, this is Mr Kody. He has brought us something rather fine. I think. Please make us a little window so we can look inside it."

Hector took the stone respectfully and went out. Stuart asked what he was going to do.

"Come and watch, if you like," Grobelaar answered affably.

In the cutting room, Hector placed the stone in his *dop*, a rod with a tacky paste on the end which held the stone simply by adhesion. The *dop* was then hooked over a metal arm and lowered so the stone came to rest on a spinning table like a brown gramophone record.

"There's diamond paste on a bronze plate," Grobelaar said, "that's how you render facets. Hector will polish one small window for us to see its heart. It will take some time. Do you have a hotel booking? Oh, well, most couriers stay at the Eurotel, just across the *chemin de fer*. You'll want some new clothes, I dare say. Do you have money or cards? Good, I'll telephone you later, to tell you how it is. In the meantime, do not despair, I know many people in this business and we depend on each other greatly. I'm afraid you look like a man sentenced to the guillotine. Console yourself that it is not so, eh?"

He gave a thin smile and ushered Stuart out, giving him a brief diagram of directions.

"I suppose it's improper to ask for a receipt?" Stuart ventured with a pale smile.

"*Certainement*. Have no fear. It looks a most notable piece, let us hope so. If it is, it's worth the kind of money that people kill for. I hope you don't know such people?'

"Presumably I've seen one or two of them today, hired of course. I take it you mean, would I kill to keep it, to break my bargain?" Again his pale smile came through reluctantly. "No. That's out of the question."

"Yes, well, preferences are not necessarily moral judgements. Diamonds cut diamonds and cut-throats cut throats."

Stuart chuckled nervously and went out, feeling a great lost despair in an unfamiliar city.

He bought jacket and trousers at surprisingly low tourist rates and amid some sympathy, allowing him to check into the Eurotel looking more presentable. He had a long hot shower and lay down on the bed, drowsy and fighting the misery of his hopeless commitments. Some time later the bedside telephone jarred him awake and the receptionist connected him without giving a name. He naturally assumed it was Grobelaar.

"Stuart Kody?" The voice was quite different, deep and hesitant, slightly accented.

"Who's that?"

"My name is Alexei Simonov. I was wondering if we could meet and talk."

Stuart hesitated in surprise. "Did Grobelaar contact you? Have you news for me, or some deal?"

The voice chuckled an interruption. "Perhaps. If we could meet, a nice public place if you wish, for dinner? Let's say La Pérouse at 9 o'clock, or earlier if you wish, a more English hour?"

Stuart was roused enough to say, "Why not now?"

"I cannot. You must have patience."

"I . . . All right. How will I recognise you?"

There was an audible sigh. "I suppose Ludmilla doesn't keep my picture any more?"

Simonov, Simonova. "Go-od heavens!" Stuart said slowly. "Yes, indeed I'd like to meet you. You know what I look like?"

The voice chuckled deeply. "Certainly, I have seen several photographs of you."

"Hey! Was it your lot who –?"

"Questions later, please! There is much to talk about." He gave the straightforward directions from the station to the river and rang off.

Stuart lay back on the bed, bemused. A dozen years he'd been gone, he estimated, and Lucy hadn't seen him in all that time. She would have been a sensitive 11 or 12 herself, but Alicia hadn't allowed her to go to Belgium for fear they might take her away. The chaperoned class visits to the Soviet Union were actually a safer bet. As far as he knew, Lucy didn't keep a picture of him anywhere and seldom spoke about him, nor did Alicia exhibit one in her apartment.

He slept for a couple of hours and woke in a strange, dull frame of mind until he remembered the meeting. It revitalised him completely with both interest and optimism which he tried to curb, and Grobelaar called a few minutes later.

"Are you rested and more sanguine, my friend?"

"Rested anyway, thank you. I've had a call, your contacts must be excellent."

"What? You have news?"

"A Russian. He didn't say anything but I'm meeting him later."

"But I . . . anyway, your stone." His voice took on a gravity which renewed Stuart's bleakness, spreading inside him like a cold puddle. "It has two or three inclusions which cannot be seen with the naked eye which means that we can legitimately pronounce it IFF, internally flawless. Its colour is a top E which means we can call it a D, first quality pure white, and its shape is a flattened octahedron which means Hector can cut it with a carat loss of possibly less than 50 per cent. Quite exceptional. It weighs 47.6 carats and we should end up with a brilliant-cut piece of between 22 and 24 carats."

Stuart had drawn in his breath and was about to exclaim but Grobelaar droned on smoothly, "Regarding price, may I call you back in the morning? I have a possible opportunity but I cannot verify it until later tonight."

"Can you give me a rough idea now?"

"I suppose . . . but forgive me if I quote you the barest minimum, for obvious reasons. Let us say a quarter of a million dollars, but probably much more."

He rang off after formalities leaving Stuart slightly breathless and his thoughts in a new turmoil at the workings of another world and the casual mention of enormous sums. He reflected that he would have been far less distressed had he remained ignorant of the real value of his loss; as things stood, he held only a vague hope that he might salvage enough to pay Rollo's bail and settle with de Hoek, but this illusion didn't last beyond dinner.

Ten

Every country has its constitution. Ours is absolutism moderated by assassination. Yours is decadence aggravated by necessity.

A. A. Simonov

It was quite dark by the time he set out but still warm and instead of taking a taxi, Stuart decided to walk off the stiffness of his bruises, not realising how far it was to the river. He thought of Lucy with every shop-window he passed, wanting to buy her armfuls of bright clothing. Close by the Maritime Museum in the Steen Fortress he found La Pérouse, one of a fleet of river restaurants. A shadow materialised as he approached the gangway, making him wary until the same deep voice spoke reassuringly.

"The British deplore our way of hugging and kissing so I'll restrain myself. You see, I feel I know you quite well."

"Your advantage. How do you do?" Stuart said and the other man chuckled. His hand was grasped firmly before he was ushered up the gangplank. The ship was quite full but Simonov was affably recognised and shown to his reserved table. They settled themselves opposite and smiled with some shyness as the waiter handed them menus.

When he left them, Simonov chuckled and said, "This is the awkward part where we both speak at once. Everyone talks like conspirators in Antwerp. That's a Steinway Grand behind you, they had an excellent pianist but people kept giving him 500 francs to be quiet. If there's background noise, you can't tell if you're being overheard."

Stuart smiled agreeably. The Russian had thinning black hair washed to softness, brown eyes with a very slight odd cast, a longish but hardly curved nose; his chin was broad and whisker dark but he had two bushy patches unshaven on his upper cheeks. There was a distinct resemblance to Lucy which he couldn't put down to any particular feature.

"I can't tell what gives her the look of you," he said, "But it's certain. And she's got your hands, Alicia's are much shorter."

Simonov nodded and looked down at his hands. They were hairy but slim and well tended.

"I don't expect she does keep my picture any more. There came a time when she stopped writing, after she was approached in London to work for us."

"Who is 'us'?"

"The Soviet Union. She didn't tell you?"

"No. Who jumped me in the taxi?"

"I don't know yet. I believe our people are trying to find out and I would say we have the best contacts. I'm sorry to hear of it, naturally. How much did you lose and what form did the package take?"

Stuart wondered why he hadn't asked that question on the telephone and in a sudden flash of clairvoyance he realised there was an untruth in the air and that Grobelaar had almost certainly been too preoccupied to have called anyone at that stage, in fact had almost told him so. He regarded his father-in-law with stony cynicism.

"Leading it back: you knew where I was staying, I was followed from Deurne, I must have been followed to Heathrow as well. That sounds like pretty co-ordinated surveillance to me, wouldn't you say?"

"I knew nothing about it," came the soft answer. "I'm not embassy staff. I was only informed after you were reported visiting Grobelaar. I am a *diamantaire* myself, that is why."

"Come on! I wasn't followed into the building and Grobelaar isn't the only one on that staircase. You were expelled from Britain on spying charges, what's more."

"In a situation like that, in 1971, we had no chance to state our innocence. The traitor Lyalin said whatever he liked. I'm sure he left out a few." Simonov smiled cryptically. "Anyway, how is my beloved daughter?"

"Beloved . . . I hadn't known she was part Jewish, though. That's a very interesting facet, maybe explains her character a little."

"Tell me about her, please, Alicia sends a couple of cards every year but doesn't say very much."

"She's electrifying, bewildering, brilliant." Stuart shook his head wistfully. "Not easy to describe, really, but she makes me terrified of being stodgy. I've only been married to her just over a year and I'm still in a kind of fantasy. The happiness is frightening, I've a terror of spoiling it. I can't believe – she only just told me she was married before – I can't believe anyone wanting to be violent with her. She feels guilty about the suicide, I'd like to dissuade her from it but I don't kid myself it would be easy."

"It would be, if I thought it right." Simonov paused and with lips and eyes gleaming said, "It wasn't suicide, it was an execution."

"Oh, come *on!*" Stuart exclaimed in furious astonishment.

"No, no, not by her," Simonov said hastily. "I did it myself. I heard from our London people what was going on so I slipped over and fixed him up."

The expression sounded almost quaint in the accented English; Stuart stared in horror. "My God, you sound even matter-of-fact about it!"

"Perhaps." Simonov shrugged. "I regarded Grady as vermin, even though we had him set up to work for us, them."

The slip wasn't lost on Stuart but he didn't pounce on it, tacitly accepting the other's duplicity.

"Did your masters know about it then?"

"Of course not. A wasted asset for them, so to speak. Would you not kill if anyone molested her?"

Stuart took a deep breath, considering. "In passion, yes I would. But to cross the Channel and cold-bloodedly blow his head off, that's something else. I was away recently and she was 'molested' then, and when I heard about it I did feel pretty murderous. However –"

"Yes, the South Africans. The man is blind in one eye, regaining partial sight in the other."

Stuart gulped and swallowed. "But she's blaming herself still, for Grady. You could have told her he was murdered."

"I feel it's preferable what she thinks, rather than to know her own father did it." Simonov made the statement flat enough to discourage further argument.

The waiter came for their order but neither had glanced at the menu. Stuart asked for Scotch, Simonov a dry Martini.

"You may not wish to eat with me in a moment," the

149

Russian said, "but I'd prefer to say it first. If any harm comes to her because of what you are doing, then I shall take action against you. I might have done so already except that you seem to treat her properly and she is apparently happy. It must stay that way, you understand?"

Before Stuart could answer, Simonov picked up his menu, stared at it and said, "Let's have the *Canard*, it's usually excellent. I'll let you chose your own starter."

Stuart glanced down the list of *hors d'oeuvres* and had just decided on a half dozen Zélande oysters when Simonov spoke again quietly.

"What did Mr Adrian Stayres want to see you about?"

He didn't look up and was apparently unaware of Stuart's struggle for composure. Only the top of his head was visible with its soft, friendly hair. When he lowered the card, Stuart was staring at the table-cloth, his thoughts in turmoil again. "Naturally, it's nothing to do with me really, but our people know many things and they asked me to ask you, that is all. I gather your father was Czech, naturalised British."

"I don't think you need me to tell you anything, with sources like yours," Stuart answered bitterly. "God help you if you've – wait a minute, that's it, you've got devices in my house, that's how you knew, isn't it?"

Simonov shrugged. "I don't know. What difference does it make? It's no use threatening me. The whole thing came to my notice only because there were diamonds involved."

"But when this Irishman beat Lucy up, I suppose you knew about it the same way, you bugged his place?"

"No. That's how I confirmed it; Alicia wrote to me but I was in Moscow, that's why it took so long. I assure you that the recent surveillance has not been for, let's say, prurient reasons but because you are now activated for British Intelligence, a world which Ludmilla rejected several years ago. It seems we Westernised her too thoroughly, she lost her respect for the *vlasti*, the bosses." He chuckled. "And her new husband is working for the other side! Come, let us order."

He signalled the waiter, who came eagerly since there were people waiting in line for tables. "In Russia you learn all about lines, or queues as you call them," Simonov said, looking over his shoulder. "The Russians are a patient people. It is estimated that they spend 30 billion man-hours a year in queues . . . *Oui, le canard sauvage au miel et aux citrons verts, pour, deux,"* he said lingeringly to the waiter. "And you, Mr Kody, Stuart may I call you, to start?"

"Des huitres," Stuart answered.

Simonov saw the waiter nod before adding, *"Pour moi, le Caviar d'Iran Osciètre,* perhaps, no I don't think so." He grinned at Stuart eyeing the price of 1850 francs, over £20. *"Non, les crevettes à l'ail."*

The waiter nodded with a slight grimace and left. Simonov seemed pleased with his decision. "Good, yes they are perfect. They boil the prawns with the oil and garlic keeping them covered with stiff bread, it keeps the steam in. They don't give you much which is very clever. So good that more would spoil your appetite."

He next ordered a Pouilly Fumé '81 and a Vosne Romanée '76, then asked casually, "Do you drink much?"

Stuart shook his head. "Average English by habit. You mean, do I go in for bouts of self-destruction in the good old Slav tradition?" He shook his head. "I understand vodka benders cost the USSR a lot more than 30 billion hours, so Alicia told me. Were you very unhappy with her?"

"No, not really, but I made her miserable. She's limited, she became desperately boring. I don't know whether the television addiction was symptom or cause but it was certainly an eye-opener. She told me about your habit of taking turns with Ludmilla to hide the TV from each other, so you only watch under extreme compulsion. I think that's a delightful discipline ... Alicia was mesmerised as if it was another world, one she could hardly comprehend, the new lack of respect for order, morals, fear of authority. The Soviet system depends on this fear, the people respect the powerful; you know, there are hordes who still think fondly of Stalin because he had the strong-arm approach. The Russian likes to feel it takes a powerful man to rule him, and even if you managed to convince – not easy – the old Stalinist that Uncle Josip was responsible for the murder of uncountable millions, he would still say, 'Well, if it was OK by him, it's OK by me. They must have had it coming to them!' They don't want the truth, they want iron security, even if it means hardship."

Stuart considered this as the *hors d'œuvres* arrived. "But when you suppress, what happens to brilliance, creativity, contribution to mankind? And you've had a huge delinquency problem ever since you banished religion."

151

"Not true, religion was another control for them to be mischievous about, like the Irish."

"I don't know . . . but if it had been allowed to be benign, simply a source of dignity and goodness rather than medieval control, it could have aided and even humanised communism. The idolising of the butcher Lenin was official, *de rigueur*, and therefore part of the control, no willingness. If . . . but there's a hundred 'ifs'. Tell me where you prefer to live."

"Frankly, I like my own people better and I like the country, though it helps to have a position to get decent food and privileges. The West is more comfortable, more luxurious, but I grew up with discomfort, it doesn't bother me, in fact I rather like it, stoicism has a good feeling of its own. I have a function but I do not belong here, yet the trouble is I've been away long enough not to belong there either. I've also become decadent in my use of women which may be why Ludmilla is a prude."

"A prude? Don't be absurd!"

"I'm sorry. I mean she was never loose. How are the oysters?"

"Perfect. Try one."

"All right, if you try one of these prawns."

Stuart did so and said, "You were right, I'd have scoffed a plateful." He put the fork down and sipped his wine. "I'm not going to live with the bugs and surveillance, though, even if I can treat it as a joke."

Simonov snorted and smirked slightly. "You chose your life. 'He knoweth your sitting down and your rising up.' Do you want to know what Ludmilla was doing this afternoon?"

Stuart put his glass down carefully and hissed, "You are all bastards, reptiles. How could you ask me such a shitty question?"

Simonov held up his hand placating. "Listen, I was just illustrating a point, not making crude suggestions."

"So you've invaded my privacy and strangers pry maybe even into my bedroom, the thought turns my stomach. Orwell's famous year already, it's quite repellent!"

Simonov's smile was indulgent, with only a hint of mockery. "An honest man like yourself has nothing to be ashamed of, surely? Anyway, you're not on vision yet, domestic gymnastics chez Kody." He saw the fury mounting and held up his hand again. "But the point is, it's not us, I should say 'we', who are doing it. It's Stayres' people, or maybe the people who watch him, I'm not sure."

Stuart felt on the verge of shouting. "But it must have been you, you knew everything from the time I got up this morning!"

"No, no. It's quite simple, a word here, a suggestion there. *They* put the equipment in and we plug into their system. Much cheaper and far less risky. The other way you get incidents, like with the South Africans, and we don't need any more bad publicity."

Stuart paused, almost breathless. "You're not seriously trying to tell me that the Brits have Gomorrah'd my place and you've penetrated their system? I just don't believe you."

A flicker of uncertainty showed in the Russian's face but was quickly covered. "What was that word?"

Stuart waited some moments before answering, realising that nothing would be gained by over-reaction. He had nearly thrown the table into Simonov's lap before he realised there might be a purpose to the baiting. As he explained Lucy's euphemistic invention, he realised that the surveillance must have been more recent than his first day home, unless Simonov hadn't heard the tapes verbatim.

He watched him put his glass down and chuckle again. "She says some very funny things, that little one. Hah, I heard her, she described your Queen as being 'rather middle class, in a nice sort of way'." He grinned broadly and succeeded in getting a wan response from Stuart. "I've made you quite angry, I'm afraid. I won't do it any more. Let us drink to your, no, 'our', Ludmilla, Liuba, Lucy, Lu, however you want it. Alicia said it was changed because Ludmilla is too Russian and not very pretty-sounding in English, is that right?"

Stuart nodded. "A bit heavy, yes." They clinked glasses and a look of delighted mischief crept into Simonov's face. "Are you sure you don't want to know what she was doing this afternoon?"

Stuart couldn't help a jaundiced smile, more at the other's facial expression than the teasing. "You might make me curious but I don't want to have to hide my knowledge from her. And if it was something risky, I certainly don't want to know, I live in terror for her."

"It's certainly risky. But you're right, it's better you don't know. Too many secrets would be confusing."

Stuart shook his head in bewilderment. "With all your inside knowledge, you must know who has my package."

"Not yet."

"You mentioned harm coming to Lucy ... there is a threat to her if I don't pay someone off."

A look of understanding crept into Simonov's face. "Ah ... de Hoek?"

Stuart shook his head first in disbelief and then nodded his confirmation. "How much do you know, then?"

"Nothing except that he closed the file on you, even though he'd discovered your nationalities. Tell me."

Stuart explained about the deal and his hope for what the big stone would fetch. As soon as he mentioned Rollo's bail, Simonov chopped the air with his hand.

"Don't do it. Find the money some other way. The diamond world will know all about your piece by tomorrow and de Hoek would have no trouble discovering that you cheated him."

Stuart's pessimism sank back to his low point of the morning and even his bruises started to ache. The psychosomatic effect was amusing enough to spark a sardonic humour, one small hurdle against Simonov's bantering expression.

"I'll squirm for you if it gives you pleasure," he said, a little annoyed at the man's ability to charm. "Did you tease Alicia much?"

"Yes, quite a lot, I suppose, until I finally realised she couldn't take it. Ludmilla also had a phone call this morning, from the Soviet Embassy. They had a proposition for her."

"Oh yes?" Stuart felt a sudden grave suspicion.

"She said the same as last time, a rank obscenity: '*I di kibeny matier*'. But this time it was for the benefit of the British microphones, I believe she was briefed to say it. Ah, here is the duckling."

Stuart wanted to guffaw loudly and had difficulty controlling his reaction. He found himself abruptly relaxing in the absolute certainty that Simonov was lying or that others had lied to him. Calmly he said, "So you don't actually know her real response?"

"No, I suppose not. We'll have leverage but don't get angry, I'll explain in a minute. First try the dish."

He swirled the taste of burgundy offered to him, mur-

muring and nodding his approval, then carefully he cut a testpiece of duckling.

"The chef is on top form. *Mes compliments.*" The waiter inclined his head agreeably, finished serving and disappeared. Simonov ate for a couple of minutes in reverent silence; Stuart did the same, his agitation nearly quelled among the delicacy of flavours.

With pleasure in half-closed eyes, Simonov drank and put his glass down. "I'll tell you what we're engaged in at the moment. It's a kind of espionage pathology, quite separate from the classified information-gathering. Naturally, we like to know what the West knows about our activities and we also try to find out in advance what they intend to do about them. When it works, it has a marked defusing effect and can save a great deal of embarrassment. If we'd had a proper system running in '71, probably I'd still be in London. It was this very system that picked you up in Johannesburg: we wanted to know why BOSS was interested in a couple of Brits with altered nationalities. Somehow I have a feeling that the South Africa thing is not so significant as that you work for W section and that Stayres has found out about it. Either he's head-hunting, desperate for Czech speakers or he's seeking a way to protect his flanks. Very interesting, wouldn't you say?"

With difficulty, Stuart kept his face expressionless, trying not to betray his confusion and astonishment. He wanted to laugh but Simonov's confident words rode over him.

"The point of pathology is to find preventive medicine. We know you have agents in all the Communist countries, we even know who a lot of them are. The same applies to ours, no doubt. South Africa is becoming a sensitive area for us and it's naturally useful if we know their reactions and their interest in whatever we might do there. If necessary then we can stop or change it to avoid embarrassment."

"Or feed in some false information?"

"That's not my department. Our brief isn't so much towards cold war as towards a new détente, if you follow?"

"You mean, you want me to go home and tell them you're all nice guys working for friendship? Don't forget your admission a few moments ago, that if you'd had foreknowledge of Lyalin's defection or Britain's sniffing, you wouldn't have been caught – that has to be an admission of your real

155

masters' identity! You of all people must know that in the West, those three initials are symbolic of all that's ogre-ish and terrible, exactly equivalent to Hitler's Gestapo."

"Too many spy novels – but you're right, I know. Not about me, though. I'm not with the KGB, I'm in extreme disfavour with them because of my two ladies' lapse of loyalty. I think Alicia only did it to spite me and jeopardise my position."

"How come you were all three allowed out together, anyway?"

"Alicia and I both had parents in Russia but, now they are dead, my situation is, let's say, all uphill. I need results, and better than I'm getting now. I bribe people in semi-sensitive spots, mostly. They're not traitors really, they believe in the medicinal aspect, though the greasing of the palm does help persuade them they are working for the good of humanity. Which they are, of course."

"Your piece of it, anyway."

"Hm. Alicia has misunderstood you all along, I think. You have grit and fibre, my friend. The notes she sent me were not too complimentary, that you were unemployed but at least better than the Grady rat. Not that anyone could ever be right for her quicksilver *dochka* – little daughter – but I think you might be just the job. I'm afraid I asked her was the Czech certified but she didn't get it."

"Just as well."

"Yes, making jokes in another language is a bit risky. Did you have a pun nickname at school?"

"All of them, variously. Only Lucy had one that was apposite. They called her The Mad Rush."

Simonov nodded. "Yes, I heard that. It was a good school for her, too good. I'm glad I didn't have to pay the fees – yet."

"Oh, who did?"

"The Embassy, naturally. They still have hopes that their investment will bear fruit and I don't mean grandchildren. If it, she, does, then I will get my promotion. Things were a little tricky for me when she first turned them down, it was probably a good thing I'd already been 'ponged', as Adrian Stayres would say."

"Is that all it means to you?"

"Yes. Why?"

"That Lucy is simply for your advancement?"

"No, no, I thought you meant in terms of patriotism and ideology." He dropped his voice. "It doesn't bother me who does what and with what as long as we all have a good time. I just happen to be paid by one side, you by the other. Neither of us is thinking about war or victory, though it would be nice to eliminate the fear, I suppose. The point, indeed the coincidence, is that you are in a unique position, one of enormous value and we could be very useful to each other. Especially if I can find what you are looking for."

Stuart eyed him gravely, feeling like a simpleton and trying not to show it. "I'd make a pretty good guess it was you or your people who took it in the first place," he said tersely.

The Russian betrayed no duplicity in his response, nodding seriously. "I suppose that's possible, yes. If I find out, those responsible will be severely punished of course, severely. You know, it's an astonishing oversight that Moscow didn't run a scan on you before. I must admit I never thought of it myself; after the Grady fiasco I was sure that Ludmilla would be unapproachable by any service. I might be accused of driving her towards the British, if they knew what I'd done. I trust you'll respect that confidence?"

"For her sake I'd have to, wouldn't I? You haven't given me a lever." Stuart closed his eyes and exhaled with a long resigned sigh.

"I've shown willing. The word is out around all the chemists for anyone asking for benzine and alcohol. I think that was the other solvent you required, no?"

Stuart looked at him sharply, realising it was the final conviction. The only time the solvent had been mentioned was on the telephone from his house. Inside, he felt a pugnacious hardening against being played like a fish and having his whole life laid bare. He changed the subject abruptly back to Lucy.

"She told me about the fighting training, part of your educational package. It doesn't sound like a preparation for your preventive medicine."

"I suppose not, but just because something's lethal doesn't mean you have to use it – in fact quite the opposite. The chances are you don't as long as people know about it. The South African didn't."

"Nor did Grady."

"He didn't know about me either, until he saw me squeeze the trigger."

"She said it was a special bullet, a chopper or something?"

"Yes. Didn't you come across them in Ireland? You tip all the round pellets out of the cartridge and replace them with little slices, like you might hack off a lump of lead with an axe. On contact they go every which way, terrible mess. I got it from another Irishman ... You know, it amazes us that you put up with those people. They worked with the Nazis against you, they tried to do deals with the Japs as well, they don't co-operate at all if they can help it, they don't benefit you in any way except as the butt of stupid jokes and now they work for us, espionage, drug traffic, arms deals, all flowing through the Republic. I'd like to think they were covering themselves in case of a Communist take-over but they're not, they just like working against the Brits, harbouring grudges and being subversive. It'd be the same whoever their neighbours were, and I can tell you straight off, when we fulfil our Plan for Europe, one of the first things on the agenda is to wipe them out. They don't know which side to oil their bread."

"Lucky for them it won't come to that. Trouble is they'll never believe they're better off with us."

Simonov ignored the bravado. "I was just reading what Churchill had to say about them when the war in Europe finished. He was very restrained ... But about my daughter, does it scare you, knowing what she can do?"

"Not in the slightest."

"No, I can see that. So tell me, what does scare you?"

"Losing her, that's – my God, Simonov, I just felt my blood stop! That was your leading question, wasn't it, the veiled threat, you dirty bastard!"

The Russian had been shaking his head, his mouth full of food. He swallowed hastily and put his hand out.

"Easy, take it easy, my boy. Your fuse is too short. You don't have to react like that for me to know what your answer would be, it's what I told them. I know that any threat is useless unless you guarantee to carry it out, by which time it has evidently been useless. Takes a bit of nerve, that's all. I'm talking about stick blackmail, which is negative, use once only or permanently. The positive, or carrot blackmail on the other hand is much less resistible, wouldn't you say? For

158

instance, you would be open to some kind of proposition which involved getting your property back, wouldn't you? Many a man would do something quite craven in the circumstances, something regrettable perhaps. The thinking, intelligent man would try to find a means to get back at the snatchers or at least establish a Mexican stand-off and do a deal."

Even in his anger, Stuart was beginning to feel scared about where the talk was leading, since he had no fall-back position and no one to support him. He considered telling Simonov that he worked neither for Stayres nor any W section, nor for anyone else; the decision to defer it seemed to steady him up.

"In other words," Simonov went on, "if someone took something away from you and told you you could have it back on certain conditions, the chances are you would comply."

"No." The answer was flat and absolute.

"What do you mean, 'No', like that? Of course you would."

"No, I wouldn't. It's the whole 'beat the hijacker' principal. If you don't give in, there are no more hijacks."

"You're not much up on revolutionary tactics. You mean to say, 'Sure, blow up the plane, and yourselves, go ahead.' Yes, that would work after a bit, after you lost a few planes. But suppose you get a call and an Italian voice says, 'Hey, mister, this is Stiletto Snatch Company, we gotta you little boy, you buy 'im back, one million bucks cash, or 'e goes in the *tagliatelle*,' then you say, 'Go ahead, stick him in the *tagliatelle*,' so they do, then they ring up and say, 'Hey, mister, we gotta you little girl, tonight we have the *canelloni*, you gonna pay now?' All of a sudden, Stiletto has credibility, hasn't he?"

"What the hell are we talking about, Simonov? What's this got to do with your guff about preventive medicine?"

"Ah. Please call me Alexei. Did you enjoy the meal so far?"

"The wild duckling was perfect. Let's say some of the side dishes were unpalatable."

"Yes, I should apologise, but you are smart enough to see a trend. I won't make doubtful protests, protestations about being honest with you, I'll simply say that I had a brief, to

159

find out if we could do business. I was instructed not to be soft just because you are family, so to speak, and if you are asked you can say I obeyed instructions."

Stuart considered him for some moments before answering. "The people you bribe, you don't go round threatening them all first, do you?"

"Oh no, we do that after they've taken a bribe!"

"So you only have to pay them once?"

"No, we go on paying them but they're so grateful for that, they make special efforts. It's a capitalist carrot with a little Red pepper in it."

"So where does that leave us?"

Simonov smiled. "You're interested? You really want to know?" He paused and shook his head, adding, "I think not. I think if I read you correctly, you are very close, like a pressure cooker at full chatter with the safety valve bulging. I think you are about to make a scene, maybe throw something or make an anti-Semitic remark, so may I suggest you try the raspberries and strawberries mixed? They're fresh, of course, they have them flown in from, oh, somewhere or other."

Stuart began to relax and finally smiled, nodding. "I'm sure you're very good at your job. You'll get your promotion without Lucy's co-operation."

The other shook his head. "No, and what's more they are going to make me pay for her schooling. I will give you a very strong lever against me and tell you that I have been using the stick a little so as to keep some of the carrots which I'm supposed to hand out, salting it away for the day of the reckoning."

"Tricky, but you're wise. Lucy wouldn't change her mind, she has great clarity."

"Really? What about what I heard?" When he got no answer he asked, "Are you any more flexible?"

"I didn't say she was inflexible, just that on one level, yours I suspect, she's able to see the joke and the futility of it all while on the other she has disgust and horror for the evils of ideologies, systems purporting to be for the good of man."

"It's not very attractive to be righteous, even if you're right." He paused to let Stuart see himself, then went on, "People sense these things, if they're given the chance – for instance, 'dogma' was simply a benign expression for 'things taught', but the word 'dogmatic' is not benign now. I'm going

160

to give you another lever against me and tell you that I don't take seriously much of what I do, in fact I'm quite naughty and often walk the high-wire. I have the mischief of the Russian and the sparkle of the Jew, I think that's probably why they don't send me home, come to think of it. I might be an embarrassment. Did she tell you her father was half-Jewish?"

"No." Stuart remembered then where he first heard it, from de Hoek's tape-recorder at the Swaziland crossing.

"I wonder why not?"

"Same reason I didn't ask about the Simonov, probably. It isn't a factor."

"You mean you don't feel strongly about it, neither of you?"

"Not at all. Would you like us to? I mean, do you feel less 'Chosen' if we don't care?"

Simonov laughed happily. "Well done, well done, you've got bite." He lowered his voice slightly and added, "You might need it."

Stuart made no reply and the waiter came to clear their plates, followed by an achingly buxom blonde towing the sweet trolley. Simonov contrived to brush the edge of her hand as she served him and when she didn't flinch, he murmured to her and she coloured slightly. She served Stuart and then crouched quickly between the trolley and Simonov, whispering something. Simonov glanced at his watch as she moved away, then looked up with a satisfied smile.

"What did you say to her?"

"Something about strawberry blondes and cream. At least you needn't worry about me going to your hotel and making you destroy a litre of vodka with me. I have a prior appointment."

"Just like that?"

When Simonov nodded complacently, he asked, "How old are you?"

"Forty-nine. I enjoy philandering and she didn't have to say yes."

"What will you talk about?"

"Listen, not everyone is so fortunate to have a relationship like yours, a girl of such élan – and remember she was very expensive. And you'll get bored eventually, everyone does."

161

"Maybe, but I think one can spice it. I hope she's going to get a lot of good surprises."

"Thirty years wait for Official Secrets. She'll have some for you first."

Stuart nodded. "Yes, quite likely. She's given me a few already – and no, I don't want to know what she was doing this afternoon, I don't want to spoil her pleasure in surprising me."

"A clear motive, good. I won't tell you then. Something I will tell you, though: I am allowed to give away a certain amount of Classified as a *quid pro quo*, bits to take home with you. It pleases your masters and eases your conscience about what you tell me, and if used intelligently can save a lot of unhappiness. Here's one: we do not have a source in W section, where of course one would be *most* valuable, so you can tell them they're secure."

Stuart felt lightheaded and laughed abruptly. "Can you just see it? I go home and say, 'OK, you've got no worries. I met this Boris in Antwerp and he tells me the outfit's clean.'"

Simonov smiled indulgently. "Ah yes, but then you tell him that you've been approached for the job and ask him what you're allowed to give us. For instance, who is the chief of W, how many operatives are there, where are they based and so on?"

"You mean you don't know?"

Simonov shook his head. "Eat your dessert. Do you want some more cream? It's very frustrating because 1971 could happen again. If you've got a watchdog section sniffing out moles and we don't know about it, how are we supposed to protect our tails? We expect you to help us out a little and we'll do the same. Having a *secret* secret section is downright devious, my masters are not pleased about it, I suspect because it downgrades all the other departments and so reduces their own status and importance. You are heaven-sent, do you see? I'm also authorised to match your pay, pound for pound and no taxes, just to stay where you are and keep your ears open. How much are you getting?"

"Hold on, I need to think." Stuart felt almost bloated on the rich food but the raspberry–strawberry combination was irresistible. He ate quietly without looking at Simonov, his thinking in a kind of pandemonium.

Simonov misunderstood his deliberation. "It's too much pleasure, isn't it? Let's order some more."

Stuart shook his head firmly and when he'd eaten the last raspberry he was able to give a smile of genuine delight. "Just superb, thank you."

"Tell me, have you done many courier jobs? I find the expenses are quite good and you get to sample all the best cooking in Europe."

"Without getting fat?"

"I'm not the sort. But have you been sent abroad much?"

"I find it strange you don't know, I thought you had proper tabs on me."

"For once, no we don't. This is the odd thing, the real nuisance factor of W. We know you were in the Army for a while but otherwise nothing. My colleagues would perhaps object to my admitting how little we actually know about this new section. Your Prime Minister was setting it up with responsibility just to herself or a very select few of the Cabinet, and it was, of course, quite a shock and very unpopular with the heads of departments. A bunch of busybodies with unlimited access to all departments and records, past and current files. Instant retribution and a probable jail sentence for non-co-operation. That's all we know." He grinned happily. "Can you imagine what a score it would be if W was our man, or even anyone in the section?"

"And you want me to go home and suggest to them that I be your man, your mole-above-the-ground? Huh, I've no idea what they'll say."

"They?"

Stuart had a sudden devious idea. And his deceit began to spawn another down-spiral within itself. "Yes. W is two people."

"Really? Why?" Simonov leaned forward eagerly.

"The position is too sensitive for one, hence the double letter. They hate each other, that's why they were chosen."

Simonov's eyes opened wide as if to maximise his input.

"Fascinating," he breathed. "This is a great score, I'll be able to eat at the Sir Antony van Dyck tomorrow, or maybe 't Fornius. They'll put the processor on to all known enmities in Government Service and probably have the names by breakfast. Are you sure you should have told me that? Would you prefer if I kept it to myself for the time being?"

"I'll ask. It's good of you to suggest it, I think the sumptuous meal has marred my discretion."

"No, I think you're getting the point quite well, that we're serious about the medicine, that our business is all about accommodation. 'The world was made for people but unfortunately a lot of them are foreigners.' I'm quoting an English MP, I forget his name but no doubt he was Tory." He attempted the difficult accent of the English aristocrat. "I always rather felt the Tories could afford the wider view, but didn't usually bother, um? Coffee and cognac?"

Stuart smiled and nodded. "I'm afraid you wouldn't make much of a spy among the toffee-nosed without some speech training. Anyway, you'd be terribly frowned on for pinching all the maids' bottoms."

"Probably – and that's not all. But they do have quite a few Jews among them, don't they?"

Stuart shrugged. "It's just not something I'm very aware of, I'm afraid – no, don't be indignant. If it doesn't matter to me, that's all it means, I'm not being condescending, supercilious. I appreciate it must give you a good many difficulties."

"Yes. A curious unfairness about an inheritance, because for us it doesn't work the other way. Americans have money and family, the British have Class, for the Russian there's only status, privilege, power – but he has to work for it, it's supposed to be impossible to hand down status or to use *nomenklatura*, father's influence, what's it called?"

"Nepotism."

"Yet Jewishness is handed down . . . I'm sorry, it's all too sad a tale, I'm not for a moment imagining that you don't realise it."

"OK . . . But Lucy told me there is one vital factor, that the influential Russian is able to get his child into the best schools which is more or less a guarantee of good position."

"Well, yes. That's unavoidable."

"There must be a thousand unavoidables. But every good Communist would cry 'Unfair, unequal!' In Siberia, someone is living on black potato cakes and nettle beer while you still have the taste of duckling and raspberries in your mouth and are wondering whether to spoil it by finishing that magnificent burgundy."

Simonov smiled, twirled his glass, sniffed again and drank

164

with decision. "Why does your department need money, running diamonds like that?"

"Don't ask."

"All right. Did they get Grobelaar's sight stopped in Charterhouse Street?"

Stuart assumed he meant de Beers in London but decided it was a good opportunity to look enigmatic. He didn't answer, instead shifting his eyes around noncommittally.

He shrugged, and the gestures said quite neatly, "mind your own business". Simonov accepted it without any visible disappointment, in fact he smiled as if satisfied that the game was being played properly.

"Do you know what you'll be doing next, or is it all surprises?"

"Training. I need lots more training, they said. I don't mind. I quite enjoy it."

"Why don't we say that you were thinking of transferring to, say, Stayres' department but I persuaded you, eventually, to stay where you are, that you went for the extra money. I'll get a commendation. How about it?"

"OK."

"Great!" Simonov was plainly delighted. "Naturally you must tell them about our discussions but not about the money, that's important. The Brits are peculiar that way, about graft. They'd make you hand it in like a good boy. Tell me something, though: with her attitude, what does Ludmilla think about you doing this kind of work?"

"We don't discuss it, I'm not allowed to. I'll have to invent something to explain the lumps I got, say I fell off a bus."

Simonov smiled and then suddenly rattled off a guttural phrase, watching for a reaction, but Stuart understood the test. "I don't speak it, I haven't been to Russia, I don't know it at all. But I know what happened to Czechoslovakia, just when they thought they were coming back into the sunlight."

Simonov nodded. "The Soviet bloc is in a real bind, a Catch Situation, from which it can't escape. The only way for it to defend itself effectively when under deadly pressure was through organised cohesion. It worked, at a price, but only half the people are Russian, the rest are a motley bunch, there were over a hundred different races, creeds and so on. To keep a diverse, backward and sometimes downright primitive people from anarchy and chaos, you have to control

165

them somehow. Lenin and Stalin, they chose terror because it was instant, it didn't require decades of turmoil and revolution. They actually preached terror quite openly, and as a result Russia hauled itself into the twentieth century and is a cohesive world power, run on lines which are completely effective and completely repugnant to the West. Without the Soviet harness, they'd forfeit their ambition to match the Western model, they'd slump back into Class B.

"Having been underdog so long, they are hyped up to believe that the bosses have at last made them top dog, and God knows just how proud and patriotic they are – *nasha luchshe* – ours is the best. So they continue with what they call competition which is, in reality, a breathless and endless business of trying to catch up. 'We will overtake and surpass the capitalist countries' – what is that but an admission of a model? But they will keep on trying and keep on imitating because, as you say, they have sacrificed their spontaneity, their individual creative genius, their heart, their exuberance, as well as their art and literature. Would that spark have survived the dominance of foreign armies? They sacrificed it and everything just to survive so a few disapproving gurgles from the West don't mean a thing. How many people die every day, half a million, a million? They just shot down a Jumbo-full of two hundred and sixty-nine innocents for flying over their airspace – the West screams 'FOUL!', the Russian shrugs and says 'Tough'. Westerners don't realise how fortunate they are in centuries of security, that they can afford such high-mindedness. You must be tired, I will stop boring you and let you go, only please don't imagine that those are my views or the views of any individual. You mustn't equate the man with the system, do you follow?"

When Stuart nodded, he clinked glasses and said, "I think it's been very productive. Let's drink to our détente."

They finished their brandy and Simonov called for the bill. With a twinkle and an elaborate flourish of fine leather, he extracted a gold American Express card and laid it on the saucer. The two men smiled and said nothing, but Stuart felt curiously mature as he resisted the frantic urge to ask when he might expect to hear about his stolen treasure.

At the foot of the gangplank, Simonov nodded repeatedly while shaking hands, smiling all the while.

"Just don't try to kiss me on our first date," Stuart said,

releasing his hold. Simonov chuckled again and turned away, buttoning up his collar tightly in parody of the sleuth. Stuart took a taxi to the Eurotel and, before sleeping, gave his home number to the hotel operator. She sounded irritated when he told her to break the connection after one ring, pretending not to understand his French and complying with eventual reluctance.

Eleven

Finding a mate is like trying to find one of a pair in a bombed-out shoe shop. The trouble is there are always those who can't wait or who'll settle for something just wearable and they screw up the whole system.

Lucy

Stuart slept very late and was awakened by the telephone. It was Simonov sounding eager and very pleased with himself.

"Alcohol and benzine, didn't I tell you? Someone bought them, at an *apothèque* in Rifstraat."

When Stuart didn't answer, he went on, "Great news, eh? We haven't found him yet, but we're on to it, don't worry."

"Sure I won't."

"What's the matter, you sound different?"

"I was asleep, that's all."

"Oh, sorry. I thought you'd be pleased."

"Yes. Thank you."

"And another thing, the Australians took the America's Cup last night, isn't that terrific?"

"Why?"

"Because now the Americans will have to spend like maniacs to get it back. They'll lose prestige and credibility and the Russian press will be righteously disgusted at the capitalist idiocy of it all. I think it's splendid, don't you?"

Stuart wasn't certain he detected irony. "Listen, it's a sport, that's all. Your lot would do it if they had a chance. Have you noticed how Russians tend not to go in for things unless they're likely to win."

"Yes, I know. Hertz and Avis. I wonder what *Pravda* will have to say about it. *Pravda* means 'truth', you know."

"It's the same in Czech . . . How was your tryst?"

"Delicious. She keeps interfering with me and I was trying to look up that bit about the Irish for you. Never mind, he made up for it with some nice things at the end. It was his last speech to the Commons in May '45. I realised then why Stalin walked all over him."

"Oh, Churchill?"

"Yes. It was because your system wouldn't let him get enough power to put his foot down properly. Mind you, it was also the reason why he wasn't corrupt. Aargh! Listen, I have to go, good luck with Grobelaar. Call me in a day or two when you've had a word with your bosses and I'll see if I have any news for you. Hug Ludmilla for me."

He gave the Russalmaz number and a strangled goodbye.

Stuart found himself trembling with frustration and annoyance, his suspicions gathering their own conviction. He rang down for coffee and croissants, admitting the waiter wearing just a towel; the Belgian showed clucking concern for the abrasions on his right arm and leg which felt more stiffly painful than the previous day.

He took a long soak in the bath before calling Grobelaar, but the *diamantaire* was out and had left a message that he would call if a deal was concluded. By inclination a loner, Stuart abhorred the feeling of being at others' behest or controlled by them let alone being supplicant and he swore grimly to extricate himself as swiftly as possible. Simonov had left him with only the merest doubt about Russian complicity in the snatch, just enough to prevent him wasting his breath with outright accusation but far more than enough to stimulate him to unspecified exchange. He speculated also that if the Russian discovered he had nothing to barter with, no job, no secrets, no information, he would never see the cache again, while the predictable reaction from Rollo made him grimace whenever he thought of it, let alone his own imminent ruin in the form of his friend's bail. He would have to take a full mortgage on his house to provide it, and for that he would have to supply an income. Under any other circumstances he knew he would have short-changed de Hoek over the big stone but Simonov's warning had been quite unequivocal. It might have been said to tighten the stranglehold but with Lucy as the pressure point he couldn't take any chance.

He wandered round the town, had a light lunch in a bistro and on his fourth call was summoned to Grobelaar's office for a 5 p.m. appointment. Unless it was quick, he stood a good chance of missing the evening flight, but the secretary said she couldn't bring it forward. He arrived punctually in Vestingstraat and again the huge Rolfe led him into Grobelaar's office.

"You're looking satisfied, Mr Grobelaar. What happened?"

Grobelaar explained that he'd been getting offers in order to persuade his bank to lend him the purchase price. Apparently things had not been going well for him since falling out of favour with de Beers.

"The price I can give you is $325,000. I hope we can agree?"

"Yhes." Stuart's quick reply was slightly aspirated but Grobelaar appeared not to notice.

"Good. Then you must say '*Mazel tov*', as I do. It seals a bargain unbreakably."

They exchanged the formality and Grobelaar asked why he didn't smile. Stuart reminded him that the proceeds were not for himself and had already become the price of his freedom. They arranged the necessary bank transaction more stiffly but just before showing him out, Grobelaar said there'd been a message from Simonov. Stuart almost brightened in eagerness but the words weren't hopeful.

"He said to tell you it was a false trail and please to call him again in a day or two. I'm very sorry and I trust you'll come back to me if you find your property. 'To them that hath shall be given.'"

"Something should be done about that," Stuart said dourly but with a straight face. "That Book has a lot to answer for, wouldn't you say?"

"The New one?" With a sly grin, Grobelaar ushered him out and touched his skull-cap saying, "Lies, all lies."

His taxi ran into a rush-hour jam, increasing his fuming exasperation to screaming point. He was now desperate to get home and take stock of his disaster in some familiar comfort. More than ever he wanted to confide in Lucy but realised it was hardly fair, just when everything was right up the creek, to share his fiasco and force her into a position of helpless sympathy. Besides, he was vividly aware that until Grobelaar had actually opened and funded an account for de Hoek, the BOSS-man's threat against her still hung fire. He was at least glad that he hadn't told her anything already.

His fury mounted against Rollo for cornering him in the first place, more strongly than fury against himself for losing the hoard.

Moreover, he realised that Simonov or his masters could decide to play him like a trout whether or not they had possession of his stones. For certain they were going to try to compromise him' and his only card lay in their astonishing belief in his position as a highly clandestine W-section agent. The prospect was frightening and confusing. Meanwhile, he had to find Rollo's bail and then legal fees, very soon, somehow without breaking himself and without giving Lucy a hint of impending disaster.

They cleared the jam eventually but by the time his taxi had forced its way to Deurne, the last flight for London had just taken off. Darkness was closing in and his mood was hardening in a way that felt almost dangerous. He strode with grim purpose through the tiny concourse thinking back to a trip to Le Mans in a private aircraft with some student friends when, clearing from Gatwick, a complete stranger had approached with casual confidence and asked for a lift to Le Touquet. Quickening, he took the left passage towards the cafeteria where he had seen two Air-Taxi offices; both were shut but opposite, next to a door marked Kommandant was a doorway leading on to the apron, emphatically No Exit. It was closing behind a suited man with a familiar but indefinable air, carrying an overloaded briefcase. Stuart prevented the door from closing and saw the man stride confidently towards a UK registered Piper Seneca, so he ran out after him. An angry voice shouted to him to stop, so Stuart waved an agreeing, placating gesture.

The pilot heard his running footsteps and turned.

"Are you going to England?"

"Yes, actually." The plummy voice made it sound like "ekchwaleah". "Wha-y?"

"Cadge a lift?"

Stuart took a moment to decipher the next question which sounded like "Wheahr?"

"Anywhere. Oxford for choice."

"Ao." The man considered for a moment and offered Tyne-Tees and then said something else difficult to catch. Stuart had to ask him to repeat which brought a puzzled frown; eventually he gathered that for another fifty "pynds",

171

an extension could be arranged to Kidlington and the man had introduced himself as St George Wennersley-Farquhar, apologised for the fee and explained with some disgust that one had to work for one's living "naa-days" because of the *fahk*ing socialists, probably, but he didn't much care for politics so he wasn't sure.

They went back inside, altered the number-on-board on the flight plan, placated the ruffled Kommandant and were airborne inside ten minutes. Stuart noticed that "Sen-George", as he called himself had to modify his accent to be understood in the universal plain English of flight controllers. He smiled to himself and decided not to remark on it.

It was a clear evening and once they'd reached their cruising level, St George locked in the autopilot, checked the panel thoroughly and lit a cigarette. He held it out in his fingers with a marked affectation, as if unfamiliar with smoking and disdainful of it. When inhaling he held the cigarette directly in front of his face, looked at it, and then irritatedly advanced his head with puckered lips until a quick sucking contact was made. After each puff he tapped ash in the tray with a stiffened forefinger, and Stuart was easily able to imagine him holding a tea-cup. His flying, however, was an alert and sensitive perfection, the log on his knee board frequently referred to and updated, the Jeppesen charts handy, constant references to VOR and ADF beacons and the second radio pre-set to the next onward frequency.

St George finally put out his cigarette with the correct measure of disgust, turned his head and smiled with what seemed like shyness in the dim glow from the instruments and the red map-light overhead. He was about to say something else when he noticed Stuart's injury so he interjected, "Bang your head, did you?" politely, but without waiting for an answer.

"Quite awkward being brought up to leisure, y' know. Having to work, I mean. But at least I've got good contacts, and m' friends use me when they can, 'Fly Farquhar and faster', merrily we sing. All pater's fault of course, wasn't organised. Do you know what he left me, um? Four-fifths of five-eights of FA. But there was one barn which the Infernal Retinue didn't know about, it was stuffed with about two square miles of revolting, vomit-coloured, cut-price carpet, he could never resist a bargain. I managed to flog it on the

172

sly for about seventy-five grand, that's when I bought this plane. Might as well work sitting down and it keeps me off the demon booze. Do you know what happened then? Little chap comes along and says, Could he have some more *money*? What for? I cried in much distress, sort of get-thee-hence, know what I mean? For the Spit, sir. Ao, I said, what Spit was that?

"Turns out the old man bought this Mark Five Spitfire and was restoring it. Sometimes I fondly imagine he was doing it for me, damn decent if he was, 'cos I spent most of m' time at Magdalen learnin' to fly and pollin' a punt. How much? It turns the loins to jelly just thinking about it, y' know. Couldn't tell if it was good money after bad, but if I can only finish her orf, she'll be worth half a million. Allock, can you imagine, he's doing every single nut and bolt and rivet and all of it has to be supervised by the CAA. Right now I don't know what to do, we need £44,000 to finish her and I just can't seem to find it. Most of my real friends are a bit strapped, like me, and those who aren't one wouldn't want for partners."

"Why don't you sell it as it is?"

"Lust. Plain lust! I want to fly it m'self, pay its way at exhibitions and film work. It's bound to lose money, I know it in my bones, but still, I mean, what can one *do*? Nowadays one needs a couple of million before anyone who's anyone will even speak to one. If you see what I – no, I must stop saying that, it's too silly."

"Are you married?"

"Why? Because I sound like a poofter?"

"No . . . er, I suppose I mean in spite of it."

St George laughed merrily. "I say, good thing I'm not, I'd have to toss you out. Or off, as they say. A rich woman, you mean? Thought about it, naturally, but it doesn't work. I call it auto-scrotumitis, letting them get the squeeze on you. Anyway all the gels whose families one actually knows seem to look like those revolting things they ride, have you noticed, same smell, everything? . . . I was born too late, I should have been one of the Few, the old boy would at least have been proud of me, downed in blazing glory over the Kentish Weald, a last transmission, 'Tell Felicity to forget me.' In those days they had to take you if you knew someone, *noblesse oblige*, y' know. I sometimes wonder if that's why he bought

173

the Spit, prang m'self out in something with a bit of pedigree."

"My old man was one of them," Stuart said with slight diffidence. "He survived the war but his best friend went down right at the finish, just over the Czech border."

"Really?"

"He didn't talk about it much, but he did say the Mark Five was the best, the very best. He was on Nines at the end, more power, more weight, not so delicate, he said. It made him sad to talk about it because I think he had such a good time. Life was very intense then, I suppose. Forcibly."

"That's it, exactly. I mean nowadays one can hardly be bothered to even gather-ye-rosebuds, um? Everything's so pale. Well, I want to change it, for me at least, and this is a start. I simply refuse to languish in a musty old manse and have people paying to murder the beasts and the grouse, I just won't do it. What did you say your name was?"

"Kody."

St George muttered cryptically, nodding his head. He took out another cigarette, looked at it in hostile surprise and fumbled it away again.

"Proposition," he added "Got one. For you. Might need pluck. Got pluck, um? Assume you haven't flown one before, but then who has? Listen! You give me £44,000 and I will give you a Spitfire. Mark Nine. About seventeen hours on the clock. All you have to do is go and sort of, er, pick it up, um? What do you say?"

After the last two days' bizarre events, Stuart now felt his mind begin to slide away. His nervous laugh in reply sounded inside like a madman's cackle. The North Sea slid blackly beneath them, faintly dotted with the lights of ships and fishing boats, while their little world in the muted cockpit seemed too remote from reality. Like the sums of money discussed in recent days.

"Unfortunately," Stuart answered with a bitter flavour, though secretly pleased to have an ear bent to his misfortune, "I've just become insolvent, otherwise your proposition would be irresistible. Would the Mark Nine in question be sitting upside down in a wood in Azerbaijan with only one wheel and a cannibalised engine?"

"As far as I know, not. And you can pay me later. What's more, if you don't want to keep it, Tuffy Beauchamp is

174

looking for one so I can guarantee you a buyer the moment it's liberated, so to speak."

"Tell me more, do!" Stuart thought of Lucy and kept the sardonic laughter in his voice, but St George was quite serious.

"Are you current, your licence, or grounded by poverty?"

"I – no, it's lapsed." Stuart decided not to mention his paltry 15 hours student training from two years before.

"Well, just paperwork, red tape. Shouldn't take you long to get it back, might get arrested without it, that's all, pity if you're just then in the money." He shook his head in the gloom disbelievingly. "You often hitch like this?" Without waiting for an answer, St George changed tack and blundered on, though his head turned in a ceaseless sweep for other traffic.

"Unfortunately there's no two-seaters left, there was one flying but it's being converted back, some purist reason."

"You mean Spitfires, I take it?"

"Airce," came the answer, presumably "yes." "Look, won't say any more, false hopes and so on, but if you can scrape up to get current, we might be in business. Give me your phone number and I'll make some more enquiries. What d'you do, by the way, reg'lah job?"

"No."

"Splendid." St George touched the squelch on his No. 1 Com Set, listened a moment and reported crossing the English coast south of the Wash. He was cleared on his way with a height change which he described as "vexing". A little later he returned briefly to the subject while Stuart tried to ward off his own disbelief and discomfort at St George's presumption. He understood later that it was a mannered habit, allowing people to correct wrong impressions rather than seeming to pry for personal details, and Stuart, in his confusion, had failed to disabuse him.

"Been meaning to rustle up one of those Air Display wizards to brief me, but waiting till me own Spit was nearer the mark. If you beat me to it, I should vomit. You fly something hot in the RAF or anything?" When Stuart admitted he hadn't, St George shrugged. "Well, it's only a plane, that's what I tell myself. I say, what d'you think about those dreadful Australians trouncing the Yanks?"

Twenty-five minutes later they joined the Kidlington cir-

175

cuit, exceptionally busy with students on night training. St George muttered something derogatory about showing the ropes to dago fighter pilots and that they were usually confined to Perth or at least Tuesdays; somehow he jostled the Seneca in among the erratic patterns of the slower Cherokee and Tomahawk trainers, then his wheels locked down and kissed the grass with rare delicacy.

He taxied to the CSE tower and made an abrupt decision. "I'll stay the night with Tuffy, in town. Listen, forget the fifty, go and work on your pluck, here's my card. Where's your place?"

"Carsey. Half an hour. I'll get a taxi."

"Splendid." He flipped a frequency and thumbed the transmit button. "Oxford Grind, Ground sorry, can you get on the trombone and rustle up a couple of cabs, good chap?"

The tower came back with a laconic affirmative as if they were quite used to him but St George took it in his stride without a smile. He put on the park-brake, checked the panel and the cut-offs then leaned out the mixtures. The Lycomings faded out with sharp contractions.

It was shortly after eleven when he got home but there were no lights showing. The front door was locked but the car was there and the kitchen door open. It was a joy that there were still parts of the country where you didn't need to lock things, but now it struck him forcibly that they were being naïve in their poor defence against intruders. While pleased to know about her skill, he felt it was up to him that she should never have to use it.

He crept in, drank a long swig of orange juice from the fridge to take the staleness from his mouth and then went quietly upstairs. In the darkened room he could hear the faintest of breathing and the slight familiar scent. It seemed an agony of relief to have her sweetness to await him after his bewildering and crushing experience, the lamb sent to slaughter, or tethered as Bear-bait, he thought bitterly.

After a furtive undressing he slid under the duvet with minimal disturbance, on the opposite side from the breathing. This was her normal side and he wondered if she wanted a swap. Lying quietly in an attempt to settle his thoughts, he became aware that her breathing had changed, was still changing, then it stopped, an alert for listening. A small

176

movement, a hand reaching out tentatively, then fluid as a sidewinder she slithered herself across his body in murmurs and caresses. All the problems and strain assumed minor roles; he said nothing but simply held her, wondering what limit there could be to love, the vanishing point when one simply evaporated at the peak of tolerance, the final brush-stroke from the hand of the artist of creation.

Later in the night, Lucy whispered, "I want to go for a check-up."

"What do you think that was?"

"Ha, ha."

"Sorry . . . What for, do you think you're –?"

"No, for my heart. I don't think I can stand any more of this. I thought I was going to die then, of heart failure. I can feel it, it sort of slithers around inside my chest like a greasy fried egg. Just before."

"Mine does that sometimes. Perhaps I better ask someone."

"No, don't! He might tell us to stop it, not to risk it . . . I think Queen Victoria thought it was too good for the common people, do you suppose it's like this for everyone? It frightens me a little, that making love could almost distract me from loving you."

"I've only just got home, I've had a hard day and you're telling me all your problems already, for heaven's sake!"

Lucy smothered his face with kisses, relaxing and then renewing her concern. "Hey, there's a bump on your head, what have you done?"

"You won't believe me but I fell down in the road. Someone made off with my bag."

"I'm surprised they'd dare, but I believe you, *lyubimy*. So you went down gamely, fighting for a couple of pairs of underpants?"

"Sure. It's the principle."

"I suppose . . . Any other damage?"

"My knee and elbow, but they're OK. I got the handle. Next time I'll just let go."

"Promise?"

"Promise. Have you been good?"

"No, very wicked and I'm not going to tell you about it. You can't be the only one to have secrets, I've decided and Russians are particularly crazy about them. You were right."

"Their own or other people's?"

"Both, but mostly their own. If you know something others don't, you've got the drop on them, or at least some status. Anyway, mine's only a surprise for you. You remember the parable of the Ten Talents?"

"Yes . . . it conflicted with the ban on usury."

"Never mind that. It was you who mentioned the lump sum; you see, if I had some money I could make some with it and then you'd love me a bit more because you could give up this dangerous work you do, luring bag-snatchers and so on. And coming back all pent-up after days and nights away has got to be bad for you as well as for me, surely?"

"I love you."

"That's all you've got to say? I suppose I believe you. But then I'm all you've got, aren't I?"

"Just about. I want to . . ."

"What? Hey, don't fall asleep, I haven't finished talking. Hey! Oh, all right." Her last thoughts before sleeping were all about risks, how frightened they were for each other because the loss would be too great to bear. If there was a child at least something would be left to a shattered survivor, but for the thousandth time she told herself you can't think like that, you have to live, be alive, take all of it. The bomb could be tomorrow or next week and for her would make any reservation seem ridiculous. And the Kremlin had recently given assurances that they wouldn't use it first . . . She was surprised the Americans hadn't come back with an assurance that they *would* do it first – what the hell difference did it make? She shook her head in bewilderment at such fatuity and remembered a Western where a gunfighter, explaining why he'd just shot someone after promising not to, said simply, "Well, I lied."

She was still smiling as a huge slow wave of euphoria tumbled her back into oblivion.

Twelve

Love is God and God is everything. Even a bomb
in a shoe-shop.

Lucy

It was frying bacon which roused Stuart the next morning.
He awoke with a smile that seemed to spread his face apart
but he became aware of it and promptly frowned before
getting up and lurching through to the bathroom. Lucy crept
in behind him as he finished brushing his teeth, putting cold
hands softly on his waist. He tried not to react but couldn't
disguise the charge it gave him. He rinsed his mouth and
turned to her.

"What is it now?" he asked sternly, then smiled, "I was
just thinking how worrying it can be to be happy."

"So what do you want to do about it, buddy boy? Wonder
or worry, such is your choice. And what is desire all about?
It strikes me that people are mostly happy in retrospect.
The only way to cope is not to care, not to seek safeguards,
just to be satisfied whatever happens – since it's going to
happen anyway, whatever your attitude. A test case is right
now: would you prefer to be about to eat bacon, to be eating
bacon or to have just eaten it? Or can you enjoy each stage
in equal measure as you come to it?"

"It's a metaphor? Would you prefer to be about to make
love, to be –"

She slipped away. "Come on down, it's ready. Shower afterwards."

"OK. What's this?" He held up the hand mirror with the
sketch on it.

"I was wondering when you were going to notice that.
What do you think it is?"

"I don't know, it's just a nice shape."

179

"Describe it."

"Well, it's somehow churchy, church window, or a statue, an angel's wings. An ikon."

"Bingo. What else?"

"Trick question?"

"No. Come on down, I'll show you." She went out and double-thumped down the stairs, making him flinch as usual. With a spontaneous reverence, he replaced the little mirror on the dressing table, pondering a few moments as if at a mystery.

In the kitchen she laid the volume of the *Thousand and One Nights* alongside his place, translating lines followed with the breadknife. After her explanation of *historia*, he stopped eating and looked at her with awe.

"Amazing," he said, and then asked quizzically, "What does it look like when she's not a virgin?"

"Oh, ghastly! Here it is, just above: *'... aparecerá hinchada y abierta cuál un abismo, y también verás que se empaña el espejo,'* – 'it will appear swollen and open like an abyss and also you'll see the mirror steam up,' Just as well, if you ask me." She gave a tinkly laugh and shut the book.

"And the reverence, is it conditioning or instinct, do you think?"

"I think it's instinct, hence the universal appeal of the shape. I remember I was at an exhibition last year and the artist was trying to chat me up, in fact he took me round explaining a few things, what he meant by this and that. They love to shock you, it's their vanity, so I had a great time. Anyway, there were several sexy paintings but one of them did have a peculiar attraction in spite of being messy and obscure. When I said so, he whispered oh, so intimately that all the women went for that picture but they didn't know why, and that he'd show me if I promised etcetera. I remember now, he was thin and his name was Bones. Well, near the middle of the picture was an egg-shape with a dot in it, 'What's that?' he demanded with a piercing eye, pointing. I shrugged so he told me, 'It's the head of a penis, looking at *you*, that's what!' In his excitement he forgot to whisper and people shushed at him. And he told me about El Greco, who was highly religious of course, but one of his, in Toledo I think, has a man doing something manipulative through his saintly robe. He said people chose not to notice it."

180

"In Church?"

"Why not? Didn't you, once upon a time?"

"Er, yes actually. It must have been all those windows and statues."

"Exactly. Here endeth the lesson. Now eat your bacon."

Stuart tasted and rolled his eyes. "It's Sunday," he said suddenly. "Are you working?"

" 'Course not. But, um, I've arranged to go off somewhere."

"Secret?"

"Yep."

Stuart put his head down to disguise the sudden dark, roiling fear that swept through him. He remembered Simonov saying that Lucy had received the Russians and had acted her repudiation for the British microphones. He had ignored it at the time. Should he mention it now? In spite of his own incessant urge to tell her everything, especially the meeting with her father, he again held back because of his earlier resolution and he knew it would be too complicated to tell only part of it.

"Weren't you going to get another car?" she asked ingenuously. "I don't want to leave you stuck. Do you need it?"

"No thanks, it's all right. I'll be able to read the papers in peace without all the usual interruptions and clamouring for attention. When are you going?"

"Ten minutes"

"Church?"

"Don't pry. Church is only one of the places where people get up to things. I will admit something though." She came and put a hand on his shoulder.

"What's that?"

"Since you're here, I don't really want to go. I'm torn. I love being here with you."

"Tough," he said, pretending hardness, but he put his hand on hers and leaned his head into it. Quietly he added, "You in for dinner?"

"Sure." She held his head, kissing the top of it. "I'll be back about seven, I expect, or earlier."

"Lu, your mum's a bit stodgy at times, where did you get all your zing?"

"I don't think she was always like that, she was good fun

181

when I was little. She's half Finnish and they're all a bit wild. And my father was half Jewish, or is, I suppose. I never told you that, did I? But you're a mix yourself."

He nodded and grinned up at her. "They say mongrels have the most character."

"Right. I was thinking if it all got broiled up enough, racism and nationalism would disappear but actually what would probably happen is that all the mixes would get together and form a new country called Outer Mongrelia or something and defy the rest of the world with their own racial exclusiveness. They'd have to, just to have someone to be different from. If the Brits for instance would only admit to being half-French, they'd get on with them a lot better. Look, I must go."

"Well, keep it safe, whatever it is."

"And yours."

He was left almost startled when she'd gone and the day stretched ahead emptily. The name Simonov was burning holes in his head and he forced away the urge to pick up the phone and bleat to Antwerp. He cast around for a moment before remembering St George. At least it pointed the way towards something to occupy him which required full concentration.

He picked up the telephone and was nearly through dialling when he remembered the listeners. Almost self-consciously he replaced the receiver and walked round to see Horrocks; his portly friend always stuck to the pub and television on Sundays and agreed equably to lend his car. Stuart was back at Kidlington airfield before midday, noticing that St George's Seneca was still there. Half an hour later, his medical certificate fortunately still current by a few weeks, he was airborne in a Cherokee trainer for an hour's dual and re-appraisal to go solo. Then they sent him on a cross-country with two landings away, Sywell and Thruxton, although he'd done it twice before, but quelling his annoyance at the unnecessary expense just for completed "hours", finally set him off on a course of reactive extravagance.

Something his father had said compounded it; "Under real pressure, go for broke." He had naturally resisted the notion until this moment but now it gave him wry amusement to

182

wonder how much pressure was required or how broke you had to be. After landing, he went to the helicopter school and signed on at once. After an hour in the classroom he was defiantly airborne in a Bell 206 on his first familiarisation flight. It was nearly £200 per hour, and they were going to ask for his passport as surety for payment until a tired-looking instructor said he'd seen him arrive the previous evening with the Hon. Wennersley-Farquhar. Without another word they simply opened an account for him, much to his amusement, and then a club member who was going abroad offered him a fifth-hand Datsun 280Z at a fraction of its worth. Stuart gaily haggled to half the figure and succeeded, although Lucy later described the car, condescendingly, as "frightfully phallic".

He arrived home just before her and they greeted each other with sly smiles especially after she had spotted the pile of untouched newspapers. Each admitted to having had a nice day but with no details. Stuart still wanted to know why she hadn't told him about the approach made to her while he'd been in Antwerp but he couldn't reveal his knowledge of it. He also wanted to ease her mind with the information that Patrick Grady hadn't committed suicide but he couldn't tell her that either without her demanding to know who had murdered him. Lucy's very infrequent references to her father might have been indifference or the result of some locked-in suffering, he couldn't tell, and he didn't want to probe once he'd given her enough opportunity to discuss it. If the two men in her life before him had both let her down badly, he felt wildly fortunate that they didn't seem to have soured her, even apart from the influence of her mother's own disillusion.

Surprisingly, the opening came from her when she called through from the kitchen. He went and stood in the doorway as she began to peel potatoes.

"Mama said something about a special new section, Double-U, or something. Are you allowed to tell me about it?"

"How did she know?"

Lucy shrugged. "She didn't say, but she sounded a bit foxy."

"That's possible," he said pointedly. He went in and

183

elbowed her gently aside, taking the peeler from her and turning up the flow from the water-tap.

"It was a guess, maybe," Lucy parried. "There was nowhere else to look. Something about a watchdog department, created by the PM to stop all the nonsense. Can't you turn the tap down?"

"In a moment. Did she get in touch with them?"

"No, she couldn't, that was the problem, apparently it's all anonymous. You're well protected there, that is if – but listen, what happens if I *really* need you?"

Stuart raised an eyebrow but surprisingly she didn't wait for an answer. "It's all right, I'm sure I can manage and it's nice to know you're safe, from the daily ring – if you remember to do it. Mind you, any more lumps and cuts and I won't think it safe. Why are you wasting so much water?"

He turned the tap down and changed the subject. "Apart from this rapid daily job, are you going to be busy every weekend as well?"

"I don't know yet, it depends." She flashed a smile at him. "What about you?"

"I'll try to go nine-to-five for a bit," he said, thinking of his flying training. "Takes some getting used to, doesn't it?" He threw away the peels and dried his hands, then Lucy shoo'd him out, suggesting a drink. He assumed the white noise of the running tap had drowned their questions but he found his eyes constantly scanning walls and crannies in the vain hope of spotting a planted bug. He determined to get them removed as a priority. He wasn't yet clear about telling someone in SIS about the Russians tapping into the British surveillance system since it would mean disturbing the absurd status quo, but his biggest problem seemed to be how to get in touch with someone in the mysterious W section. He wondered if the man Adrian Stayres might know.

Somehow, he realised, he must ingratiate himself enough to provide bona-fides for some effective deal with Simonov, if only to recover enough to avoid total ruin and Rollo's disgusted fury even after he'd fronted the bail money. In spite of his expensive commitment that day, he was old enough to be sceptical of any hope from St George's wild and only half-stated proposal, yet the man's infectious eccentricity had provided sufficient inducement to resume flying lessons even in the face of poverty. The further inclusion of the hideously expensive helicopter training was out of character, he knew, yet now that it was begun, he actually felt more lighthearted about his disastrous loss, like shedding a winter skin. Finally, though, he knew it was Lucy and the thought of surprises for her which coloured every move.

She came through then and found him staring at the wall.

"Why so preoccupied, or can't you talk about it?" she asked lightly. "You were going to get us a drink."

"Yes, coming up." He jerked back to normality, to be promptly thrown again by her next remark.

"You know, I've been thinking they might deceive us into deceiving each other."

He looked at her, startled. "Who might?"

"The people whose business it is to deceive. I call them the Ministry of Misinformation."

"With respect, my love, what do you know about it? I mean, who is them?"

"The professional deceivers who work for all the governments, you must know the kind I mean. I'm not trying to find out what you've been doing, but somebody did come and offer to tell me, isn't that amazing?"

"Why on earth would they do that? Who was it, anyway?"

She gave him an enormous, exaggerated wink and said, "Now that is something I can't tell you . . . but only because they didn't say."

She took his hand and led him out to the front door. The expected warm front had arrived and they could hear the rain spattering lightly in the dark so they went out together under the umbrella.

"If you bugged all the umbrellas in England, you'd have all the world's secrets in a week," she said, holding tightly to his arm. "Darling, the house is once more bugged. It must be something to do with you, but I was approached again, sermons about détente, doing my bit, expensive education, all that stuff. I told them what they could do with it. They said 'all right', but perhaps if I could at least get you to talk inside the house, some good would come of it because you are in a very sensitive spot. I don't know how you became so important so quickly but I always said you were wonderful, didn't I? But listen, I don't like it, I don't want any of it, I don't trust any of it, or them – and I don't want bugs in the house. So is there some way we can get them to Gomorrah off?"

185

"You mean you refused to co-operate?" Stuart felt a flood of gratitude, not needing to ask the question.

"Of course, absolutely. They only need the merest 'yes' to get you started, that's all, then you're mainlining in a month. My so-called husband Grady told me all about it, that's how they got him, they were going to use him to compromise me. That's why the booze and the violence. I wouldn't go along with it, do you see? He was backed into a hole but I couldn't get him out. I keep wanting to ask what's happening with you. I fear the same pressures although I trust you completely, it's quite different. Just tell me we'll be all right, that we can keep them away. My little secrets are different, that's just fun. Just secrets, not deceits, yes?"

"Sure. You're shivering, shall we go back?" As they turned, he asked casually, "Was your father part of it?"

He felt rather than saw her nod. "They miscalculated there. I was eleven or twelve when he was thrown out and I had no contact with him anymore. I remember him as great fun, very playful and bright, but Mama was already separated from him so it was infrequent visits, then none at all. I got used to it and there was very little time for brooding anyway, too busy. After University, maybe during, the first time the Embassy approached me I gave them a flea in the ear and later they came back saying I could see my father very often if I'd agree to work for them."

"What were you supposed to do?"

"Get recruited by the West, I think. Fortunately it meant little to me, the time for missing my father had gone. Anyway, I didn't like the visits. I liked it when he lived with us, but I think he was very randy, I smelled different perfumes sometimes, mother crying and so on. Not much fun really."

"What about my question?"

"Was he part of it? I don't know, but almost certainly. You get so little out of these diplomatic types, they ought to sew up their mouths, all except one corner for speaking surreptitiously out of."

Stuart chuckled. "Crytomaniacs, your word. Who told you about the listening devices?"

"Nobody, but it's a reasonable assumption since they asked me to get you to talk. I don't want people listening to us making love, it's too private, too sacred. Anyway, I like a good howl now and then and it puts me off."

"Didn't last night."

"Hee, you crept up on me and then I forgot about them. God, I feel all trembly just thinking about it. Tonight I'll stuff a sock in my mouth."

She giggled and hung on his arm outside the gate. "Dinner first, roast potatoes, it's absolute heaven having someone nice to be nice to, don't you think?"

"Very nice, yes."

"Indeed. Just one thing, before we go in?"

"Um?"

She spoke with unusual vehemence, clutching him. "I'm not going to play at all. I won't even follow the game. If anyone tries to make me, I'm gone, and that applies too if anyone tries to use you to compel me. I'll be gone. I'll die first, I'll lose everything first."

Stuart swallowed. "Why don't you tell them?"

"I did. They know it. You make sure everyone knows, OK? That makes you safe as well."

"How do you mean?"

"Just treat me the same way. Just go. No regrets, we'll hold on to our spirits, we'll be dolphins, you remember the joy of them around *Sailor*'s bows? They're unique, you know, they have no enemies. Fearless life . . . I'll be a Bottle-nose dolphin and . . . hey, what about that drink?"

"A secret one?"

"Yes, with Sch . . . the phone's ringing."

He left the umbrella in her hand and hurried inside.

"Hair?" The voice was unmistakable. "Kody?"

"Oh, St George. Where are you?"

"Oxford still. Why'nt you come and have some dinnah?"

"Because ours is in the oven. Why don't you come here? Just a minute." He turned as Lucy came in shaking out the brolly. "Have we got enough for a third?"

When she paused and nodded confidently, he said, "Yes, plenty. St George, come on over."

"Áo. You didn't tell me you were married."

"I wasn't hiding it. Here's how you come." He gave him directions and glanced to see if Lucy was out of the room. Quietly he added, "Don't mention your proposition, will you?"

"Ah. Nary a word."

Stuart poured two Scotches and took them through to the

kitchen. Lucy was laughingly incredulous at St George's name. "It's not just the name, you may not be able to understand his speech. Rather far back."

"Oh, don't worry, my school was full of them. Where did you meet him?"

"On a plane somewhere."

"Oh. Would you set another place for me?"

When St George arrived in a borrowed car he was impeccably dressed as before, this time wearing brogues, a coarse-weave sports jacket and a Guards tie. Lucy looked up at his gangly height, taking the raised eyebrows and the thin nose which seemed almost to quiver with sensitivity. After shaking hands and being offered a drink, St George endeared himself at once by looking carefully round the drawing-room and instead of a predictable remark said simply, "Non-smokers. Good, then I won't."

He turned to Stuart and said, "Couldn't go. Weather's gone clampers up north. Saw you in the Bell, thought I'd look you up."

"Oh, where's the Bell?" Lucy asked with a smile, "Nice barmaid?"

"Oxford," Stuart answered crisply.

St George's head went back sharply on his long neck, a deep crease of suspicion almost theatrically dispelled when he caught Stuart's wink. Lucy excused herself without noticing it and went to the kitchen.

St George said almost hoarsely, "What an *enchanting* lady. Walks like a dancer. Are you deceiving her?"

"Not really. It's a surprise. I would have told you not to mention the helicopter but I didn't realise you'd seen me there. She doesn't know about the flying. We're having secrets, it's fun."

"God, yes." St George nodded eagerly like a schoolboy planning a midnight feast.

"And I wasn't in Antwerp, OK? And I'm not broke, either."

"God. Anything else? Don't want to put the old foot in it."

"That'll do for now."

"When are you going to tell her?"

"I may not have to if I can recoup my losses, if there's

188

anything in this scheme of yours. When are you going to tell me more?"

"You can't get hold of people on Sundays, they're all shooting."

Stuart raised an eyebrow at the wondrous narrow-thinking but St George was oblivious. "Secrets," he said, "I don't know how you can *bear* it. I'd get too excited, I just know I'd blurt!"

Lucy came back in then and reclaimed her drink. "You've gone silent," she said. "What were you talking about?"

"About you, my love and what you were up to this afternoon."

Lucy whirled on him in a flash but then saw their bland faces. "If I thought you'd been spying," she said, and left the sentence unfinished. St George looked quite delighted. "Ooh, what fun!" he said, his face squeezed in delight.

Lucy gave him a quizzical look and retreated to the kitchen again. St George leaned back in his chair to check she was out of earshot, trying to peer round the door.

"What *were* you doing in Antwerp, you didn't say?" he asked in a low voice.

"Secret."

St George's head went back again in sharp surprise before he grinned. "Ah. Like I shouldn't have told you about the deceiving the Taxman with the old boy's carpet investment?"

"That's right. You should have made something up. I might have been a freelance tax-inspector for all you know."

"God. Somehow one doesn't meet people like that in the normal run. What do you do really?"

Stuart felt his exuberance growing. "I spy," he said from the corner of his mouth.

"Oh, no! You mean peep and tell, informer?" St George chortled. "I say, that's really disreputable. Good thing I don't believe you."

Lucy came back in then and said, "If we tried to catch each other out, would that make it even more exciting?"

"You're not allowed to pry, Lu. They'd have to lock you up. And as for yours, I don't want to know because it's probably something dangerous. Just knowing that gives me a sharp pain in my nethers when I think of it. St George you had a word for it?"

"Oh, I say, *pas devant*." St George inclined his head respectfully towards Lucy. "A crudity. But it didn't mean that exactly, it meant the direct action of the squeeze."

Lucy seemed awkward using his name. "Er, St George, I'm not squeamish."

"P'raps not, m'dear, but I am. Anyway, the thing about secrets is that you have to have someone to keep secrets from, otherwise they have no value."

"That's true. Dinner's ready, if you are."

As they sat, St George said, "Have you told, ah, Lucy what I do?"

"No, I don't think so."

A wolfish expression crossed his face when he saw she was busy at the sideboard with her back to him. "I'm a gun-runner," he said in a deep bass tone for a sinister edge, then more brightly. "I liked the sound of it. I really wanted to be an absolute bounder, one of those awful jet-set voguey photographers, I'd use my title shamelessly, spend my life peering at naked females and lunching with the chic. I even bought a wizard camera with all the kit, but I'm just no good at it, the composition and so on. And naked ladies make me shake, rather. The secret I'm sure is what the pros do, they have about five cameras with engines in them, you rattle off about three hundred shots and slope off to the dark-room to see if you got a good one. Emerge triumphant and all that, claim your prize."

Lucy turned and beckoned to him. "Come and help yourself to vegetables. So you've got a title as well as being, what is it, canonised?"

"My dear, do I detect just the right hint of mockery in your expression? I'm afraid the old boy's passing made me a baronet, yes. Sir St George is a bit much so nobody bothers."

"How did you manage at school with it, surely they must have razzed you half to death?"

"Ah, well, at places like Eton and Marlborough, the snobbery works differently. It's quite out of order to notice eccentricity, it's almost *de rigueur* to have one. Down in the village of course you just had to stick your nose in the air and pretend there was no one about. One is not aware at the time of snobbery's existence, it's just us and them and quite right, too, if you see what I – oh, sorry. Anyway, it took a long time to discover there was another point of view."

"I suppose poverty helped," Stuart ventured.

190

"Oh, no, not at all. It's quite acceptably eccentric to be broke, merely a trifle inconvenient."

"Is gun-running acceptably eccentric?"

"Oh, absolutely. There's the slight social stigma that the business is full of very dubious types, Red Infiltrators, Marxist saboteurs, Cuban murderers, bog-trotting knee-cappers and so on."

"Of that ilk."

"Quite so. Comrade Kalashnikov has come up with a new one, the AK74 to replace the 47. Smaller bullet but ultra-fast, and tumbling. Makes a revolting mess. He must have a very dubious turn of mind, don't you think? An extremely sinister-sounding name, too. But then even the word Russia sounds sinister in English, don't you think? If it was called Florida or Steppes to Heaven, one might want to visit it and other people would have a different attitude to it, don't you think? It must be a dreadful place. I mean, just on the sound, one would rather drop anchor in Peacehaven than say, Grimsby, don't you think?"

"Yes," Lucy said firmly. "And if we call you a gentleman gun-runner, that should cancel the stigma."

"Oh, rather."

Stuart said, "In turn, you might think of ex-Ludmilla, my lady, as a Russian flower, transplanted."

St George stopped with a forked roast potato in mid-hoist. He looked from one to the other without moving his head, then put the fork down.

"God," he said in a low voice, "I'm trying to remember if I said anything horrid."

Lucy laughed and reassured him but St George continued frowning. "I don't think there is one."

"What?"

"A Russian national flower." He saw her head shake in agreement. "If all the Russian ladies looked like you, we'd have an instant war for the oldest reason. I have a feeling they don't, though. But in any place, if there are enough women and enough home comforts to lure them with, you don't need to fight, do you?"

"Stuart would agree," Lucy said, "to him almost every action has a sexual motive, as long as the urge lasts. But tumbling bullets and expressions like 'overkill', 'megadeath', 'nuke 'em', they're simply obscenities."

Stuart sensed that St George wanted to tell Lucy he wasn't really a gun-runner and was torn up by the game of secrets. He changed the subject for his sake and the meal finished amiably.

At one moment, while Stuart was out of the room, Lucy whispered, "St G., can I borrow, or rather rent your camera?"

He agreed readily, sensing a conspiracy and squeezing his face in delight when he confirmed it with a finger to her lips. He said he would phone first and bring it to her. He left at half-past nine and promised to come again, his gaze lingering.

"I think he was rather taken with you. Perhaps you're a born lady," Stuart said later, but Lucy declared archly that she preferred to have become *his* lady than to have his Lordship thrust upon her, so to speak.

"And since you've started going away, I'd like our evenings shorter and the nights longer, like in Russia. I want to go up into our lair, share a lair. It isn't boring for you?"

The idea was so sweetly naïve to Stuart that he felt he must avoid a cliché. He looked at her without expression then went to his desk, pulled out an old cigar box and emptied it of keys and assorted junk. COMPLAINTS, he wrote on the lid with a red felt marker, holding it out for her to see it was empty before putting it on the mantelpiece. He knew from her clasping reaction that he was learning the kind of unpredictable caprice that delighted her and he hoped the ideas would always come lively. And flowers aren't the only way of saying you remember, he thought, when next day Lucy was delighted to receive a young silver birch, the Russian national tree, consigned according to barely legible scrawl, by Mr Wednesday Farker. She gave it a daunting inspection and a heavy pep-talk like a Soviet Sergeant-Major before allowing it to join her growing regiment. Stuart had often seen her berating a less than vigorous plant, brooking no excuses and sometimes digging them up and moving them even at the wrong time of the year. She called it punishment yet was so solicitous with her transplants that she had no failures; nevertheless he could almost feel for them when she did her rounds, clumping in her wellies and glaring at the border with beady suspicion.

Thirteen

Lucy: "All the accidents in life are caused by men –"
St George W-F: "Oh, I say, that's not fair."
Lucy: "– by men taking their trousers off!"

Number 3 Carlton Gardens overlooks Pall Mall and St James's Park but Stuart reflected it would be a lot more pleasant if you didn't have to look out through sneaky net curtains. Adrian Stayres received him affably enough and ordered coffee for them both, saying, "Nice of you to come."

"It wasn't really. I wanted to find out what you knew about me and how."

"A curious anomaly about being completely under wraps. By elimination: if you've looked everywhere else, there's only one place you can be. There were enquiries, as you know, and it may have been assumed because of your Czech that you must be in my department. Naturally I scoured the various corridors and found no trace of you and since there is apparently only one outfit which for obvious reasons isn't going to divulge the names of its personnel, you, Stuart Kody, would appear to have been found out."

"What?"

"Come, don't let's hedge. You have to be working for them, have to be. W Section. Lloyd George did something similar back in twenty-two, it was called the garden suburb, he had prefabs in the grounds of Number Ten for all his sneaky people. I don't need to tell you it was extremely unpopular. Kennedy had something like it. Surprised you didn't succumb to the temptation to brag to your wife about it."

Stuart looked away thoughtfully. Two tattered and hardly airworthy-looking pigeons were entwining grubby necks on the window-sill, one of them pecking the other repeatedly.

"So what do you want from me?" Stuart asked eventually.

"Ah. Two things, actually. I'd like to know if your chaps are watching any of my chaps, if there's any suspicion about us. We're finding irregularities in some incoming messages about which we can do nothing at the moment. Obviously we process our stuff and pass on what's relevant. We believe the fault's at source, but possibly someone else believes the misinformation starts here. Do you know?"

"I don't," Stuart answered with feigned concern. "I could try to find out, I suppose. How extraordinary!"

"What is it?" Stayres turned to follow Stuart's gaze at the two net-blurred pigeons, one of which was on the other's back, kneading away steadily with its feet. "Oh, that. They're always at it."

"Yes, but the one doing all the pecking and nudging is the one underneath. Feminine aggression."

"Hmph . . . find out, you said. Splendid. Very good of you to take it like that. Would you say a whole sentence for me in Czech?"

Stuart frowned for a moment and then spoke very rapidly.

> *"Papír bíly, až to zebe,*
> *Jeník po něm chodí bos,*
> *Z modré barvy stoupá nebe,*
> *v černe křídla koupá kos,*
> *v žluté se sluníčkem bzucí*
> *zralá hruška plná bos."* *

Stayres looked bewildered. "I didn't understand a word, hardly. What was it?"

"Hrubin. A kind of nonsense nursery rhyme, unusual for Czechs. 'Little Johnny walks barefoot on white paper, feeling like it's freezing.' It goes on about a blackbird and a ripe pear full of wasps."

"Metaphor?"

"For what?"

"Nest of vipers, something like that?"

"Oh . . . could be."

"Don't." There was iron in Stayres voice warning him not to push, though he continued affably. "Well, your accent seems faultless. Do you have Russian as well?"

* František Hrubin. Říkejte Si Pohádky. (Melantrich 1943.)

"No, hardly at all. The odd word. It's compulsory in school although they're not keen to learn it. I didn't go to school there."

"Ah. Well, to my second point. I can pay some special rates for one-off jobs even though our basic salaries are meagre, so if you should feel like doing a little moonlighting for us, your language would be a great boon, not to mention your special skills. You didn't even go to our nursery school in Gosport: where do they send you for your small-arms and hand-to-hand?"

"I'm not allowed to say."

"Um. Johannesburg must be chilly at this time of the year." It was a statement rather than a question and Stuart made no response, although he felt more than mere flickers of apprehension.

"Do you know Prague well?"

"Fairly, but it's been a few years. I did some holiday exchanges at school and once a whole summer."

"Um. Have you got any leave coming up, do a little sort of trial run for us?"

"Well, I'm a bit tied up at the moment."

Stuart looked out of the window while Stayres played with a paper-knife. The two pigeons were side by side again, shuffling uncomfortably as if in the embarrassment of post-coital politeness.

"What I don't like," Stuart said, "is the fact that someone has bugged my house."

"Not guilty," Stayres said quickly, before adding, "Your own people, perhaps?"

"No, it can't be. I have it on the best authority that our section is still clean but the other side is plugged into your surveillance system. Thus they're not only getting the same information as you but they also know what you're getting."

"Absolute nonsense. And certainly not us."

"In that case how did you know I'd been in South Africa?"

"We just rang the airline, that's all."

"Why?"

"Because your family was trying to find you, remember? What an interesting stone it turned over – you working for W *and* married to an alien." Stayres looked as though it was an affront.

195

"Enough to get you interested in tabbing me, obviously."

Stayres bristled visibly. "We did nothing of the sort. I think your people could easily check it out and I'm perfectly willing. We can't sit here all day playing 'I-didn't-you-did'. Run along to Number Ten and tell them I'm just trying to do my job. I've got my very best operative holed up in Plzen, on the run with no papers and I've run out of retreivers."

"Do the other side know who he is?"

"Yes, I'm afraid they do."

"So he's expendable."

"Are you suggesting I *ditch* one of my own people? Why don't you get out of here!"

"Just testing," Stuart said easily, "Can't you go yourself?"

"I'm sure you know perfectly well that I was blown and ponged some time ago and I'm here because I wasn't expendable. We don't behave like that, it's counter-productive."

"Otherwise you would?"

"Believe what you like. But I'm quite confident about your listeners, they're not ours. Maybe it's the South Africans again. If you find out, do let me know. Now, if you'll excuse me?"

Stuart walked disconsolately through the park. He found a call-box but the bright sunlight made it insufferably hot with the door shut, the traffic too noisy with it open. After getting the number from enquiries, he made his first call with considerable misgiving and diffidence.

"Number Ten Downing Street," the voice said with brisk efficiency. "Can I help you?"

"I hope so. I want to speak to W."

"I'm sorry, I don't understand."

"Letter W, W Section chief, how can I find him?"

"One moment, please."

Stuart chewed his underlip nervously, wondering what was happening. After a while a youngish-sounding man came on the line, his voice very clipped.

"Can I help you? I'm Wicket, one of the Private Secretaries, you asked for W, alphabetical, is that right?"

"Yes, I have some interesting information."

"I see . . . I suppose you'd better come round and see me. Today, can you do that? Fine, about two o'clock, I'll leave your name at the door so you've no problem."

196

"You don't know it."

"Ah."

Stuart chuckled with relief and gave his name, then rang off and made another call to Kidlington to cancel his afternoon's flight training. It felt a pity to waste such a fine day. He strolled again in St James's Park, had a sandwich and a beer in a pub and was outside the door to Number Ten just before two o'clock. The barriers were up against the small collection of pedestrian sightseers and his arrival on foot brought preventive gestures from the constables on duty. They treated him with courteous suspicion until he gave his name, then the dark Georgian door was opened at once and he was met by a lively-stepping young man with a schoolboy face, wavy brown hair and an immaculate suit. His hand-shake was automatic and quick with reluctance, then he led him out of the small foyer with the Chippendale hooded chair into the inner hall. There was Gainsborough's *The Watering Place* but the young man plainly didn't want him to linger, taking him quickly to an office on the left and introducing himself as Julian Wicket.

He turned and leaned one hand on an elegant table-top. Behind him, the door was open to the sunlit garden, stirred by an afternoon breeze. "Now, if you'd like to tell me what you have to say, I might then be in a position to advise you whom to see."

"Thanks. I realised something on the way over here that if I don't present this correctly, I'm in danger of incriminating myself. The person I should be speaking to is, I think, in a sufficiently sensitive position that what I have to say shouldn't go beyond his department."

"But you can only be incriminated if you're guilty of some misdemeanour, surely?"

Stuart shrugged. "I need to speak to the head of W section, and no one else."

"Ah, well now, identities of certain section heads are completely under wraps, known only to a few cabinet ministers. We can't organise a meeting for you, we know nothing about you."

"I see." Stuart felt himself bristling at Wicket's supercilious manner. He said quietly, "You're an impudent little shit. Go and get someone else to speak to me, and you clear off."

Wicket was completely taken aback. He looked as though

197

he was going to retort when Stuart added, "You're a civil servant and that means you work for *me*." After a short pause Wicket turned and walked stiffly out of the room.

Stuart waited in silence for about five minutes, gazing out into the garden. A quiet and awesome dignity seemed to pervade the whole building until he heard voices and a stage cough from the doorway. Wicket was back, standing behind and to one side of a big-bellied, round-faced cheerful-looking character with a *pince-nez* hanging from a lapel-string. He was easily recognisable from the media pictures as James Breakspeare, the deputy Foreign Secretary, but realities often carry an unexpected jolt. Stuart felt intimidated, as though Wicket had reported him to the Headmaster for impertinence, but he managed to hold out his hand, giving his name himself. Wicket, his introduction not needed, quietly withdrew.

"I understand you have something to tell someone but you need a precaution," Breakspeare stated affably. "Unfortunately, we have to take precautions ourselves and we use all the means in our power to protect certain identities. As far as incrimination is concerned, you have my word that what you have to say will be treated in strictest confidence. First give me a little background, as quickly as you can because I have an appointment just now deferred for you."

"All right. I was out of the country recently on a private matter. I disguised it from my wife by telling her that I had a job with a secret Government department. The information got to others, to Adrian Stayres in SIS and also to the KGB. Stayres couldn't find me on any MoD or SIS staff lists and concluded that I must be working for this new W-Section. The KGB received the same information. My father-in-law is a Russian diplomat, or commercial attaché as he prefers me to think; he was one of those thrown out from here in '71 and he's now in Antwerp. I met him last week for the first time. He told me several things which could interest seekers of détente. Shall I go on?"

Breakspeare glanced at his watch. "Please do."

"Briefly, he said they didn't have a plant in W Section, they didn't even know any of the staff names until mine was handed to them. I did not deny that I was on the staff."

"Why on earth not?"

"Because I had to have something to bargain with, frankly, and I'm not so likely to be compromised."

198

"But as things are you can't be compromised at all. Ah, but they think you can, is that it?"

"Yes. I was attacked and robbed in Belgium and it could help greatly to leave him with his illusions. I'd rather not elaborate, if you don't mind. He implied threats as well as being friendly, which was rather confusing. Anyway, I made up a few harmless things out of the blue which seemed to please him a lot."

Breakspeare frowned suspiciously. "Such as?"

"I said that W was headed not by one but by two people, chosen deliberately for being hostile to each other."

"How extraordinary. What else did he want to know?"

"Nothing specific yet, though he wanted to know more about the section. He hoped to establish some kind of working system, a sort of mutual backscratching for what he called preventive medicine. He led me to believe that was his function, to head off embarrassments like the one which involved himself."

"Hmph." Breakspeare nodded ponderously and glanced again at his watch. "Your little acorn of deceit has grown branches already. You appear to have appointed yourself an unofficial double agent. Did he offer you money or stay with the pro-good-relations sermon?"

Stuart hesitated a moment and decided on the truth. "He offered me money, yes, but there's no arrangement yet. He told me not to tell you that."

"Fair enough. Let's say you didn't. What was your motive in trying to get in touch with this W, or in coming here?"

"It's a bit over my head, I wasn't sure of being able to keep up the front. I also felt there might be something worthwhile to be gained, simply because I am unofficial. As far as I know," he added with a rueful smile.

Breakspeare didn't respond to it but considered for a moment before finally shaking his head. "Very dangerous, very thin ice, I'd say."

"Well, supposing you gave me something quite untrue about this new section, I could pass that across for you."

"Hmph, main-chancing, aren't you? And you could double your money by *telling* him it was untrue ... Pointless, like a dog chasing its tail. No, I'm sorry, we cannot play this game or give you any status whatsoever ... You say Stayres believes it too?" He gave a short rasping chuckle. "That's

199

not bad, spread a little paranoia, keep the departments in line ... You said something about implied threats. Are you married? Oh, of course, it's your father-in-law ... Problems for your wife here? No? Good. You don't need to worry about threats, then."

"I'm not certain. He only threatened me if I hurt her but he also showed a ruthless side and he's pretty cynical."

"Right. I'll try and get a word in the Boss's ear but I'm certain we can't help you or give you any backing. That would have to be my advice, I'm afraid." Breakspeare looked at his watch again and made to leave.

"Just a minute," Stuart said quickly, "my house is wired. Simonov, that's his name, said they were British plants and that the KGB had tapped into your circuit. If you wanted to get something across –"

"Mr, er, Kody, I have to tell you that whatever you say is entirely your own business but I suggest you be very careful indeed."

Stuart's anger came near the surface. "In that case, I want the listening devices removed from my house immediately."

"Can't be ours, can't be. Look, I must bid you good day. Please leave your address and phone number with Master Wicket."

With a frown and a nod, Breakspeare reversed out into the hall and disappeared down the corridor towards the Cabinet Room. Stuart watched forlornly as he went, feeling devoid of support or encouragement. He was ready to explode at one wrong word from Wicket but the young secretary defused him with a timely apology.

"Mr Kody, I'm sorry for giving you offence."

"OK." Stuart took the proferred pad and wrote on it quickly, then gave it back and held out his hand. "Shake it properly, it means something if you mean it."

Surprised, Wicket did so and it was clear he felt a new response. Stuart was led courteously through the foyer and for a moment he considered sitting in the hooded chair, knowing he'd never come here again. "Doesn't look very comfortable," he said, pleasing Wicket with the conversational indulgence.

"No, sir, it isn't, but it's frightfully surreptitious."

Stuart had to smile at this and at the chair's placing near the door, the first object to be seen on entering. The sun had gone as he emerged past the constable's arm but he could see several cameras raised his way and not only at the line of placard-bearers, protesting about the Cruise missile delivery to Greenham Common. It gave him an eerie feeling and then his irritation with them all and his own apprehension suddenly flowered an idea which at first seemed stunning in its dimensions.

On the journey home he examined it from every angle available to his limited experience. He couldn't see any flaw and gradually realised he was feeling the dry-throated fear which comes the moment a dangerous dare is accepted. Since he even thought he had the means of pulling it off convincingly, he found himself driving faster and faster, hounded by the thought that Breakspeare's people might actually co-operate and remove the listening-bugs too soon, while his notion of the spiral seemed more perilous by its necessity, tightening in acceleration.

Roaring into the village he felt an instant let-down at the absence of Lucy's car, but inside the house was a note from her which he read shakily for the second time clutching at the kitchen table:

Gone to station to collect Mama. Don't be cross. Two calls.
1. Man called Hook (?) v mean 'n' moody, says he's got powers. Bully for him, I said. Told me not to interrupt! Says he knows how you did it. (Pry: did what?) Says you can double up, by the end of the month, or something about my Knees (???) Just rang off, his number on hall pad.
2. St G in Ox tomoro lunch.
3. Tonite you will be my Prisoner.
  Former slave and concubine.
                                    Burn this note.

Her lightheartedness evaded him in the face of another new crisis. He wondered helplessly if they'd damaged Rollo to get Powers' name or to discover their real method of running the stones. For a brief moment he even wondered if the two of them had planned it precisely that way from the beginning, using his ignorance. It was too uncomfortable a thought to dwell on, and no longer relevant.

Besides, he couldn't be absolutely sure that Simonov really

held the solution by possession of the cache of stones, but if the Russian appeared to have all the good cards, only Stuart's new idea held any hope of trumping them. Otherwise he could just about raise the bail money from his own property but little in the way of legal fees. For de Hoek's apparent double demand he had no resources at all, but it wasn't hard to understand the South African's fury at being duped with such apparent cunning. It even offended Stuart's image of himself to seem such an accomplished and professional liar.

Adding three hours to the time for Johannesburg, he reckoned de Hoek would have long left his office. Thinking of the initial faltering success ending in this impasse led him to the two "fancies"; on the phone, his lawyer confirmed that a declared package of spectacles for Alicia had in fact arrived. Stuart agreed to collect it from the man's home that evening although the news seemed incidental in the face of other pressures. He didn't consider the value of the coloured stones in his despair for a solution and even St George's airy promise of riches suffered similar jaundice.

He poured himself a drink and sat down to brood in the gathering gloom, noticing that Lucy had put the television on display as a kindness to Alicia; she would become distressed at the game of trying to find it, let alone its small size. He switched it on and got a weather forecast, a complex low pressure with another behind it, a firm pointer to high winds and rain, unflyable days for trainers. It merely added to his depressing thoughts since if de Hoek was inflexible about the time element, he had little over two weeks to raise the sum demanded – on top of Rollo's bail and legal fees. He had a crawling feeling about the mention of "knees" in the note but his mind refused to dwell on it. His anger began to feed on de Hoek speaking that way to Lucy; added to the thought of supplication to those conniving Russians, it charged his fury and frustration until his forearms began to ache, and he had to hide all of it when Lucy and her mother arrived. In the enforced calm he was later to feel fortunate that there was nothing to be gained by sharing his despair, since it would perhaps have dissipated this hardening anger.

Fourteen

Lucy came bubbling through the front door just as he put the lights on.

"Economising?" She kissed him heartily and said, "Mother's here, to cheer us up. Did you get my note – what was that about my knees, please?"

"I've no idea. I'll find out tomorrow, I expect." He pecked Alicia's proffered cheek.

"Well," Lucy went on. "We got held up by a protest march and then we had to stop for a very small, spiky animal. Mama says it's typically Western not to worry about ordinary chogs."

"What?" Stuart frowned but Alicia had gone into the cloakroom.

"Exactly my word. She said they only worry about the Head chogs! That's so silly, I told her, only Head chogs get run over. The others have rights and get protected."

Stuart struggled to match her mood. "Quite right," he managed to say seriously, in case Alicia could still hear.

"And she can't understand about the Greenham women, why the authorities don't remove them and lock them up. Or shoot them. When I told her it was the essence of this free society to be allowed to protest, she said that was why it was decadent."

Stuart nodded, surprised at the topical cue for his primary revelation. He followed her through to the kitchen and said quietly, "She's probably right. The trouble is they're all wasting their time."

"That's what I told her. Whatever your sympathy with

203

their principles, the thing is a *fait accompli*. What she won't admit is whether she voted in the Government which ordered the missiles in the first place. I told her what St George said and she was outraged."

"I didn't mean that." He kept his voice very low as if withholding something from Alicia rather than any outside listeners. "It's a waste of time because ... look, this is top secret, I really shouldn't tell you except, well, for peace of mind it's pretty incredible."

She arched her eyebrows quizzically, a smile playing as she opened the fridge and looked back at him.

"The missiles," he said. "They won't be *armed*."

After a moment's anxious incredulity, her face wrinkled up with delight. "What ... what happens when someone finds out?" She was on the edge of laughter.

"Who?"

"Well, let's say Them. The 'enemy', whoever they are?"

"It was the 'enemy' who gave them the idea in the first place. Why waste money on something unusable, which is to say if you ever have to use it, we're all up crappers' creek anyway?"

Lucy stood up and hung herself joyously on his neck. "It's a delicious secret. You must let me tell Mama."

"Lucy, no!" he hissed, looking over her shoulder.

"Why not?"

"Well ..."

"She won't tell a soul. I'll make her promise. Oh please, she'll be so thrilled."

"I really don't think you should."

"Oh, come on, please! It's too delicious."

After further pleading, he shrugged and relented. Lucy flew out of the room and he heard their exchange distantly, wondering how much conviction it would carry to the outside, and by which conduit. After a minute he went into the drawing room and Lucy stood up from arranging the fire. It was obvious she had forgotten about possible bugs, but Alicia was looking at him strangely.

She sat down and lifted the beady-eyed terrier. "But what will happen if our, if the Russians find out they are just dummies?"

Stuart gave a long enigmatic shrug while Lucy finished her bustling and lit the fire. Alicia persisted. "How could the

American President or the Senate do this without everyone knowing?"

"They didn't. They don't know about it, that's the point. It was natural selection, or if you like, natural corruption: the contractors got paid for warheads which they simply faked. Quite logical really, they figured that if they had to be used it was all over and they'd frankly rather spend the money on a yacht and a few mistresses and extra goodies like that."

"You mean they have explosive, conventional?"

"No, they've got nothing. There's no point in using ordinary explosive on a global scale because your oppo can't tell which one it is when it's coming at him. I doubt if he'd believe you if you tried to reassure him, so they reckoned they might as well leave them blank."

"Lyuba, what's *kompromis*?"

"Compromise."

"*Da*," she said, confused. "Compromise is good sometimes, but the Soviets would never believe it if you told them."

Stuart nodded at her. "They would, you know. They'd have good reason as well. I really shouldn't say any more."

"I agree," Lucy said. "It's super. Mama, come and help me in the kitchen. Darling, Harvey Smith is going for his nuptials tomorrow, did I tell you? I wish I could tell him, just to see his expression."

"He wouldn't sleep. Anyone like a drink?"

Both accepted and then Lucy added, "I could try drawing him a picture, I suppose," which earned her a sharp "Ludmilla!" in response. They both had more questions for Stuart but he refused to be drawn further, repeating that he shouldn't really have said anything at all, that it was just for them. He kept away while they prepared dinner because when they were co-operating they would use him as a common nuisance. He sat staring into the fire wondering if he'd caused even a fraction of the havoc he required and from where the first ricochet would come.

After the meal, he went out and drove the few miles to see his lawyer, Hamish Browne, a rotund and bouncing little Scot. He accepted the familiar package without opening it and then startled the lawyer out of a brandy languor.

"Tomorrow I might have to ask you to negotiate a total

mortgage on the house, big as you can get. Borrow on the holdings as well. Everything you can find."

"That seems a great shame. Have you been gambling, Stuart?"

"Not exactly. I was humping the chips and now I've a friend in trouble. I'll get it back someday, maybe. Can I use your phone, privately?"

"Of course."

After the door shut, Stuart dialled the Antwerp number, wondering if Simonov was again out to dinner. In fact he'd had to cancel it and was doing his utmost to control his agitation.

Stuart kept his own voice calm. "Alexei, I've got a big problem with de Hoek. I need help. Have you any news about my – what?"

The voice on the line seemed to quaver slightly. "I said, never mind that! Listen, you've hit the fan here, it's like a trail of gunpowder all the way to the Kremlin."

"What is?"

"Don't be stupid! Your information about Cruise not being armed – can you verify, quickly, and give the source?"

"How the hell . . .? Did Alicia tell you?"

There was a pause at the other end and Stuart later realised that Simonov had speculated briefly on whether he could blame her. "I would like to say yes, but no, I'm afraid she didn't."

"Has anyone rung me since?"

"No – aren't you at home?"

"They're almost certainly *your* bugs then, you were lying to me and making trouble."

"It's not important now, listen –"

"*You* listen, dammit. I thought they'd been removed. I was going to use that information to bargain with you, either for my property or for your direct 'influence' on de Hoek. Preferably both."

"It's true, then! The Chairman will have another relapse, I don't know what's going to happen. The Geneva Arms talks still going on . . . it's the biggest coup for twenty years, I'm reeling. We could make you a Hero of the Soviet Union. Look, we have to have verification and source."

"What about de Hoek, Simonov? I can't take any chances with him, he's vicious. If I had enough to buy him off, I'd do it, but you could stop him just like –"

206

Simonov brusquely interrupted again. "One thing you said, 'The enemy gave them the idea ... they'd have good reason to believe it.' What does that mean?"

Stuart paused to blow his cheeks in relief that he'd held a card in reserve. "I'll tell you on the two conditions, but first that you get de Hoek's mind away from Lucy, I don't care how, I want you to scare him until his Jaapie blood freezes, I want a fucking cast-iron guarantee, do you –"

"I said, all right, you've got it."

"Don't be flippant, Alexei, She's your *daughter*."

"I am aware ... Don't you understand what's at stake here? Listen, this conversation is being recorded for onward transmission to Moscow, it's them you'll have to convince so start talking like a grown-up. We want to know what you meant, what else you've got and above all where you got it from. As for your property, we are getting very warm."

Prepared for this Stuart said firmly, "No. You get me more. I'll keep calling you until I get my assurance and my bag and contents intact. Otherwise forget it."

"Stuart, they'll go to someone else for the information!"

"Oh yes? Who? And what do they ask for?" Without another word, he hung up and exhaled hugely with relief. Hamish Browne saw him out with some concern but Stuart tried to reassure him about the mortgage. "It may be only a precaution. I'll know tomorrow."

"All right, good luck then."

When he got home Alicia was just preparing to go up to bed. Lucy jumped up with disappointment on her face.

"You missed all the excitement, screams over the gymnastics, the World Championships, the poor Russian girl pranged on her vault and the Czech won with a ten on the Floor. You'd have come to blows!"

Alicia shook her head in denial. "But she was just like my *dochka*, so beautiful, elegant, really a woman, not like some of these beanstrings and tumblers. Dressed in white too, looks better than the red. Ah, she was lovely. But the Russian would have won if not for the leg."

"Of course," Stuart said, knowing how it mystified Alicia to be uncompetitive.

Lucy added wistfully, "She wasn't just beautiful, she was a magic gymnast, with an amazing full-in-back-out. We were both yelling on her last diagonal, she had to be perfect to win, she put half a foot out but they gave it to her anyway."

"She looked so like you, except the hair, and not so naughty perhaps." With a little smile Alicia kissed them both and started up the stairs.

Lucy took Stuart's arm and looked at her. "If you hear a lot of noise in the night, it's only me being strangled."

Alicia replied with a severe look as she went up but clearly enjoyed being tolerated.

"You seem anxious about something," Lucy said, holding him away from her in the low light. He had nothing to say to this understatement and to cover his silence, she added, "Do you find you look back to laughter love-making more readily than the heavy?"

"Yes . . . but like everything else you have to have both to know the difference, I suppose."

"Mm . . . Well, I think I'll save my new invention till you're in the mood. You must've had a hard day at the office. Where did you go today?"

He didn't want to remind her. Thinking of the cameras and watchers in Downing Street, he saw no point in evasion.

"Number Ten, actually."

Her eyes widened because she knew it was the truth in the way he spoke. It made him smile suddenly. She replied with a wicked grin and pushed down the duvet.

"Prisoner . . . spread your arms out."

He did so, delighted at the swift distraction. She sat on his stomach, placed a foot in the crook of each of his elbows and grasped his wrists with her hands before straightening her legs. Then she bent slowly forward until she was completely double, stretching herself until her torso was pressed flat on to his. She nibbled his chin and then inchingly moved herself down, flexing her feet as well as being pushed by his arms. It almost broke up when she muttered, "I hope there's no one standing behind me with a bucket of ice-cubes!" but the convulsion brought them together in an ecstasy as taut as violin strings.

Grimacing, Stuart said, "How come you get to put *your* feet up after *my* hard day at the office?"

"Because I'm in charge here." She giggled and then whispered, "Are you dying to share more secrets?"

208

"Oh, how! And you?"

"I mean, do you have others, apart from your working ones?"

He nodded slightly into her hair. "Um, yes, I suppose so."

"Just for me? It's unbearable," she said, quivering. "How long shall we wait?"

"Officially it's thirty years."

"Oh, God, you'd better still love me then."

"Why, are you doing something dreadful?"

"I might . . . I got a new Spanish phrase book the other day, it's got a supplement of swear-words and unmentionables."

Stuart snorted softly. "What made you think of that?"

"Well, English is so rich, you'd think they'd have something prettier than the word to 'come'. In Spanish there's *gozar*, which is much better, it means more like to rejoice. It's a different aspect, instead of the anticlimax of having arrived, it's more of a Yah-Hoo, a celebration."

"You're right, you know. And the French have *jouir*. Is that hurting you, you're like a vice?"

When she shook her head against his chest, he said, "Please free my arms so I can hold you. This is incredible."

"We-el, I don't know . . . Promise you won't try to escape?"

"Promise," he chuckled and then slipped his freed hands down. He felt the muscles forced out from her hips like small hard fruits, but she lay on him so lightly, so precious that his emotions began to whirr. In extreme tension he could only give a strained whisper.

"Don't move, whatever you do."

"Gozas?"

"Quizas."

"I didn't know you had any Spanish?"

"I don't," he said. "It was a song. *Quizas*, Perhaps. By Cliff Richard."

"If he could see me now!"

"Ssh . . . Did you feel like the girl gymnast as well as look like her?"

"How did you know?"

"Your eyes were shining."

"Minor identity crisis. They'll show it again, I expect, then you can see if she's like me. They shouldn't give their names."

"Why not?"

"Because she's Czech and because she's much fitter than I am."

"I don't want you any fitter."

"And about eight years younger –"

"Or any younger either."

"– that's why. She's a little princess and you'll go and find her, rescue her. I'll have to keep you prisoner."

"I wouldn't mind. What's her name, anyway?"

"Ekaterina Szabo."

"Szabo, that's not a Czech name. It's Hungarian or Romanian."

"Oh, don't tease ... are you sure? Mama said she was Czech but the telly's too small to see the writing."

Stuart found it hard to believe she could have less than total confidence. "Lucy, you sound almost serious. Anyway, you know better than to think like that, controlling the uncontrollable."

"What's uncontrollable?"

"Emotions in others, things you can't change ... Heaven's, I'm so crazy about you I have to stop myself slobbering. Just thinking of you, I'm like a starving timber-wolf with a photo of a T-bone steak."

She raised her head and looked at him, her hands smoothing his face. All the rest came from reflection of feelings because her eyes began to glow and then to glaze.

"Oh ... ohahoo ... This is too good for mere mortals ... Let us rejoice."

"Gaudeamus igitur."

"That's what I said."

"Amen."

"And *delirium tremens.*" Then pretending, like a running child trying to catch up, she cried out, "Wait! ... Wait for *me!*"

At breakfast the next morning, Lucy said, "Mama, I think my husband's a poet. He said I was tungsten filigree, isn't that peculiar?"

Alicia watched them narrowly over her teacup. "I don't understand."

"Never mind." She touched Stuart's shoulder. "I think you are like volcanic rock."

210

"Kimberlite."

"That's what I said."

He smiled. "Not this time. Kimberlite is diamond-bearing ore."

"Oh."

Alicia ventured her own thoughts. "Hundreds, thousands must know it, that 'secret' of yours."

Stuart raised his eyebrows. "Why? In everyone's mind, an ICBM is precisely that."

"What is it, please?"

Lucy put in sweetly, "Intensely Catastrophic Bloody Menace."

Stuart inclined his head to her. "Thank you my love; so you see, people just don't expect a ballistic missile to be like a harmless arrow with a sucker-pad on the end."

Alicia shook her head. "You don't understand, Soviet's reaction when KGB finds out, what happens then?"

"What do *you* think?"

"I do not know. I think at once they won't believe it, they'll have to check."

"Um . . . I wonder how, it would be very difficult. You and I couldn't tell even if we were allowed to take one to bits. I mean, from the Army I know how to dismantle a hand-grenade but I still couldn't tell if the explosive is explosive, except by setting it off."

"Ah, but they have detectors for the radio-active."

"Yes, Geiger counters. They've thought of that. They put a small amount of U-235 in each nose-cone so that any Boris with a Geiger on the end of a very long stick will hear a clicking noise, that's assuming he's allowed to stand next to a Tomahawk or a Pershing without anyone saying *Oi, you!*" He shrugged and buttered a piece of toast. "I thought you'd find it a comfort, that's all, otherwise I wouldn't have told you. Did you sleep all right?"

"With my head in a *navoloka*, a pillow-bag, yes." She smiled then. "It was comforting."

"What was?" Lucy asked quickly. "The noise, the bag or the secret?"

"They were all nice . . . I could not hear you really. I am so happy that you do not fight, or only in whispers."

Lucy looked at Stuart and raised her eyes in cherished amusement.

"Are you going to meet St George? After my, er, morning clients, I promised to take Mama to Cheltenham for Harvey's big performance."

Stuart nodded abstractedly, trying to think out his day. The fact that there'd been no British reaction left him reasonably certain that only Simonov's people had bugged the house; nevertheless as a precaution, when Lucy had gone on her mystery errand, he walked out and called Antwerp collect from the village call-box.

With no progress overnight, Simonov was agitated and pessimistic; it was only then that Stuart fully realised his father-in-law was nearly as supplicant to KGB connivance as himself. Until then he'd subconsciously nourished the idea, since his ruthlessness over the Grady affair, that her father wouldn't see Lucy endangered but it was plain now that he had far less influence than he'd suggested. He was clearly desperate for something useful to reinstate himself in favour.

Stuart also understood then how dangerous was his own charade as an agent, not to mention his missile invention as well, should it be discredited; their willingness to believe something of the kind, however, stood well in its favour. The second part was much more tricky, being less to their liking, and he now felt a distinct hesitation about putting it forward.

Simonov pressed him uncomfortably, making airy promises, but Stuart insisted it was their turn.

"And if we find your diamonds?" The voice sounded almost to leer in his taut imagination.

"You take them to Grobelaar for me, quick sharp. I'll call you later." He hung up abruptly and walked back to the house, the wind swirling the leaves viciously and threatening to bring rain. He heard his telephone ring while he was still in the road but as he went in he heard Alicia speaking a breathless, rapid Russian. He could only make out the name Sasha repeated twice in attempted interruption before she became aware of him standing there. She hung up and looked at him briefly before her eyes slid away and fastened on the little terrier looking up at her. She gathered him and spoke distractedly, or so it seemed at first.

"He's a champion, you know."

"Yes, you told me," Stuart replied.

"He has the temperament, you see."

212

"Yes."

"Not like Lud – Lucy."

"What do you mean?" He looked at her curiously.

"At the school they said she was the best . . . Do you know there are ten applying for every place and of course they have to be beautiful, who wants to see an ugly dancer? In the class for the thirteen-year-olds, my God they are like a roomful of flowers to see and she stood on her own almost, perfect physique, hip turn-out exceptional, such grace you could cry. She got it from him." Alicia stabbed with her finger towards the telephone. "She was too naughty as well, too bright. A real ballerina is steady, not too imaginative, she has to conform, to be moulded. Legs of steel and arms like willow-wands but no, she wanted it all, she used to do gymnastics, sneak to secret training. They saw her arms growing muscles, her shoulders, she became too flexible for a dancer, can you believe? They were so angry, but . . . in the end they had to allow her, she had the gym in her heart from a little girl, always daring. And then the fall, it was the end of her hopes, she lost two years."

Stuart looked at her mystified.

"You didn't know . . . I wondered. She fell off the asymmetric and broke her neck. It wasn't her fault, the apparat broke."

He gulped and said, "I wonder she never told me . . . I almost wish you hadn't, I can't bear to think of her hurting herself. You must know that."

"That is why I told you."

This time she met his gaze evenly and he looked at her for a long moment. He nodded and was about to speak but Lucy's arrival ended their dialogue. She bounced in, flushed in her tracksuit, and her slim neck looked as poised and confident as ever. She ran upstairs to change, stopping halfway to tell him something.

"They're showing it again, the World Championships. You'll be able to see her for yourself."

He followed her up to the bedroom and said, "I don't want to see her, my love. Why should I?"

"Because . . . Oh, no reason. I just wanted you to know I'm not jealous."

"All right," he chuckled, "but it's jealousy of a myth if I don't see her. Do you think I could suddenly want somebody

213

else, just like that, when you're so perfect anyway? Has someone been giving you dark thoughts about men's constancy?"

"No more than usual. I'm sorry. Maybe all the mysteries make me insecure."

He snorted and said, "The Complaints box is still empty."

"I emptied it because of Mother, some of them were a bit seamy. There's one for every day you go away. Why did you say Kimberlite?"

"Because I'll bring you a diamond."

"Oh . . . I've got one, thanks." She held up her hand. 'I'll dance for you, not like the lady in the song."

"We'll see . . . I'd better go."

"All right. You're still tense, aren't you?"

Knowing not to simulate, he nodded but gave her a reassuring smile. "Don't worry, there's just something on. They said they might call me."

"Oh," she answered sadly, "is it to do with what you told us?"

He shrugged with genuine uncertainty. "Could be."

Fifteen

If one has a secret, a lifelong secret, one can't afford
to be married.

Bones. (*Anthony Johnson*)

St George was late and Stuart waited in the flying club, chatting
to one of the instructors. The television was on in the corner
out of sight, but when there were several exclamations coming
from it, they leaned round to take a look. Stuart saw a video-re-
play of the pretty but stoically expressionless Russian champion
carried off with a damaged knee. A bit later he caught his
breath and ignored a nudge from the instructor who was
making some point about gear-up landings. He watched the
ethereally graceful Szabo complete a faultless routine on the
floor. He noted she was, in fact, Romanian but apart from that
they were right, he thought, she's very like Lucy. He was
unmoved otherwise and wished Lucy was there to be cuddled.

He sensed a presence by his shoulder and turned to see St
George staring horsily at the screen with his teeth showing.

"I'd like to buy one of those little things and take it home,"
he said, still watching.

"What things?" Stuart asked.

"Little contortionist ladies."

"What would you do with it, her?"

"I'd ... I don't know, well, I'd *dandle* her, I suppose.
You've got one, what do you do? I shouldn't ask, I suppose.
I'm jealous enough as it is. To be quite frank and above
board, I think I'm in love with your wife."

"So am I."

"Oh ... well, there we are, then. I haven't even got one to
swap with you – I suppose a sister of sixteen hands is *hors de
question*? Sixteen two, actually. Anyway, not what I wanted
to talk to you about. Let's go and get some coffee."

"OK. Before you say anything, I've got a really serious priority. Are you genuinely able to offer a chance of a biggish lump of cash, and quickly?"

St George looked a bit flustered. "It depends, I mean, how quickly?"

"Say, two weeks? I expect I could stretch my man to a bit more if all else fails."

"Mm . . . Don't see why not. As I said, I've got the buyer and the rest of it all seems to be checking. So far, we've only shoved out a few gentle questions, nothing panicky, you understand? Here's the background. At a place called Kbely in Prague is a museum where they have a Mark Nine Spit in almost flying condition and –"

"St G, I've just had a thought. You could save the hairy part till it's a 'go' situation, so to speak. I've got enough on my plate right now. I'm very practical, I do things, but thinking about them gets in my way, so I only need to know what to do straight off, OK? Let's allow there's a very valuable aircraft somewhere which simply needs liberating."

"Splendid. This is where nepotism raises its rightful head. Have you heard of the Confederate Air Force?"

"Yes, in Texas. World War Two aircraft collection."

"Right. The Ghost Squadron, in Harlingen. Lovely bunch of right-wing die-hards." His voice dropped to closet level. "One of my Uncles is a Colonel in the CAF. They're all Colonels. He said he could fix me with a ride in one of their Spits and no questions. I'm sure if I asked he'd fix it for you as well, just produce your licence."

Stuart shook his head in agitation. "I'm not current yet and look at the weather." He didn't think it was the moment to admit he'd never even had a licence.

"Go to Texas, look in any of the mags. They have much cheaper flying schools, rapid courses, no bull and guaranteed sunshine. When you're feeling up to the mark again, shunt down to Harlingen and take a whizz. You're right, there's no point in even thinking about the rest of it till you're sure. It's a one-off, see, it would have to go on the button first time." Only then did St George look at him seriously, considering the risk. "I take it you're desperate enough?"

"It's looking that way, yes."

"Well, that's the main thing." He looked out of the window at the rain but his eyes were glazed with distant speculation.

"Nothing to it, really. You'd just have to hug the deck and go like a turd off a trowel for about fifteen minutes, whizz over the wire. Piece of gâteau."

Stuart gulped. "That's called thinking about it?"

"Oh, sorry. Well, what do you think?"

"Right now, I'm not certain if I have a choice. I'll know later today ... Do you often go to Antwerp, by the way?"

"Sometimes. You 'wan gehr'?"

"If I give you an address, you might pick up a small item for me. I'm going to get a man to make something, for Lucy."

"No prob. I was going to ask what, but obviously it's a secret."

"Right."

"Feel like lunch?"

Stuart shook his head and St George understood at once. "Mm, I'm not sure I would either."

"I did think of something, though. If we went together, I did the talking and you did the flying..."

"Well now, that *had* occurred to me but ... put yourself in my place, wouldn't you want the lion's share for the risk? I would. Apart from that, my schedule's chokker for a month. Thank God," he added with deliberate double meaning.

Stuart's next call to Simonov was almost the clincher. His father-in-law was so evasive and demanding of more information that he seemed to be making an agreement impossible. Stuart, in his lawyer's office, was about to hang up when the Russian asked quickly, "Where are you? They tell me you're not calling from home."

When Stuart told him, he said, "Give me five minutes."

He waited in the empty room, staring bleakly at a solitary copy of *Good Housekeeping*. After a full ten minutes, he was called back, the voice gasping and surreptitious.

"Stuart, there's a problem. I didn't want them to know about me telling you this, so I'm calling from a café. Listen, we found your bag."

A wave of relief engulfed him so hugely that he didn't take in the next words and Simonov had to repeat them.

"The rubber flange, it was glass ... Only glass in it, do you hear?"

A red mist of fury surged in front of his eyes. "You

217

thieving bastards! Simonov, I'll get you for this if it's the last –"

"Bargain, man, bargain! Give us what we want from you. After that we can try to find what happened to it."

"Get stuffed!"

"Stuart," the voice pleaded, "I've even got something for *you*. Because of what you told us, our conference team is about to be pulled out of the Geneva talks, they're going to walk, they won't have the Americans laughing at us, still bargaining over dummies. Tell W that, they'll swing all the influence you need. Maybe you can even stop the walk-out."

The spiral had changed from a slippery helter-skelter to a baffling, inescapable maelstrom, charging Stuart's answer with cold fury.

"No! No deal. Goodbye."

His blood was racing as he pounded down the receiver. Hamish Browne had heard the raised voice and was standing next door looking concerned. Stuart's determination alarmed him further.

"As I asked you, Hamish. Hock the lot. Send 75 grand immediately to my friend's lawyer in Johannesburg. The rest into my current account. I'll be away about a week or ten days."

Quickly he wrote down his instructions and signed a power-of-attorney. From the classified in a flying magazine, he picked a number in Dallas, Texas, and booked himself on a PPL course beginning the next day. From a travel directory, he found a cheap direct flight from Brussels at 11 pm the same evening, after which he dashed home to gather a few belongings. Lucy and Alicia were still out so he left a brief note that he'd been called away at short notice, and by intention rather than remorse, he left her a cheque for £5000. "Ten talents," he scribbled and was going to add that he didn't want it back before he realised that it might detract from the zest and energy of whatever she had in mind. The telephone rang twice but he ignored it; as he left, he said simply and loudly to the wall, "Take care of her, Simonov, or I'll see you get the chopper cartridge yourself."

He caught a late afternoon flight to Eindhoven and took a car to Antwerp, where he briefed Grobelaar and gave him the two coloured stones. The proceeds from the big white were put into a Geneva account for de Hoek, whom he still fiercely resisted contacting, believing it pointless.

"Friend Runyan told me not to sell these two, Mr Grobelaar, but I will if all else fails. Add them to his spoils and contact de Hoek for me, if you don't hear from me by the end of the month. Tell him that's all there is, the Russians have got the rest. I'll be an optimist meanwhile, and ask you to make something for me and enhance the value of this one."

His instructions for the pink stone were specific to a diagram; Grobelaar accepted the commission gravely and without demur, but only because the lozenge shape of the rough permitted it. When he asked the significance, Stuart told him it was a secret; bowing, he seemed content with the mystery and that an English nobleman would come to collect it.

"A jewel is full of dreams," he said whimsically but after having the idea Stuart felt a huge reluctance that it might have to be used as a last-ditch bargain. It served to harden his determination and to resist any last calls to Simonov, however close by. The wisdom of this only occurred to him later, that his counterparts were ruthless enough to snatch and prise from him his only remaining lever. He drove the hire car to Brussels and just before boarding his transatlantic flight, dialled his home number with a single ring. He found it wasn't a case of remembering. She was like a stereo track in the unreeling of his life, only she wasn't able to see it yet. He wondered when, if ever, there'd be a time to savour and to share it.

The relay tail which had picked him up in Eindhoven lost him in Brussels quite by accident since he was unaware of it. He therefore had several days lead as not even his last contact, Grobelaar, knew his destination.

From Dallas/Forth Worth it was only about ten miles south to Grand Prairie airfield and its Regional Aviation Training Centre. The cab driver was friendly, the flying school people were friendly, and somewhere he even recalled passing a road-sign which said DRIVE FRIENDLY, not easy to decipher because of the heavy calibre of the bullet holes which riddled it.

The flying staff were variously laconic, cigar-chewing and overflowing still with hair-raising or cynical tales of action in South-East Asia. Everything moved at typical Texan pace, fast and efficient, with an easy flamboyance. As it wouldn't slow him down significantly and it seemed pointless to

219

cheesepare at this stage, he kept on with his helicopter training, for which his main instructor was Dan Yorick. Inevitably known as Meaty Yorick, he had flown both big 'copters and bird-dogs under VC fire; he seldom smiled and looked as though nothing would ever surprise him again. He taught with the assurance and fatalism of a seasoned preacher, but flew even the tiny R.22 with a finger-tip delicacy that made his movements, followed through the dual controls, barely perceptible.

The fixed-wing cross-countries took Stuart to places sounding of old romance, Abilene, Wichita Falls, Waco, Cisco and even the 200 miles to Austin, over what was once endless, unfenced prairie but from the air was seen now as an orderly patchwork of squareholdings broken up by small growths of suburbia, a hundred similar throw-off houses crammed together in litters without a city to suckle them. He felt the huge distances would have demoralised any prairie horse which knew in advance, but now it was all multi-geared jeeps and pick-ups, the tough competition demanding efficiency. Money was the yardstick, the password and the final word. The men were hard in the eyes as once they had been in leathery hides, and they were proud of their short history, showing him the vast acres of disused stockyards at the North Edge of Fort Worth – the hell-raising oasis at the end of legendary, punishing cattle-drives – and the extraordinary vigorous skills that lived on among the rodeo professionals, riding the furious broncs and bulls, roping calves and steers and earning sometimes a luxury living in prize money.

The days passed in supercharged activity. An ebullient club member called George "Bear" Creek befriended him noisily and lent him an old Volkswagen to commute to his motel, the Trade Winds, chosen because it was nearest and cheapest and easy to find by the tall Whataburger chalet. For himself the Texan roared proudly in a throbbing, high, four-wheel-drive turquoise rancher with an over-sized chrome-plated rollover bar, twin fur-padded gun racks and great bristling tyres called Gumbo Monster Mudders. "The Bear" was over-sized in everything, six-four, broad, wildly hairy and making his current fortune from multiplying outlets for his Famous Grandpa Grizzlyburgers. "None but the Brave" was the motto, although he was careful to use only the finest of prime "beeves".

They still kept their guns with pride; each man seemed to have several and spoke nonchalantly of stopping power, magnums, calibres, plinking. House robberies were few in suburban areas because nearly every home contained several loaded handguns and were not often locked. The logic ran simply, that an unlocked house probably had someone in it, who was only too happy to make it easy for you to get in, since once inside the Law allowed him to shoot you dead. One club-member showed them a small hole in his fur-lined boot where his eighteen-month-old daughter had found and fired a loaded .22 in the bottom of the cloakroom cupboard. He'd forgotten it was there. Another was having wife trouble because he insisted on keeping is .38 Special under her pillow, instead of under his own, his reason being that she drank less.

The Bear was particularly proud of a rare possession, a .45 stainless-steel Magnum automatic, of which only some 300 had been made. It was a huge piece which yet seemed to nestle in his hand. Among his other eccentricities, the Bear usually sported a roll of toilet-paper in the windscreen of his rancher, apparently to show that he'd come up in the world and didn't need to vandalise telephone directories like some of his hill-billy drinking pardners. He also had a second trailer-hitch fixed to the *front* of the machine so that when close to dead drunk, he could call up the wrecker on his radio-phone and have himself trailed home, "all nice 'n' legal". He slept off most nights in the cab and sloped inside for his breakfast Grizzlyburger.

Stuart went out with him on one evening only, swept on a tide of no-refusal to hit several Dallas singles bars but escaping early when it promised to be little more than a lost tomorrow. He felt almost foolishly jealous of his time away from Lucy and he found the bars depressing for the hungry loneliness on so many faces, the compulsion to seek comfort in casual sex or alcoholic oblivion when the unrealised goal was more likely affection and reassurance. The Bear told him gleefully that Dallas women, because of the business demand for secretaries, outnumbered the men 5:3, "so even a horse's ass like me can get hisself a piece, time to time". He lined up several for Stuart and became exasperated with his smiling refusal to commit himself, accusing him of faggotry and other deviations. Stuart had to explain that the problem was far more serious even though five thousand miles away, wondering why it should make him sheepish in front of a man. On his third night in the motel a girl knocked on his door and apologised for disturbing the wrong room, yet showed no inclination to leave. On that occasion there was neither embarrassment or put-down in his simple statement, "Sorry, I'm in love with my wife."

There were sometimes long devoted queues for the more popular bars, an extraordinary willingness for an otherwise impatient people, cramming up by the hundreds immediately after the working day, to drown heads with weak booze, deafen ears with country music and distract the lonely eyes with topless propaganda.

He loved the exacting side of helicopter flying, especially the judgement skills in positioning and emergency auto-rotation even though the cigar-chewing Yorick insisted it was just a question of going by the book. Although several hours short of his helicopter rating, he had reached almost enough for his fixed-wing licence and was on the point of calling St George for the Harlingen contact when he was summarily interrupted.

Knowing that the Bear was out on the town, the knock that came he expected to be another saleswoman. He had his answer ready but the figure standing there was a broad-shouldered, crew-cut All-American, who snapped open a card-holder and said, "Mister Stuart Kody? The name's Randolph. CIA. May I come in?"

"What do you want? I thought you guys only operated abroad."

"That's right."

"So how does anyone know I'm here?"

"Don't ask, it took us long enough. God, I feel torpedoed."

"Sorry, yes, come in. Like a beer?"

"Yuh, solid."

"What?"

"Uh, means yes, thanks."

Stuart reached into the cooler and produced two Budweisers, favouring the brand after discovering it was originally Czech. Randolph wearily slid a Colt Python out of his shoulder holster and threw it on to one of the double beds. "Stickin' inta me," he explained, but his eyes were very deep set and quite unreadable. He nodded his head up and down as if pondering, though it seemed more like an affectation.

He swigged some beer and wiped his mouth backhanded. "OK, I got some questions you may not want to answer. You gotta Russkie for a father-in-law, right?" Stuart nodded warily.

"An' you been cahooting with him." It was a flat statement this time. "I understand certain information passed between you of a Classified nature?"

"Not exactly, no."

"Not for me to judge, don't know what it was. My boss wants to know where you got it, because your boss doesn't know anything about it."

"I haven't got a boss."

"Your Mister Breakspeare. He bossy enough for you?"

Stuart stood uncertainly, not knowing whether Breakspeare had changed his mind and decided to acknowledge him after all. Randolph emptied his Bud, watching him calmly.

"OK, you were gonna tell me where you got the Classified." Another statement.

"No, I wasn't."

"Right. Get your things together, we're leaving."

"But I haven't – who says, exactly?"

"My boss, me, Deke outside and Betsy here," the agent said briskly, scooping up the Python. "We're takin' a little trip. You don't ask where, you keep a clean nose and you speak to no one on the way. Any action out of line will be extremely prejudicial to your circulation, get me? If you think you can take me, I've got back-up muscle in the car with a big gatt. Let's go."

Stuart packed his few clothes in silence, bristling at the hostility, then stacked his pilot training notes and manuals into the shiny new briefcase provided by the school. Incongruously, he wondered how to hide it from Lucy.

Outside there was a Plymouth sedan with another agent at the wheel. Randolph opened the rear door and motioned Stuart inside, taking one of his bags.

"Wait a minute, I've got to settle my bill."

"We'll take care of that," said the voice from inside. "Seven nights, ninety bucks. Let's go."

223

"Thanks. Next time I'll stay at the Rodeway Inn, that's about forty a night. What about the flight school?"

"You're in credit there, so they'll take care of it."

"The Volkswagen belongs to George Creek. I've got to give it back and thank him –"

"Gimme the keys. We'll leave them at the desk and call him. Just get it into your Limey skull, we gotta priority here, OK?"

"You mean if I'm bad, you won't shoot to kill?"

The driver ignored them and thunked the shift into drive with the brake still on so the car bucked and snorted. Stuart shrugged tiredly and got in, feeling a great longing to be home.

With Stuart out of the picture, the enquiries for his source and verification had been stepped up to an intense degree so that inevitably there were spillages. From regular sources in the Kremlin, his information eventually reached Washington and then back across the Atlantic where Breakspeare soon came under bombardment as being the Ministerial end of W Section. Reluctantly and under orders from the Prime Minister, he didn't deny his rôle but immediately instigated a search for Stuart Kody, becoming thoroughly embarrassed that he couldn't produce him. Repeated calls to a puzzled and affronted wife yielded no results beyond alerting Moscow to the search through the still "live" house bugs. Lucy was understandably distressed especially when Alicia told her there'd even been a call from Simonov. It made her thoroughly uneasy and she had even begun to think of her promise to be off the scene when she had a call from St George. He wanted her to meet him in Oxford, ostensibly to collect the camera, but his voice too was full of affront.

"Did you tell anyone about me being a gun-runner?"

"Of course not!"

"Well then it must have been that rotten stop-out husband of yours, with all his secrets he can't even keep one of mine. He should be made cuckold or somesuch – with your permission of course."

Lucy chuckled nervously. "What happened?"

"A Boris," he said ominously, "approached me in Amsterdam, wanted me to take something unspecified into Eire, threatening to tell the Gobbies about the old boy's carpet investment."

"Stuart wouldn't have blurted on you, St G. What did you say to the threat – what's a Gobbie anyhow?"

"Oh, Cornish smugglers' word for an Excise man. I told him I didn't like the cut of his jib, frankly."

"How *fierce* of you."

"Ye-es rather, I should say so. He also asked me where Stuart was. Has he been in touch with you?"

"You too! All I get is a single bell on the phone every evening. Why is everyone trying to find him, that's what I want to know, even from some Minister downwards?"

"Ah."

"What do you mean, 'Ah'?"

"Nothing . . . just that it seemed right they should ask you first, I suppose. Lunch tomorrow, um? Are you going to tell me what the camera's for?"

"All right, but it's secret."

"Splendid."

With difficulty, he restrained himself from troubling her about his further interrogation. Having failed to move him with the blackmail, they had bundled him into an empty office in Schipol airport, two burly men with a Voice Stress Analyser, a wickedly sharp hunting knife, a syringe full of some clear fluid and some potent physical threats. St George chose the Analyser because he couldn't give an exact answer and Texas seemed a vast haystack for a search. He was relieved that they didn't ask him about flying since flight centres would have narrowed the search enormously; meanwhile he felt sure that Stuart would call and so be alerted before going down to Harlingen. Nevertheless, he began to feel the remorse of Judas when the call never came.

The next morning, Lucy was just in from her class when the telephone rang.

"Mrs Kody?" The woman's voice was accented, clipped but soft. "You don't know me. I'm calling from Johannesburg, at great risk."

"South Africa?"

"Yes." It sounded like Yiss. "Now listen, please. I don't know the reason and I'm afraid I don't know when but I do know there's an order out to have you damaged. It's some kind of revenge, to do with your husband."

"Where is he?"

225

"I don't know. I think that's the problem. He hasn't done something he's supposed to do for someone here. A vengeful man."

Lucy gulped. "What kind of damaged?"

"'Well, last time, I hear you put up a pretty good scrap yourself, so this time it's coming with a gun. Been told to shoot you in the knee. You won't walk again. So I suggest you get out of there and hole up until it gets sorted."

"You don't know how much time I have?" she asked, shuddering.

"No, but the order just went out, as I understood it."

"The order . . . is it someone you work for?"

"You could say."

"Why are you doing this for me?"

"Because . . . I hate and despise him, he's a disgusting animal. And because I'm free of them all. I just love a spirited girl, wherever she is. We will probably never meet but I want you to get clear. Don't tell anyone at all where you're going, I'll put a Mollie-to-Lucy in the London *Times* if the situation changes. Just don't mess around."

"I won't, I'm very grateful. Can you tell me how you know all this without knowing where my husband is?"

"I'm afraid not. I assume my boss was trying to force him in some way."

"He couldn't know about it then," Lucy choked. "Stuart would never –" She stopped then, creased in puzzlement. "Thank you . . . Mollie. I'll split right away. I owe you."

"No you don't. Take care."

"Who's going to take care of my plants?" Lucy bleated softly, but the line was already dead.

Sixteen

Flying is the safest way to fly.
Susan Koerner Wright
(Mother of Wilbur and Orville.)

They drove east for about twenty minutes, towards Dallas. Stuart wondered if he'd ever be back, still feeling some bewilderment from a city of such vibrant energy. It had only existed 80-odd years yet was known the world over for more than one infamy. By the "Grassy Knoll" over which Oswald fired his killing shot at John Kennedy, there is a sign with an arrowed diagram showing the action and Stuart had heard more than one Texan refer to it as a very competent shot, speaking only professionally. He supposed the locals felt a huge and lasting shame that it had happened there.

At Love Field they swept up to a sleek, twin-jet 8-seater, only one among dozens. Randolph took his elbow to the steps as the driver watched and then left them. Stuart was aware that Randolph expected hostility but he offered none, feeling a light acceptance. Randolph pulled aside the concertina partition and said exhaustedly, "Let's go, guys." One of the pilots came back and shut the door, nodding to them as they strapped in, but Randolph maintained his wooden lack of expression.

"We can't go all the way to Europe in this, can we?" Stuart enquired but the American only shrugged. They took off in a searing blast of acceleration and after about twenty minutes levelled at cruising height, the stars clear in black sky. The seats were very comfortable and across the aisle Randolph spread himself in weariness and eventually fell asleep. Stuart was wide awake, his mind full of questions.

He got up quietly from his seat and went forward, tapping

on the partition. A voice beyond said "Yeah?" so he slid it back and looked inside.

"Just come for a peep at your baby," he said easily as the two pilots turned to look at him. "You fly friendly?" he asked and they grinned back. "Surely do," said the captain in the left seat, waving his arm airily. "Here she is. You're a Limey, right?"

"Right. I was over on an instant flying course. We don't have the weather for it back home. Have you been told why this special treatment?"

"Nope. We're just the drivers, which means we do nothing but tell the little black box where to go."

"And what did you tell it this time?"

"Oh, take a little ole and, hopefully, little-used route up-country some, carry on four, five hours and wake us up and slam her down some place I forget . . . I gotta go to the can, you wanna sit here for a minute? Sure, why not? You want coffee? I can do everything a stewardess can except two and they're both over-rated."

The captain got out of his seat and squeezed past him. In the dim light he saw the flash of grinning in a darkly handsome face. Both pilots wore uniform shirtsleeves and trousers.

Stuart lowered himself very carefully into the seat and tried to take in the huge confusion of dials and switches. To orientate, he focused his gaze on the T, the basic essential flight instruments normally grouped close in front for ease of scan. Altimeter 39,000, airspeed mach .65, heading 044°, attitude indicator, straight and level. It was eerie, like a magic carpet, the raging fires in the tail barely audible, the black porcelain dome of sky studded with silver dots of vital clarity and far, far below, faint and humble light signals of the earthbound. He looked across at the co-pilot who was making notes on a clipboard.

"Enthralling. You ever get fed up with it?"

"I guess. I never get fed up with trying to recapture first feelings, first impressions. I –"

There was a sudden commotion behind them, Randolph's voice shouting, "Where's Kody? Not in the goddam can with you?"

More distantly the pilot's furious answer, "He's flying the plane, you dumb jerk!" There followed a couple of heavy

228

thumps, a pause and then the forward partition was wrenched aside.

"Raise 'em up and come outa there, Kody, or I blow you away."

Stuart grimaced at the fatuity and started to get up but there was the sound of a heavy blow behind and the gun wavered before clattering to the floor. The partition slid almost shut and there were grunting sounds from beyond, ending in a decisive thud. The aircraft lurched slightly but the outraged co-pilot was already half out of his seat, scooping up the Colt. He was a slight but wiry figure and looked determinedly angry as he reached out to slide the door. Instead it was wrenched open again and Randolph stood there with blood on his face, panting. Stuart realised that the agent's next action was thoughtless and instinctive, the pure result of intense training – coupled probably with a rage to have found himself waking to some kind of conspiracy. His left hand chopped down fast on the wrist behind the gun and immediately afterwards a bloodied right came straight out and fragmented the co-pilot's nose. The man collapsed raggedly, half out of his seat, blowing red mist as he fell.

Stuart had shouted his protest but now sat transfixed as Randolph picked up his Colt, checked it and glanced behind him into the cabin.

"Shit! *Shit!* SHIT!" he roared in ferocious outrage. "What the hell? What the good god damn are you doing there, Kody? You're not supposed – Kee-rist! Can you fly this thing?"

Stuart shook his head dazedly as Randolph looked behind him again to verify his catastrophic handiwork. He leaned to one side and groaned. At once he straightened and went back into the cabin, returning a few minutes later shaking his head.

Stuart had seen the speed and force of the blow which felled the co-pilot and Randolph's next words froze the unreality in mid-frame, badly focused.

"Didn't need to look. His neck's broke," he said and bent down to look at the co-pilot. He felt a pulse unnecessarily because the man was breathing in short rasps through still-flowing blood. "This one's nose is all over, if he hasn't got bones in his brain, he'll still need surgery. He's unconscious.

Hey, look, you were just on a pilot's course, can you get us down, huh?"

Stuart wasn't sure about his own voice control and he fought against shouting pointless insults and accusations. Eventually in forced quiet, he said, "Randolph, I'm still technically a student. I fly in daylight, in good weather at about 100 miles per hour, not far from the ground. This is not quite the same thing. We're seven or eight miles up, doing two-thirds of the speed of sound, it's dark outside and I've no idea where we are."

"Huh. Are you scared?"

"What kind of a damn stupid question is that?"

"I mean, are you gonna sit there and piss your pants or are you gonna get us the hell down on the goddam deck, that's what I'm saying!"

"Where were we headed? The course is more or less north-east."

"Washington. Dulles. But that must be another thousand miles. We gotta get down."

Stuart considered. "I don't think so. The longer we stay up, the more time the cope has to recover or the more I can learn, the more we can warn people. I take it you don't know anything about this?"

"Not a rev."

"Well, get this poor guy stretched out in the back. See if there's a First Aid kit. Let me know if he comes round. Otherwise just leave the door shut and leave me alone."

"You mean you want me to just sit back there not knowing what's happening? How the hell can I do that?"

Stuart found himself coldly furious. "Suppose I got up from here and started thumping you, Randolph? What would you do, kill me as well?"

"You're –"

"Just fuck off, will you?"

Randolph stared for a moment in the gloom, agonised yet still inscrutable, then he bent to the crumpled figure and lifted it out by the armpits. He left the partition open but after a moment it closed itself to a small movement of the aircraft. Stuart found himself eerily alone, his pulse still racing and his thoughts in a centrifuge.

He closed his eyes to shut off further input and spent the next half minute composing himself and dispensing with needless questions. He realised as he gained clarity that it was no use examining every switch, button and dial, straining in the low light to understand everything when only a minute portion would have any practical value.

He opened his eyes cautiously but nothing had changed. The jet still whispered through the night sky, occasional tiny movements from the yoke showing that the autopilot was active. The height, heading and airspeed remained the same. He looked first for conventional headsets and saw none, not even a microphone clipped to the panel. He tensed for a moment then found on his left a draped headband with a slender stalk-microphone at right angles to it. Awkwardly he fitted it over his head and adjusted the stalk in front of his lips, all the time scanning the panel and feeling the confusion returning. So many things he'd recognised while the co-pilot was there seemed to haze out now the responsibility was transferred. His eyes began to flit between dials so he closed them and with clenched fists willed the calm to return.

The muted rushing noise was one constant and the column was vaguely reassuring with its occasional slight movements. The panel glowed like a dark mystery in green luminescent figures while outside was midnight blue. Against the starlight he could see the powerful strobe flashes of three other aircraft, none closer than five miles, their levels unknown. There were no longer any lights visible below and he assumed a bank of cloud cover. He thought of his single hour of instrument flight in a simulator and quietly shuddered.

At the rear of the console between the seats two green lights showed "Engage" and there was a trim wheel in front of them. Looking closer he could see it was the autopilot control which ought to be reasonably intelligible, but just in front of it was a green display screen, a cathode ray tube with push-buttons alongside and below it. On the right the legend stated "VLF Omega", and his mind, uncomprehending, wanted to faze again. He knew he should call on the radio but he wanted some calm assimilation first, mainly so that the controllers wouldn't panic him. Lucy filled his thoughts suddenly and the possibility of failure freaked him for a wild moment before mysteriously evaporating.

Call sign . . . where was it usually? There, at the top of the panel: N57OOCF.

Microphone switch . . . he adjusted the stalk again while

231

looking for the switch but he couldn't find it. Radios ... in the centre of the panel were three sets of figures familiar in the VHF range, the left hand one with a green button illuminated and pointing to it, "Select 123.75." Transmit button *must* be on the control column, can't see it, there are three with crazy lettering next to them, XPDR ident, A/P TCS, TFM DN/UP, all meaningless except for the word UP, and the one he wanted wasn't there, should say W/T or MIC or TX, panic rising again. A gong pinged suddenly and a light flashed on the panel: SELCAL, SELCAL.

Stuart sat with his hands quivering, his body frozen, helpless in ignorance. The button continued to flash and the gong sounded again. He wanted to press it timidly just in case and the thought made him livid. He stabbed the button sharply and heard "... Zero Zero Charlie Fox, Memphis Control, do you copy?"

"Yes!" he wanted to shout but still couldn't locate the transmit button. Frantically he ran his hands over the yoke, taking care not to nudge the other buttons, searching desperately for some other projection, hideously conscious that these aircraft were not designed for beginners or even solo professionals. At last, unmarked and out of sight on the back of the left handgrip, he found a tiny knurled button, not responding to pressure at first then suddenly springing sideways and back again. He was about to shout with relief when Memphis ATC came back with their query now urgent. Shakingly, he had to wait them out.

"Memphis this is November Fife Seven Zero Zero Charlie Fox. I have an emergency."

"Well, now, Roger Charlie Fox, Are you Mayday, what is your emergency?"

"I ... er ... low-time pilot in control of a fast, high jet, on auto. Both regular pilots out of action. I'm ... going to need a lot of help."

"Char-lee Fox, this here's Memphis ATC," the voice drawled calmly, "Roger your Mayday. All other aircraft on this frequency change at once to 133.00 and wait to be called. Charlie Fox, what is your aircraft type?"

Stuart searched wildly for some indication: he hadn't asked either pilot that question ... There, dammit, it should boast itself on the column but the legend was missing from the groove where strands of glue still adhered. There was nothing visible on the co-pilot's side either, just a stop-watch bracket and a clip board.

"Er, Charlie Fox aircraft type not known, sorry."

"Charlie Fox, you *have* to know! How else can we find someone to help you . . . Beg pardon, wait one, we'll get it off your flight plan." There was silence for about two minutes then, "Charlie Fox, you are Cessna Citation Two, from Dallas Love Field to Washington DC. We'll get ourselves a high-time and hopefully sober jet pilot and whip you into the handiest, biggest, lovin' mother of an Air Force Base in no time flat. Take it easy, buddy, right?"

"Memphis, Charlie Fox. Thanks. I suggest you don't rush me. I'm OK up here, let's get sorted out quietly."

"Uh, yeah, Roger. What's your fuel state?"

"I don't know, I'll try to find it. I presume more than enough to get to Washington."

"You can relax, Charlie Fox, there's no way you're going up there with all the conflicting traffic, it gets real crowded. We'll jes' call 'em up and say you won't be comin' in, not this way anyhow. Stand by. Do you locate your radio panel?"

"Affirmative."

"Somewhere there you'll have a read-out in thousands, should say transponder over it."

"Yes, got it. It says 5270."

"Roger, Charlie Fox. Switch it now to 7700, this is the emergency setting, we'll all see you clear on the screens, bleepin' like a lil' lost sheep."

Stuart turned the first three knobs cautiously and on the new setting, a small green light began to pulse steadily.

"Good Boy, Charlie Fox, we got you clear at flight level 390. Give us your airspeed and heading, just for a check."

"Airspeed is a Mach Number .65, heading is, let's see, 056°."

"O . . . kay, Charlie Fox. We gotta bright boy here, found hisself a Cessna Citation bro-shure, Citation One but what the hell? Now we can see where you're at, till we get ourselves a- airman . . . You're all on course for Bowling Green, serene and high, in the purple sky . . . hey, that's like a country song, well it's no surprise, you're over Country country, with all the might and technology of Uncle Sam's fair land to help you. You still there, Mr Charlie Fox?"

"Where else, Mr Memphis?"

"No scare, no sweat, Mr Fox?"

"Yes to both, Mr Memphis."

"O . . . kay, why not? You sound like an Anglo to me, right?"

"Correct."

"Well, we sure cain't be jes' leavin' you right up there, 'terferin' with our native airspace, you's coming in, y'hear?"

"Suits me, Mr Memphis, just so long as it's not sudden."

"For sure, for sure. That's a pretty fancy panel you got there. Ol' Flight Director in front, you used one o' them?"

"Like an Artificial Horizon?"

"Yeah, but there's a difference. As well as the horizon and the little airplane, you gotta command bar, you feed stuff in and it tells you how to fly it. For a new set heading, say, you follow the bar with the little wings and get a perfect turn-in and turn-out. It's a bossy one, see?"

"Yes, glad you told me." Stuart felt his mouth go dry even more, since the time would surely come when he'd have to cancel Autopilot and control the machine himself, one of half a dozen terrifying novelties he'd have to face, including instrument flight, flight in cloud, night flying, two engines and bewildering speed. He didn't even think about landing, feeling already overloaded.

"'Fraid that's about all I know, Mr Fox, but it sure looks a pretty panel. Hey, what does the GNS say to you?"

"Er, what is it, Mr Memphis?"

"Global NavSet, called VLF Omega, between the seats, a CRT."

Cathode Ray Tube. "Ah." Stuart kept feeling impulses to reach out and take hold of the yoke whenever it made a tiny movement. He watched the Flight Director to see how it followed but in the steady conditions the variations were undetectable. He looked down at the glowing tube.

"It says: From BWG. To CRW. Dis 206, ETE 48, BRG 068, DTK 058."

"We copy, Charlie Fox. You gotta problem. You are on Jetway 6 and you have passed Bowling Green waypoint without changing your heading. We'll clear your air and come back to you." To Stuart this wasn't comprehensible but was so worrying that it cracked the last kernel. His mind seemed to emerge into crystal air with a vital and certain piece of

234

knowledge, that letting ignorance cause worry is counter-productive and in circumstances like the present, probably fatal.

Pressing his mike switch he said quietly, "What does it mean, Mr Memphis?"

"Simple, Mr Fox. You are en route Bowling Green to Charleston. Nashville's on your starboard side and Little Rock's behind you. Farther to the right and famous for the Choo Choo, Chattanooga. But I digress, it being in the nature of us country folks. Distance to Charleston you gave me 206. Estimated time en route 48 minutes, bearing to Charleston 068°, but unfortunately you are flying your previous track of 058°."

"So what do I do?"

"Well, Mr Fox, I wasn't going to ask you to do anything. I was going to clear the air for you but since you ask, why don't you move the bug on your heading indicator, just below the Flight Boss, on to 068°? Check the global to see it's still zero six eight."

"Zero six nine."

"Roger, so move the bug to zero six nine and let's see what happens."

Stuart carefully turned the small knob at the base of the dial, not too unfamiliar because it resembled a small plane's gyro. A little notched bracket slipped to the right over two divisions and the wings on the flight director promptly tilted to starboard and very slowly levelled up again. A small window stated Course 069° and the Omega confirmed it. His tiny action felt like a triumphant foray through the border of ignorance and a grim little smile broke his pursed concentration.

"I have a new heading, Mr Memphis."

"Attaboy, Mr Fox. Senior controller wants to know your situation on board, just what we gotta salvage."

"One pilot dead, one injured. One moronic government agent confined aft."

"Roger. Nature of injury?"

"Prolonged unconsciousness due to severe thump on the nose. Definite breakage, hold one, I'll check condition."

He strained round in the seat and slid the partition. Randolph was kneeling on the floor, swabbing the co-pilot's still-bleeding nose. Sensibly he had the man half face-down to prevent inhalation of blood.

235

"How's he coming?" he called out. Randolph looked up quickly.

"No change. How're you doing?"

"All right." He slid the partition back, closing off the scene and the brighter light. He reported the situation over the radio, hearing it read back with less solemnity.

"O . . . kay, four souls on board, one busted beak, one stiff and two amblin'. We have a good go situation but there's been some rag-chewing in Powers-That-Be about changing your flight plan. Hold one, Mr Fox."

Just as Stuart clicked his acknowledgement the aircraft lurched slightly and a red light began to flash in front of him. Scared again, he took a quick look at the flight instruments and saw the "Off" flag showing on the flight director and a yellow sign warning: Autopilot Off. The heading indicator began a slight rotation, the airspeed began to increase and the altimeter to count down. Beneath it, the Rate of Climb showed a negative 300 feet per minute.

Panic dug into him like a dozen tiny, hooked flails. A major failure of some kind had affected the power source for essential instruments and the aircraft was no longer controlled by its own systems. Must get straight and level, that's the first, most important thing, he muttered to himself, stiffly calm. He took hold of the yoke and eased it slightly back. The altimeter's fall ceased abruptly and began to climb, rather rapidly, the speed reducing. The flight director was useless and toppled sideways but the heading indicator continued its swing up the compass scale. Very cautiously he eased the column left and the swing stopped, reversed itself and then steadied.

Glancing down he saw the NavSet screen reading OFF OFF OFF USE CAUTION!!! SYSTEM TURNING OFF OFF. It was too panic-seeding so he ignored it. The red warning continued to pulse and then clearly over the loudspeaker he heard the ATC call anxiously.

"Charlie Fox, Memphis, you deviated, what is the problem, did you disconnect autopilot?"

Stuart felt explosive relief that at least the radio was still working. His voice came out less calm than he willed it. "Memphis, I have a major system failure, loss of autopilot, director, gyro, Omega, radar, several warning lights showing. I think I'm in a real bind."

"Roger, take it easy Mr Fox. We found you an airman, Captain Jethro Gain, a Citation test pilot no less, patched into you on ARINC all the way from Wichita, Kansas, this is Memphis handing over to you, Cap'n Gain. Good luck Mr Fox, we're all kinda with you and –"

A voice that seemed from a massive chest broke in with a deep, compelling resonance. "The boy's in deep trouble, Memphis, calm the Deejay spiel, get off the air ... Charlie Fox, Gain here. Sounds like inverter failure. Is the flight director still working in front of the right seat?"

"Er ... oh, yes, it is!"

"Roger. You got a group of thirty-five winkers just above the radar, do you have top left stating AC fail?"

"Affirmative."

"Are you straight and level?"

"More or less, I think so."

"OK, but you're gripping like a fiend, huh? Just slack off a little ... Now, on the left side of your panel there are lines of switches, start at the bottom, walk your fingers up, one, two, three, four and one left. Can you read the legend to me?"

"Yes, peering. Says AC power, Inv 1 above, Inv 2 below."

"Position of switch?"

"Up."

"Put it down, please, to inverter 2."

He did so and the red light continued flashing but the flight director suddenly unscrambled itself. The autopilot still read Off but the AC fail was extinguished. Gain's deep voice reassured him at once but he found himself panting wetly.

"Flashing red Master warning reset, press please, tell me if it goes out."

"Uh, pressed and out."

"Right. Centre console, at the rear, Mr Fox, autopilot engage, press the two greens, they should light and cancel yellow flag. Tell me."

"Affirm ... and thank you." His voice cracked slightly and he tried to disguise it from Gain. "Heading and attitude resumed and steady."

"Good." The bass voice paused for another interrogative "Mr Fox, how do you feel? I understand you've been flying all day and have approximately 40 hours fixed wing, all light singles."

"Correct. I feel spaced and cornered, if that's possible."

237

"We appreciate you are in an exceptionally stressful situation, Mr Fox. However, I have been requested not to alter your flight plan, reasons given as political, except to change your destination from Dulles to Andrews Air Force base. Runway's long and wide. They didn't even want you to talk on the radio but I overruled them. You don't sound like a big mouth to me. OK, you done good so far and if the flames keep hot, we're gonna get you down, that's for sure. So you just settle and take it easy. You copy, Charlie Fox?"

"Roger. Thank you."

"OK. We got this piece of air to ourselves and I'm gonna take you quietly round the cockpit for essentials only. First of all you'll shortly be passing Charleston, please reset the heading bug on your directional gyro to 076°. There's a digital readout as well as the needle. Got it?"

"Zero seven six. Done."

"Good. You see where the engine instruments are, top centre? Read them to me."

"First I've got Fans, left and right, per cent rpm. Hey they're both reading 104 per cent!"

"That's OK, Mr Fox, they, er ... upgraded the engines and left the instruments as they were, get me? You'll find you're still in the green, right?"

"Humph ... OK, next is ITT, left and right, both in the green, six hundred and sixty. Is that turbine temperatures?"

"Check. Next?"

"Turbines rpm as percentage, again at the top, in the green. Fuel flow 450 pounds per hour both, fuel quantity left and right both 1200 pounds, oil temp. and press. both green."

"Dinkum dandy. Go down a handspan to the radio panel. Which window reads 123.75?"

"The left."

"That's us. Towards the end we'll change you to 129.1, turn the centre knob to give that, 129.1 preset. Lower left is a green select button to change frequencies. When ordered, simply press. Not now, OK?"

"OK."

"Switch off the radar to the left, you won't need it. Click when it's done, and now don't acknowledge any more unless I request it specifically. Below the radar is a big white knob at present in the UP position, that's landing gear. I guess you never had moving gear yet? To operate, you lift it deliberately out and down, when locked you'll get three nice comforting green lights. To the right of that you have cabin pressure. During the latter part of descent you have to depressurise. At the moment you are probably pressurised to about eight thousand feet.

"Below this comes the real business, throttles. You may have heard that jets just fly flat out so you can't burn 'em, that's not the case here and you're limited to the green. When reducing, do it slowly and don't let the power get below what I tell you. Turbine response is slower than piston in the pick-up and at low speeds this can be critical. Just to the right is flap control, 3 positions, Up/Take-off-and-Approach/Land. Idiot-proof. Just below is engine synchronisation, has to be off before power reduction for landing. Before flaps down, go there and cancel it. Now, take another breather. How do you feel?"

"OK, in fact good."

"Dandy. You have less than an hour to run . . . You know, it's a helluva thing, I fly most every day and I ain't had an inverter failure in four, five years. Couldn't blame you for thinkin', Why me? But you handled it, son, so you're gonna be fine . . . landing will be real good fun but you do it by the book, none of your Texas flash-boy air-jocks and kangaroo-bangers. No sir. We set up the speed, trim to a hair and fly it into the ground, a small concession right at the end, you ease back so, so slight to get zero descent at touchdown – by the way, you won't realise now but from your seat you can't see the nose-cone, so when you reach the runway, you are simply looking out of a window and you have no reference points. Used to be the other way – I was down with the Ghost Squadron last week at Harlingen in a P.51 Mustang, like a bigger version of your Spitfire, and with those you can't see past the nose at all, all engine . . . When it's time to descend, you don't have to go on instruments, by the by. How much instrument time have you, or simulator?"

"Mr Gain, I have about 45 minutes, sort of demo really."

"Right. We pull the altitude hold, trim the autopilot wheel forward and reduce the throttles to about 65 per cent so we don't overspeed in the dive. Please note that when you level off again you gotta increase throttle so you don't get too slow. And don't forget that with too little power she can just stop flying."

"You mean stall?"

"Yup, if you set her up wrong. You know what a Standard Rate turn is, in England it's called a Rate One?"

"The first notch on a Turn-and-Slip, 3° per second?"

"Righty. If and when you have to turn – one notch only on the Turn and Slip. You only have to watch the basic instruments, just the Flight Boss, then airspeed, then attitude and VSI, vertical speed. Finally compass heading. Let's do a turn. On the column is a button marked A/P TCS, see it?"

"Yes."

"Touch control steering. Press it and then move the column to the right – gently. Tell me what's happening."

"The wings on the little airplane are banking to the right. The altitude is steady, the airspeed is down slightly at point six two and the compass is swinging upwards, 085°, 090°, 095°."

"OK, bank left gently to your original heading, zero seven six, level off and release the TCS. Autopilot will resume. If I was up there teaching you, I'd now give you an overspeed situation, fifteen degrees of left bank and 1000 feet per minute height loss. You would then take remedial action. We're not going to do it, you have enough stress, just tell me what you would do."

"Take off the bank, pull up out of the dive."

"Check. And the opposite is more critical, climbing with a turn and insufficient speed or power, the deadly stall. First preventive action, please."

"Nose down, full power, straighten up."

"We got ourselves an airman. Mr Fox, have you heard of 'The Leans'?"

"I don't think so."

"Right. When you are on instruments your reflexes usually try to tell you that you're turning, or banked, or climbing. Weird feeling, once it starts it gets worse and makes you nuts. Turning blind in a void, a human cannot reorientate so he has to trust his instruments. Total, implicit trust. Sounds risky, but you have nothing else, I repeat, nothing. You cannot fly in cloud without instruments – unless trimmed straight and level, of course, but then how can you be sure? You feeling OK?"

"Yes. Could do with a leak."

"No way. Stay put. You got a placard says not to leave the cockpit unattended on Auto. That what happened to your crew? Pay it no mind, son. The feeling will go away, we gonna have you working soon, you gonna have to earn your ride in that fancy millionaire's plaything, right, Mr Fox?"

"Whatever you say, Mr Gain."

"Better believe it. Do it wrong and you'll never see me in court."

"Are you doing all the navigating for me? The Omega system went off and it's scrambled, or waiting for me to re-start it."

"Don't worry, we're all watching you. The Omega runs on its own batteries for one minute in case of error or failure and your emergency lasted quite a bit longer than that. We'd have it right by touching a few buttons but it's all taken care of. I'm going to leave you for a few minutes. Just a couple more points for you.

"We'll bring you in on a long, long final but Andrews has ten-tenths cloud cover down to 2000 feet. You may not see the runway until you're a coupla miles out. No sweat. No icing reported either, ha. Speeds are important for gear and flap so don't touch 'em till you're told. You are now at Flight level 390 and we are different from Europe, the flight levels become feet below 18,000. So you are going to descend, de-synchronise, slow down, select second radio frequency, deploy gear and flap, depressurise, disconnect autopilot and smear it on the tarmac. You change frequency because you will be out of Memphis line-of-sight once you descend behind the Appalachians. Your new frequency will be Andrews AFB but ARINC will still patch me into you. On approach, two people will talk to you, myself and the ground controller. Have a think about it all, ask what you want, otherwise we'll have a few minutes scratch and blow. OK?"

"Sounds good. Are you going for a leak?"

"How d'you guess?"

Stuart grinned in the gloom and then sensed that the partition wasn't fully closed; he glanced round and saw the left half of Randolph's curious face peering through and a momentary stab of feeling overcame his first impulse to be brusque again. He gave a small nod of reassurance instead.

"How're you going, kid?" the agent asked.

"They say it's a question of doing what I'm told. We're

going on up to Virginia, under the direction of Captain Jethro Gain. Jethro is a pretty smart cookie because he's in Wichita, Kansas, where we can't fall on his head. How's the second pilot?"

Randolph shook his head. "Still out. How long?"

"Half an hour, three-quarters maybe."

"Can I come up front now?"

"No." Stuart's reply was quite emphatic so Randolph didn't argue. "Go back and relax. I'll rap on the slide when you've to strap in, then you'd better anchor the man down as best you can. In case we stop before we slow down."

The face disappeared after a shake of disbelief and Stuart was glad not to have weakened. He felt highly charged but vulnerable to distraction since he lacked the instinctive skill from proper training. He didn't want Randolph there at all, let alone accidentally nudging something vital and causing another emergency.

His little capsule still whispered cleanly through the night sky at over five hundred miles per hour; all round the fascia, the lights behind the matt black glowed through with their information both confident and mysterious. Because he had no habit of it he felt a profound unreality; the ache in his bladder had gone, the cabin temperature was exactly right and the seat superbly comfortable; he could have been in a good cinema except that aeroplanes have special smells and he had enough knowledge to realise how close his position was to lethal.

It gave him a short-lived feeling of detachment so that he saw himself as if from outside and, inevitably, through Lucy's eyes. It was then that he was able to consider the whole sequence as an affront; it seemed almost like a conspiracy against him which had led him through torments and finally placed him in this precarious position when all he was trying to do was clear the threat against Lucy and somehow compensate Runyan for the stupid loss of a fortune. Suddenly he realised that right here there was more to be saved than just his own life and those of the other two. There was a sleek, modern machine worth a prince's ransom, and thinking back he recognised what had spawned the thought. First the Memphis controller and his word salvage and second, Jethro Gain's assurance that a catastrophe wouldn't bring him to court. The problem was that he had no bargain,

242

not like an option to salvage a vessel at sea, since he was doing his utmost to get down safely for his own survival.

At sea ... Through his dark, brooding and desperate thoughts, a possible solution shot like a sunbeam through dispersing clouds. He reached for the captain's flight bag, found a chart of the eastern seaboard and studied it carefully until the radio voice came back to claim him.

Seventeen

Times are changed with him who marries. There are no more by-
path meadows where you may innocently linger but the road lies
long and straight and dusty to the grave.

Stevenson

Deep and resonant, Gain's voice came through the air like a
comforting miracle.

"Charlie Fox, Uncle Jethro, do you read?"

"Affirmative, Captain."

"Hmph. Show a little respect, could save your life, is that
it?"

"Sure."

"Why not? You got about twenty-eight minutes to live,
then you start again, one way or the other. How do you
feel?"

Stuart snorted quietly at his matter-of-factness. "Still good,
if a bit unreal. Captain, do you know who owns this aeroplane?"

"Well, I can look it up, but why the hell do you want to
know, it's nothing to do with our job here."

"It is if they want it back. I'd like to get in touch with the
insurers."

"At this time o' night? Forget it. What's your game, Mr
Fox?"

"Just this, Captain. I really don't like the idea of a hard
concrete runway, not with my limited experience."

"Huh, so where do you think there's a grass field with
runway lights and radar approach, plus you can't dump a
thin-wheeled hot ship on grass."

"No, I'm asking salvage."

"You're *what*?"

"Please call up the insurers, I'm sure it can be done
somehow. Maybe even the Government is carrying it. Tell

244

them there's an option. For salvage, I'll do as you want, otherwise I'd much prefer to do a long, long flat approach down the Potomac and put her down in Chesapeake Bay. Safer for us, perhaps, but not so good for the plane."

Gain's voice filled with despair. "Oh my, no ... Please, Mr Fox, tell me you're not some kind of crazy!"

Stuart didn't answer and after a long silence, Gain's voice spoke again with forced normality. "OK, Mr Fox, I got someone chasing it for you. Meanwhile, may I suggest we go to plan?"

"Roger."

"Right. Let's have a panel scan, heading and height, then engine instruments. Ignore gyro against magnetic for precession, by the way, they're slaved."

"Check, they're the same."

"Good. To the left of the landing-gear control are two white switches, you press these up for landing lights but not yet, not till we're below cloud, the glare will distract you. The next switch to the left is your beacon, you can leave this on safely. You should have no conflicting traffic anyway if the boys are doing their job. Finally, underneath those switches is a big red knob which you pull for emergency braking. Let's be optimistic about you not putting her down on the last quarter mile of runway, so you won't need it. Just know that it's there. You have foot brakes just as in a trainer, right? Next step, alter your heading to 090°, now please. The wind is south-easterly, drifting you north. Tell me about crosswind landings, did you crab it or wing down?"

"We did both. Crab till the last moment, straighten up and touch. If you don't touch at the exact point of zero drift, then windward wing down for sideslip."

"Righty, then that's what we'll do. Andrews has wind 140° at 15 knots. Your runway southbound, One-Niner Left. Means there's two of them, wide as a prairie and nearly two miles long. The only lights will be on yours. No sweat, right?"

"No smear."

"Uh ... O-kay. Sounding perky. I think you are ready to go to work, Mr Fox."

Stuart felt his fingers flex involuntarily, accompanied by a slow scalp crawl. Gain didn't wait for acknowledgement but continued with resonant calm.

"Below the thirty-five winkers is a small panel of greens. Bottom row, second from left says ALT SEL, altitude select. Press to cancel, click me when you've done it."

Click.

"Roger. Autopilot trim wheel, that's on rear centre console, wind it slightly forward, note the airspeed increase? Now, right hand on both throttle levers, draw them back and watch the fan speeds, that's the first gauge on the engine panel, take 'em down, down to 65 per cent. Wait while everything settles down, then tell me your VSI, vertical speed, that is rate of descent."

"VSI shows down 800 feet per minute."

"Thank you. Crank on some more trim, see if you can round out at 2000 feet per minute. What's your heading?"

"Er, zero nine zero, steady."

"Airspeed, Mach number?"

"That's . . . zero six eight."

"Good. You can expect to enter cloud in about four minutes. Feel OK?"

Click.

Stuart sat on in steady silence as the height peeled off. The autopilot still dealt with the heading so he was apparently sharing control. Behind him he heard the partition slide back and Randolph's strained voice asking what was happening.

"On our way down. Fifteen, twenty minutes. You can strap in and start praying."

"The co-pilot's starting to mumble, I'm trying to bring him round. What do you think?"

"I should leave him be, he'd have a helluva job to switch himself on again, he's been out nearly two hours and he'll have a headache like a dropped melon."

"Shit, you're enjoying this, aren't you – want to do it all on your own."

"Sure. Why don't you go and abuse yourself, instead of me?"

There was a sudden reflection of white through the screen as the enveloping cloud picked up the rear interior lights. Randolph flinched and then tried to peer through it, looking bewildered. After a few more moments he closed the partition and disappeared.

Except for the muted sound of the airflow, there was almost complete silence. Altimeter 28,000, VSI down 2100 feet per minute, heading and attitude steady. He had a sudden unreasoning suspicion that all was not well. Jethro Gain, however, seemed to read his thoughts.

"Still with you, Mr Fox. Radar has your heading good, transponder is reading off your height. Click me?"

Click.

"Right. Mr Memphis would like his frequency back so he can fill the night with country wisdom and a few Gospel readings."

Before Stuart could answer, Memphis interrupted. "Captain Jethro Gain, Methuselah of the Jetways, mind your mealy mouth or the Mississippi mud-men gonna come and beat yo' feet. On your way, Charlie Fox, gimme back my freeque, you got two wings and a prayer and Tennessee don't hold with unbelievers. And Charlie Fox, you goin' fer salvage is what I call *believin'*!"

"Mr Memphis, do you have a tape running?"

"Ah, evidence? Sure do, Mr Fox, I'm your man. Meanwhile see-lect your new life-line, One Two Niner Decimal One. Go, go. G'night."

Click. Stuart reached out and pressed the second green radio select button and at once heard a crisp military voice ringing with authority and confidence.

". . . this frequency until further notice, we have a priority, emergency situation. November Fife Seven Zero Charlie Foxtrot, do you copy?"

"Charlie Fox, over."

"Right. Heading and height is good. We have you 23,000 computed descent rate 2120 feet per minute. You'll receive instructions from us and from Captain Gain, not conflicting, we can over-ride the land-link. Our cloud-base is down to 2000 feet, RVR three miles in light rain, wind 140° at 18 knots. Captain Gain?"

"Gain here. How do you feel, Charlie Fox?"

"All right. Panel seems good. Heading the same, height loss as stated, just over. ASI is Mach point six eight, fans are 65 per cent, temps all green."

"Hey, hey, sounds like you made first base still running. Do not attempt to look outside until you are told. Stick with the panel, faith and hope. OK, at five miles out we're going to reduce airspeed to one hundred fifty knots, you'll be flying her then, you'll need to feel it. From now on I want the speed in knots, not Mach. You come over the hedge at 110 and flare at 90. Tell me about speed and descent, from the classroom."

"Nose up or down, that is elevator controls the speed, throttle controls the rate of descent."

"Good. The problem is when you get too low with not enough height to pick up speed, understand? Assume that you cannot accelerate back to flying speed on engine power without height loss. Therefore, I emphasise, you must not let the speed get too low. Er, hold one."

After a short pause, Gain called again. "Mr Fox, we have Edson Whinniker on the link. He's Vice-President of Kentucky Premium CorpJet Leasing. He is appraised of your situation. Speak now, Mr Whinniker."

A shrill voice broke in excitedly. "I understand from the agency leasing our Citation that you are Mr Stuart Kody from Gloucester, England and that you have feloniously skyjacked this aeroplane in contravention of US Federal Law. The only thing I have to say to you is advise that you get yourself down and turn yourself in quietly. It may help to mitigate your just deserts."

"Sorry, Mr Whinniker. You are in error. I have not hijacked this aircraft, I am a passenger who has been requested by a Government agent to take control, due to pilot's indisposition. I am not qualified and this is an emergency. There are two ways I can solve it, and our chances of survival would be favoured in ditching. Can you speak for your insurers?"

There was a long breathless pause and Stuart was aware of the airwaves full of tensions, dozens, maybe hundreds of ears straining to hear Whinniker's answer. Eventually the words seemed to tumble out, rapid and shrill.

"Mr Kody, I believe I can speak for the insurers, yes, if you will accept twenty per cent of hull value for a successful runway landing at Andrews AFB without damage. Your answer please!"

Although the percentage was way down on a full salvage claim, Stuart was in no mind to haggle. On a rapid estimate he reckoned it might be enough to solve his immediate problem, given a value on the Citation of between two and three million dollars. The only other problem was time.

"On condition that payment is immediate, Mr Whinniker. Two days maximum and no hassle."

"Yes, yes, very well."

"Then I accept. Goodnight."

Whinniker clicked off without pleasantry, presumably in an attempt to register his disgust. The Andrews controller managed to distract from any further thoughts on the matter, apart from his initial exclamation.

"Doggone ... Andrews: Charlie Fox you are passing 18,000, change your altimeter setting now to airfield height, QNH 1019."

Click.

From Kansas came a deep chuckle. "Gain here, you gotta damn gall, Mr Fox, and you even got me a fee – for which I'll be thanking you when you've got the bird down with her bits nicely bolted ... Righty, to work. Your Flight Director shows you with about 8° nose-down, right?"

Click.

"Right. You appreciate that you are on autopilot trim, so if you cancel autopilot you will have to set aircraft trim, up/down button below the red on the column. So press the red to cancel Auto, then thumb on the trim to take the pressure off the column. Do it now, please."

Stuart picked up new stiffness in Gain's voice and wondered if it was worse for the man on the ground. Watching the Flight Director for its reaction, he paused and then firmly pressed the red.

The nose came up at once and the descent rate, after a short lag, fell off sharply. He pushed the column forward, waiting to get the correct attitude back, then in small squirts, he thumbed the trim forward until the pressure against his hand disappeared.

"Gain: Charlie Fox, how did it go?"

Stuart had to seek out the transmit button again, his finger now slippery, explaining why the buttons were so deeply knurled. "OK, I'm trimmed forward. Should I re-engage?"

"Up to you. How's your heading?"

"Er ... it's gone up, 095°. OK, I'll bank left to correct it ... 090."

"Andrews: Thank you, Charlie Fox, try to maintain your heading, we want to get it right on the button. This is busy airspace."

"Gain: Mr Fox, take the stress off and re-engage, heading only."

Click.

"Gain: Mr Fox, do you reach the pedals comfortably?"

Click.

"Andrews: Passing 11,000, you have just over four minutes to below cloud base. We compute on passing 6,000 feet you turn right onto track 186 for runway 19, your heading against drift 180, we call corrections as necessary."

"Gain: Charlie Fox, remember it'll seem a bit fast for you at the end, a much hotter ship than you're used to. Accept it, just do as I say, OK?"

Click.

9,000 feet. He wiped his palms on his thighs and felt drops running down inside his shirt. He thought about his tenuous lifeline and his one option if it should fail, full throttle, back on the yoke, try to hold the climb steady, back upstairs and try again. On impulse he tuned the second radio also to 129.1 Just in case. He continued scanning, almost numbed by so many instruments, willing hard to understand.

"Andrews: approaching 6000 feet on QNH."

"Gain: Turn cabin pressure control to slow depressurise ... Next, cancel autopilot, very steady right turn onto 180°."

Stuart thumbed the red again and watched rigidly as the heading indicator crept round the dial in response to his pressure. He remembered to level up before 180° so as not to overshoot the turn. He called, "Charlie Fox is 180°, Altitude 4800."

"Andrews: Roger, you are just to left of extended centre-line for runway 19 Left, hold for the moment."

"Gain: Charlie Fox, trim back now to reduce your airspeed, just little touches, then ease your throttles forward to give fanspeed seven zero per cent. Wait twenty seconds then tell me what you have."

Click ... He ran his eyes over the panel again, scanning tensely. "I have one hundred and eighty-five knots, VSI 1200 feet per minute."

"Gain: Roger, want you slower. Column back to give 150 knots, pressure off with trim. Tell me."

Click ... "150 knots, 900 feet per minute."

"Andrews: Charlie Fox, alter your heading to starboard, 3° you are too far left."

Click.

"Andrews: Three thousand feet. You have twelve miles to run."

"Er, Captain Gain, my speed is down to 140, even less."

"Roger, Charlie Fox, let it settle. Tell me when it's holding."

"Er . . . seems to be holding. VSI 650."

"Gain: Good enough. Wings level, heading steady?"

"Yes, I –" The Citation lurched in sudden turbulence and the VSI needle jumped. On the flight director the wings were no longer level. Tentatively he corrected, feeling a huge outside pressure as though probing unfamiliar circuits in his brain. He had a massive desire for some external reference to remove all the doubt and strain of imagination and he had to fight the urge to peer into the grey-black outside.

"Some turbulence encountered. Steady now."

"Andrews: Roger, Charlie Fox. Heading is good, you have 2200 feet."

"Gain here: cancel engine synch."

Click.

"Andrews: Charlie Fox, we have you exiting below last reported cloud base."

"Gain: Wait ten, Charlie Fox, then look ahead."

Click.

Lights! Everywhere lights, gleaming in drizzle, orange and white, reality as a violent intrusion after hours of subjective intensity.

Calm, speak calmly. "Surface in sight."

"Gain: Roger, Charlie Fox, don't look for the runway, it's there. Switch your landing lights, then cycle undercarriage, just to the right."

It was somehow the most significant action, the one he'd been anticipating most, he realised, having lowered gear only once before, with Desouches into the strip near Kimberly. It seemed like ten years ago. He pulled out the white knob and slid it downwards. There came clunks and a whirring sound from below and there was a marked increase in wind noise.

"Gain: Do you have three green lights for landing gear?"

"Gear selected down, negative greens. Yes, there they are!"

"Flaps down to approach indent, please. Mechanical marker to left of control will show you. Trim back to counteract."

The Citation's nose dipped slightly but the speed fell off in the increased lift/drag from the flaps. Stuart thumbed back trim to restore the correct attitude. "Flaps to Approach. Trimming."

"Gain: Roger, Charlie Fox. Look ahead, do you see the runway, red or green lights and extended yellow centre-line? It will be slightly to your right because of your drift allowance."

"Andrews: Heading is good. Check height."

"I see it! Red lights, then two lines of white coming this way, miles."

"Gain: Red means you are too low on the runway visual. Increase throttle to 75 per cent, do it now."

Stuart responded at once to the serious order, easing the two levers quickly forward and watching the percentage indicator. The aircraft lurched again violently but this time he corrected more easily by outside reference.

"Red is gone to pink, fading . . . Now I have green."

"Gain: Reduce throttle again, 70 per cent."

Click.

"Andrews: wind backing on descent, alter heading now 3° port, steer 177. You are to right of track."

"Gain: Bank left, Charlie Fox, small-small, till they tell you you're back on centre-line, then fix new heading 177°."

Click.

"Andrews: You are back on extended centre-line."

"Gain: Select heading 177 on giro, look outside again and pick it up visual."

Click.

"Andrews: Three miles to run, height and heading good."

"Gain: Airspeed please, Mr Fox."

"One hundred and thirty."

"Throttle back to 65 per cent."

"Andrews: Two and half miles to run. All good."

Click.

To the left of the runway he could see an array of emergency vehicles, blue and orange strobes flashing in urgency.

"Charlie Fox to Andrews, can you cancel all the flashers, it looks like a stampede."

"Wilco, Charlie Fox, it's your party. Be advised you are below glide path."

There was now red showing on the VASI lights and real

concern in the voice from Wichita. "Gain: Check your airspeed and that you have 65 per cent power!"

"Airspeed is, oh shite, 90, power is 60, just under!" He fought the rising tide again: open throttles, increase airspeed by lowering the nose but logic said there was no room, it would take him even lower. Gain called again, deep and taut.

"Gain: Power on, nose down, then slowly up. Read it to me."

Stuart had to swallow before the words came out. "Full power, airspeed 100 plus, climbing."

"Andrews: Charlie Fox back on glideslope, going high."

"Gain: Full flap now, trim back."

Click.

Half a minute . . . Salvage . . . Life . . . Gain was right, he couldn't see the nose but the runway seemed to be coming up straight and steady, a little to the right because of the drift vector, but very fast. Too fast. The flashing lights had all gone out.

"Gain: tell me how it is, Mr Fox."

"Black holes, lots of lights, runway clear in sight . . .'

"No, your airspeed, Mr Fox!"

A glance at the panel, quick with reluctance. "Airspeed 190, 300 feet, whugh! More turbulence."

"Gain: reduce, reduce, get the speed off! You're much too hot!"

"Andrews: one half mile, heading is good, height is way over, be advised you are too high, Charlie Fox."

"Gain: nose down, cut the power!" Tension in his voice, clamped in control.

Unreality again, no experience of night landing, everything happening too quickly for less than trained reactions.

"Gain: double-click when you're over the lights. Airspeed?"

Surely too fast, the ranks of coloured guides whipping below. Click-click. Look at the panel. "165 knots."

"Still way too hot. Get it off, Mr Fox."

It was Gain's warning about slow pick-up, he came to realise, which gave him a serious reluctance about bringing the levers all the way back. He pushed the column forward and willed the aircraft down but it kept resisting him.

The runway streamed wetly between the lights, just there but unattainable because he already knew that forcing the yoke farther forward would only give ground contact at a still unmanageable speed: at the moment of levelling she would promptly fly again.

Controller's voice now urgent as well. "Andrews: Charlie Fox, passing half way, less than one mile remaining, decision time for go-round, you should overshoot, overshoot, right hand."

"Gain: Do it! Full power, leave the flaps. Gear up!"

Stuart obeyed, his mouth closing drily on sandpaper. It struck him forcibly that he really might be safer to turn left and follow the Potomac river to the sea.

"Gain: get 300 feet before half flap, throttle hold at 200 mph, at 500 feet right turn, circuit height 2000, correction, stay below cloud base. Mr Fox, you've got to watch that airspeed."

At full power the rate of climb was astonishing and Stuart realised he was late for his second right turn for the downwind leg when the Air Force controller over-rode the beginning of Gain's calm reassurance.

"Andrews: Mr Fox you are entering a conflicting zone exit lane, you may encounter wide-body wake vortices, tighten your circuit immediately."

The call had come just too late, for the lethal wake turbulence of a loaded 747 is up to two miles deep and twenty miles behind it. An invisible fist came out of the dark like a great sledgehammer, smashing at the beleaguered Citation as a fractious child a toy. The column wrenched his hands and the aircraft seemed to stop dead, suspended in the air on its right wing-tip, still shuddering before the nose arced over and it fell like a shed leaf spinning to its foredoom.

Stuart was aware of the tight, calm, but meaningless voices even in the panic-laden juddering of the Cessna. He knew enough from his short training that he had mere seconds to live. Lights spiralled anti-clockwise and crazily beneath the nose, almost numbing him. The voices ceased and then he seemed to hear beside him, as if in the right-hand seat, distorted by a cigar, the laconic, unsurprisable preacher's voice of the Texan instructor, Dan Yorick.

"Full left rudder, stick forward, throttle all the way ... spinning stops, centre pedals, back on the stick and ease her out of the dive. If y'all lose more than three hundred feet, then you can pretend you're dead ..."

But that was in practice a mile high over sunlit prairie, and here there was only dark stone and concrete, people living lives of tension in an enforced trust of those above their heads, and no height margin to spare.

The airspeed indicator seemed to whirl round the dial as the ground lights rushed upwards. Stuart had the column all the way back now, feeling such overstrain that he knew with a vague relief that he would black out before they struck. His right hand, unable to hold up against the G-force, had to finger-crawl its way to the throttle levers to ease the engines down from their perilous overspeed. In a huge searing parabola, the Citation lifted from its swoop at the imagined rooftops, levelled still in exquisite jeopardy and finally arrowed upwards into the black sky like an act of redemption.

Level at last, feeling his whole body wanting to burst from hypertension, he managed to bank the jet gently onto a northerly heading, keeping carefully below the loom of ground lights on the base of the cloud. He pressed to transmit even though he could sense the radio was dead. There were no voices, no more lifeline to experts on the ground. The training aircraft had always been fitted with a single set and Stuart was about to turn for the sea in hopeless resignation when his thoughts unscrambled. Almost sheepishly he remembered the second NavCom and thumbed the pre-select button. The ATC voice came in a blast that made him jump in his seat.

"... read, Charlie Fox. Do you read, over?"

After a pause, he found a grim satisfaction in speaking calmly. "Charlie Foxtrot is back level at 1500. Lost you for a moment. Wake turbulence ... All right, shall we try that again?"

The controller's voice sounded parched. "Andrews: You went off-screen, Charlie Fox. Your squawk now clear ... heading is good, continue north for positioning. Where were you hiding?"

"Er, behind a house, I think. Is Captain Gain still with us?"

"Gain: Mr Fox, I just got up off the floor. What did you do?"

"Incipient spin, as far as I could tell."

"Moses ... All righty, you must be fair shredded, let's get you on the carpet. Andrews will position you five miles out, present height, turning southbound on centreline. You still got half flap, Mr Fox?"

Click.

Off to starboard and behind he could just see the distant runway lights beckoning a welcome. He took a moment to look back and slide the partition a couple of inches. Randolph sat suffering, his face in his hands and vomit down his shirt. The co-pilot lay tethered securely on his side in the aisle, his chest moving. The pilot's body was out of sight. Stuart turned back to the panel and found himself scanning with a new and clear detachment.

"Andrews: Charlie Fox, stand by right turn base leg. You are clear to finals No. 1."

A little later, after the second turn was completed and he was lined up again on the 19L approach, Gain's voice rejoined him with all its depth and confidence renewed. The sequence of power reduction, lowering gear and flaps and trim setting seemed to flow with clear precision. He watched in fascination as the lights grew, following Gain's instructions in a robotic trance, accurate to every nuance, reading the picture clearly.

"Trimmed out. I have 130 knots, 70 per cent power. VASI is green, heading 175°."

"Andrews: heading is good, trending slightly high."

"Gain: Not again, Mr Fox. Give me 65 per cent and keep on the VASI."

He could see the lights had paled and he reduced power slightly; after a short wait, they commended him with vivid green again. The height shed away rapidly in his semi-trance and suddenly he was scything in over the threshold.

"Andrews: you should flare now, Charlie Fox, you are too –"

"Gain: zero throttles, ease her back gently, float her in. Take off any drift now and get ready to straighten up."

As his hand slid back the throttle levers, the flashing truck lights erupted again just below and to the sides. He gave the right rudder pedal the merest touch then sensed rather than saw he was crossing the centreline, moving right with the wind. The end came suddenly, in a blur because he could hardly see the runway surface, his landing lights were so outgunned by the markers.

A touch of bank took the drift off and then the port main wheel struck the tarmac and threw him level, airborne again but forgiven as the Citation sat squarely on its main gear. He held the column back until the nose wheel gently made contact on its own as the speed fell away. He reached his toes for the brakes, softly at first before sensing their power, an incredible confidence of perfect machinery. His body came hard against the straps as he stiffened his feet on the pedals, his gaze fixed beyond the screen where the side lights seemed to converge in heaven's infinity.

All the tightness in his body seemed to flow away in elated exhaustion, like the backwash of a wave which has teetered too long before breaking. On hissing wheels, the Citation careened wetly down the vast black runway in precise deceleration, for the controller just another landing, his next orders almost routine.

"Good one, Charlie Foxtrot, down at 10.48, take the next exit and follow the flashing blue."

Jethro Gain's relieved voice carried a restrained exuberance. "Mister Fox, tha-ank you. Raise your flaps and welcome to the Jetways."

"I've no words, Captain Gain."

"That's OK, son. Try 'click'."

Click.

Eighteen

I know that's a secret for it's whispered everywhere.
                                                    Congreve

"Stearman, Central Intelligence." It was all he'd said so far, partly because of the helicopter's noise and because he appreciated Stuart's exhaustion. "Langley, Virginia." The way he answered the obvious question seemed to hold the same lilt as if he'd intoned "Land of the Free."

"Home of the Brave," Stuart responded in an attempt at revival. "I always wondered if that meant the Red Indian warrior."

The Sikorsky's rotors slowed as they ducked out to see a vast floodlit spread of low building. Over the whining-down of turbines, the CIA director said, "You want that large Scotch, you better button your limey lip. The hand that holds the bottle rules the night."

Stuart followed him inside and two minutes later, in Stearman's office, the American was pouring as good as his word. He looked slight, with tired eyes, an attractively crooked smile and thick, springy-looking silver hair.

"Before you take a shot at me about Randolph and the whole grab, I should tell you we did you a helluva favour." He said it like an admonition. "The Ivans hit your motel a couple of hours after you left. We picked them up."

Stuart covered a gulp and waited in silence.

"At this very moment they're starting to tell us what they wanted from you. It's not quite the same as what we want ourselves, get me?"

"No, I'm afraid not."

"Well, previously they wanted verification and source, right? They don't need that now, they verified it for themselves."

Stuart frowned in puzzlement as the American grinned long and wickedly before supplying an answer.

"They got a man inside, at Greenham in England. He got a good look at two Tomahawk cruise missiles before we nailed him down." Stearman nodded in triumph. "Yep, your blanks. Dummies. The first three delivered as diversions for the protest groups. If there was going to be trouble on the roads during deployment exercises, we didn't want anything lethal to be exposed. Our first question for you is: How did you know about it? How did a Limey agent get in among our lot and *why*? It shows a distinct lack of trust. Breakspeare sears you were acting on your own and you certainly hadn't told him about it. He did admit there'd been some attempt to establish a liaison between you and A. A. Simonov, but that it was early stages. So . . . where did you spring the leak?"

"You won't believe me, but I made it up."

Stearman eyed him coldly. "You're goddam right I don't believe you . . . Suppose, no, let's pretend I do. Why did you make it up and then why did you tell him?"

"He was trying to blackmail me so I tried to give him something they could never check on, without being a traitor."

"I get you . . . sort of. What about the other stuff they seem so desperate to hear?"

Stuart sipped his whisky and stayed silent for some while. He was too tired to think clearly and all he had left was a tenuous instinct not to give it all away.

"Phew!" he said finally. "One small acorn, as Breakspeare said. Look, can I do a deal here or do I get the slammer anyway? Or the chair maybe?"

Stearman shook his head affably now. "London might hang you, I suppose, but we've no cause. Yet. It depends entirely on what else you were going to give them. I figure it must be connected. A deal . . . Boy, you've had a pretty good night of it so far . . . Right, if it's square, it'll get you out of here and on your way." Stearman freshened both their glasses as Stuart began in hesitation.

"I don't know if I was going to use it. Simonov wasn't playing ball with me, after the first instalment, he pretended not to have some property of mine, but they stole it, for sure."

Stearman nodded. "Nice father-in-law. Somehow he got

the access number of that Geneva account and emptied it, using a false passport. Your money, I take it?"

Stuart's head whirled in the implications like fumes from the whisky. He was almost shouting in his new anxiety. "No, it wasn't mine, dammit, oh God in heaven, he's really done it! His own daughter – and that fucking South African is going to, I don't have enough to –"

He slammed his fist on to the low table and the glasses both jumped. "I'll kill him," he said with hard conviction. "I'll – what time is it in Johannesburg, I've got to stall somehow, explain, I don't know . . ."

Stearman looked at his watch. "Early morning. Look, is this anything to do with what we were talking about?"

"What? No, not really."

"The rest of it, you were going to tell me. Our deal, yeah?"

Stuart pressed his eyes with a closed fist, as if trying to squeeze out his disarray.

"All right . . . I was going to tell him that you had followed suit with the dummy Cruise plan, after the Soviets had deployed blank SS22s. I was going to tell him you'd found out about it."

Stearman exhaled a pent-up breath. "Jeez . . . but it wouldn't wash, they could check it."

"Maybe . . . but it would take a helluva time, going round all the sites. Especially as I was going to say that about a dozen of them were armed. I think they've deployed nearly three hundred so far. They'd have to get a team and dismantle every one."

He looked up and to his surprise he saw Stearman grinning at him like a modern Macchiavelli. "I like it!" he said, thumping the table in his turn. "In fact, I goddam love it! . . . And then, when they'd checked out every one, you could say we had a mistaken belief. Or . . . you cunning little skunk! You were going to tell him *you'd* mislead us, misinformed us, is that it? And they'd think we followed their lead and left Europe defenceless. And you get all the credit, hotshit-damn!"

Stearman's voice had risen in his excitement. He controlled himself quickly and sat down again. Stuart took a great pull on his whisky and drained it.

"Something like that," he grinned palely. "They might even disarm, you never know."

"In a pig's eye."

"He said they were going to walk out of the Geneva talks."

"They did it. Today. But their pretext was the continuing deployment of Cruise and Pershing. You really think the reason was embarrassment at your information?"

Stuart shook his head diffidently. "It's hard to believe but it's what he told me. The talks were deadlocked anyway."

"Yeah . . . We can chew some more in the morning. You look ready to crash."

"Crash?"

"Huh-huh," Stearman gave a gravelly chuckle. "Me in this business. I should chose my words more carefully."

Stuart didn't smile as his anxiety overrode the humour. "Can I call Johannesburg first?"

As Stearman pushed the telephone across to him he thought wearily that none of this would have happened, could have happened, not even Rollo's hasty call for help, if it hadn't been for this infernal instrument. He pointed at it.

"Alexander Bell must have been the devil incarnate . . . How do I get overseas enquiries?"

Stearman turned to look it up for him so he dialled his home number. Not trusting himself to speak, he let it give one single ring.

"What was that," the American asked curiously as he put the handset down.

"Home. Daily reassurance."

"Ah." Stearman seemed to catch himself, a strange look on his face, covered by passing across a jotting of the code. Stuart dialled it and gave the operator his request for the Department of National Intelligence, the new name for BOSS, in Johannesburg. Stearman looked at him curiously.

"Who do you want in particular?"

"Kobus de Hoek."

"Well now, you're out o' luck. His 'copter ran out of fresh air. Yesterday. Sabotage, we think."

"Dead?"

"Yup. Not even lumps. Hyena fiesta."

They kept him at Langley for the best part of three days while he had medical treatment for bouts of shaking and over-tensed muscle cramps. He lost his appetite and slept a great deal, and worried away most of his waking moments.

They allowed him multiple calls home but there was no reply. The Telecom people assured him they were checking for faults.

At his last meeting with Stearman, the American handed him an envelope and favoured him with a wry smile. Stuart looked inside the envelope and saw it was a draft on the US Treasury. He raised his eyebrows with deliberate exaggeration and put it away without looking at the figure.

"The Government carried the insurance?"

"Yep. Whinniker really stuck his neck out, didn't he? With all that stuff on the airwaves, they couldn't back out of it. Feel you earned it?" Stearman didn't wait for an answer. "Anyhow, we want your assurance that you'll come back for Randolph's, er, tribunal in about six weeks. Second, if you give anything else to Simonov, let me know first, right? There's an RAF transport leaving for Brize Norton in an hour. I fixed you a ride. I'm doing you a little favour as well, I haven't told Breakspeare I'm releasing you, he'll want 'a bit of a chat' with you some time. You see, W Section never existed, it was drawn up and announced but not implemented. Breakspeare's forced to create it now, it's his official baby. He's got one single agent." Stearman prodded him in the chest with a pointed forefinger. "Good luck, mister."

It was mid-morning when the cab drove him into Carsey. Deciding it was too early for explanations, he stopped it outside Horrocks' house to hide his flight case in one of the garages. There was a large sealed crate standing there but his haste overcame his curiosity and he went straight home without noticing the addressee was Mrs L. Kody.

Her car wasn't in the drive and at first he wondered if she might be on the short morning stint which she'd been keeping to herself. The house was locked up, however, and once inside he found it quite cold and dead. The water cylinder had no residual warmth and casting around for clues, he found only one word on the telephone pad. The rest of the sheet had been ripped off under the name Rollo. It made him scowl, and in growing alarm he called Alicia's number but there was no reply. He tried St George and an answering service said he would call in from Stornoway. Finally he tried Simonov and was deluged with questions, mainly to do with his whereabouts.

"How come you don't know?"

"The Brits took our bugs out of your house. Are you there now?"

"No. Where's Lucy? She doesn't answer."

"I don't know. She just took off. Told no one."

"Alicia?"

"Not even Alicia. She's disappeared too."

"You mean I can't –"

"I don't see how. I suppose you'll just have to wait . . . did you hear about de Hoek?"

"Yes. Was it you, did you 'fix him up', as you put it?"

"Of course not!" The levity in Simonov's voice seemed to give him away. "Listen, my boy, that was a great score of yours, about the Cruises. Very, very good. Er, about the rest, I –"

"Did you find the stones?"

"No, it's a mystery. I wondered if one of our people . . . We're baffled, frankly. I asked the Bureau if they'd replace them for you. I can persuade them to do it, I think, now that you've got me back in favour. They say it depends on the quality of your next bulletin, frankly."

"I see . . . well, it's red hot, I promise. I'll be in touch. I've got to find Lucy first."

"Oh. And listen, I got your money back for you, from Geneva. He can't use it, after all. Can I have ten per cent?"

Stuart ran a hand over his face, disbelieving. "Yes."

"Thanks. Don't be long, please. There's no threat to her now. How was Stearman?"

"What? How the hell did you know?"

"Oh, we have ways. You are such a dark horse, my friend, a whole file to fill. They didn't know until then that you were a jet pilot as well."

Stuart paused in astonishment. If they didn't know the truth from the panic over the airwaves, it meant they must even have a night-scope or an infra-red camera inside Andrews AFB. Thinking only of Lucy, he muttered, "Keep it to yourself, won't you? It's under wraps."

"Classified? All right." Simonov's eager voice seemed to hug the conspiracy. "Call me very soon."

He searched the house in suspended anxiety, his emotions getting more tattered by the minute. Her clothes were all there, too evocative, her colours and faint scent making him tremble. There were no other signs to help him and while he waited for St George he dialled Alicia's number intermittently without success. At last a call came, the charges reversed, from a coin-box in the Hebrides.

St George couldn't answer his over-riding question.

"No, she didn't say, just that she had to go. I flew her to Luxembourg, she was going on from there."

"When?"

"A week, no, five days ago."

"Didn't she say *anything*?"

"Not really, but I had other people on board. I gave her that package from Antwerp. She was a bit jumpy. She said she had a complaint."

"About the package?"

"No. I thought she was leaving you. I nearly proposed to her but then she said she wouldn't open it till she saw you. Why didn't you call me, did you get to Harlingen?"

"No, I . . . got diverted. We'll talk about it when I can relax, when – hell, how do I find her?" His voice rose to a near shout. "Not even the KGB know where she is . . . Sorry. When are you back south?"

"Few days. Look, I've got to go. Bunch of nouveau and over-rich stalkers. From Lancashire. They actually *tip* me!" He spoke with the horror of the ultimate social gaffe.

Stuart tried to respond but was too distracted. "Tough. Thanks, St G., I'll be in touch."

He thought poignantly of the package from Grobelaar, at the same time puzzled and remorseful about the complaint. Suddenly he slammed his fist into his other hand and dashed to the mantelpiece. He whipped the Complaints Box open in eager expectation but it was quite empty. He slammed it shut again, realising a split-second later that his eye had registered something while his distracted brain, looking for something on paper, had skipped a synapse. Cautiously he opened the lid again and in one corner, written in ball-point, was a single word: Barnacles.

With a slow, tremulous delight seeming to spread throughout his limbs, he closed it softly and pressed his hand on the lid. Yes, he said to himself, that's right. After more than a year, she'll need scraping and anti-fouling, and then . . .

* * *

264

He talked his way into the cockpit of the Air Kenya 727 and friendly pilots even let him stay for the landing. The runway on Mahé has Victoria harbour clearly ahead some six miles distant but strain as he might, he found it impossible to pick out an individual white hull.

His chest stayed constricted when the taxi arrived at the harbour and he could see the anchorage clearly. There was again no sign of *Sailor V* among the yachts lying to the breeze around Hodul Island, although some were teasingly similar. The tentacles of doubt continued their slow creeping.

"The slipway," he asked. "Isn't it in use?"

"*Le slip, l'incliné? Mais bien sûr,*" answered the driver and Stuart realised it was out of sight behind Hodul, on the other side of the harbour.

The black Seychellois pointed and angled his head in a question. Stuart nodded drily and the cab moved off again, slow as an explorer. He wanted to get out and run. As they drove round the harbour and the palm-lined set in all its exotic shimmering, he could see only a large grey fishing boat dominating the yard; farther on, their vantage point changed and he could see it was blocking sight of the lower section where a varnished mast protruded.

Her curved stem canted upwards, she stood chocked and clean on the ways, a new coat of red anti-fouling giving her a crisp look of expectancy. He could see on his side the end of some waterline masking tape fluttering loosely but there was no one near. Then as they drew opposite he saw the top of a paint roller appear over the rudder. There were two slim bare legs beneath it, wearing flip-flops.

Breathlessly, he thrust some money into the front seat and slid out with his grip.

"*C'est assez?*" he asked, his eyes fixed towards the slipway.

"More than enough," the driver answered, following his gaze, "I have seen her, M'sieu. *Très mignon.* A change from our dark island beauties. I should be taking her away, if I would be you."

"*Merci. Bonne idée.*"

He walked towards the slip, his feet picking their own way through rubbish, timber and discarded gear. The lofted paint roller stopped and disappeared but the legs didn't move. There was a small gap between the rudder and the stern post and when he got close, he could see one gold-green eye looking through it, very still.

"You've come too early," her voice said almost querulously, "I wanted to surprise you."

"Too late to help. You've done it all."

"Yes. Launching in half an hour. You've lost weight."

"Have I? I've been rushing about. What made you think of here?"

"Your friend Rollo. And St George gave me a packet from you, can I open it now?"

"Yes, of – no, finish your job. I'll get something cold and fizzy and very expensive and we'll drink to *La Vie* as she goes in."

"All right. I've finished actually. I'm just messing. I'm covered in red spots, look."

She stepped nimbly out from behind the rudder, her face mock-serious under a spattered plastic cap protecting her hair. She wore tiny cut-offs and a paint-streaked halter torn from a T-shirt. She bent to pick up a cloth, the movement straightbacked and effortless, and wiped her hands with thinners. He put down his grip and took the cloth from her fingers. They stood very close and she watched his eyes as he looked for splashes and wiped them off, both of them wary with self-control.

When he'd finished she shook out her hair. He saw it had begun to bleach already, a marquetry of teak and sycamore.

"You're perspiring like a horse," she said. "Are you all right?"

He shook his head silently. Still watching round-eyed and cautious she reached out to touch his chest. It seemed to be thumping hugely as he covered her hand and she felt it with pretended alarm before a slow smile creased her face.

"Have you got it here, the package?" he asked her.

"Yes." She darted quickly to her bag lying by the side of the steel track and came back pulling off grey wrapping paper.

"Where's your mother?" he asked, watching her trying to be slow and graceful in her impatience.

"Greenham Common. She's joined the Ladies' Peace Camp."

"But –"

"I know, I said there's no point now after what you told

266

us. Guess what she said? She would have gone before but she was scared of one going off, exploding." Her face crinkled with laughter so she couldn't see what she was doing. "Anyway, she says their principles are OK, their hearts are in the right place and she's expanding her consciousness. And they're crazy about her *borscht*."

The wrapping removed at last, she managed to pause before opening the box it revealed. It was polished ebony with a gold tag declaring: *A. Grobelaar, Diamantaire*.

"Oh," she said in awe and suspense, and then again as she very slowly lifted the lid.

It lay as he had asked on a bed of aquamarine velvet, the pink lozenge stone nestled in a swirling skein of platinum filigree. He watched every nuance of her face as she recognised the design from the hand-mirror at home, creasing up in delight and even blushing. Passing him the box, she slid out the pendant and hung it against her throat.

"I want to see it so badly . . . And to think there you are with your heart on your sleeve, just look at me with *this*! One secret we'll have to share . . . The only mirror's on board – quick let's call them! You tear off the tape and I'll go and get Zu-Zu. He's in charge, he moved us up the waiting list when I told him how urgent it was."

"Why was it?" he started to ask but she was already flat-footing away to the foreman's office. Anxious again, he stripped away the waterline tape and climbed the ladder with his grip and her handbag. By the time he'd stowed them and hauled the headsails on deck, a faint hammering came through the hull. Lucy clambered aboard, breathless with running and anticipation, then the ladder disappeared. They sensed the beginning of movement and she clasped him theatrically in the cockpit, then the trolley shook alarmingly, gathering way in a perilous trundling. They hit the water with a great rush, throwing out an affronted stern-wave which settled as the sloop swung away out of the cradle in a carpet of bubbles, rocking gently into stillness, cupped in liquid crystal, tense as rapture . . .

"What was the urgency?" Stuart finally managed to ask, "And what was that about Rollo?"

"He called just as I was leaving. He said he needed help."

"Help for what?" He quailed inwardly, too conscious of how and where it had all begun.

267

"I don't know what he'd done, but he'd decided to jump bail, for your sake, he said. He had to chase someone for something, I've got it written somewhere . . . Towers, Powers? Anyway, he found him, or it. But now he's holed up in Durban, Rollo that is, and he wants us to sail down and collect him. He says he's got this great idea, and something you left behind, he wouldn't tell me over the phone what it was. He said you'd know. He sounded very apologetic." She turned and waved her thanks to the men on the slipway.

Stuart's mind reeled in confusion. For a brief, very brief moment he almost felt sorry for Simonov and his now-eager concern to replace a collection of diamonds which had never left the Republic at all. Or had the bugs still been in place, had he overheard Rollo's call to her and drawn his own conclusions, playing with him again? Stuart felt like a dog chasing its tail before he realised it didn't matter any more.

The confusion turned slowly to utter contentment and as Lucy watched his face, her own anxiety faded. Mollie Vrouwer had kept her word, the release note in the *The Times* airmail copy appearing just the day before. She reached up to ruffle his hair.

"I've got stores and everything. I even started the engine by myself to come over, I had to be busy, missing my forty clients, *and* I was about to launch a business with the money you lent me, and you needn't ask 'cos that's a secret too . . . Shall I start it?"

As they drifted slowly away from the cradle in almost flat calm, she stood in the companionway admiring the pendant in a salt-stained mirror and then gazing up at him, posing, her face alight and flushed. There was no sweeter thanks and no flicker of disappointment. The stone looked surely too large and exotic to be anything but costume, leaving yet another truth in abeyance for a surprise.

"I don't have to dance if it's not a diamond . . . but she said she would have loved him anyway, didn't she? Can I go on wearing it?"

"Yes, but that's all."

Gaily she complied, flinging her ruined top and shorts out into the water, now stippled darker blue by a catspaw.

"No to the engine," he said with mock decisiveness, taking off his shirt and tossing it down the hatch. "I'll get the main up and we can sail out quietly. Rollo Runyan can stew . . .

We'll head up for Praslin island to catch your *cocos* on the job, and I suppose we could have another honeymoon ourselves. If you like."

"Oh yes, I like. But –"

"Damn! I forgot the champagne."

With a look of triumph she bent to rummage in the icebox, then stood proudly with a dripping frosty bottle of Pol Roget.

"See? Qualified sea-wife. But –"

"You're an unqualified ship's siren. And no more buts."

*If you have enjoyed this book and would like to
receive details of other Walker Adventure Fiction titles,
please write to:*

*Adventure Fiction Editor
Walker and Company
720 Fifth Avenue
New York, NY 10019*